INFERNO

KAT ROSS

For Anna B.

SOLIS

White Sea

The Solitude

Tjanjin

The Umbra

Pompeii

Sand
Hills

Sinking
Sands

The Kiln

The Red Hills

The Gale

Cimmerian
Sea

Delphi

Samarqand

The Burrow

Susa

AUSTRAL OCEAN

0   50

Leagues

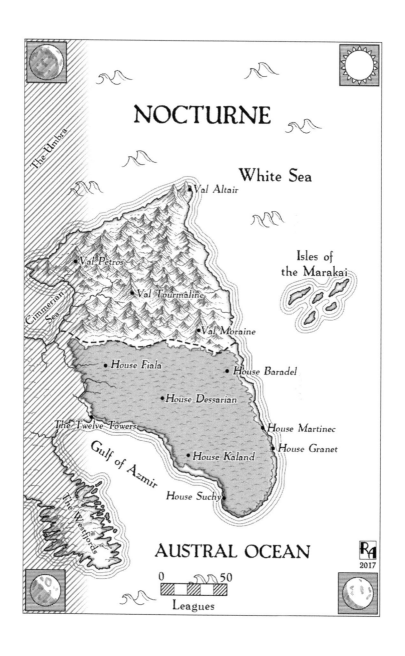

NOCTURNE

White Sea

The Umbra

Val Altair

Isles of
the Marakai

Val Petros

Cimmerian
Sea

Val Tourmaline

Val Moraine

House Fiala

House Baradel

House Dessarian

The Twelve Towers

House Martinec

House Granet

House Kaland

Gulf of Azmir

The Westfjords

House Suchy

AUSTRAL OCEAN

R
2017

0   50

Leagues

CONTENTS

Incens'd with indignation Satan stood
Unterrify'd, and like a comet burn'd
That fires the length of Ophiuchus huge
In th' arctic sky, and from his horrid hair
Shakes pestilence and war.

—John Milton, *Paradise Lost*

❧ I ❧

RED DAWN

Lieutenant Captain Arshad shaded his eyes against the low sun with one hand, resting the other on the pommel of his sword. From his vantage point atop one of the fortified towers flanking the Carnelian Gate, the seventh gate of Samarqand, he could see six leagues of the western road before it wound into a fold of low hills. Farther out lay the Gale, which appeared as a smudge of darkness on the horizon. He couldn't make out it today; a southerly wind carried smoke from the blacksmith's quarter, painting the landscape with a grey haze.

Since the Hazara-patis had ordered all the gates leading into the city to be sealed, traffic had dried to a trickle. But now he saw a group of dust-coated travelers trudging along the western road.

At first, Captain Arshad assumed they were refugees from Delphi. The Pythia ruled with a heavy hand and not everyone liked it. After the massacre of the Ecclesia, there'd been an influx of people, afoot and riding on wagons, who'd had enough of her fanaticism. But this bunch didn't look like Greeks. They all had bright red hair and wore sand-colored cloaks. Arshad frowned. Perhaps they were a troop of players in costume come to entertain the king.

"What is it, captain?" asked his second in command.

"I'm not sure." He sighed. "I'd best go down and find out."

The group neared the gates and the captain revised his opinion. Not travelling players. They had no baggage and they all wore the same odd cloaks. They were a weird-looking bunch, most likely some religious cult. There seemed no end to the number of gods worshipped by the heathen Greeks. Arshad discreetly made the sign of the flame.

He trotted down the winding staircase to the bottom of the garrison's watchtower, moving at an unhurried pace. They'd already refused other refugees fleeing Delphi, and a few country folk who'd hoped to shelter inside Samarqand's walls until things settled down. Arshad felt bad turning them away, some were families with children and he had two sons of his own, but orders were orders and there was no bribe large enough to induce him to open those gates. Everyone knew what King Shahak did to traitors.

His generals were the latest casualty. Rumor said they'd been plotting to unseat the king and replace him with one of their own. Somehow Shahak had gotten wind of the conspiracy. They were now on display in front of the Rock, their bodies rearranged in monstrous contortions.

That was four days ago and no new generals had been promoted, leaving the middle-ranking officers in charge. Lieutenant Captain Arshad commanded a garrison of a hundred men at the Carnelian Gate. Each of the six other gates was similarly guarded. The rest of the army, about a thousand men, kept order in the city and patrolled the inner curtain wall enclosing the Rock of Ariamazes. The king would be in no danger from this ragtag group.

Archers lined the top of the wall, arrows duly knocked to bows although it seemed unlikely they'd be needed. More soldiers with spears and shields occupied the garrison, sparring in the muddy yard.

When Captain Arshad reached ground level, he peered

through the ornamental grillwork of the towering wooden gates. The group had halted thirty paces away, but their leader kept coming and now Captain Arshad got a better look at him. The first thing he noticed was that the man had been burned in a fire. Swathes of scalp were bald and misshapen, with thick seams of scar tissue. The second was his eyes, which were a shade of blue so light as to be almost colorless. He seemed to have no eyebrows.

"The gates are sealed," Arshad said curtly. "You'll have to go back to wherever you came from."

The man nodded and grinned, dirty red hair swinging. Arshad wondered if he was simple.

"I'm here for an audience with King Shahak," he said.

The solders laughed at this, although Captain Arshad didn't join them. Something about the group made him uneasy. All the adult males save for two also bore the marks of fire, though only on half their faces. Arshad found that very odd—as if the burns had been inflicted deliberately. Then there were the identical cloaks, made from some tanned hide the captain didn't recognize.

"And who shall we say is here to see him?" one of the soldiers taunted from the wall.

"Gaius Julius Caesar Augustus." The man spread his arms wide. "King of the Avas Vatras."

The soldiers exploded into laughter at that.

Lieutenant Captain Arshad felt himself losing patience. His original assessment must be correct. They were a troupe of performers hoping for a crust of bread and a cup of wine in exchange for some mindless entertainment, and desperate enough to risk the displeasure of Samarqand's notoriously unstable king.

"There's a village not far from here," he said in a tone that brooked no argument. "Just walk north along the river. You'll find food and shelter there, if you have coin for it. But you won't be getting into Samarqand. Not today, nor anytime soon."

He looked at the children again. They were ragged and thin, but they didn't look afraid. Lieutenant Captain Arshad had seen a lot of refugees and they all wore the same expression, a mixture of weariness, suffering and resignation. But these children stared boldly back at the soldiers. It was eerie. The only one who *did* look afraid was a man leaning on a stick. Arshad seemed to remember him limping as the group approached. The man's intense gaze met his own and Arshad had the impression he wanted to say something, but then he cast a furtive glance at the scarred leader and Arshad realized his fear was not of the soldiers on the wall. Suddenly, he was very glad for the wall between them.

"You heard me," he said sharply. "Go on with you."

The leader crooked a finger and a little girl came forward. She couldn't be older than eight or nine, with fiery hair down to her waist, tangled and wild. She had the same pale eyes. Unbidden, Arshad thought of a story his grandfather used to tell about a monster called a wight. They were cunning things. They pretended to be human, but their eyes were like black almonds and when you realized what they were and tried to run, they were very fast....

The scarred man leaned down and whispered in the little girl's ear.

She stared at Captain Arshad, her gaze finding his through the carved grillwork in the gate.

"We don't want to leave," she declared in a high, childish voice.

Cold fingers of dread traced a path down Arshad's spine. The archers sensed it too and he heard the creak of bowstrings. No one laughed this time. A heavy silence fell on the garrison.

"Are you sure you won't open the gates?" the leader asked softly.

Captain Arshad started to make the sign of the flame. His finger brushed forehead and lips, but before they touched his heart, a wall of fire raced toward him.

The girl stepped forward, a smile on her face.

It was her, she'd done this somehow....

A wind rose, whipping the flames into a bonfire. They consumed the gates in a matter of seconds. Arshad had never seen a fire burn so hot. It quickly spread to the garrison towers. Captain Arshad grabbed a young messenger boy who stood frozen in the yard.

"Get to the inner curtain wall and send word to seal the Rock."

"Who are they?" the boy gabbled, his eyes huge. "*What* are they?"

"Just run. Faster than you've ever run before." Arshad gave him a hard shove. "*Go!*"

One of the archers screamed and tumbled from the wall, blue flames trailing from his body. The boy took off into the warren of streets, legs pumping. He didn't look back.

Lieutenant Captain Arshad drew his sword and waded forward into hell.

2

FLESH AND BLOOD

oly Father help me, he's going to sneeze.

Javid watched from the corner of his eye as King Shahak's nose twitched. His breathing sounded clotted and uneven.

Any moment now. But which way will he turn his face?

The king sat in a chair, fingers resting on a lacquered box in his lap. The box never left his custody now, though he rarely partook of its contents. He no longer needed much dust to work magic. It was transforming him — and not for the better.

Shahak's skin was ashy and peeling, his hair thinning. An embroidered robe in shades of bruised purple hung on his cadaverous frame. From the pointed sleeves emerged thick, yellowed nails, the fingers quivering with a faint tremor. Fever-bright eyes lurked deep within their sockets. His nose and cheekbones were sharp as blades, making his full lips seem vaguely obscene.

"Allow me to refresh your spiced wine, Majesty," Javid murmured, taking the opportunity to back out of range.

In the last week or so, Shahak's bodily fluids had acquired strange magical properties. Just that morning, his chamber pot spontaneously turned into a huge, hideous toadstool. The scraps of silk he used to blot his frequent nosebleeds had to be handled with tongs and burned immediately, before they tried to crawl away.

Javid took his time pouring the wine. A pair of blank-faced servants knelt in the corner, eyes cast down, waiting to do the king's bidding. But Javid encountered far fewer souls in the torchlit corridors of the Rock these days. He suspected that many of the palace staff had slipped away. Even the royal guard was diminished. Javid envied them.

The king's nose twitched again. His eyes watered and he drew a sharp breath, then expelled it in a violent sneeze. Javid took a nimble hop back as a spray of dark liquid struck a silk pillow to the king's left. A moment later, a tentacle erupted, questing delicately across the floor. The servants leapt into action, removing the offending pillow to throw it into the holy fire the magi kept burning day and night.

Unperturbed, Shahak accepted the cup with a wan smile.

"You must make a trip to Pompeii soon," he said. "To replenish our supplies before we undertake the work of reviving the drylands."

Javid gave a low bow. "As you command, Majesty."

"One day I should like to accompany you." He coughed into his handkerchief. "But there is much to be done here. We must make certain our stockpiles are adequate." He glanced at the cage hanging over the door where Javid's former employer, Izad Asabana, sat on his perch in the form of a crow, staring disconsolately through the bars.

The spell dust seized from Asabana's warehouses was dwindling. Even though Shahak used it rarely, he had an intense fear of running out. Leila said it was the only thing keeping him alive.

"And how are your sweet sisters?"

"Bibi is getting on well as Leila's apprentice. She's a bright child. It keeps her out of trouble."

"She is not performing spells, I hope," Shahak said dryly.

Javid smiled at the jest, though he kept a sharp eye on the handkerchief for signs of movement. "No, Highness. She runs errands within the palace and assists with the more mundane experiments."

In fact, Javid was grateful Leila had taken Bibi under her wing. She was too clever for her own good and chafed at confinement. Leila made sure she was kept far from the king, and she seemed to find Bibi useful for the non-magical devices she constructed in her workshop.

"Dust is not to be trifled with," Shahak said with a peevish frown. "I trust Leila's judgment, of course, but with the supplies running low...."

In their haste to remove the tentacled pillow, the servants had left the door to the corridor open and Javid heard rapid footsteps approaching. A moment later, the Hazara-patis, Master of a Thousand and chief steward of the palace, rushed into the chamber. He collapsed into the prostration, pressing his bald head to the carpet.

"There's a disturbance at the Carnelian Gate, O King of Kings. The garrison has fallen. People are rioting in the streets to get out."

Shahak's red eyes narrowed. "Fallen? To whom?"

"The initial reports are unclear—"

"Stand up, man! I can hardly hear you."

The Hazara-patis rose unsteadily to his feet. "I beg forgiveness, Your Highness. It's just that—"

"Is it the Greeks?" Shahak growled. "The Pythia? I expected her to come eventually, but how could there be no warning that an army marched on our city?"

"Not the Pythia." The Hazara-patis knit his hands together, steeling himself. "A single messenger boy survived the melee at the wall. He claims the gates were burned to cinder and torn from their hinges. He's not very coherent, but...." His voice trailed off.

"Not to fear, Your Majesty, reinforcements have been dispatched. We will restore order."

Burned to cinder? Javid knew the Carnelian Gate well. It was made of cedar planks two hands thick. He took a bracing gulp of wine.

"What else?" The Hazara-patis hesitated and Shahak slammed his hand down on the armrest. "Speak!"

"The boy claims it was a group of refugees. They sought an audience with the King of Kings and were naturally refused." Sweat rolled down the steward's milk-pale brow. "They claimed to be Avas Vatras, but of course it must be some trick—"

Shahak leapt to his feet, full of sudden energy. "I wish to see for myself."

The Haraza-patis looked scandalized. "Your Highness! It's far too dangerous—"

"Not from outside, you fool. From the Sky Garden."

The Rock itself was all of a piece and windowless, but before her transformation into a beast, the Queen had installed a garden on the battlements so her children could play beneath the sun and remain perfectly safe. Perhaps because she had loved it and he hated his mother for opposing his ascension to the throne, Shahak rarely went there. But it commanded a view of Samarqand for many leagues.

Now the three of them hurried through the inner court and up a series of winding staircases. Guards in felt hats and tunics with the sign of a roaring griffin hastily stepped aside at the door to the gardens as the king swept through. Without the Queen's guiding hand, the place had run a bit wild. Under different circumstances, Javid would have been grateful to be out in the open air after the oppressive atmosphere of the Rock. Date palms mingled with citrus and pomegranate trees, and thick-trunked cycads banked beds of roses and poppies the color of fresh blood.

Javid trailed the king as he strode along a gravel pathway to the waist-high wall at the edge of the roof. Smoke smudged the sky to the west, and in a few other places as well. Below, soldiers rushed out of the garrison adjoining the Rock and surged across the parkland to defend the inner curtain wall.

Beyond that ... chaos reigned.

The streets of Samarqand were built in spirals, all leading up to the Rock. Everywhere he looked, Javid saw tiny figures running pell-mell. Knots of soldiers tried to keep order, but they were vastly outnumbered. The flood of humanity surged toward the city's other gates like water rushing down an open drain.

Shahak gripped the stone balustrade, dark brows drawn together in displeasure.

"Why do the people flee? I see no invading force."

"There, Your Highness," Javid said faintly. "I think...."

Up the main thoroughfare called the Parthian Way, a group of about thirty figures was making its way toward the Rock. Sunlight glinted on red hair. It was hard to make out from a distance, but they seemed to be armed with crude spears. When they reached the curtain wall enclosing the king's park, archers sent a volley of arrows raining down. The assault was met with gouts of fire that turned the arrows to ash in midair. Another scorching blast struck the wall and the soldiers nearest the blaze fell back. The second set of gates blew off its hinges.

"Holy Father," Javid whispered.

He turned to Shahak, whose face was an immobile mask.

"The Vatras," the king said hoarsely. "They have come."

The Hazara-patis, who had witnessed any number of horrors since Shahak took the throne, slumped to the ground in a dead faint.

Javid was tempted to join him. Instead he found himself saying, in a surprisingly calm voice, "We must seal the inner gates to the Rock, Majesty. The doors are bronze. They withstood a siege by the fire daēvas once before. We can wait them out, there are not so many of them."

The King was silent for a long moment. Then he turned to Javid with a quizzical expression. "Bar the doors? On the contrary, we must let them in."

Javid opened his mouth, then closed it again. He drew a deep breath.

"Of course you know best, Majesty. But...." He swallowed. "Well, they almost killed every living soul in Samarqand the last time."

Shahak tapped his yellow talons on the stone. "That was a thousand years ago. General Jamadin was unwise to oppose them." His eyes gleamed with excitement as he watched the band approach. "I'll confess, I have dreamed this moment might come someday. The Vatras have been sent by the Holy Father to be our teachers, it is perfectly clear."

Yes, it is perfectly clear that you are mad as a magus shitting in a rainstorm.

"Teachers, Majesty?"

"My conjurations are child's play compared to the forging of talismans." Shahak flicked a finger dismissively. "Mere tricks to pass the time. But a talisman survives its maker for ages! The ones we have today all predate the war. Now *that* is a legacy. To forge an object of enduring power. You know only the simple remnants like lumen crystals, but I've read ancient scrolls that say in the golden age of the adepts, there were talismans that could raise the dead. Talismans to bring rain or divert the path of a thundering river. What wondrous empire can I build with an endless supply of magical devices that could be used by anyone, not only those versed in the arcane art of alchemy?"

He stepped over the prone body of the Hazara-patis and began striding back toward the guards at the door. "No, I must let them in."

Javid hurried to catch up. "But—"

"They are my brothers. Yes, yes, my flesh and blood. They shall have their audience."

Javid recognized the decisive tone. There would be no turning the king from this course. Resignation settled over him. "It is as you say, Highness." Then a new awful thought occurred to him. "But it might be advisable to keep the source of the dust a secret for now. I do not know how the Vatras would take it."

In fact, he could well imagine how they would take it.

Shahak considered this. "You mean they might not understand that I consume the dust with the utmost reverence for the souls who perished?"

"Precisely, Majesty. As usual, you have struck to the heart of matter. *We* know you mean no disrespect, but it is a very delicate matter. They might be ... touchy."

"Perhaps you're right." He graced Javid with a benevolent smile. "What would I do without your judicious counsel?"

Javid murmured self-deprecating words even as he inwardly prayed the king would not forget or change his mind — assuming they lived past the next quarter of an hour.

The guards at the entrance to the Rock snapped to attention at their approach.

"Order the bronze doors to be opened," Shahak told the captain. "I will greet my guests in the throne room."

Silence greeted these words. The captain gave Javid a bleak look. It said, *We're all going to die and there's nothing we can do about it, is there?*

Javid gave the merest shrug of agreement.

With a guttural growl, Shahak turned the captain into a fluttering moth. His gaze fixed on the next guardsman and he repeated the order. This time it was obeyed with alacrity.

Javid hoped he might slip away at this point and try to whisk his family to safety, or at least find a dark hole to hide in, but it was not to be.

"As the Hazara-patis is indisposed, you will address the Vatras on my behalf," the king told him cheerfully. "Explain that the incident at the gates was a misunderstanding and escort them to the audience chamber. We shall find common cause." He started down the stairs, then turned back. "And fetch Leila Khorram-Din. My royal alchemist should be on hand for this historic occasion."

❦ 3 ❦

A ROYAL REPAST

Small fires smoldered in the strip of sedge grass along the curtain wall. Nicodemus stepped over the blackened bones of an archer who'd fallen from the top, though most of the Persian defenders had retreated back to their impregnable fortress.

The Rock of Ariamzes hulked half a league away, casting a deep shadow across the parkland. It looked like an enormous grey boulder, all of a piece without seam or opening. The palace-fortress had defeated Gaius once before and Nico wondered how he intended to conquer it this time. Unlike the Carnelian Gate, the massive doors leading to the Rock were plated in bronze.

They could be melted down in time, but not today. The Vatras swayed on their feet, hollow-eyed and exhausted. Working fire drew on one's own life force and they weren't used to tapping it freely. In the Kiln, the wards that sustained the Gale had also dampened elemental power. Like muscles that atrophy from lack of use, using fire had depleted them. Nico experienced the same thing when he'd first emerged from the gate with Domitia two years before.

Even Gaius looked tired. It seemed to be dawning on him that he wasn't as strong as the last time he came to this city with a legion at his command.

"They need to rest," Nico said. "To eat."

Gaius gazed at the Rock, his expression unreadable. "The Danai built that," he said at last. "The fools. They were always too trusting of the mortals."

"We could make camp here—"

"No. We march for the Rock." He turned to Nico. "You'll get us inside or Atticus loses his tongue. I can still use a knife."

Nico looked away before Gaius saw his anger. "All right," he muttered.

His leg ached like a bastard, but he hadn't joined the fray at the Carnelian Gate or the curtain wall. Fire simmered in his fingertips, shivered along his skin. Enough to melt the doors? Probably not. But he'd find a way. He had to.

The children, all painfully thin, were looking around in wonder at the trees and lush greenery of the park. Atticus crouched over a bed of flowers, touching their petals with reverence. Thankfully, he hadn't heard the exchange. Nico turned to find Aelia staring at him, her son propped on one hip. The boy looked more like his mother, with the same wide mouth and strong features. Their eyes met for a moment and she looked away. He wondered what she was thinking. If she hated him for the punishment she'd almost endured on his behalf.

That was Gaius's way. Threaten others to compel obedience.

Nico started down the road to the Rock, leaning on the stout hickory stick he'd found in a farmer's woodpile. After a moment, the rest of the Vatras followed. The defenders were holed up inside, along with the royal family and its retinue of servants, cooks, messengers, scribes — in other words, hundreds of innocent people, most of them unarmed.

I have no choice. But I will see Gaius burn some day, whatever it costs me.

Once they reached the Rock, Nico sank into the calm of the

Nexus, the place where all things were one. Earth power was primarily a talent of the Danai, but he could tap a certain amount of it. Perhaps he could weaken the hinges. He gritted his teeth, feeling the particles of metal resonate. Pain shot through his injured leg. He drew deeper....

His eyes snapped open as gears groaned and the massive bronze doors slowly swung wide. At first, Nico thought he'd miraculously opened them, but then a voice came from inside.

"King Shahak bids you enter as his honored guests. He humbly apologizes for the misunderstanding at the city gates. You may enter the Rock of Ariamazes freely and in a spirit of welcome."

Gaius's eyes narrowed, a sharp, cunning expression that Nicodemus didn't trust. He'd seen Gaius in murderous rages, or full of manic good cheer, but this was something new.

A beardless youth waited in the antechamber. He wore a black coat trimmed in silver stitching at the sleeves and high stiff collar. Chin-length brown hair framed his face, parted in the middle and neatly oiled. He was too well dressed to be a servant, but Nicodemus had spent enough time in the court of Tjanjin to know he wasn't a noble either. He lacked the arrogance, the softness. Something about him said he worked for a living.

"If this is some kind of a trick, you will have cause to regret it," Gaius said coldly.

The youth paled. "It is no trick, I swear it on my honor. King Shahak will greet you in the throne room. He is most anxious to meet you."

The Praetorians went first, alert for any sign of treachery. The ranks of defenders waiting inside flinched away from the scarred faces, but none raised a weapon. Nico exchanged a look with Atticus and limped into the cavernous entrance.

"I am Javid," the youth told Gaius with an elegant bow, quickly recognizing where the power lay. "King Shahak's personal wind ship pilot. He has given me the honor of escorting you into his illustrious presence, if that is acceptable. Or do you wish to bathe and rest first?"

His tone was perfectly courteous, as though he were greeting any foreign delegation. Nico was impressed by the youth's courage.

"No," Gaius said flatly. "Lead us to your king."

Javid bowed again and brought them deeper into the Rock. When they reached a set of tall double doors, he inquired what name should be announced.

"I present King Gaius Julius Caesar Augustus of the clan of the Avas Vatras!" he said in ringing tones.

Nico scanned the throne room. A handful of nobles in silks huddled together like penned cattle who had just caught a whiff of the abattoir. More guards stood stiffly along the walls. Several made the sign of the flame as the Vatras entered.

An elevated dais held a throne carved from the same grey stone as the Rock itself, with a pair of roaring lions supporting the arms and a figure with eagle's wings across the back — a symbol of the Persian prophet, Nico remembered. Leaning forward on the throne sat a man of indeterminate age. His face bore the signs of some wasting illness in its terminal stage, but when he saw them, he rose to his feet and strode down from the dais with a broad smile that managed to be welcoming and ghastly at the same time.

"King Gaius! What an honor it is to meet you, cousin!"

There was a brittle silence. Gaius stared at him, his face a mask. Nicodemus braced for a wholesale slaughter.

"King Shahak," he said at last. "You are ... not what I expected. But I am pleased to be greeted with such courtesy and I too regret any misunderstanding."

The nobles emitted a collective exhale of relief. Shahak nodded happily, oblivious to the noose that dangled over his head.

"There has been needless strife between our peoples. In fact, I have always been fascinated by the wonders of the pre-Sundering era." Shahak beckoned and a woman stepped forward from the shadows next to the throne. She was more handsome than pretty, with dark hair in a braid over one shoulder and sharp, intelligent eyes.

"This is Leila Khorram-Din, my alchemist. Perhaps we can exchange knowledge for the benefit of both our peoples." He licked his lips. "I myself have some small skill, but it is nothing compared to the forging of talismans."

"And what would you offer in return for this *exchange*?" Gaius asked, clearly amused.

"If there is any way I can be of service, you need only ask." Shahak paused. "Forgive me if the question is indelicate, but how is it you came to be free of the Kiln? I would have welcomed you with a proper processional along the Parthian Way had I known to expect your arrival."

"An assassin came for me," Gaius replied. "The attempt failed. But the wards of the Gale were disrupted. The barrier between our lands has fallen."

Whispering erupted among the nobles until Shahak silenced them with a cold look.

"An assassin? Sent by whom?"

Gaius didn't look at Nicodemus. "The other clans, no doubt. They have always feared what they could not have themselves. It was not enough to imprison us. They sought to wipe us out."

"Well, I can assure you that you will be perfectly safe here. All within these walls know the price of treachery." Shahak's gaze strayed to pale things nailed to one of the pillars. "I too have been the target of vile conspiracies. It is the price of power that one must expect such intrigues — and deal with them swiftly and without mercy."

In the dim candlelight, Nico hadn't recognized the objects. His gorge rose as he realized they were human skins. But Gaius seemed pleased by the display.

"Very true. And my people have been victims of a far greater outrage." His expression grew solemn. "I would seek redress from those who left us to die in the Kiln. In that way, you may be of use. What is this modest skill with magic you speak of?"

The wind pilot's shoulders tensed and he watched Shahak with an intent gaze.

"I can transmute the nature of material objects," the king replied. "Among other things."

Gaius raised an eyebrow. "May I see a demonstration?"

Shahak considered the request for a moment. Then he ordered the guards to drag over three long tables. Fishing in a pocket of his robes, he scattered a handful of smooth white stones across each one. Curving yellow nails tipped each finger and Nicodemus wondered what ailment the king suffered from.

"Kashi ma bubussunu," he hissed.

The stones jiggled, rattling like dice. Romulus raised his spear in alarm and the royal guards tensed. But a moment later, they transformed into gold plates laden with food, still steaming as if fresh from the kitchens. Despite himself, Nico goggled. There were quail eggs stuffed with caviar, roast saddle of lamb, platters of truffles and nuts and artichokes, fresh figs in cream, and four roast peacocks with the tail feathers artfully arranged in a fan.

The Vatras, who subsisted on the tough, bitter flesh of bush rats, had difficulty comprehending the feast spread out before them. They sniffed suspiciously, wrinkling their noses. Shahak pressed a scrap of silk to his face and dropped it on the ground.

I must be tired, Nico thought, for in the instant before a servant hurried forward and retrieved it with a pair of tongs, he thought he saw the cloth *twitch*.

"A toast to your health," Shahak said, raising a wine horn shaped like a gazelle and pouring two cups. "To the reign of King Gaius! May our friendship prove long and prosperous."

Gaius smiled. He accepted the cup and swirled its contents, looking meditative. "I have not partaken of wine in a long time. Are you certain....?"

"That it is real? Absolutely." Shahak took a long draught from his own cup. "My wind pilot can taste it first if you have doubts."

Gaius glanced at the young man, who inclined his head. "That won't be necessary." He took a sip with eyes closed, sighing deeply. "Ramian red, if I'm not mistaken."

Shahak beamed. "You have a refined palate."

Gaius set his cup on the table. "My men are not accustomed to spirits. Better they have water." He grinned. "I cannot vouch for their behavior if they get drunk."

"Of course." Shahak made a sharp gesture and servants rushed forward to pour water into the cups and beckon the Vatras forward. The Praetorians and nobles took up two of the tables, Gaius's wives and children the third. Nico moved to sit down next to Aelia, but Romulus and Remus barred his way.

"Not you," Romulus said, baring his teeth.

Nico sighed and stepped back, leaning on his stick. He felt hollow as a drum and the smell of the food set his mouth to watering. Gaius jerked his head at Atticus, who cast Nico a guilty glance but went to sit down at Gaius's table.

Whatever initial reservations the Vatras had, they quickly crumbled. Nico watched them tear into the banquet, his stomach rolling at the spectacle. He'd forgotten how crude his people were. Forks were ignored as they stabbed chunks of meat with their knives and gobbled them down, sauce running down their chins. Only Gaius had any semblance of table manners, and even his were decidedly rusty. Dirty hands reached across the table to grab whatever morsel tempted. Teeth tore flesh from bone, then cracked it for the marrow within. Hilarity erupted when one of the Praetorians tried to eat a peacock feather.

The Persian nobles were obviously appalled, and just as obviously trying not to show it.

"Tell me more about this spell dust," Gaius said lazily, when they'd eaten themselves to glassy-eyed bursting. "I never knew mortals could work magic."

"It is a recent discovery," Shahak replied. "Leila Khorram-Din and her father were the first to make use of it." He spread his hands modestly. "My own studies have pushed the boundaries of what it can accomplish."

"But what is it made from?" Gaius persisted.

From his vantage point in the shadows, Nico saw a wary look pass between Javid and Leila Khorram-Din.

"There is a cave deep within the Valkirin range," Shahak replied. "It is guarded by an icebjorn, the largest and most fearsome of its species. Leila had the idea of feeding it milk of the poppy to cause the beast to sleep. Within lies a chamber where the dust can be found."

Gaius's gaze narrowed. "The Valkirins?" he growled, banging a fist on the table. "I'm not surprised they would try to keep such riches for themselves."

Nicodemus suppressed a laugh. A child would see through the tale, but Gaius had been in the Kiln for a thousand years. And in many ways, he *was* a child — albeit a horrible, murderous one.

"Show me this dust," Gaius demanded, draining his cup.

Shahak produced a lacquered box and opened it. Gaius peered inside. He swayed a bit in his chair.

"One must know the proper words to speak," Shahak murmured. "But I could teach you. I would place the Rock at your disposal, along with all my armies and the fleet at Susa. Only teach me the secrets of the adepts. Together, we can forge a new empire that spans Solis and Nocturne both."

Gaius's face went rigid with hatred. "I see possibilities in an alliance," he hissed, "but only if you renounce all ties to the other clans. They're liars and thieves."

Shahak snorted. "I care not for the Danai, nor the Marakai or Valkirins. If it is revenge you seek, I would not deny you."

"That is good." Gaius belched loudly, then rose to his feet and studied the nobles who sat across from him, gazing at each in turn. Finally, he pointed to a woman with shining dark hair caught up in a silver net. "There is one last condition to cement this treaty. I shall take a mortal wife. This one will do."

Shahak looked startled. "Lady Ardashir is already married. But there are many concubines in the harem—"

"Where's her husband?"

Shahak's eyes slid to the bearded man on her left, who looked green with fright. His mouth opened but no sound came out. Gaius leapt on the man, dragging him to the floor. His fingers closed around the noble's throat, strangling him with ruthless efficiency. The man's heels drummed on the stone floor. He flailed wildly and Gaius's snapped one wrist like a piece of kindling.

Chairs scraped back, hands flew to mouths, but not one of the man's friends did anything to stop it. Nor did King Shahak, though his full lips pursed in distaste.

Nico looked away, trying to silence the sounds coming from under the table. Gaius could have just burned the man and been done with it, but he obviously wanted to put on a show for the rest of them.

At last Gaius stood, sweat plastering hanks of red hair to the scar tissue seaming his skull. He gave a thin smile. "And now she's a widow."

Lady Ardashir slumped in her chair, eyes rolling back.

"Help her up," Gaius said mildly to Romulus and Remus. He wiped his face with a napkin. "I'm weary from our long journey. I'd like to go to my rooms now."

Shahak blinked. "Of course, of course," he said hastily. "Where is the Hazara-patis? Has he recovered his wits?"

A bald, pasty-faced man with a heavy chain of office scurried forward.

"Prepare the guest chambers on the highest level of the palace. See that their every need is attended to."

The Hazara-patis bobbed his head and dashed away.

Nicodemus watched the wind pilot and the alchemist, who sat at the next table. Leila's cheeks were flushed bright red. She moved to stand and Javid gripped her wrist with a quick shake of his head. She sank back into her chair, jaw tight.

They look as glad to be here as I am, Nicodemus thought. I wonder what hold Shahak has over them.

Gaius's wives rose, children nodding sleepily in their arms. They were clearly used to such violent outbursts. Nico's skin crawled as Gaius paused to stroke damp hair back from the brow of a little girl and kiss her forehead. Then he strode off without another word, his Praetorians prowling behind with the unconscious Lady Ardashir.

Nico hobbled for the double doors. As Aelia brushed past, she pressed something into his hand. He watched her walk away, back straight and head high. Nico's fingers probed the gift. His lips twitched into a half smile as he tucked the loaf of bread into his shirt.

❧ 4 ❧

SACRAMENTUM

"**H**e's a monster," Leila declared, pacing up and down.

"Which one?" Javid asked.

"Both of them!"

"That's hardly news."

She rounded on him. "How can you be so calm about it?"

"Look, we're still alive, which is more than I expected." He paused. "Well, not Lord Ardashir. That was ... awful. But I don't plan to sit around and wait to see who's next."

"I agree with Yasmin," his ma said levelly. "This has gone quite far enough."

"It's Javid," he muttered. "Please, ma."

She twisted her hands in her lap. "I'm sorry. It's just I forget sometimes."

As soon as King Shahak dismissed them, Javid went straight to his family's rooms and told them all that had transpired. Leila's own suite was not far off and she had helped her father, Marzban Khorram-Din, hobble to the secret meeting, then cast a spell to prevent eavesdropping.

They'd met no one in the halls. Even the servants were lying low.

Marzban Khorram-Din reclined on a couch, looking thin and pale, though his black bird-of-prey eyes were as fierce as ever. Javid's youngest sister, Mahmonir, played with a wooden horse at his feet. Every so often, Marzban would make a hideous face that set her to giggling. Bibi, who was too old for such things, stood next to Leila with arms crossed. Farima, the eldest, sat wedged between his parents on the opposite couch, eyes wide.

Two of the chickens roosted in a box filled with straw. The third, who had striking golden feathers, watched the door with sharp eyes. Even back at home she'd been the smartest one, flying the coop whenever Javid let his guard down.

"But what can we do?" Javid's pa demanded, making the sign of the flame. "Our fate is in the hands of the Holy Father now."

"I fear King Shahak will let the Vatras do whatever they want as long as they teach him the secrets of forging talismans," Javid said. "They will use him to get their revenge, and when they're done, they will turn on him. But we have a bit of time. If they were going to kill us all, they would have done so."

Marzban made a harrumphing sound. "I for one do not intend to sit here and wait to be immolated."

"But what can we do?" his ma echoed.

"There's a gate to the Dominion in the park," Leila pointed out. "We could escape that way."

"It's well-guarded now," Javid replied. "Besides which, getting trapped in the Dominion would hardly solve our problems. What if we couldn't find another gate to get out? No, we need to summon aid. And I happen to know someone who might be able to stand against the Vatras."

"Who?" Bibi demanded.

"A friend. Her name is Nazafareen."

"The Breaker you told me about," Leila said thoughtfully.

"Katsu said she defeated a fire worker in Tjanjin. If we could find her—"

A soft knock made everyone jump. Javid crept to the door, heart in his mouth. "Who is it?"

"Me," a muffled voice replied. "Open up!"

Javid shook his head, then slid back the bolt. Katsu stood there, looking dapper in a red coat and matching cap. When he saw Javid, he broke into a white grin.

"The city is nearly empty," he said, ducking inside. "The guards couldn't believe I actually wanted to come *into* the Rock." Katsu waved a piece of parchment. "But this did the trick."

As Shahak's pilot, Javid held a certain amount of authority. A week before, he'd given Katsu a letter with the king's seal, granting free rein to come and go from the palace in hopes they could plot an escape. But he certainly hadn't expected Katsu to use it now.

"You great fool!" Javid exclaimed. "Why are you still here?"

Katsu arched an eyebrow. "Did you think to be rid of me so easily?"

Javid made a sound of exasperation. "You know what I mean. If I were you, I'd be halfway across the Umbra by now."

Katsu gave him a lazy smile that warmed his cheeks. "No, you wouldn't. You'd be right where I'm standing." He looked at the others. "I'm here to offer my help, for whatever it's worth."

"Who is this young man?" Marzban Khorram-Din rasped.

"I am Katsu of the Selk Isle of the Marakai," he replied, bowing from the waist. "Newly come to Samarqand and master of the wind ship *Shenfeng*."

"A Stygian! Well, well." Marzban's hooded gaze took in his curly hair and dark skin. "I've heard your people rarely leave the Isles."

"That is true enough," Katsu replied lightly. "But as I am not partial to either fish or constant darkness, I decided to make my own way in the world." He turned to Javid. "When I heard the news that Vatras had taken the Rock, I feared the worst. Then a sentry at the curtain wall told me that the gates had been opened to them freely. It seemed madness, but from what you've said about King Shahak, he is more than capable of such folly. So I decided to come see for myself." His voice softened. "I am very glad to see you unharmed."

"You're a good boy, Katsu," Javid's ma said with firm approval. "A good friend. Javid should have more like you, he keeps to himself too much—"

Javid cleared his throat. "Since you are here, I think it's time everyone heard what you know of the Vatras, and of Nazafareen."

"Yes, tell us, tell us!" Bibi exclaimed.

So Katsu sat down on a cushion next to Mahmonir, nearly crushing a clutch of eggs one of the chickens had hidden, and began to relate his tale.

"After Javid bought my way out of the Pythia's dungeons, I returned to New Hope in the Isles of the Marakai, the town where I was born. From there I caught a ship to Tjanjin, hoping to find a talisman that had been stolen from the emperor. I was a fortune hunter and he had offered a large bounty to anyone who returned it." Katsu paused to pour a cup of watered wine. "I did find the talisman, but it had been in the possession of a Vatra who kidnapped a Marakai girl. Her name is Meb and she is a descendant of the fabled daēvas whose power turned back the Vatras a thousand years ago."

"Where is Meb now?" Bibi asked eagerly.

"She left with her clan."

"Will she come save us?"

Katsu took a sip of wine. "I don't know, but Nazafareen might. The last I heard, she and Darius were heading for the Valkirin range." He leaned forward. "If I can gain permission to leave the city, we can try to find her. And if not, then we go to the Marakai."

Javid nodded. He felt the glimmerings of a plan. "Shahak wanted me to make a run to Pompeii. His stores of dust are running low. Perhaps we can use that as a pretext."

"Pompeii?"

"There is no point in keeping secrets anymore," Leila interjected. "The dust comes from the old capital of the Vatras. It is the burned bones of those who died in the final battle, when the sun and moon were frozen in the sky and the Gale was forged."

Katsu made a complex sign with his left hand and muttered an oath to Babana the Oyster King. Javid's da whispered, "Holy Father!" His ma pursed her lips. Bibi gave a low whistle.

"Cool," she said.

"It's not *cool*," Javid snapped. "It's disgusting. And if the Vatras find out...."

No one spoke for a minute.

"But what if you don't return?" his ma asked. "What will happen to us?"

Javid and Leila exchanged a look.

"The king knows exactly how long a trip to Pompeii takes," Javid admitted. "It could take some time to find Nazafareen. She could have gone anywhere by now. If Shahak suspects treachery...."

"You stay here," Leila said. "I'll go with Katsu."

"Take me," Bibi said fiercely. "I won't get in the way, I swear. I'll help you—"

"No," Javid said immediately. "It's too dangerous."

Bibi shot him a venomous look. "It's dangerous here too."

"The child has a point," Marzban Khorram-Din murmured.

"You're not going," Javid said. "That's that."

Bibi fell into a mutinous silence.

"I'm not a very good pilot," Katsu said. "Although Savah has been teaching me the basics."

"Shahak doesn't know that," Leila said. "I'll tell him I've found a new pilot, one with excellent credentials. I know how to fly a wind ship. Javid, you must pretend to take ill."

As much as he wished to go himself, Javid saw the sense in this and didn't argue. "How soon can you leave?"

"I must consult the king. We will need his blessing, but I think I can manage it. Two days should be enough time to prepare for the journey to the darklands."

They spent another hour fleshing out the details. By the time they finished, Mahmonir had fallen asleep on the lower portion of Marzban's long white beard. The alchemist looked down at her fondly and Javid wondered how he had ever been afraid of the man.

"Come," he said to Katsu. "I'll escort you out."

They walked together through the twisting corridors. When they reached the antechamber to the bronze doors, out of sight of the guards, Katsu paused and took Javid's hand. "I'll find Nazafareen," he said confidently. "And perhaps she knows who the other talismans are. She was going to seek them out."

Javid looked at him seriously. "If you return with all three, I'll show you a book I have. It's called The Hard and the Soft."

Katsu laughed. "And I thought that was a fighting style taught by the monks in Tjanjin. You never fail to surprise me, Javid." Katsu drew him close and kissed him softly on the lips. "I'll hold you to that."

"Go to Savah and tell him everything. He can be trusted to help."

Katsu nodded. "I'll see you in two days."

Javid thought the guards might try to bar him from leaving the Rock, but they stood aside and let him pass with stony faces.

"Lucky bastard," one of them muttered.

NICODEMUS KNELT IN THE CENTER OF A VAULTED STONE chamber, Romulus looming to his left, Remus to his right. The brothers were identical in appearance, carrot-haired and wiry with narrow, wolfish features. The only way to tell them apart was by the ritual burns, which were on opposite sides of their faces, and the fact that Remus almost never spoke.

Also that Remus was fond of using his knife. He held it now, dangling point down at his side.

The Vatras occupied lavish rooms on the uppermost level of the Rock. Tapestries covered the walls and silver standing lamps cast a cozy glow over polished cedar furnishings. A faint breeze made the candles waver. Improbably, Nicodemus caught the scent of roses.

"Ah, my boy," Gaius said. "What a pass we've come to."

He sounded genuinely sorry, and Nico understood that his own usefulness was at an end.

My life is worth nothing, he thought bitterly. The first years of it spent scrabbling to survive like a wild beast, and then a wasted chance to make something better of myself. I deserve this.

"I wonder what Domitia would make of you now?" Gaius asked softly. "She always liked you. I did, too. When your mother died, you took it like a man. I didn't think you'd make it a week, but you surprised me. It's a shame things turned out the way they did." Gaius squatted down so they were eye to eye. "Tell me one thing. Is my daughter truly gone? And if so, did she die as you claim? Or did you have something to do with it?"

Nico held Gaius's translucent gaze without wavering. "I told you before, her body lies on the plain of the Umbra, a black-fletched Danai arrow through her throat. If you look, you'll find it."

Gaius nodded slowly. "Perhaps I should take you along in case we find something different." He paused. "Or perhaps I should just kill you now. To be honest, I'm leaning that way."

Remus adjusted his grip on the knife, his expression impassive. If Gaius gave the order, Nico knew Remus would slit his throat without a second thought.

Exhaustion crashed over him.

I could just let it end now.

But then he thought of Aelia and Atticus and all the people —
mortal and daēva — Gaius had yet to rape and murder but surely
would, and something stubborn in him dug in.

*I betrayed him and he won't forget that, but he wants to be loved. He
craves it. I've always known that, from the first time he brought me to the
burrow and sat me down on his knee to fill my head with lies. My
treachery cut him to the quick. He's not lying when he says he viewed me as
a son. I can use that. I can give him what he's always wanted....*

And suddenly, Nico knew what he had to do to walk out of
this room alive.

Maybe.

"Wait," he said.

Gaius sighed and covered a yawn with the back of his hand.
"Why?"

"Because I can help you get your revenge. Things have
changed since you were banished to the Kiln. For one thing, the
Valkirins no longer live in timbered holdfasts. They've retreated
to the mountains of Nocturne and it will not be so easy to root
them out. The keeps are made of stone, and the cold and dark are
difficult for us to tolerate. But I know exactly where the four
Valkirin holdfasts are. There was an old woman at Val Moraine
who would have welcomed our return. She told me everything she
knew about the clan's defenses."

Nico licked dry lips. "I lived among the Marakai and I learned
how to sail a ship. And I spent a year at the court of Tjanjin. The
emperor has a large talisman collection that might be of use."

A spark of interest lit in Gaius's eyes, but it wasn't enough.
Nico had expected that.

"And why should I trust anything you say?"

Nico summoned a few tears, though his heart was cold and
empty. "I know I lost my path, but you can't imagine what it was
like to be the only one of us left. After Domitia died, the Breaker
caught me. I thought she would kill me, but she didn't. Instead
she held me captive. Tortured me until my mind had broken. She

said you went mad and led the Vatras into a war we couldn't win." His heart beat faster. "You and someone called the Viper."

Gaius's face gave nothing away. "And you believed her."

"I didn't know what to believe," Nico replied truthfully. "But the claims were repeated in the mortal histories Domitia assembled."

He'd told Gaius that Domitia took a job at the Great Library, where she combed through records from the war, searching for evidence of the three talismans. He did not tell Gaius she had been Oracle of Delphi. It might lead him in directions best left alone.

"Tell me, was the Viper real?" he asked.

Perhaps the unaccustomed wine had mellowed him, for Gaius didn't react with anger. If anything, he seemed surprised.

"He was real," Gaius replied slowly. "A childhood friend. He served me faithfully for many years. Farrumohr was a good man and a staunch ally. He spoke truth about the other clans, which didn't make him popular. He died when they burned Pompeii." His eyes grew distant with memory. "We all fled, it was chaos. Much later, I discovered his fate. He fell into one of the sinkholes and couldn't escape. Some of the others fleeing the city saw him floundering there." Gaius's face darkened. "None stopped to help him. I never saw him again."

The tale matched what he heard from Nazafareen. Nico got the impression Gaius was telling the truth, though of course he couldn't be sure. But why would Gaius lie to him now?

"You say this Breaker knew about Farrumohr?" Gaius frowned. "How?"

"She said he wasn't truly dead. That he was somehow influencing events from the afterlife." Nico hesitated, then decided to throw in a bit of truth. "She believed he might be pulling your strings like a puppet."

Gaius laughed. "Then she lied to you about more than just the war. Farrumohr is gone, of that there can be no doubt." He stared down at Nico. "I wish you had come to me first. But that time has passed—"

"Make me a Praetorian," Nico said, playing his final card. "I would take the burns and swear the oath. Grant me a chance at redemption, father, and I am yours until I draw my last breath."

Emotions flickered across Gaius's face, too quick to read.

"You little shit—" Romulus snarled.

"Shut up," Gaius said mildly. "You would do that? Of your own free will?"

"Yes."

"For your mother's sake, the death I'd give you now would be clean and swift. You understand the penalty if your oath is broken?"

"I understand."

Everyone knew it. That's why so few chose to serve as Gaius's personal bodyguard.

"Get him up," Gaius said.

The twins hauled Nico to his feet. He winced as his half-healed leg buckled. Romulus scowled deeply. As usual, Remus looked a thousand leagues away.

The burning had to be done by another. When a Vatra summoned flame, it would not touch his or her own flesh. Nico's gut tightened at what was coming, but his mistakes were already writ large across his flesh. What was one more chapter?

"Do you know the words of the *Sacramentum*?" Gaius asked.

"I know them." Nico pressed a fist to his heart. "I am the flame between the king and his enemies. The spear through the heart of the lesser clans. I forsake all other loyalties, blood ties and allegiances beyond this Brotherhood. Born to fire, raised to fire, marked by fire. By these scars, I shall never forget the Day of Infamy. *Malo mori quam foedari*."

"Very good. So which side do you prefer?" Gaius asked, his eyes glittering. "Left or right?"

It was then that Nico realized Gaius had anticipated this

33

moment all along. That it was Nico who was being made the fool. Gaius didn't trust him and never would, but it amused him to see Nico maim himself.

Oh, fuck it. It didn't really matter, did it?

Domitia was right when she said he was a son of the Kiln. Two brief years in the civilized world had done nothing to change that essential fact.

I'm a hunter and a killer and I care for nothing — except to see you dead someday.

Nicodemus studied Remus and then his brother, cocking his head as if trying to come to a decision.

"I think you both left the ugliest halves," he mused. "Ah well, flip a coin if you'd like. Just watch the eye, I need to see—"

Remus's hand shot out, gripping Nico's jaw, and the world turned white with fire.

5

GAMES

Princess Pingyang threw the Senet sticks, stifling a yawn with the back of her hand.

"Oh, look. I've captured another of your houses," she said, sliding her own piece forward four squares and Meb's back to the starting point.

It was the third house she'd taken in the last twelve moves.

Meb scowled and grabbed the sticks. Senet was a deceptively simple game, yet Princess Pingyang beat her every time — probably because she'd been playing it in her father's court since birth, Meb thought sourly.

Of the thirty houses, or squares, six were marked with special symbols: The House of Happiness or Pretty House, the House of Water, the House of Rebirth, the House of Three Truths, the House of Re-Atoum and the Last House. Princess Pingyang had already gotten five of her six pieces through the Last House.

Meb almost made a stupid move so the game would end quicker, but the patronizing smile on the princess's face made her decide to fight it out. She threw the sticks. Three landed black side up, one red side up. Meb hesitated, fingers playing over the pieces, then moved three squares into the House of Rebirth.

"More tea?" the princess's handmaiden whispered with down-cast eyes.

Meb shook her head.

She was tired of drinking tea. Tired of playing Senet. Tired of nibbling the disgusting sweetcakes the princess adored.

Tired of sitting around doing nothing while the Diyat met in secret.

She shifted impatiently and Anuketmatma, the Mother of Storms, flexed her claws, sinking them into Meb's lap. Meb grunted and scratched her in the soft place behind her ears.

The room they sat in was excessive even by the standards of the Mer, every inch of it crammed with gilt fabrics and jewel-encrusted furnishings. The Marakai claimed a tenth of the goods they traded as the *Hin*. Most of the treasure went into vast store-houses overseen by the viziers, where it would eventually find its way to the bottom of the Great Green as offerings to the Marakai gods. The rest was stuffed haphazardly into the guest chambers of the Mer to impress visitors. If it glittered or gleamed, the reasoning went, the mortals would like it.

Of all the city-states, Tjanjin had the closest ties with the Marakai, so the princess had been given the gaudiest room of all.

Now she picked up the sticks in one hand, holding her cup out with the other for the handmaiden, Feng Mian, to refill. The tea set was exquisite, made from Tjanjinese porcelain as thin as a whisper and painted with tiny birds to match the ones that twittered from their wicker cage.

How does she drink so much tea without using the privy? It must be another princess trick.

Pingyang was full of them.

Unlike Meb, her heavy black hair was never mussed. She never spilled crumbs on her silk robes. And she never lost a game of Senet.

Meb sighed.

Eleven days had passed since she disembarked from the

Asperta and appeared before the Diyat, who gave her a cursory once-over and dismissed her so "the grownups could talk."

Only eleven days, yet it felt like a year. Like ten years!

When would the Diyat let her go? Meb figured they were talking about Nicodemus. Captain Kasaika said they were in disagreement, but refused to tell Meb anything else.

She longed to escape the Mer and return to her berth on the *Asperta*, even if it meant going back to her job cleaning fish. But she was the *talisman*. She had to be kept *safe*. Meb's scowl deepened.

Not that anyone treated her differently. When Captain Kasaika said toad, she still expected Meb to hop.

I should have run off with Nazafareen and Darius, she thought mutinously.

"Don't frown so," the princess admonished. "It will ruin your skin."

She tossed the sticks and swept toward the Last House.

"Why did you come here anyway?" Meb burst out, then felt her face warm. None of it was the princess's fault. She was probably just as bored as Meb. Surely the court at Tjanjin was more exciting than this!

Too well-bred to take offense — or at least to show it — Pingyang gave her a sweet smile. "As a companion to you, dearest Meb, and as a gesture of goodwill to the Marakai so they know Tjanjin is your loyal ally."

"We knew that already," Meb grumbled.

"You are tired of Senet," the princess said, setting her cup aside. "Perhaps we could do something else." She clasped delicate hands to her bosom. The nails were very clean. "What if Feng Mian does your hair? We can braid it with scented oil—"

"No."

"Or paint your face. You would be so pretty if only you—"

"I want to finish the game."

The princess sighed reluctantly. "Very well. It's your turn."

Four throws later, it was over. On her second try, Pingyang managed to toss the sticks so only the red one faced upwards, which was the only way to pass through the Last House.

Meb stood so abruptly Anuketmatma spilled from her lap. The Mother of Storms bristled, casting her a slit-eyed look. Meb bundled the cat into her arms.

"I'm tired," she declared, pretending to yawn. "I think I'll go take a nap."

Princess Pingyang inclined her head. "As you wish, Meb. If you come back later, we can tell each other stories."

Feng Mian gave her a shy curtsy. Meb heard them whispering together as the door closed.

The princess was the same age as Meb, but it was painfully obvious they had nothing in common. Pingyang probably thought Meb was an uncouth savage, and Meb thought she was a shallow priss. Why the Diyat insisted they spent time together every day was a mystery.

Maybe they want to make me into a *lady*, she thought with dread. But I won't! *Not ever*.

One of the Medjay waited outside to escort her back to her chambers. Part mortal, part Marakai, he wore a tight uniform of sharkskin and carried a short spear. He did not speak to her, nor Meb to him.

Once inside, she threw herself down on her narrow bed. The room was much plainer than the princess's but still palatial compared to her berth on the *Asperta*. Meb hated it. She missed the gentle sway of her hammock. The open air and sky. She felt the sea all the time now, calling to her, though Captain Kasaika said she couldn't do anything with it or she'd be in big trouble.

The captain had told her all about the Vatras. The fourth clan who worked fire. The War of Sundering seemed a terribly long time ago, but Meb had met one of them. Nicodemus seemed nice until he locked her up and summoned those liches. Once she'd thought he was a friend. Her mouth twisted. Stupid to think he would be. She had no friends. Princess Pingyang didn't count. She was as much a prisoner as Meb.

Suddenly, she couldn't stand being in her room for *one more minute*.

Meb crept to the thin slit of a window.

"If I only knew what they planned to do with me," she muttered, rebellion gathering in her heart.

Anuketmatma curled up on the cot and draped her tail over her nose, but she watched Meb with intent green eyes.

They all think I'm Meb the Mouse. They forgot who else I am.

Meb the Sneak.

Meb the Skulker.

Meb the Shadow.

She poked her head out the window. Her room was about halfway up the Mer. She knew where the Five met. The triangular chamber at the very top.

Meb turned sideways, sucked in a breath and squeezed out the window, fingers and toes finding hairline cracks in the slanted wall. She glanced down. Nine Medjay patrolled the grounds a hundred paces below.

She inched her way upward, clinging like a barnacle to the outside of the Mer. The night was calm and clear. Meb grinned in silent exhilaration. Years of scrambling across the pitching deck of the *Asperta* made her agile as a monkey. She had no fear of falling, only of being seen, but the Medjay never thought to look *up*.

At last she heard voices. They drifted through one of the three circular openings at the top of the Mer, each representing a phase of Nocturne's trio of moons. Meb braced her feet on a narrow ledge of gold plating. Hecate's cold light burnished the still waters of the harbor far below. Most of the Marakai fleet sat anchored there, waiting for word from the Diyat. In the distance she could see the Stygian town of New Hope, where a thousand lumen crystals twinkled like fireflies in the darkness.

Meb stilled her pulse and listened.

"WE MUST WAIT FOR WORD FROM THE OTHER CLANS," AHMOSE snapped. "I will not lead the Nyx to war without knowing what they intend. Have you forgotten what happened to Sahket-ra-katme?"

Like Sakhet, Ahmose had a sharp nose and bright birdlike eyes. She stared at the others sitting cross-legged in a circle, an empty pot of kelp chai between them.

Despite their treasure hoards, the Marakai were an austere people and the three-sided stone chamber at the very peak of the Mer was bare of furnishings except for overlapping rugs in the center. Heavy panels could be fastened shut when storms blew in, but they were not needed tonight and a fresh breeze smelling of the sea spilled through the open windows.

"No one has forgotten," murmured Nimlot of the Jengu Marakai, speaking slowly as was his habit. "But time runs short. We must come to a unanimous decision. The matter is too weighty for division."

"Ahmose is right. It bodes ill that the clans haven't answered," said Radames of the Selk, his handsome face grave. He wore tattoos of Anuketmatma on both cheeks and the backs of his hands. "Something is very wrong."

"It is no mystery. The time of Isfet is upon us." The deep, dry voice belonged to Qenna of the Sheut, a sturdy woman who wore her hair in waist-long dreadlocks.

Ahmose frowned. "That is your prophecy, not ours. Though I do not disagree that dark days have come to the clans." She glanced at the fifth of their number, Hatshepsut, who was tall and full-lipped with a swan neck and elegantly sloping forehead. "And what of the Khepresh? Is this girl the heir?"

Hatshepsut returned her gaze with cool consideration. "I

already told you, I don't know. The Blue Crown has no connection to the talisman as far as I'm aware."

The others exchanged a quick look. More than one wondered if Hatshepsut spoke the truth. She had commanded the Khepresh for more than two hundred years and might be hesitant to relinquish her power to another. Or Meb might not be the one. And if she wasn't, the consequences of a claim would be disastrous.

"It doesn't matter," Radames said. "That is not what we are here to discuss. The question is whether we leave or shelter here." He paused. "The Isles have no gates. The Vatras cannot come upon us without warning."

"And it would be madness to sail forth without knowing where the other talismans are!" Ahmose exclaimed. "The three must be united. We cannot risk losing Meb on a whim!"

Qenna's face hardened. "It is hardly a whim. You would hide and do nothing while the world burns—"

They all started squabbling again.

"If I may?" Captain Mafuone interrupted diffidently.

She knelt outside the circle with Captain Kasaika. Qenna had argued for them to be present because Kasaika knew Meb the best and Mafuone had sailed with the mortal Breaker and her companions. Like Qenna, Mafuone was Sheut Marakai. Their prophecies foretold the Vatras' return and the chaos that would follow. Both women agreed the Marakai needed to act, but only Nimlot of the Jengu was leaning their way. The others sided with Ahmose. Eleven days of argument had failed to break the impasse.

In the meantime, none of the birds carrying messages to the Danai Matrium and the four heads of the Valkirin holdfasts had returned.

Mafuone cleared her throat. "By your leave, I can take the *Chione* to House Baradel. Kasaika can approach the Valkirins—"

"No," Hatshepsut said with finality. "It's too dangerous. We don't know where the Vatra went."

"Or if there are more of them," Radames added. He gave Mafuone a brilliant smile. "Though it is a brave offer, captain."

"Birds are notoriously unreliable," Nimlot grumbled, swirling the dregs of his chai. Like the Giant Carp Who Shakes the Seabed, the Jengu's patron deity, he was slow to anger but deadly when roused.

"And so are the other clans," Ahmose muttered darkly. "They feud like children. I wouldn't be surprised if they have already gone to war with each other."

"Are you certain the Breaker didn't know who the other talismans were?" Radames asked.

Mafuone shook her head. "She was going to seek them out."

Qenna sighed. "I propose we wait three more days. If no news comes, we must assume the worst."

"And what of Meb?" Radames asked. "Will she do as she's told?"

Nimlot studied his chai. Hatshepsut shifted uneasily. Ahmose and Radames shared a troubled look. None liked to think too hard on the power the child wielded. If she grew headstrong....

Captain Kasaika folded heavily tattooed arms across her buxom chest. In the moonlight, the ship inked on her biceps seemed to toss atop a curling wave. "The girl's scared of her own shadow," she growled. "Leave Meb to me. She'll do as she's told, or she'll be scraping whelks from the bottom of the *Asperta* until she's sixteen!"

OUTSIDE THE WINDOW, MEB MADE A HIDEOUS FACE.

I oughtn't be surprised, she thought, flexing the numb fingers of one hand, then the other. I should be glad they're not sending me off to fight the Vatras alone.

Just the thought made her ill.

Captain Kasaika was right. She'd never stand up to the Five.

And why should she want to? They knew what was best for the Marakai.

Meb stared out at the dark horizon. The wind was picking up. She could feel a storm coming, though it wasn't the cat's making. Just one of the regular gales that blew in from the White Sea.

I'd best head back down before it catches me, she decided.

That turned out to be trickier than going up. Meb clung to the Mer, toes blindly probing for cracks. Sleet prickled the back of her neck and her thin arms trembled with exhaustion.

A little further.

She reached the juncture where two sides of the great pyramid joined and paused to rest for a moment, shivering in the icy wind. An unpleasant thought occurred to her. What if Captain Kasaika came to check on her? She did sometimes. The captain was a hard woman, though she'd hugged Meb fit to break her ribs when Nazafareen brought her back to the *Asperta*. But if she found Meb gone now....

She braced her legs to start down again when the clouds parted and moonlight streamed through. Meb's breath caught.

A lithe figure descended the opposite side of the Mer. It was clad in black except for the eyes, which met hers for a fleeting moment. Before Meb could shout, it vaulted through a window and vanished.

Meb regained her composure and climbed the last twenty paces to her rooms, squeezing inside as the wind began to blow in earnest. Anuketmatma arched her back and leapt from the bed, rubbing against Meb's leg with a demanding purr.

That was no moon shadow, Meb thought, warming her chilled hands in the cat's thick fur. I know what I saw.

Someone else was listening too.

❧ 6 ❧

THE FIVE

Ragnhildur flew ahead of the storm, aiming for the lights of New Hope. Culach couldn't see them, of course, but Mina assured him they were drawing close.

"They'd better be," he muttered, as the wind buffeted them this way and that. "I don't fancy a swim. Do you see the Mer yet?"

"I.... Yes! It's a bit off to the left." She took his hand and pointed.

Culach leaned over Ragnhildur's neck and whispered to her. She screamed and banked.

"Is Njala still back there?"

He felt Mina glance over her shoulder.

"She's following."

They'd arrived on the Isle of the Jengu the day before only to learn that the Five were meeting on the Isle of the Selk. Culach wanted to leave for Selk immediately, but both mounts and riders needed rest after the long journey from the Umbra so they'd taken rooms at a Stygian inn, which reeked of some foul brew made from black kelp.

Culach had expected retaliation for punching Victor in the face and then having him tied to the saddle, but the Danai sat drinking quietly in the common room until he passed out. He'd hardly spoken a word since finding the bodies of his wife and mother. Both his sons were missing as well, Galen presumably a prisoner of the Pythia.

Once I would have taken joy in his suffering, Culach reflected, except that he helped me save Mina from the cold cells.

Of course, he did it in traditional Dessarian style, wreaking the most damage for the smallest reward.

After carting an unconscious Victor off to their rooms, Mithre told Culach that he and Mina should do the talking when they met with the Five. To everyone's surprise, Victor had agreed when he woke up. The indomitable Victor Dessarian had died on the Umbra with his kin and Culach found he almost missed him. Victor could be a first-class prick, but this new, meek version made his skin crawl. He wondered how long it would last — and what Victor intended.

Now Culach felt Ragnhildur flex her wings as she prepared to land. A moment later, she skidded to a halt on the Isle of Selk.

"The Medjay are coming," Mina whispered. "We're near the base of the Mer, in a sort of clearing. They look stern but not unfriendly."

Culach slid from the saddle, offering his hand to Mina. She dismounted but remained at his side, fingers resting lightly on his elbow.

"I am Culach of Val Moraine," he said when the approaching footsteps came to a halt. "My companions are all of House Dessarian. We carry news for the Diyat."

"Welcome to Selk, cousins," a polite voice replied. "May I take your mounts?"

Culach was surprised. On Jengu, he had simply permitted the abbadax to fly off and fend for themselves. Both were good hunters. He just hoped they hadn't eaten someone's dog.

"You have a place for them?"

"We are not often graced with Valkirin visitors, but we keep a stable just in case. They will be well cared for."

Culach whispered calming words to Ragnhildur and Njala. "Go with these men, my darlings. And behave yourselves."

The mounts hissed and snorted, but permitted themselves to be led away.

"You may follow me," the Medjay said.

Culach let Mina guide him over the rocky ground. She'd described the Mer on Jengu to him, a vast pyramidal structure plated in gold. He knew they'd passed inside when the wind died and the echoes of their passage indicated walls.

Culach wondered if the child named Meb would be there. He'd heard about her extraordinary powers from the patrons at the inn. A few rounds of kelp ale loosened tongues and the local Stygians were happy to relay the latest gossip. Everyone knew about the wave she'd summoned, though none had seen her since the fleet returned from Tjanjin. The good news was that the Five were still meeting, so there was a chance their decision could be influenced.

They took a ramp that wound upward through the Mer. At last, the Medjay ushered them into a larger chamber and bade them to wait.

"I think we're supposed to sit on the floor," Mina said, tugging at his hand.

Culach sank down, feeling thick carpet beneath his palms.

"I somehow thought it would be fancier," Mithre remarked dryly. "The *Hin* and all that."

Culach laughed. "Oh, the *Hin* goes straight into the deep. Gerda used to say even the lowliest hagfish wear crowns of gold and ropes of pearls in these waters—"

"A Valkirin and three Danai," a thin voice interrupted. "And not just *any*. Culach Kafsnjór and Victor Dessarian, if I'm not mistaken. I thought you two had some sort of blood feud."

Culach scrambled to his feet. He heard the others do likewise.

Bloody hell, the woman must have *run* to have gotten there so quickly.

"Strange times make for strange allies," he replied.

"Indeed. Well, we are glad to see you. I am Ahmose of the Nyx."

Hurried footsteps signaled the rest of the Five, who made courteous greetings and introduced themselves: Nimlot of the Jengu, Radames of the Selk, Hatshepsut of the Khepresh and Qenna of the Sheut. Culach quickly memorized each of their voices. Nimlot, ponderous and deep. Radames, rich and musical. Hatshepsut, a hint of arrogance. And Qenna, forceful and with a brisk edge that suggested she didn't suffer fools.

"What news do you bring?" Radames asked eagerly, once they had all settled themselves on the carpet. "Have the talismans been found?"

"My son Galen inherited the power," Mina said, her grief plain. "But last I knew, he was in the hands of the Vatras."

Culach heard gasps of dismay.

"Then there is more than one," Nimlot said. "We know only of Nicodemus."

"The Oracle of Delphi is his accomplice," Mina said grimly. "They escaped from the Kiln together." She paused. "But that is not the only blow we have suffered. She burned the Matrium on the plain of the Umbra, and three hundred of our best scouts with them."

"By faceless Sat-bu, it cannot be true," Ahmose hissed.

"That explains a great deal," Hatshepsut said sadly. "We mourn your losses, cousin. Things are far worse than we feared."

The others murmured similar sentiments, but Culach noted that they didn't offer to avenge the dead.

"And the Valkirins?" Nimlot asked. "I hope you are not the last of your clan."

"Not the last, no," Culach said carefully. "But there was ... an accident at Val Moraine. Someone blew the Horn of Helheim and summoned revenants from the crypts. Halldóra of Val Tourmaline was already dead, killed by my great-great-grandmother Gerda. Runar and Stefán fought bravely, but there were so many risen.... We barely escaped with our lives."

"An accident," Radames said in a flat voice.

"It was me," Victor said hoarsely. "I did it."

The Five fell silent. Culach would have given much to see their faces.

"Would you care to tell us *why?*" Ahmose finally asked.

"I didn't know what it did. I...." Victor trailed off and cleared his throat. "It seemed like the right thing at the time."

Someone drew a deep breath.

"And the Valkirin talisman?" Qenna demanded.

"Is a woman named Katrin Aigursdottir," Culach said hastily. "She went with Nazafareen to hunt the Pythia."

"And?"

"And they've both disappeared."

"This is a disaster," Ahmose muttered.

"But Meb is safe?" Mina asked.

"Yes, Meb is safe." Culach winced at the acid tone. "The Marakai are not in the habit of losing their talismans."

"Be easy, Ahmose," Nimlot muttered. "It is her son you speak of."

"I'm sorry," Ahmose said, chastened. "But you!" That must be directed at Victor. "They said you were arrogant and feckless, but you've managed to outstrip even your own reputation. Of all the stupid, selfish—"

The tirade went on for several minutes. Culach expected Victor to erupt, or at least speak in his own defense, but he said nothing.

"If you are quite finished, Ahmose, I have some questions for the Kafsnjór," Qenna said at last.

"Very well. I think my point is made."

"Yes, I think so too." Culach sensed Qenna's gaze. "I don't

wish to offend, but it's clear you've lost your sight. Was that Victor's doing?"

"No." He drew a deep breath. "But it does have a bearing on things."

And so Culach started from the beginning, from that fateful day at the lake with Nazafareen, and told them all he knew of the Viper, and of King Gaius. Qenna of the Sheut pressed him for every detail he could remember, especially regarding the serpent crown, though the others were mostly silent.

"It all fits with what Sakhet told me," Radames said at last. "She believed the Viper wielded an evil influence over his king. But you no longer suffer from these dreams of the past?"

"They stopped when I reached the end of Farrumohr's life." Culach scratched his head. "Or rather the beginning. When he was just a boy. It all ran backwards, you see. I told Nazafareen everything. But there was one last dream. It came after she'd left for Solis and I was alone in the cold cells." Culach hesitated. "She was right when she said the Viper wasn't properly dead. I saw him in the Dominion."

"But if he's in the shadowlands, how can he harm us?" Nimlot wondered.

"I don't know. But I thought I ought to tell Nazafareen. We hoped you might have some idea where she is."

"I'm afraid we don't." Ahmose sighed. "Setting the matter of the Viper aside for the moment, what you're saying is that with only two Vatras loose, both the Danai and Valkirins are in disarray and have already suffered horrendous losses?"

Culach had to concede that this was indeed the case.

"So if, or more likely when, the rest of the fire clan appears, we have only Meb to save us?"

"There's Nazafareen—"

"Who has vanished," Ahmose said tartly.

Culach bit his tongue.

"We can still try to rescue Galen," Mina said, her voice urgent. "I know where he is. If Meb takes the fleet to Delphi—"

"Sakhet-ra-katme sacrificed her life to protect the girl," Ramades said gently. "She was the oldest and strongest of us all, and it did her no good when the Vatra came. I understand your desire to find Galen. We all wish he were here with us right now. But I can only assume he is unable to access his power, else he would never have been captured in the first place."

"So unless Galen is handed to you on a silver platter, you will turn your back to him?" Qenna demanded.

"And you would send Meb, not to mention the entire Marakai fleet, to their deaths for a slim chance that the Danai talisman *might* still be alive?" Ahmose retorted. "And if he is not?"

"Really, Ahmose! His mother is present."

"It is a cruel truth, but someone must speak it," the mistress of the Nyx muttered.

Nimlot cleared his throat. "This bickering is unseemly. Culach has given us much to think on. I think we should take time to discuss it further."

Without strangers listening to every word.

Sensing an imminent dismissal, Culach played his last card.

"I would like to see Meb," he ventured. "Perhaps my knowledge can be useful to her."

"She is a child, not yet thirteen," Hatshepsut replied. "It would only frighten her."

Culach disliked the condescending tone.

"With all due respect, she is the talisman," he persisted. "Doesn't she have a right to know the threat we face?"

"The Diyat will ensure Meb knows all she needs to," Ramades said smoothly. "I imagine you are weary from your journey. Rooms have been prepared with food to suit the tastes of your clans. You are welcome to remain as our guests for as long as you choose."

Culach forced a smile. "I hope we can speak more later."

"Of course. We are grateful for your candor and the news you brought, bleak though it may be."

The Five murmured a few noncommittal parting words and the Medjay led the four of them to a lower level of the Mer, escorting Victor and Mithre to separate chambers.

"You heard them. They will do nothing," Mina seethed once she and Culach were alone. "If the Marakai won't help my son, I'll go to Delphi myself."

"If it comes to that I'll go with you, my love," he replied. "But until they announce their decision to the fleet, we still have a chance. If we could only appeal to Meb directly. Nazafareen had faith in the girl."

"A child of twelve." Mina exhaled softly. "And the hopes of the world rest upon her."

"I was only eleven when my father led a raid on Val Altair's breeding stock." Culach smiled. It was a fond memory. "We snatched a dozen of their mounts before Stefán knew what was happening. I bloodied an opponent, though I didn't earn my first kill until I was fourteen."

Mina snorted. "Yes, well, you Valkirins were born for war. This girl is Marakai. They're a peace-loving people."

"Until the battle arrives on their doorstep." Her kissed her temple. "At which point it's usually too late. So let's hope it doesn't come to that, shall we?"

❧ 7 ❧

ICEBJORN

M eb was in an agony of indecision.

"If I tell Captain Kasaika what I saw, she'll know I was spying too. But what if it's someone who wishes us harm? What if it's a Vatra?"

The cat finished washing one paw and started on another.

"*You're* no help," Meb muttered.

Anuketmatma sneezed. She leapt up to the table and stalked over to the small leather bag where Meb kept her few belongings. The new knife Captain Kasaika had given her (which wasn't half as good as the one she'd bought with the black pearl). A comb Meb rarely used. Some shells she'd collected from the lagoon where she lived before her parents died. Sundry other items.

Anuketmatma began nudging the bag toward the edge of the table.

Meb sighed. "Do you have to?"

The Mother of Storms might be an inscrutable and pitiless deity, but she was also a standard feline. Meb often found gifts of dead mice on her pillow. If she threw them out, they would be faithfully returned until she pretended to eat them.

The bag teetered toward oblivion.

"Don't," Meb warned.

Looking her dead in the eye, Anuketmatma raised a paw and gave it a final push. The bag fell, spilling its contents across the floor. Anuketmatma peered down at the mess in fascination.

"You rotten...." Meb dropped to her knees. The cat yawned and resumed her washing.

Meb began shoveling things back into the bag. Her fingers touched a pair of fish bones and she paused.

The Medjay always locked her in at night — for her own safety, they claimed. But she'd used the fish bones to escape Nicodemus when he held her captive in the emperor's palace. Maybe she could pick the lock and do some investigating on her own.

"Are you telling me I should try to find out who the spy is myself?"

Anuketmatma ignored her.

It didn't take Meb long to reach a decision. The alternative was losing at Senet again — or worse, getting her hair done.

"I'll take that as a yes."

She pressed her ear to the door and heard nothing. Meb slipped the fish bones into the crack of the door jamb and wiggled them. In a matter of seconds, the tumblers clicked and she was free.

She slipped through the Mer, cloaking herself in shadow. Being invisible came as second nature and she had little trouble eluding the Medjay, who made so much noise she could hear them coming a league away. Anuketmatma padded along behind, her eyes gathering the moonlight.

It was fun to creep around the Mer unseen. Meb avoided the treasure rooms on the lower level, knowing they would be heavily guarded. And whoever she'd seen wasn't a thief. She felt sure they'd been eavesdropping on the Five, a thought that filled her with righteous indignation despite the fact that she'd been doing the very same thing.

She prowled through dusty storerooms that tickled her nose with the smell of strange spices and explored passages so cramped even Meb could barely squeeze through them. The Mer was a giant maze, deliberately designed to befuddle intruders. Sometimes a cold breeze would brush her cheek from some hidden shaft to the outside. She stepped carefully, knowing the ancient builders had set traps for the unwary and a wrong step might bring the ceiling down on her head.

After a while, Meb found herself in a series of small, tight chambers she'd never visited before. Some of the walls had pictures, the paint old and flaking, images of Marakai offering the *Hin* to the gods and other scenes of daily life. But then the pictures took an ominous turn.

She traced a finger along one huge mural of the fleet racing across the waves, flames leaping from the shore behind. Meb gave a little shudder. She continued on, reading the tale of the Sundering by the dim light of tiny lumen crystals embedded in the floor. The last panel showed three daēvas standing together in a city with topless, half-built towers. One had fair hair and a sword. The second was dark like Meb, the third olive-skinned.

The three talismans.

A wall of fire raced away from their outstretched arms, devouring the city. Their faces were hard and pitiless.

Meb jumped as Anuketmatma leapt from the shadows, snaking between her legs.

"Can you *not?*" she muttered, following the cat from the chamber with jellied knees.

Cobwebs festooned the doorways of this deserted section of the great pyramid and she saw no sign anyone had passed through in a long time. Another hour or so elapsed of fruitless searching. Meb retraced her path back to the inhabited quarters. She was growing bored. The storm still raged so climbing up the Mer again was out.

"We ain't even found a mouse," she whispered to Anuketmatma, who suddenly hissed and laid her ears back, staring at the juncture of the corridor just ahead.

Meb crept forward. She stuck her head around the corner and yanked it back, pulse pounding.

A figure in black crouched before one of the guest chambers, ear pressed to the door.

Meb had barely made a sound, but when she peeked again her quarry was already running in the opposite direction. Meb swore a vile oath and pursued. She had no idea what she'd do if she caught them — scream for the Medjay, most likely — but after the unrelenting tedium of the last two weeks, she wouldn't let a chance at some excitement slip through her fingers.

She dashed through the corridors, catching glimpses of the shadowy figure ahead. They were fast, but Meb was faster and she gained ground. She skidded around a corner and stopped.

The corridor ahead lay empty.

She frowned, then realized with a stab of dread that she'd reached Princess Pingyang's rooms. Meb had been only a few paces behind the black-clad figure. They couldn't have reached the next turning without being seen.

What if they'd taken the princess hostage? What if they were an *assassin*?

She ran to the door and pounded on it. No one answered.

"Princess!" she cried. "Don't worry, I'll fetch the Medjay—"

The door cracked open. A hand shot out and hauled her inside.

"Meb," Princess Pingyang said, her cheeks flushed with color. "Such a pleasure to have your company. What is all this talk about the Medjay?"

Meb looked around. The rooms looked undisturbed, their last game of Senet still laid out on the ivory table.

"No one came in here?" she asked.

A small crease appeared on the princess's forehead. "Why, no. I was just...about to take my bath."

Meb narrowed her eyes. "Where's Feng Mian?"

"Drawing the bath."

"You never open the door yourself."

Pingyang gave a small laugh. "Well, you were making such an awful fuss—"

Meb pushed past her, striding into the bedchamber, the princess trailing behind.

"Really, Meb, this is most improper, I have to insist—"

The princess's sleeping quarters were even more ridiculous than the sitting room if that was possible. A gold and purple striped canopy bed warred with crimson silk wall coverings and a vanity table carved in the shape of an enormous bejeweled butterfly.

Meb stalked to a wardrobe and threw open the doors.

Feng Mian glared back at her.

She'd unwound the cloth from her face. Gone was the meek maidservant who never spoke above a whisper and took little mincing steps. Black eyes flashed dangerously.

"Well," Princess Pingyang said with a sigh. "I suppose we'd better talk."

"YOU'RE SPIES!" MEB MUTTERED FROM THE DEPTHS OF HER usual puffy chair.

Anuketmatma had slipped inside with Meb and now she prowled the room, poking her head into priceless urns and batting at the fringes of a tapestry.

Feng Mian thrust a cup of tea at Meb with a scowl. She'd changed out of her sneaking-around uniform of loose black pants and tunic, but her demeanor remained defiant.

"Spies is a strong word," Princess Pingyang objected cheerfully. "I didn't lie when I said my father is an ally of the Marakai. But the Five tell me nothing." She sipped from her own cup. "Truly, they left us no other choice."

Meb's lips tightened. She glanced at the large cage next to the window. There seemed to be fewer birds inside than she remembered.

"So you were sent to make reports, not to be my companion."

"Both, dearest. Is that so terrible?" The princess paused and regarded Meb with shrewd eyes. "And you would never have caught Feng Mian if you hadn't been … seeking information yourself."

"That's different! I'm the talisman. I have a right to know what they're planning."

"If you're the talisman, why do you let them treat you like a swaddling babe?" Feng Mian inquired sweetly.

Meb opened her mouth for a sharp reply, then closed it again.

Princess Pingyyang shot her companion a quelling look. "What she's trying to say is that we share the same goal. To defeat the Vatras. But we cannot help when we are left in the dark."

"All right, then. What were you doing when I saw you out there?" Meb asked Feng Mian. "Tell me, or I'll get the Medjay."

Princess Pingyang gave a quick nod.

"A Valkirin and three Danai just arrived on Selk," Feng Mian said. "They bore tidings for the Five. The storm prevented me from listening to the meeting, but I followed two of them to their room."

"And?" Meb leaned forward.

"They want to see you, but the Five won't let them." Feng Mian crossed her arms. "I might have learned more had you not crept up on me."

Meb considered this. "What should I do?"

Princess Pingyang cast her a pitying look. "I cannot say. But you are the Marakai talisman. It is wrong that they exclude you from their council."

Meb squirmed, then forced herself to meet the princess's eye.

"It is wrong, isn't it?" she whispered.

"In the court of Tjanjin, if the princess were treated with such disrespect, the offender would be flogged!" Feng Mian growled. "You must demand an audience."

Issue demands? To the Five?

Meb felt the world tilt beneath her feet.

Could Meb the Mouse do such a thing?

She'd never talked back to Captain Kasaika. Not even to the *cook*. Meb glanced down at her tattered leather vest and trousers. She still had a tea stain on the left knee that dated to a week prior.

"You disobeyed them twice already," Feng Mian pointed out. She gave a short laugh. "I'll admit, I didn't expect to meet you at the top of the Mer." She tilted her head. "You're an agile climber. And fearless."

"So are you," Meb conceded.

They regarded each other with frank appraisal. Meb decided she liked the new Feng Mian a good deal better than the old one, even if she *was* a spy.

Still, she hadn't considered climbing the Mer to be particularly brave. Meb had a good head for heights and a natural talent for stealth. But to stand before the Five and make them do what she wanted....

Anuketmatma vaulted onto her lap, licking Meb's finger with her rough tongue. When Meb failed to respond, she gave it a hard nip.

"Ow!" Meb pushed the cat away. She drew a deep breath. Princess Pingyang looked at her expectantly.

"Okay," Meb said, eyeing the Mother of Storms, who seemed to grin. "I'll do it."

By the next day, Meb was very close to regretting her decision.

Restless, she paced her chamber waiting for Captain Kasaika. She'd asked the Medjay to find her what felt like *hours* ago. The princess thought Meb should go straight to the Five, but that prospect filled Meb with abject terror. No, she owed it to Captain Kasaika to tell her what she intended first. Most likely the Five would blame the captain for Meb's insubordination. At least she'd have fair warning.

Now Meb wished she'd never gone spy-hunting in the first place.

The Mother of Storms had abandoned her after breakfast, sneaking out the door without a single sign of encouragement.

Rotten cat.

Meb froze as footsteps halted outside her room. There was a brisk knock.

"Meb?"

She wiped her palms on her trousers and pulled open the door with a sickly grin. The captain peered down at her, brow creased with concern.

"They said you wanted to see me. Is everything all right?"

Meb nodded.

"I brought Captain Mafuone." Kasaika stepped aside to reveal the mistress of the *Chione*. "May we come in?"

Meb nodded.

Kasaika wore her hair shorn to the scalp, but Captain Mafuone kept hers in a dozen tight braids adorned with bits of shell. A tattoo of tentacled Sat-bu, She Who Strides the Waves, coiled around her left arm. She gave Meb a friendly smile.

"So what's all this about?" Kasaika asked, glancing at Meb's unmade bed with faint disapproval.

"Well, I...." Suddenly her tongue went dry.

"Out with it, girl," the captain snapped.

Meb thought of Feng Mian and straightened her spine. "I heard people came to the Mer," she burst out. "Asking for me."

Captain Kasaika's eyebrows shot up. "You *heard?* From whom?"

Meb looked past her, out the slit of a window, where the sea murmured beyond the breakwater. She let its song fill her. Her nerves steadied.

"Never you mind where. I heard it and I want to know what's going on."

Part of her scarcely believed she'd just said "never you mind" to the captain. Kasaika didn't seem to believe it either. She just stared at Meb like she'd grown a second head.

"I have the right," Meb said, her courage gathering momentum. "And if you won't tell me, I'll go find out myself."

The captain rubbed a hand across her scalp, her silver bracelets jangling.

"Now you listen to me, Meb—" she began. Captain Mafuone laid a hand on her arm. They shared a look.

"The kid's right," Mafuone said quietly. "You know it."

Kasaika frowned.

"There's prophecy being revealed now and we'd better heed it. No disrespect to the Five, but they'd keep her stowed in the hold until the storm hits, then tell her to jump in when she never learned to swim."

Meb cast the captain of the *Chione* a grateful look.

Kasaika grimaced. She was Selk. "If Radames finds out, he'll knock me down to swabbing fish guts off the deck."

"And if we don't pull the clans together and find those talismans, the Vatras will do a lot worse. You think they can't sail a ship?"

Kasaika looked at Meb, her face softening a little. "I suppose I ought to be relieved you had the guts to speak your mind. I wondered when you would."

"The Mother of Storms is on my side," Meb said. "I think. You know how she is."

"Well, that's something." The captain laid a hand on Meb's shoulder. "If you really want to know what we're facing, best you hear it from Culach Kasfnjor himself."

Meb drew a breath. "All right."

"Might as well go now," Captain Mafuone said. She winked at Meb. "Think you can manage to make yourself invisible?"

THE VALKIRIN WAS ONE OF THE SCARIEST PEOPLE MEB HAD ever laid eyes on.

He was huge for one thing. And he had a terrible winding scar down one side of his face. He looked like he could snap Meb's neck with two fingers and not break a sweat. The wickedly gleaming sword at his waist had probably chopped off a lot of heads. Arms and legs, too.

He had bright green eyes like Anuketmatma, except his were fringed with silver lashes. She recoiled as his gaze swept to the door ... and straight *through* her, to some distant point.

Then she realized he couldn't see her.

Meb relaxed a little.

A small, dark-haired woman hurried forward. She took Meb's hands in her own, tears in her eyes.

"Thank you," she whispered. "Thank you for coming."

Captain Kasaika had told Meb on the way that the woman's name was Mina of House Dessarian and that the Vatras had taken her son.

The Danai talisman.

"Okay," Meb mumbled, feeling awkward. To her relief, Mina dropped her hands and went to sit down next to Culach.

"The Five don't know we're here," Captain Kasaika said. "But we decided Meb ought to know everything we do." She barked a laugh with a note of wonder in it. "Actually, the kid insisted. So here we are."

"I'm glad," Culach said simply. "Where is she?"

"Here," Meb said in a small voice.

He smiled and she was startled at the transformation. He was almost ... handsome.

For a Valkirin.

"You met Nazafareen," he said.

"Yes. Is she your friend?"

He gave a small, secretive smile. "She is now. I wish I knew where she went."

"Me too."

Meb had felt safe with Nazafareen, even if she'd gotten a bit scary at the gate with Nicodemus.

Meb remembered the taut faces of the emperor's guards as they gazed up at the wave she made, though it seemed more like a dream.

I guess *I* can be scary sometimes, too, she reflected with some surprise.

"Tell her, Culach," Mina said softly. "Tell her all of it."

So he did. Meb listened to his tale with a sinking heart. She had often wondered about the other talismans. If they were young or old. What they looked like. How their weakness in the power had shaped them. It had never occurred to her that she might be the only one left alive.

The burden of that possibility weighed heavily on her now.

"You must gather the clans," Culach said. "They will follow your banner."

Meb looked at Captain Kasaika, her fear hardening to anger. It wasn't fair. She didn't know how to be this person they would make her into.

"But what if the Five don't want to go to war? They're still the Five! Their word is law."

"Not if you claim the Blue Crown," Mafuone said quietly.

Meb stilled. "Oh, no. You don't expect me to...." She gave her worst scowl. "No."

"In three days, the Diyat will address the fleet. We already know what they're going to say. That the Marakai must shelter in the Isles and stay out of it."

Meb said nothing. Her pulse fluttered like one of Princess Pingyang's songbirds.

"If you try to sway them now, they will listen and nod and give you a pat on the cheek and tell you they will give your words due consideration. Then they will do exactly what they intended in the first place." Mafuone paused. "But if you stake your claim before the entire fleet, they cannot refuse you."

"And what if I'm not the heir? The Nahresi will kill me!"

Everyone knew what happened to false claimants. They would be trampled beneath the wave horses' razor-sharp hooves.

"I'm certain you are."

But Meb thought she saw a glimmer of doubt in Mafuone's eyes.

"How do you know? *How?*"

"Because the Sheut prophecies say the Blue Crown has another name. The War Crown. And in the time of Isfet, when all seems lost, a new heir will rise. Who else could it be but you?"

"It could be someone else," Meb muttered. "And I'm not even Sheut."

Kasaika crouched down before her. "No one will force you. But I agree, it seems the only way. The fact that you are the talisman is not enough. If you were older, perhaps. But you are not yet of age. I fear the fleet won't listen to you otherwise."

"You *knew*," Meb said bitterly. "And you didn't tell me."

Kasaika had the grace to look ashamed. "Mafuone and I discussed the possibility, yes. Qenna, too. But the choice was always yours to make."

I won't cry, she thought savagely. But her throat felt very tight.

She looked at the Valkirin. He seemed to sense her gaze, for he turned his face to her. Something about him reminded her of Nazafareen. Solid and trustworthy.

"What do *you* think I should do, Culach Kafsnjór?"

He seemed surprised she would ask, but took the question seriously, thinking for a moment.

"My father was a hard man, Meb. He valued fear over love. I've tried not to make that same mistake." His face grew sad. "I can't say I've done the best job at it. But he told me a story when I was a boy that never left me." Culach's eyes moved restlessly, as though they saw things beyond the thick walls of the Mer. "Once there was an old icebjorn who lived in a cave on Mýrdalsjökull glacier. It was a fearsome beast, fourteen paces tall with claws the length of daggers, and the cunning of its kind. Two young Valkirin bucks decided to take its pelt for a rug. When they reached the cave, the bear was waiting for them. She reared up on her hind legs and gave a mighty roar. It echoed across the glacier, triggering snowslides for leagues around. The first Valkirin fainted on the spot. Well, icebjorns won't touch anything that looks dead, so the bear ignored him."

"What happened to the other?" Meb asked with wide eyes.

"Oh, he got eaten. When the first hunter woke and saw the icebjorn gnawing on his friend, he begged for his life. And the bear said — for in this story icebjorns can talk — the bear said, 'Only a fool seeks mercy from an icebjorn.' Then she ate him, too."

Meb squinted. "I ain't sure I get the moral of the story."

"Me either. I thought *you* might." Culach laughed. "That's why I've never forgotten it. At least you had the courage to say so. I just nodded like I knew what the hell he was talking about."

Captain Kasaika sighed.

"But know this," Culach added in a sober tone. "Whatever you decide, we stand with you." Pain flashed across his face. "I'm not sure what use I'd be. But I guess it's better than nothing."

His sincerity touched Meb's heart.

"Thank you, Culach Kafsnjór," she said formally. "And I think I do know the moral. They shouldn't have messed with that old icebjorn in the first place."

He looked alarmed. "I don't mean you should hide from the Vatras—"

"Don't be silly. The Vatras aren't the icebjorn." Meb smiled, though she knew he couldn't see it. "I am."

———

BRAVE WORDS, YET MEB HARDLY SLEPT THAT NIGHT.

After breakfast, which she pushed around the bowl, Meb went to see Princess Pingyang and Feng Mian. For once, her steps didn't drag as the Medjay escorted her through the halls of the Mer. She needed advice.

The Senet board sat untouched as Meb told them everything that had transpired. When she finished, Princess Pingyang looked at her gravely.

"So you will seek the Blue Crown?"

"I guess so," Meb said miserably.

"You *guess* so?" The princess arched a perfectly painted eyebrow. "That is no way for the Queen of the Marakai to talk."

"I'm not queen yet. And I might never be if the Nahresi break every bone in my body."

Feng Mian narrowed her eyes. "But that is not what troubles you the most."

Meb looked up, startled. "No."

"What does, then? The Vatras?"

"Not them, either. I mean, they scare me to death, but...." She twisted her hands in her lap. "I'll have to stand up there in front of everyone. Everyone! And talk."

Feng Mian started to laugh, turning it into a cough when Princess Pingyang shot her a dirty look.

"That is nothing to be ashamed of, Meb. You simply lack practice." Her eyes gleamed in a way Meb distrusted. "Let me help you."

"Help me how?"

Pingyang looked her over with a critical eye. "You slouch. When you talk, you have a tendency to mumble and address your feet. Your hair needs washing and the way you walk...." She shook her head. "It won't do."

"You're not painting my face," Meb snarled.

The princess laughed. "I would not turn you into a Tjanjinese lady, no. I doubt that would go over well. But if you are to win the respect of your clan, you cannot be Meb the Mouse any longer."

Meb scowled. So they'd heard of her nickname.

"You should listen to the princess," Feng Mian advised. "When she walks into the court, the nobles tremble. They call her the Jade Dragon!"

Pingyang made a modest noise, but Meb could tell she was pleased by the name.

It was definitely better than Meb the Mouse.

"I don't know," Meb said, chewing her lip. "We only have two days. It doesn't seem like enough—"

"Stand up," Pingyang ordered, a note of steel in her voice.

Meb sighed and rose to her feet.

"Walk to the window.... No, not like that! Lift your feet, don't drag them along the floor like rice sacks. Shoulders back, head high.... Now you're looking at the ceiling. Here, I'll show you."

They took turns drilling her for the next three hours until Meb sat down on the rug and refused to budge. The princess *was* a dragon and Feng Mian even worse. How could she ever have imagined them to be soft?

"It's hopeless," she moaned. "This will never work. They'll laugh me right off the pier."

Her tutors exchanged a troubled glance. But Princess Pingyang wasn't one to give up so easily.

"There must be a time when you felt strong. Invincible! Like you could do anything. Perhaps when you called the wave?"

"Not really. I only did that because the Lady wanted me to." The princess looked disappointed and Meb thought for a moment. "But there is a place.... Never mind. It's stupid."

"It's not stupid. Tell us, Meb."

"Well, you know the aquarium? Of course you do. Sometimes, when I had a day off in port, I would go to the shark pool."

"It's my favorite," the princess said with a delighted laugh. "Feeding time?"

"Yes!" Meb sat up. "I would gnash my teeth and pretend I was Meb the Shark."

Pingyang grinned. "Then that is who you shall be. Forget all the rest of it. Just be Meb the Shark."

They tried again. This time, Meb tried to imitate the flat, deadly gaze that always sent chills through her bones. The sinuous glide as the great fish sliced the water with their fins. Feng Mian gave her a curt nod, which was better than Meb had gotten before. The princess clasped her hands.

"I felt a certain something. A presence! That is what you want. They must be a little bit frightened of you."

Meb nodded in relief. She just wanted to get her mind off the Blue Crown and the Nahresi and all of it. In two days' time, she would either be dead or commanding the whole Marakai fleet, and in truth, she wasn't sure which would be worse.

"Can we play Senet now?"

"Soon, dearest." Pingyang's eyes were gleaming again. "But first we must work on your speech!"

———

A DAY PASSED. THE DIYAT DID NOT CALL FOR CULACH AGAIN, nor did Meb.

He liked her. She was yet a child, but she had hidden strength. He only hoped it was enough.

Mina had gone with the two captains to meet in secret with Qenna of the Sheut. If Meb succeeded in her claim, they would sail for the darklands and rally what remained of the Danai.

Culach strode to the door of their room and stuck his head out. "Medjay?" he asked.

"Here, Culach Kafnsjor," he replied.

Eirik had called him Culach No-Name. But Eirik was dead, eaten by his own abbadax.

I am a dynasty of one, he thought with dark amusement, and my subjects are all dead. Or rather, Undead.

"Would you take me to the stables? I'd like to visit my mount."

"Of course." The man paused, clearly uncertain how to go about it without causing accidental offense.

"If you promise not to lead me over the edge of a cliff, I can simply follow your footsteps."

The man gave a nervous laugh. "I promise, Culach Kafsnjór. The path to the sea is well-groomed and level."

There were no stairs in the Mer, only ramps, which made things easier. Culach followed him outside and took a deep breath of sea air. The Isle of the Selk was windy but no worse than the mountains. As the Medjay said, he found the path easy to navigate. The steady pulse of waves grew louder. They had reached the shore.

"We are standing before the door," the Medjay informed him.

"Yes. I can smell them." Culach turned to the man. "If you don't mind waiting for me—"

A harness jangled inside.

"Who's there?"

"It's me," Victor said.

Culach hesitated. He hadn't expected company — particularly Dessarian's.

"I'll take you back when we're done," Victor offered curtly.

Culach could hardly refuse. He thanked the Medjay and heard the man walk away. Ragnhildur made a noise of greeting, butting her beak against his chest. Culach cupped it in his hand. "How are they treating you, darling?"

The abbadax had a broad range of vocalizations, from ear-splitting screeches when they attacked to soft trills that indicated contentment. Culach was pleased to hear one of the latter.

"And Njala?" he asked.

Victor no longer had the bitter stench of the diamond, but he reeked of grief, a flat, *empty* scent that tickled Culach's nostrils.

"She is well."

"You didn't go to their council with Mithre," Culach ventured cautiously.

Victor was unpredictable at the best of times and when he veered off on his own, the results tended to be disastrous. If he did something to turn the Marakai against them now....

"Don't worry, I'm not going anywhere," Victor said, reading Culach's thoughts. "I only wanted to ensure Njala was fed and sheltered."

Culach sensed no deception in his words. "Will you help them unite the Houses?"

"I will," Victor replied without hesitation. "It's what Delilah and Tethys would have wanted."

Culach stroked Ragnhildur's neck feathers, which lacked the deadly barbs of her wings. He heard Victor moving around the stables, the clatter of a water bucket being lifted.

"I did care for your sister, you know," Victor said quietly.

Culach stiffened. The sea rushed into the silence, then rushed out again.

"I only left because you would have killed me."

Culach couldn't disagree with that.

"But I didn't take her through the gate," Victor added. "She followed without my knowledge."

"I know."

Now. I didn't then.

It was all so very long ago. He had been a different man, more like Eirik than he cared to admit. Culach supposed they'd both been different men.

"I can still see your bare ass running off into the woods," he said. "Unfortunately for me."

Victor laughed. With some surprise, Culach found himself laughing too.

They passed the rest of the afternoon trading stories of old times. Victor told him about Delilah and the sort of woman she had been. He wept, but there was no shame in it and he seemed better when he was done. As they walked back to the Mer together, Culach thought of the strange and winding path that had led them to this moment.

If not for Nazafareen, neither of us would be here. Whether by accident or design, she was at the heart of it all.

He remembered her voice when they parted, so full of life and determination.

Goodbye, Culach Kafsnjór. Goodbye!

Will you come back in our hour of need? he wondered now.

The damp wind of the White Sea crept inside the collar of his leather coat and Culach shivered.

Wherever Nazafareen had gone, he just hoped she still had his mother's blade.

❦ 8 ❧

THE HOUSE BEHIND THE VEIL

E verywhere, she heard the sound of water.

Slipping over stones, trickling through mossy crevices, splashing beneath her boots. Its murmurs followed her as she circled pine-shadowed lakes and waded through stagnant bogs. She forded rivers, leapt across streams. Whether swift or meandering, the water all flowed in the same direction.

Toward the Cold Sea.

The current tried to sweep Nazafareen along with it, to make her obey the natural order of things.

She walked in the opposite direction.

She didn't feel tired or hungry — nor much of anything — yet it took great will to resist the tidal pull of the sea. Resisting caused a sensation akin to pain. A tearing of the soul. It grew worse the deeper into the Dominion she went.

Now she followed the bed of a shallow creek. The wood it ran through was dark and lifeless. She heard no birdsong or rustlings of small animals. No sighing of the wind in the trees. Certainly no human voices.

Only the water.

Every now and then she sensed a gate nearby and circled

around to avoid both the newly dead and the great hounds who herded them along. Nazafareen took grim satisfaction in the fact that her awareness of the gates meant she hadn't lost everything.

She was still a Breaker, even beyond the veil. The magic was still part of her essence.

As Nazafareen walked, she muttered softly to herself, repeating what she knew to be true.

The Gale is down.

The Vatras are loose.

She had done that.

Gaius should have been dead but wasn't.

Darius.

Oh, Darius.

Her steps slowed. The water rushed against her boots, tugging.

Don't think of him. *Don't.*

Nazafareen tried to focus.

"I'm going somewhere because Culach told me something important," she whispered. "He said…. He said…."

What?

She had a moment of panic when she couldn't remember.

Nazafareen felt her memories fading around the edges, like a parchment curling in flame. She rubbed her stump, biting hard on her lip. Then it came back to her in a rush.

"Culach said Farrumohr forged a crown and I saw it. I saw it on Gaius's head. Only for an instant, but it was there."

I *saw* it.

She started walking with purpose again.

That was the biggest problem with being dead. The Dominion wanted to lull you into complacency. To soothe you into forgetting who you were. Until you gave up and let the water take you.

So she walked and muttered.

The Gale is down.

The Vatras are loose.

I did that.

Farrumohr made the crown.

But Gaius carried no talismans.

The crown must be *here.*

If I find Farrumohr, I'll find the crown.

And I'll fucking Break it.

Thoughts of the Viper stoked her temper, which helped fend off that awful blankness. She stayed in the middle of the stream to hide her scent from the shepherds. She'd been lucky so far, but she knew they were hunting her. And they were not constructs of magic. They lived here, in every sense of the word. She couldn't break *them.*

The mountains in the distance grew closer. The stream turned away from her path so she abandoned it. Pine boughs wove a tunnel over her head as she entered the foothills. The sounds of water faded for the first time.

"I must be leagues from the Cold Sea by now," she whispered, though she still felt its pull.

And then Nazafareen heard something strange.

A steady thumping sound, not far away.

Part of her — the cautious part — wanted to keep going. But it was the only sound that was any different she'd heard in such a long time. Not the panting of a hound, she felt sure. Not the tread of their paws. It wasn't moving.

Nazafareen crept through the trees. The thumping grew louder, accompanied by a rasping noise.

She peered around the bole of a white oak.

Darius sat against a tree, sharpening *Nemesis.* He wore a shirt with the sleeves rolled up to the elbows and travel-stained boots. Both his arms were whole. He'd discarded the shadowtongue cloak. She supposed it wouldn't do him any good in the forest anyway.

The sight of him filled her with so many conflicting feelings, she could only stare in wonder for a long moment. He must be dead too. Was he hiding from the shepherds? But, oh, at least they could be together! She hated for him to be dead, but all in all, it wasn't so bad.

And she wouldn't have to do this alone.

Then, after they'd vanquished Farrumohr, they could go to the boats and find out what was on the other side.

Nazafareen rushed from her hiding place. She tripped in her haste, tumbling to the ground before him. Her palm broke the fall, though it didn't hurt.

"Darius!" she cried, bursting with sorrow and happiness both.

He didn't look up. Her smile faded.

"Darius?"

Understanding took her with brutal force. Nazafareen rocked back on her heels.

"Oh."

He did raise his face then, but his eyes looked straight through her. She saw pain there, and weariness.

The sound thundered in her ears. His heartbeat.

Nazafareen crawled closer. She touched a lock of hair that had tumbled across his forehead. It passed straight through her fingers as if *he* were the ghost.

"I'm glad you're alive," she told him softly. "Truly, I am."

She sat and watched him for a while. He ran the whetstone down the blade, his mouth set in a stubborn line. She didn't want to leave him, but he shouldn't be here. The gulf between them was impassable. And if he stayed much longer, he'd get himself killed in truth.

Her aching grief turned to anger. "Go back where you belong," she said roughly.

Of course, he didn't answer. He just kept sharpening that stupid sword.

"Go!" she screamed.

Nazafareen leapt to her feet. She tried to shake him, to pull him to his feet and drag him to the nearest gate. He slid through her fingers like smoke. She cursed him. He finally set the whetstone aside, carefully wrapping it in a cloth and tucking it into his pocket. He ran his fingers along the edge of the blade. Then he rested his head against the tree. As she looked into his wounded blue eyes, her rage ebbed. The tidal currents of the Cold Sea rushed into the void, threatening to pull her back toward the boats.

"No." Her jaw set. "You won't take me yet."

Nazafareen turned her back on Darius, the only man she had ever loved, would ever love, and started walking again.

The Gale is down.

The Vatras are loose.

I did that.

Her fist clenched. How she hated them all!

Much better to focus on those she despised. Love was a dangerous thing in the Dominion.

And who did Farrumohr hate enough to linger for a thousand years? Nazafareen thought she knew.

She climbed the mountain. From the top she caught a flash of the sea, turning away before it tempted her. A valley lay on the other side and in the center of the valley, a lake. It reflected the grey skies like a dull mirror.

"I found you," she whispered.

THE GARDEN WAS MADLY OVERGROWN. VINES HEAVY WITH crimson flowers covered the ruin of the House Behind the Veil like splashes of blood. Some of the walls still stood, but the twisted tower had tumbled down, leaving heaps of rubble. She felt the echoes of old magic in the stone, but it was no longer potent, more like puddles of rain after a storm that were slowly seeping into the earth.

She wandered through what remained of the house. Vague memories surfaced of Culach and of feeling terribly weak and ill. Those memories were still her first. Even death had not restored what the ward took from her.

It didn't take Nazafareen long to find the well.

It waited in the garden, the sides slick with moss. Shattered stones formed a ring around its mouth, as if something had broken *out* of it.

The question was whether that something had gone back *in* to lick its wounds.

Nazafareen thought it had.

She stared into the depths. After only a few paces, the darkness was impenetrable. She had no idea how far down it went, or even where it led.

Nazafareen knew that if she went down there, she might never come out. No, worse than that. She might become like Farrumohr. Her essence would fade away until nothing was left but pure malice.

Shadow and flame.

Nazafareen felt true fear for the first time since Gaius killed her. She had more than her life to lose this time.

Will I risk eternity in the lowest levels of the Dominion to hunt this creature?

A wind swept through the garden, smelling strongly of the sea.

In the end, it was not hatred that made her swing her legs over the edge.

It was all those she'd left behind. Darius first and foremost, but also Meb and Kallisto and Herodotus. Javid. Culach. Victor. All the mortals and daēvas she loved. She would not abandon them now.

Nazafareen took a last look around at the lush gardens. Then she pushed off the edge and fell into darkness.

THE DROWNED LADY

Darius slid the sword into its baldric, satisfied the edge was keen. He rubbed his arms, seized by a sudden fit of goosebumps. That sensation of being watched he always felt in the Dominion seemed worse than usual, though at least this time it lacked menace.

It was ebbing now anyway. He stooped to drink from a stream, cupping the tepid water in his hands. It had barely touched his lips when a thin howl broke the silence. It was answered by another, even closer. The water trickled through his fingers, forgotten.

The hounds had caught up with him again.

They'd been chasing him since he came through the gate. Darius thought he'd concealed his trail, but they must have found it again. It was time to go. He started running through the woods. He had no idea how to find the Drowned Lady but didn't doubt her existence. He couldn't afford to. She was the last shred of hope he had.

He flashed through the trees, flat-out sprinting now. The howls grew louder. He wouldn't lose them so easily this time. Just ahead the land sloped into a bowl-shaped depression. Darius half-slid down the hill, hoping to gain ground and hide in the dense forest below, but shepherds must have anticipated this, for the sounds of pursuit came from all sides.

A full pack.

The trap closed. Dark bodies streaked through the trees. He didn't bother drawing Nazafareen's sword. Whatever the hounds were, his gut told him iron would have little effect. And elemental power didn't work in the Dominion.

Four more loped toward him, silent now. Holy Father, they were big.

Their hindquarters were bunching to spring when Darius launched himself at a low branch and swung his legs up. Jaws snapped and snarled below. He scrambled up the tree, heart hammering in his chest. Eight Shepherds circled the trunk below. Yellow eyes stared at him balefully. One of them whined and settled down on its haunches. The rest followed suit.

Darius swore.

It was the bloody chimera all over again.

He couldn't afford to be stuck here. He had to find Nazafareen before she was gone forever. How long did souls stay in the Dominion before passing on? It was another question he had no answer for.

But he couldn't fight a whole pack.

So Darius settled into the crook of the tree to wait.

Time passed. He dozed fitfully for a bit, tedium and exhaustion overcoming his fear. When he woke, the hounds were still there.

"If you'd take me to your mistress, I'd come down," he ventured.

They snarled, fur bristling.

"Okay, okay." Darius held out his hands.

He was trying to figure if there was a way to move through the treetops when the hounds rose to their feet, heads lowered. Darius caught movement through the branches below.

"If you're a necromancer, you have two choices," a voice called out. "Climb down and face me, or wait until you fall from weariness and the Shepherds butcher you."

Darius frowned.

"The first would be a cleaner death, though I'll admit, I fucking despise Antimagi."

He knew that voice, yet he couldn't quite believe it. Darius swung his legs down and descended to one of the lower branches — though still out of reach.

A tall woman stood at the base of the trunk, one hand resting on a hound's head. The other gripped a sword. A cloud of dark curly hair framed her stern features. Darius blinked.

"Holy Father, Tijah, is that you?"

She squinted into the branches above, her face registering almost comical surprise.

"Darius?"

He waved. One of the hounds gave a low, rumbling growl.

"Knock that shit off," Tijah snapped. The Shepherd looked at her, red tongue lolling. "He's with us. Goddess, Darius, get down here!"

The moment his boots hit the ground she rushed forward and grabbed him by the shirt, looking him over with big eyes, then pulled him into a hug, laughing.

"Where's Nazafareen?" she asked.

Darius didn't reply. Her grin dissolved.

"Where is she?"

"Dead," he said hoarsely.

Tijah pressed a hand to her mouth. She searched his eyes, tears springing to her own. They'd fought together as Water Dogs for the satrap of Tel Khalujah. Darius had been there when Tijah's first daēva died. She understood exactly what it meant to lose your bonded.

"I'm so sorry, Darius," she whispered.

He brushed her pity aside. "You thought I was a necromancer."

Tijah wiped her eyes and nodded. "Most are dead, but a few got away. I've been hunting them down in my spare time."

"Spare time?" He glanced warily at the hounds. "And these things listen to you?"

"We've been tasked with locking the gates, Darius. When.... Ah, damn." Tijah swallowed. "When Nazafareen broke the wards, some ghuls started coming through. But never mind about that. Tell me everything that's happened."

Darius had left her at the gate to Nocturne all those months ago. Six? Seven? It seemed like longer. He gave her the quick version, explaining about the Vatras and the search for the talismans. When he told her about going into the Kiln after Gaius, Tijah shook her head.

"Sounds like Nazafareen," she muttered. "Leave no asshole unpunished. Except this one was more than she bargained for."

"You would have done the same," Darius said defensively.

Tijah met his anguished gaze. "Yeah, I guess I would have. Where's the fucker now? Gaius?"

"I don't know. I don't give a damn." He turned away, his voice ragged. "I just want her back, Tijah."

Her gaze sharpened. "What do you mean ... *back*?"

"You heard me."

She sighed. "That doesn't happen around here."

Darius felt his composure fracture. "Where's the Drowned Lady, Tijah? How do I find her? I bet you know." He seized her tunic. "Tell me!"

He heard the distinctive sound of a sword leaving its scabbard. A figure melted out of the twilight.

"What's going on?" a male voice asked. It wasn't friendly.

Darius let go of Tijah and stepped back.

"Darius," she said. "I think you remember Achaemenes." She held up her wrists. She wore cuffs on both now. One had linked her to Myrri. The other.... Darius raised his eyebrows.

"Yeah, he's my bonded." She seemed annoyed by this fact. "So try not to piss him off."

Achaemenes sheathed his sword, walking toward them with a rolling gait. He was young, barely out of his teens, but the cool gaze that met Darius's seemed much older. Darius did remember him now. The light brown hair had grown longer and he'd filled out a bit from the skinny kid they'd met in Karnopolis. The limp was the result of the bond. It deformed his leg, just as it had once withered Darius's arm.

He wondered how such an odd pairing had come to pass, but the look on Tijah's face discouraged him from asking.

"What are you doing here?" Achaemenes asked in a milder tone. "It's dangerous."

"Is it?" Darius replied coldly. "I'm here to see the Drowned Lady. I have business with her." He turned to Tijah. "You can't refuse me this."

She gave him a level stare. "Okay, I've met her. Only once and that's because she sent her kennel to bring us in. The woman's scary as shit. I know how you're feeling right now, but—"

"Where is she?"

Tijah sighed. "There's a tower."

"Tell me how to get there. *Please*."

For a moment, he thought she'd dig her heels in. Then she grimaced.

"I'll do better." She gave a whistle and the hounds perked their ears up. "Come on, we'll go together."

Achaemenes shrugged and followed as Tijah started off through the woods, the shepherds trotting at her heels.

"How's your father?" she asked.

"Alive as far as I know. That's the best I can say about him."

She laughed fondly. "Good old Victor. Still starting trouble?"

"You have no idea."

"Well, give him my regards. And your mother?"

"Gone."

She stopped. "You're serious?"

"Gaius ordered it. That's why…. It's why we went after him."

"*Fucker.*" She looked murderous. "I wish I could hunt him down with you. If we chop him into little pieces and feed the scraps to some starving cats, that might do it."

Darius said nothing. Tijah scowled at him.

"What are you planning to ask the Lady?"

When he still didn't reply, she grabbed his sleeve. "You're going to offer yourself up, aren't you?" She shook him. "Aren't you, Darius?"

"My soul is mine to dispose of," he snarled.

Tijah rubbed her forehead. "And I'll be back here getting Nazafareen out of a damn tree when *she* comes after *you*!"

Darius smiled. "You think she'd do that?"

"Of course she would," Tijah muttered. She pointed through the trees. "There you go."

Darius stopped in surprise. A slender black tower rose just ahead.

"I didn't realize I was so close," he said.

"Who knows if you were?" Tijah responded cryptically. "It's never in the same place. Take it as a good sign. If she didn't want to see you, we'd be walking in circles."

They approached the tower. It seemed to have no windows or doors. Darius wiped sweaty palms on his tunic. He refused to contemplate the possibility of failure, though he could tell Tijah was only doing it out of pity.

"I'd better go alone," he said.

Tijah nodded. "I figured so. We'll wait for you out here." She laid a hand on his arm. "Good luck, Darius."

"How do you … ?"

"Get in? Try 'round the back." She scratched one of the

hounds behind the ears, then gave it a pat on the rump. "Go show him."

The Shepherd padded toward the tower, disappearing around the corner. Darius hurried to catch up. He counted four sides. As they reached the fifth, he saw a narrow archway. From the slender shape of the tower, he'd expected stairs. But when he stepped through, he stood in a long corridor that seemed to stretch to infinity in both directions.

The hound waited about ten paces away. It looked at him with intelligent eyes.

Darius squared his shoulders. "Coming," he said.

As soon as he started walking, the hound stood and trotted down the corridor. Darius followed. The interior of the tower was made of the same shiny black stone as the outside. They passed closed doors, hundreds of them. He could see his own reflection swimming darkly in the walls and floor, but not the hound's.

After many long minutes, the hound stopped. It rose on its hind legs and scratched at a door that looked exactly like all the others. The door swung open. Darius steeled himself and went inside.

The chamber beyond was cavernous, with a high vaulted ceiling. Hundreds of tiny white sparks floated just above the floor. He stared.

But it wasn't a floor.

It was the Dominion in miniature.

Darius could see mountains and prairies, forests and rivers and lakes, all ghostly pale. The sparks of light were thick in some places, sparse in others. Darius realized they were streaming through gates. At the far edge of the chamber, the sea lapped at a dark shore. Tiny ships gathered there, holding the brightest clusters of lights. As they sailed away, the sparks grew dimmer and dimmer until they vanished into darkness.

A woman walked among the lights. Her skin was the color of

bleached bone save for a network of blue veins running beneath the surface. Water ran in a continuous stream from her hair and mouth. She held a silver goblet in her hand. Her face was not kind.

Darius gave a low bow.

Holy Father, Tijah was right, he thought.

She's scary as shit.

"Who are you?" she demanded. "How did you come to the Chamber of Souls?"

He didn't want to get Tijah in trouble, but he sensed that lying to this woman would be a bad idea.

"I met two of your servants. They guided me here."

Her eyes narrowed. "The girl from Al Miraj, was it?" Water flowed from her mouth, puddling on the ground. He could see it through the spectral landscape.

Darius nodded.

"She should not have done so. Leave at once."

He hesitated. The Shepherd no longer looked tame. Its hackles rose.

"I have an offer for you," he cried. "Please hear it before you send me away."

She looked him over. "Why should I, daēva?"

Darius had no answer for that so he dove right in. "There's a mortal woman. She would have come through the gate in the last few days—"

The Drowned Lady turned away from him with an irritated expression. "So you're one of those," she muttered. "They find me occasionally. Some poor sap who thinks they can bargain their beloved back from behind the veil. Well, it doesn't work that way. *You* shouldn't be here at all and the dead only travel in one direction. Across the sea." She made a shooing motion with the goblet. "So let's not waste each other's time."

His desperation mounted. "Listen, if you'll take me instead—"

"No."

"Then let me die now so I can find her before she's gone."

Darius fell to his knees and unsheathed *Nemesis*, laying it against his throat. "I do not wish to bloody your chamber, madam, but I will if I must. Or command your hound to rip my throat out. I will not resist."

The Drowned Lady sighed heavily. "So you're not only one of those. You're one of *those*."

Darius had sharpened the blade to within an inch of its life. A trickle of blood ran into his collar.

"Who is this woman you would die for?"

"My bonded. Her name is Nazafareen." His eyes devoured the lights moving through the chamber. *Where are you, my love? Which one?*

The Drowned Lady looked at him sharply. "She wields negatory magic."

"Yes."

"Put the sword down." Her voice was tart. "If I want your soul, I'll let you know."

He lowered the blade. "You may remember her. She, uh, destroyed the wards on the gates."

"Oh, I remember that one all right."

"She didn't mean to. She was fighting a creature named Farrumohr."

Her face darkened. "I know who he is."

"Can you try to find her?"

"If she died three days ago, she'll be gone by now."

"Please. Just try."

She drained her goblet. The water trickling from the edges of her lips ran red. "It's all I can offer you."

The Lady strode to the tiny shore, studying the lights there. A slight frown creased her pale face as she worked her way back across the chamber, finally pointing to a spark some leagues away from the tower, in a valley by a lake. Darius rushed over, gazing down at the light.

"She shouldn't be there," the Lady said angrily.

He reached out to touch it when the spark winked out.

"Where did she go?" he demanded.

The Lady's lips set in a thin line. "Into the Abyss. Forget her, boy. She's lost to you now."

It was too much. To be so close.... Darius balled his fists.

"What is that? What is the Abyss?"

"The place of the restless dead."

"Is that where Farrumohr lives?"

She didn't answer, but he knew he was right.

He sat back, stunned. "She's gone after him. Holy Father, of course she has." Part laugh, part sob escaped his lips. Darius jumped to his feet. "You have to help me now! Do you know what he's been up to? I'll tell you. He—"

A frigid hand closed around his neck, lifting him from the floor. Her eyes blazed.

"You dare command me, boy?"

His legs kicked. Spots danced before his eyes. He was on the verge of passing out when she released him. Darius fell to the floor, coughing.

The Lady paced up and down, sparks eddying around her feet. She seemed to have forgotten he was there. Darius rubbed his throat, watching her warily.

"I cannot break the compact," she muttered. "But perhaps there is a way around it...."

She spun around. "I will offer you a bargain, if you truly want Nazafareen back."

"Name your price," he said thickly. "Anything."

As soon as the words left his mouth, Darius knew they were a mistake. He didn't have much experience haggling with deities, but *anything* probably wasn't a good starting point.

"No one has ever returned." She paused to consider. "Not in good shape, at least."

He wondered if she was thinking of revenants. Wights and

liches. Some other monsters Tijah called *ghuls*, whatever the hell that was.

"You want her body and soul — and that's the tricky part." Her eyes grew cunning. "It'll cost you."

"I don't care," Darius said wearily. "What is it you want?"

"I'm not sure yet." She drew closer, until they stood eye to eye. She smelled like the bottom of a muddy pond. Not stepping back required every ounce of courage Darius could muster.

Tijah was wrong.

Scary as shit didn't begin to describe her.

"You have a darkness in you," she murmured. Darius stilled. He felt cold fingers riffling through his mind. It was one of the most unpleasant experiences he'd ever endured, in a lifetime of unpleasant experiences.

"Ah," she said at last. "I've settled on my price. Would you like to hear it?"

He didn't.

"Yes."

The Drowned Lady gave him a chilly smile. "If I let Nazafareen live again, you will be my pet. Just as you were Thena's pet."

She held up one hand. An iron collar dangled from her fingers.

Darius stared at it. He tried to speak and couldn't.

"Or is that too high a price for you?" She opened her hand and the collar vanished, to be replaced by the silver goblet. "Go on your merry way, then."

She turned her back to him, walking among the lights.

Just the sight of the collar had dried his mouth to ashes. Fury and panic warred inside him.

"I don't need your blessing," he said. "I'll go after her myself."

"Oh, but I'm afraid you do. The living may not pass through any portal to the Abyss. Go ahead and try it, if you don't believe me."

She might be lying. But she might not. And if she spoke the truth, he would waste precious time confirming it. Darius didn't even know where to find one of the portals. How he loathed this woman! But to leave Nazafareen to face Farrumohr alone?

"I'll do it," Darius whispered.

She glanced at him over her shoulder and flicked her wrist in a dismissive wave. "Go wait outside. I'll send a Shepherd to lead you. Then you will return to me, pet."

Darius strode to the door. He turned down the corridor the way he'd come in. Blood pounded in his temples.

"Will you chain me to the wall too?" he muttered savagely. "Will you tell me stories while you torture me? Or do you have something else in mind?"

He wanted to punch the wall until his hand shattered. To scream until his throat gave out.

Oh, but he knew just what that felt like.

Maybe she saw you were Druj, a vicious voice whispered. *Unclean. Tainted. Maybe it's only what you deserve—*

Darius stopped walking.

No.

He wasn't any of those things. Once he might have believed it, but not anymore.

And he would not accept her bargain. Nor would he cede his love to the Abyss.

Darius spun on his heel and marched back to the Chamber of Souls. The Lady looked up in faint surprise.

"Listen to me, you.... I won't be your slave so you'll damn well have to come up with something else," he spluttered. "Your bargain is fucking.... It's barbaric!"

Perhaps not the eloquent speech he intended, but it would have to do.

The Drowned Lady stared at him. Then she started to laugh. It sounded rusty, as if she hadn't laughed in a long time, but she didn't seem quite so scary anymore.

"Well, good for you," she said. "I was hoping you'd grow a backbone, but one never knows."

————

AND SO DARIUS FOUND HIMSELF SITTING IN A COMFORTABLE chair in a much cozier room adjacent to the Chamber of Souls, balancing a cup of tea on his knee while the Drowned Lady reclined on a divan with a bowl of grapes.

"I'm sorry if I was a bit rough, but I had to be certain of you, daēva," she said. "Those who are weak would be quickly turned in the Abyss. It's a lawless place."

"Please, my Lady," Darius said, still feeling decidedly lukewarm towards this creature. "Just tell me how to find her."

"First, you need to understand how things work around here. You die, you get in the boat, you go on. Simple." She popped a grape in her mouth. "Your Nazafareen chose not to. Only a very few souls do that. Only a very few are *capable*. Something powerful must tether them to the living world, and it's usually nasty." She spat some seeds into the bowl, along with a good deal of water.

"After a while, they get tired of trying to elude the Shepherds. They realize they have to either cross over or go to ground. If they're really determined, they find a portal."

"Can't you bring them back? Make them cross over?"

She shook her head. "There are other realms than mine, daēva. The Abyss is beyond my aegis. And the longer they stay, the more twisted their souls become. None have ever returned that I know of."

"Except for Farrumohr."

"Yes, except for him. He moves between the two realms." Her face hardened. "He is not welcome here. The Shepherds watch for him now."

"You said the living couldn't pass through," Darius said. "Is that true?"

"It's true."

His heart sank.

"But I could give you a special dispensation." She popped another grape into her mouth.

"*Will* you?" he asked, conscious of the difference.

"I might. There's still a price. Don't worry, it won't be as bad as the first one. But know this. If you die there, you will be condemned to the Abyss for all eternity." She held out the bowl. "Want a grape?"

"No, thank you." Darius shifted uneasily. "What are the new terms, if you don't mind my asking?"

The Drowned Lady smiled.

❧ 10 ❧

NECROPOLIS

Nazafareen fell through darkness.

Or was *falling* even the right word for it? She had a sense of movement, but not in any particular direction. Then she saw a point of grey light somewhere far off. The darkness pressed against her, squeezing, choking. She clawed for the light. Her essence screamed....

She stood beside a dry cistern. Nearby sat a large stone building anchored on one side by a squat tower. It was not collapsed like the House Behind the Veil, but the lines of the structure disturbed the eye, as if all its joints and corners were slightly out of true. Gardens surrounded the cistern — if they could be called such. The flowerbeds were withered husks. Skeletal white trees rubbed their branches together like monstrous crickets. The sky was a putrid yellow.

She didn't want to go inside the house. The small, oddly-shaped windows reminded her of blank eyes, dozing but sentient. But Farrumohr might be there. And if he wasn't, she needed a vantage point to get her bearings. She walked to the tower and pushed open the door. Circular stairs led up. Nazafareen followed them.

She saw no sign that anyone lived there. The house felt as utterly dead as the grounds. But from the chamber at the top of the tower, she saw a road. And at the end of the road, a city.

It could have been Delphi or Samarqand. A mixture of stone and mudbrick buildings, some grand, others humble. It stretched as far as she could see. Unlike those mortal cities, no wind ships plied the skies above. There was no smoke from fires. She detected no activity at all — at least none that was visible.

Nazafareen left the tower and took a path through the gardens leading in the direction of the road. She finally reached it.

And met her first restless dead.

A woman, trudging toward the city. She muttered to herself, words too low for Nazafareen to make out. She wore a cloak with silver and gold thread and kohl around her eyes. One foot was bare, the other clad in a dainty slipper. Nazafareen waited for her to pass, then fell into step with her.

"What is that place?" She pointed to the city.

The woman stopped walking. Her head slowly turned to Nazafareen. She would have been pretty if there wasn't such deep bitterness in her face. "Have you seen him?"

"Who?"

"Have you seen him?"

"Do you mean Farrumohr?"

"*No.* Have you seen him?" Her hand reached out and grabbed Nazafareen's sleeve. A wound gaped at the wrist. "*Have you seen him?*"

Nazafareen pulled her arm away. "I don't know who you mean."

The intense light in the woman's eyes faded. She turned away and started walking again.

Nazafareen waited until she'd moved ahead to follow. As they neared the city, others appeared on the road, first in a trickle and then a torrent, until she found herself jostled amid a river of souls.

A few studied her with a hungry light, but she made her face vengeful and they left her alone. She did not try to speak to them.

In the city, the dead were everywhere.

Some had bodies and looked relatively fresh, but from the corner of her eye, she saw thin shadows flitting through the ruins. The rest lay somewhere in between. They looked like people at first glance, but close up they were insubstantial. *Fading.*

Nazafareen wandered through a warren of crumbling streets. She passed a man crouched in a puddle, shoving handfuls of mud into his mouth, his belly swollen and distended. Beside him, another man with a pointy beard stared at his own reflection, entranced. The sounds of fighting echoed from the mouth of an alley. She saw faces slack with apathy and twisted in anger. Eyes glazed with lust and greed.

To her relief, Nazafareen did not encounter a single child, though the adults were bad enough. She felt her spirits sinking. As hellish as this place was, none of them had been condemned here for their sins. They'd chosen it.

Of course, so had she.

Nazafareen rubbed the stump of her right wrist, clinging to a sense of purpose amid the petty pointlessness of it all.

The Gale is down.

The Vatras are loose.

I did that.

She traversed slender bridges with gaps in the crumbling stonework she had to leap across. She passed domes of flaking gilt and forests of topless marble pillars. In one small, desolate square, she saw a shrine to a strange god with snakes for hair and a forked tongue. An old woman abased herself to it, murmuring words in sibilant tongue.

On and on the city went. It seemed to have no end.

I'll never find him this way, she thought.

So Nazafareen started asking for Farrumohr, choosing the

ones that looked like they still had the power of speech. Most ignored her. The others seemed afraid and ran away.

She moved deeper into the necropolis, until all that remained were the shadows.

Nazafareen lurked in the off-kilter doorway of a hovel until one drifted past. Then she seized it. The shadow writhed in her grasp, making a sound that would have set her teeth on edge if she weren't dead herself. As it was, she found it rather beastly.

"Stop that," she growled, shaking the shadow hard.

It subsided, wreathing her arm like smoke.

"I want Farrumohr. Tell me where to find him."

The shadow suddenly elongated, striking at her like a snake.

Nazafareen laughed. "Tell me and I'll release you." She spat on the ground. It sizzled and smoked, eating through the paving stones. "Or I'll unmake you right now, shadow."

More of the beastly hissing. Yet there were words this time, if one only listened.

He is one of the oldessst of us, Breaker.

"I know that," she snapped. "Where is he now?"

The tower. He sleepsss.

"How do I find it?" She scanned the streets ahead but saw nothing that could be called a tower.

The creature squirmed and Nazafareen tightened her grip.

There.

A tendril of darkness reached toward a pile of rubble in the distance.

"You little liar—"

Down.

Nazafareen shook it again. "What do you mean down?"

Into the earth.

He sleeps.

Crystals of ice were starting to form on her fingers. The thing must be terribly cold, though she couldn't feel it.

Free me now.

Nazafareen nodded. "I'll keep my promise, shadow."

Blue fire arced from her palm to its heart, leaving a fine grey ash that slowly settled to earth. Nazafareen rubbed it out with the toe of her boot.

Her essence *shriveled*.

It was not the sickness she'd once felt when she used the power. Her body felt nothing. Hunger, thirst, pain — those were all distant memories.

This was worse.

Nazafareen held up her hand. She could see the faint outline of the street right through it.

Using breaking magic in the Dominion had wiped her mind clean. Using it here seemed to speed up the process of becoming one of *them*. Still, it was the only weapon she had.

She walked down a wide avenue and surveyed the heap of rubble. It was made of stone blocks nearly her own height, as if a large building had once stood there and been torn down. Nazafareen clambered to the top. On the other side she found a deep pit. It had five sides hacked crudely into the earth.

The shadow hadn't lied. It was a tower, of sorts.

Only this one stood on its head.

Nazafareen started to climb down, blue fire licking at her eyes.

❧ II ❧

A BARGAIN

"Don't you like grapes?"

"I do, it's just—"

"Let's get you some proper food." The Lady strode to the door of the chamber, trailing water as she went. "Is there any of that stew left?" she called.

Darius heard a muffled reply. It startled him. He couldn't imagine who else would live in this place. He wasn't sure he *wanted* to imagine.

"He'll be right along," she said, returning to the divan.

"I should probably get going—"

"Nonsense. There's nought to eat in the Abyss. May as well make your last meal a decent one."

The door opened and a young man came in carrying a tray. He looked ordinary in all respects, with a neatly trimmed dark beard and pleasant features. He wore a long purple robe with astrological symbols embroidered on the voluminous sleeves.

"I may have put too much thyme in it," he muttered, setting the tray on the table. "And not enough salt. But it's hot."

The stew smelled wonderful. Darius suddenly realized he hadn't eaten in days.

"Thank you," he said, reaching for a bowl and spoon.

The man watched him eat with a worried expression.

"It's really good," Darius managed, swallowing a mouthful. "I like thyme."

That elicited a smile. He finished the first bowl and started on a second.

"My name is Darius," he ventured. "Of the Danai."

Not Karnopolis. Not Tel Khalujah. He might have been raised there, but they had never been his home.

The man nodded courteously. "And I am Nabu-bal-idinna."

The name struck a chord. Darius struggled to recall where he'd heard it. Something to do with Herodotus....

"You were the alchemist to King Something-or-other," he exclaimed. "King Teispes!"

Nabu-bal-idinna's cheeks flushed a bit. He smoothed his robes. "You've heard of me?"

"Holy Father, yes." Darius frowned. "But didn't he rule more than five hundred years ago?"

A vague expression crossed the alchemist's face. "It hasn't seemed like such a long time." He brightened. "Some of my works survived then?"

"Not many, but some. You wrote a treatise on the talismans. That there were four, rather than three." Darius turned to the Lady, who watched in amusement. "Nazafareen is the fourth talisman. You knew that didn't you."

She nodded. "I did."

"My Lady gave the three talismans their power herself," Nabu-bal-idinna said.

She folded her arms. "That's the reason I don't meddle anymore," she grumbled. "I only meant to stop the war. When I learned what they did with it.... Freezing the sun in the sky! Well, I couldn't take it back, but I added those wards so they wouldn't work more mischief."

"She didn't intend for the Vatras to be punished so," Nabu-bal-idinna said softly. "Gaius perhaps. Farrumohr. But not all of them. Not for generations."

"Yet you wrote of the fourth talisman," Darius said. "You knew she might be needed to break the wards someday, if the Vatras returned."

"And look what she's done with it!" the Lady nearly shouted. "Got herself killed and now she's gone into the Abyss."

"Nazafareen didn't *get* herself killed," Darius replied, disliking the Lady's tone. "I don't believe she ever stood a chance, not even with her negatory magic. Gaius has some source of protection we don't know about. Something she couldn't break." He paused. "Is it connected to Farrumohr?"

The Lady shared a troubled look with Nabu-bal-idinna. "The Viper draws the restless dead to him like moths to a flame. Their numbers are growing. And the Abyss shares a border with *my* aegis." She gave Darius a hard stare. "I'm letting you go because I want him found and dealt with."

"That's not an answer."

"It's the only one you'll get from me, daēva."

Darius's temper rose. "Why?"

"I told you, I don't meddle with the living world. And it wouldn't help you if I did." Her face grew thoughtful. "I'll admit, I did not foresee Nazafareen's death, though it might be the only way—" She cut off abruptly.

"The only way to what? Stop Farrumohr?"

She said nothing. Darius drew a deep breath. He was tired of riddles.

"Tell me this, then. How can we kill him if he's already dead?"

"You can't. But you can drag him back through a portal. Shepherds will be waiting." The Lady smiled. She looked scary as shit again. "You just bring him to me."

"And if I do, you'll let Nazafareen return to the world of the living?"

"I will. Though there is still the matter of price."

"I thought you just named it."

"No, that's the price for your special dispensation."

Darius set the bowl down. He'd lost his appetite.

"Just tell me," he said.

Nabu-bal-idinna perched on the end of the divan and started rubbing her feet. She sighed happily.

"Well, here's the thing. You'll find out what it is after you complete your task."

"Not the bond," he said instantly.

"Not the bond," she agreed.

Darius thought of the stories he'd heard. "And not my first-born child, either."

She made a face. "What do I want with a squalling infant?"

"Say it."

The Lady sighed. "Not your firstborn child. And not your second or third. You can have a dozen for all I care, I don't want any of 'em."

"I really wish you'd just tell me what it is now."

"I'm sure you do."

"Is it something I'll hate?"

She smiled. "Hate is a strong word."

"I think it's unambiguous."

She shrugged. "Maybe. Maybe not."

Darius wanted to keep haggling. He had a bad feeling. But every moment he delayed, Nazafareen would be deeper into the Abyss.

"Do we have a deal?" the Lady asked sweetly.

"Yes," he said through his teeth. "We have a deal."

"And you swear to return to me when this is all done? I need to make sure everything is settled to my satisfaction."

"I swear to return."

And if you've screwed me, I'll have something to say about it.

She smiled in a way that made it clear she knew exactly what he was thinking.

"One more thing. I know who's waiting outside. The hothead and her daēva. But you'll go alone or not at all. They have another task to complete."

"I'll go alone."

"Good." She rose. "There's a portal into the Abyss not far from here. The Shepherds will lead you there."

"Will they come with me?" he asked hopefully.

"They cannot."

"Then how will I track her?"

"That's up to you." Her tone softened a little. "If I knew, I would tell you plainly. I cannot say what you will find in the Abyss. You are the first to be given free passage. But remember this, daēva. You possess the will of a living being. That makes you stronger in such a place."

"But I can still die there."

"Of course." She patted his hand. "Though I strongly advise against it. Nabu-bal-idinna will escort you out."

Darius rose and followed the alchemist into the corridor.

"What is this place?" Darius asked, eyeing the doors to either side as they walked.

"The Lady's tower is the physical manifestation of the Nexus," he replied. "There are other gates, other worlds, even other Dominions. Some mirror each other, like those we were each born into."

The thought made Darius's head spin. "But daēvas were new to the Empire," he said. "The first ones came with my father."

"As I understand it, the world you call the Empire was meant for mortals, and Nocturne and Solis for daēvas. So it remained for a very long time. But the gates allowed passage between the two, if one was willing to brave the Dominion. I believe General Jamadin led the first Persian forces through. They settled in what is now Solis. And then your father went the other way."

"Why do you stay here?"

The alchemist was quiet for a moment. "Put yourself in *her* place. Eternally surrounded by the dead and burdened with making sure they go where they're supposed to and don't make a nuisance of themselves. Wouldn't you get a little bored? A little lonely?"

Darius suppressed a smile. "I suppose so."

"She means well. And we enjoy each other's company."

"Do you know anything about the Abyss? Anything that might help me?"

Nabu-bal-idinna sighed. "I'm afraid not. You must love this Nazafareen very much to risk going there."

"More than life itself," he replied simply.

"Perhaps that will help you, then."

They walked in silence for a while.

"Nabu-bal-iddina?"

"Hmm?"

"What's on the other side of the Cold Sea?"

"Oh, you'll find out some day." He glanced at Darius. "I hope you will, at least."

When they reached the archway leading out, Nabu-bal-idinna stopped. "I cannot go any further. But I wish you luck, Darius of the Danai. The Lady will keep her word if you return."

Darius nodded at him, stepping out into the half-light of the Dominion, the alchemist's steps fading away behind him.

Tijah leapt up from a tussock of grass, her face taut. "What did she say?"

"Nazafareen went to a place called the Abyss. The realm of the restless dead. She's hunting a creature called the Viper. Dead — but not dead, if you know what I mean. I must follow her there."

Tijah frowned. "We'll go with you."

"You can't."

"Why not?" she demanded, black eyes flashing.

"The Lady said the living can't pass through the portals. She's letting me go, but she said you have your own task to do."

Tijah shared a look with Achaemenes. "We'll see about that."

The Shepherd at her feet gave a low bark. They followed it to an old overgrown cistern in the woods. Five more of the hounds sat in a circle around it, watching the still black water. It didn't reflect the trees or sky above.

Tijah sat on the edge and swung her legs over. When her feet touched the inky darkness, they hit an invisible barrier. She stomped her boots down in frustration.

"It's solid as rock," she growled.

"Let me try."

Darius leaned over and dipped a hand in. His fingers slid through the surface. It didn't feel like water though. Just an icy, formless cold.

"Shit!" Tijah glared at him. "What's down there, Darius?"

"I don't know. But that's where she went."

"You be careful. Get her and come straight back. We'll be here."

"Thanks, Tijah."

Darius's heart raced as he eyed the cistern.

A lawless place.

None have ever returned.

He drew a deep breath and jumped in.

12

THE VIPER'S DEN

A rough path led down around the edges of the inverted tower. It started as bare dirt, but as she traveled deeper the walls and ground grew smooth and black with a polished sheen. Nazafareen heard her own footsteps but nothing else.

She'd never gone into a fight without Darius guarding her left side. Nazafareen touched the cuff. It felt solid and real — more than the arm it circled.

She descended into the pit until the curdled sky was only a tiny point above. Thick dust coated the floor of the tower. It looked undisturbed. She saw no other passages leading out. The place was empty.

He sleeps.

So claimed the shadow.

But where?

Her gaze moved to the center of the octagonal chamber where she saw a low wall. Nazafareen approached warily, halting a few paces away.

It was a well like the one at the House Behind the Veil. Runes wound around the mouth, pitted and old as time itself. A rime of black ice coated the surface. Could Farrumohr be hiding inside? The prospect of entering the well made her soul shudder.

"Farrumohr!" she shouted.

The walls threw her voice back in a cacophony of echoes.

"You coward!" she screamed. "Come out and face me!"

....*face me*....

....*me....me....me*....

The shadows at the edge of the chamber thickened. They stirred.

She saw a spark of flame in the dimness.

No, two sparks.

Nazafareen waited.

The shade moved closer, growing more solid as it crossed the vast chamber until it no longer drifted but walked, raising little puffs of dust. A tall, slender man with close-set eyes and spiky red hair. He wore a white robe and sandals on his feet. A crown of gold circled his brow, formed in the shape of a serpent with jeweled eyes. His movements were graceful, yet there was an indefinable strangeness to him as well. A hint of cruelty in the bland features. Even if she hadn't known the sort of monster he was, Nazafareen would have instinctively disliked him.

The breaking magic roared inside her. She raised her hand and forks of black lightning lanced from her fingertips, snaring him in a web of corrosive power. The flames of his eyes flared.

Farrumohr laughed.

Mindless rage boiled. She unleashed another blast of huo mofa even stronger than the first, aimed directly at the crown. It crackled outward, blindingly bright in the gloomy chamber, sparks spitting against the black walls.

When the afterimage faded, he continued to walk toward her.

"Did you truly believe you could come to *my house* and destroy me?" He shook his head. "Stupid child."

Nazafareen retreated, cold fire coursing through her veins. She could barely hold it in check. The crown shimmered in the half-light, the jeweled eyes seeming to watch her with sentient malice.

Farrumohr halted ten paces away. "Your hatred only makes me stronger here," he rasped. "But you cannot separate the magic from your own heart, Breaker. And *that* is its flaw."

He waved a hand. Fluted glass columns in all the hues of the rainbow soared to dizzying heights above. A throne appeared behind him, forged from glass of a smokier hue, all sinuous curves with a high back. He sat down, hooking one leg over the arm. When he spoke, his voice was amused.

"You came to destroy me. But did you not stop to wonder why I have survived a millennium in this place? As long as Gaius lives, our ties protect me. And Gaius is beyond your reach." He grinned, showing pointy eyeteeth. "But by all means, try again if you're not convinced."

The lightning leapt in her. Before she could stop it, a sizzling bolt burst from her fingertips. Again, his eyes flared for an instant, then faded. Her essence felt ... thin. Insubstantial. Like gossamer floating in the wind.

He's baiting me.

With a great effort, Nazafareen forced the magic down.

"There is no leaving the Abyss, Breaker," he murmured. "We're both stuck here." He studied her with a flat, reptilian gaze. "It's happening already, can you feel it? You are becoming one of us."

She shook her head in denial, taking another step back.

How is it I cannot sense the talismanic crown he wears?

How?

His voice was low, hypnotic. "The process is inevitable. You forget who you were and care only for one thing – the thing that led you into the Abyss. In time you forget even that thing. You drift in a state of frustration and misery."

He waved a hand again and she saw the decaying necropolis. Some of the dead tore at each other like ravening dogs. Others walked alone with burning eyes and clenched fists. A woman sobbed quietly to herself in a deserted alley.

In the deepest part, only the shadows remained. They moved aimlessly, like wisps of smoke in a soft breeze.

"The Drowned Lady would condemn us here forever," Farrumohr said. A flicker of hatred crossed his features. "She doesn't care a whit for these poor souls. Many are guilty of petty sins. Jealousy, vanity. Is it fair that they must suffer until the end of time?"

He beckoned and the darkness at the edge of the chamber gathered, pinpoints of flame appearing within it. Shadows drifted forward. They seemed afraid of him, shrinking in on themselves to grovel at his feet.

"These are my pets. They helped me build this place. Shadows cannot feel pain as the living do, but there are ways of ... coercing."

Nazafareen felt a stab of pity for the poor creatures, but also gnawing fear. If she released her grip, the negatory magic would strike at him again and again, devouring her until there was nothing left.

The Viper's right. I am a fool. I should never have come here.

Her eyes flicked to the well.

The Viper barked his harsh laugh. "You are wondering if that will lead you back to the Dominion, like the portal you came through, yes? You see your mistake and wish only to escape." He gazed at the ice-covered rim. "I discovered it during my excavation. At first, I thought it might be a way out. But then I deciphered the runes." His eyes sparkled with a merry light. "The Abyss is not the end. No, the levels go on and on, each worse than the last. There's not even a name for the next one. And I fear it makes the Abyss seem pleasant."

She sensed the truth of his words. A fathomless lay void beyond that skin of black ice. Even the huo mofa recoiled from it.

"So here we are. You came to end me, but you cannot. And

the doors only open one way. Down." He grinned. "Ah, Breaker. You know so little. You don't even know what you are."

Nazafareen looked at his leering face. "Tell me, then," she said, and was surprised to hear strength in her voice.

His mouth tightened in distaste. "*You* are what happens when the bloodline of my people is polluted. It's a very rare thing, because unlike the mongrel clans, we avoid mortals. But someone must have strayed." He sighed. "The law of unforeseen consequences, child. The resulting offspring became something new. I don't hold it against you. It is simply your nature." He leaned forward on the throne. "But I would offer you a chance."

The bloodline of my people....

Nazafareen's hold on the huo mofa started slipping and she severed the thought.

He tries to distract me with lies. I must remember that.

In the bright light, a hundred Farrumohrs reflected back from the crystal columns, the floor, the walls. All the images of him were clear and sharp, but hers was a faint outline. Blue fire flickered along its edges.

"What chance?" she growled.

"The Lady has set Shepherds to guard the portals to the Dominion. She sits at the center of her web in the Nexus like a fat spider, feeding off the souls that come to her." He bit off each word, his lips pulling back from his teeth. "It's a travesty the Lady holds the keys to all worlds. But if we gathered enough of our brethren, we could get through."

Her web in the Nexus.... Keys to all worlds....

He spoke so quickly, Nazafareen struggled to follow his words.

"Already you draw them like flies to a midden." Long fingers stroked the arm of the throne. The air behind him shimmered and she saw a legion of restless dead moving through the city. Thousands of them, ravaged faces turned toward the inverted tower.

"My father died a broken man because we lost our homestead

when the Marakai refused to raise water from the sands. I was only a boy. They sent me to live with Gaius."

Once again, his train of thought darted like quicksilver.

"Sometimes I see through his eyes. Part of me lives in him." He laughed. "The crown was more potent than I imagined. Gaius still doesn't even know its true purpose. If I'd been him, I might have thought twice about accepting a gift from the most skilled maker of talismans in the history of the Vatras. But he was never very bright."

Farrumohr's mouth twisted. An edge of anger crept into his voice. "I was betrayed, too. I know what it feels like to die alone, though mine was far worse than yours. I was days in dying. *Days*. But in the end, it made me stronger."

He stood and walked towards her. "Gaius sustains me now, but once I am free of this place, I will no longer need him. Take your revenge, I won't stop you." He gave a thin smile. "Kill me then, Breaker, if you can. I know it is your heart's desire. The thing that led you away from the Cold Sea. But I assure you, in the Abyss it's impossible."

Nazafareen glared at him, the breaking rage muddying her thoughts. Something tugged at her, something important, but when she reached for it, it slipped away.

"A temporary alliance only." He looked at the well. "But I won't have you running loose. So that is your choice. Help me gather an army to storm the portals or be banished forever to the nameless place. Think hard, Breaker. Your decision will be final."

Nazafareen saw the shape of it now. Once she agreed, he would pour poison into her ear until she was his to command. He would use her to cast out the Drowned Lady and give him the run of the place. Of the Nexus itself.

"So you would make me your new Gaius." She laughed softly. "The shadows won't follow you, will they? They despise you as much as I do. You set yourself on a throne, but you're still king of nothing."

His face darkened.

"You are a coward, Farrumohr." She glanced at the cringing shadows with contempt. "And I don't fear your servants."

"They are weak," he agreed. "But you *should* fear me."

He leapt forward and seized her, dragging her toward the well with an iron grip. The shadows drifted along beside them.

Shards of thought rattled around, puzzle pieces that almost fit together, yet the full shape eluded her. Then they stood at the rim and she saw white things moving beneath the ice. They looked like hands. Sudden and complete terror of what lay inside left her mind a blank.

"Goodbye, Breaker," he hissed.

The huo mofa sizzled between them, lighting his face in a fey blue glow. It looked like a mask.

A mask....

The shards fell into place.

He claims my magic won't work against him in the Abyss, but how could he know? How could he be *utterly certain*?

Would he risk himself after all this time?

Coward, he's a coward.

You're becoming one of us.

Nazafareen twisted her head to look at the shadows, truly look at them, for the first time. Five were dim, starveling things, but behind the sixth, she saw a reflection on the onyx floor that didn't belong. A faint Farrumohr. A hint of gold touched its brow. She hadn't noticed it before amid the dazzle of reflections in the chamber.

Their eyes met. He realized she knew.

Nazafareen flung her hand out. The shadow almost got away, but she grasped a tendril and held on tight. It writhed, hissing in anger. Her boots slid on the black ice and they tumbled over the edge into the well.

DARIUS'S EYES FLEW OPEN. HE STOOD ON A PLAIN OF TRACKLESS stone. It stretched as far as the eye could see in all directions. The weight of the sky pressed down. His shoulders slumped.

There's nothing here.

Nazafareen is gone.

The Lady tricked you.

Just lie down for a bit, his mind whispered. Rest. Then you can search for her.

He felt his knees buckling.

No.

"No!" he shouted into the void.

The sound was oddly muffled, dying within seconds.

Darius made himself start walking.

The first step was the hardest. It took all his will to break the inertia. But once he got started, it was easier to keep going.

Where he was going, Darius had no idea.

The landscape never changed. The horizon remained a blank slate. Despair — never far away — bubbled up again.

He walked and walked, putting one foot in front of the other.

He might have been walking in place.

How do I find her?

How?

The Lady said he was stronger than the dead. Or that's what he interpreted her words to mean, at least. But what if she meant the Abyss itself?

Darius held an image of Nazafareen in his mind, not as she was at the end but in life, the day after they met and she came striding down to the river, ready to pick a fight.

The first time she gave him the water blessing.

The first time he made her laugh.

He closed his eyes and held tight to the memories, teasing out every detail, until they burned brightly in his mind. And he felt a subtle shift around him.

Darius opened his eyes. An impossible structure stood in the distance. A tower balanced on its spire. His heart leapt and he started running toward it, but it drew no closer.

He stopped immediately. I have the hang of this now, he thought.

Darius remembered Nazafareen when he found her in Samarqand, her hair damp and the way she jumped up to greet him, a fragile smile on her face and her skin warm from the sun. The joy that flowed into him when she slid the cuff around her arm....

This time, when he opened his eyes, the tower loomed before him.

It stood on its head, the point tapering out to five sides in a mockery of the Drowned Lady's home. But this tower was the color of old bones, and it was not finished. He craned his neck, following the lines to the very top — bottom? — which ended in jutting fragments.

A flash of movement to the left made Darius turn.

Something loped across the plain.

Make that *several* somethings.

Darius narrowed his gaze. They were men, but they ran on on all fours — quite nimbly. He slid *Nemesis* from the baldric over his shoulder, the iron blade shining with a dark light.

Could he find a way into the tower before they reached him? Darius hesitated, and by then it was too late.

The dog-men were naked and hairless, with heavy purple phalluses that swelled in excitement as they caught his scent. He could see their eyes now, solid black like wights. As they closed the final paces, they let out howls that sounded all too human.

He couldn't touch the Nexus here, but he'd been trained as a Water Dog to fight similar creatures. Once that memory would have filled him with loathing and shame. Now he embraced it.

"Come dance with me, Druj," Darius whispered as the vanguard hit.

NAZAFAREEN HIT THE ICED-OVER MOUTH OF THE WELL ON HER side, the shadow – the true Viper – writhing in her grip like a snake. She clutched a thin tendril in her fist. The rest of him stretched away, desperate to escape.

Bit by bit, her hold was slipping, yet she felt a little stronger than she had before. Less like one of the shadows. Outwitting him gave her a slender thread of hope.

If only I had two bloody hands....

Nazafareen managed to get up on one knee, bracing her boot on the sheet of black ice as she struggled to hold the whipping shadow. She heard an ominous crack. A thin fracture appeared beneath her.

From the corner of her eye, she saw the avatar he'd conjured hopping up and down in a panicked fury.

"Let go!" it screamed. "You stupid girl, they're coming!"

A blurry white face pressed against the ice, then vanished. More cracks spiderwebbed outward across the mouth of the well. Nazafareen sensed a void yawning open beneath her. She tried to gain both feet and slipped, landing hard on her back. Pure terror came hurtling back.

The ice was so slick. She couldn't get out without using the edge for support, but if she let go of Farrumohr, Nazafareen knew he'd flee into that endless necropolis and it might be another thousand years before she found him again.

The ice groaned as she grappled with the shadow, but it was like fighting smoke. Its icy reflection scowled at her, pure venom in its eyes. The golden serpent flicked a forked tongue, its coils tightening around Farrumohr's brow.

The crown.

A jagged bolt of power ripped from her hand, shattering the rime of ice. As it cracked wide, she felt her negatory magic hunting the ghostly talisman, running it down like a hound with a hare. The serpent reflection exploded into fragments and fell away. Farrumohr's screeching avatar winked out.

Darkness poured from the mouth of the well and a black wind seized the Viper, drawing him down into the depths. His shadow elongated, tendrils curling around the lip, but some force had hold of him now and wouldn't let him escape. Frantic, Nazafareen hooked her fingers over the pitted stone wall. She hoisted herself up as the ice fully gave way, the wind roaring in her ears.

Something grabbed her ankle.

She looked back, stuck halfway over the rim. A pale hand with sharp black nails dug into her essence. She screamed and hurled another bolt into the depths. The grip slackened for an instant and she yanked her leg free.

Nazafareen tumbled over the lip of the well. She scrabbled back, away from that terrible wind. White frost coated her boot where the thing had touched her.

For one endless moment, she heard a cacophony of guttural howls, hungry and triumphant.

Then a thick coating of ice covered the well again. It was still and dark.

Nazafareen stared at it until she was certain whatever lived in there wasn't coming back out. She felt dizzy with exhaustion and relief.

I have done what I could. Let it be enough.

How she wished she could just step into one of the boats and let it carry her away, but she had to walk through the city again and find the well and hope it let her return.

She allowed that it might not.

And what then?

Sudden anger filled her. How dare the Drowned Lady condemn her to the Abyss after all the sacrifices she'd made? The Viper was a liar, but he'd spoken true about that.

There was no justice in this place.

Only the justice she made herself.

The other shadows had fled to the recesses of the chamber when the wind came. Now they crept forward, whispering in her ear. They twined around her, embracing, caressing. She pushed them away but lacked the strength to unmake them.

Come.

Come, daughter of the Abyss.

Come, Breaker.

You will take his place.

You will stay with us.

They nudged her toward the throne. Nazafareen settled into its curving lines.

They felt right and good.

Soft, coaxing voices filled her head.

Our dark ruler....

Stronger than the last....

A good queen.

A just queen.

Nazafareen leaned back. Beads of power dripped from her fingertips, hissing where they struck the stone. The shadows genuflected before her.

She felt a wave of adoration, not only here in this tower but in every decayed corner of the necropolis as word spread that a new ruler sat upon the throne. Oh, the gnashing of teeth and cries of rapturous terror! She saw statues torn down and new ones raised in their place.

Of a woman with a hard face and empty eyes. A woman with only one hand.

I will not be like Farrumohr. Not some petty construction of shadow and flame. No, I will be a queen of cold blue fire—

Her new subjects keened in alarm. Nazafareen looked up. A young man approached. He moved with a light-footed grace that made the shadows seem feeble and repellent. How bright and clear his face looked in the dim chamber. Nazafareen half rose from the throne, drawing strength from his vitality.

Darius.

My soul.

A cacophony of panicked voices swirled around her.

He cannot be here. He cannot!

His heart yet beats.

It is not possible!

Darius hefted a short sword. Black ichor dripped from the blade. The shadows shrank back.

"Oh, but it is, Druj," he said with a wintry smile that warmed as he looked at Nazafareen. "I have a special dispensation."

13

THE LAST THREAD SNAPS

At the Mer on the Isle of Selk, Culach moaned in his sleep, twisting in the feather bed he shared with Mina.

"What is it, my love?" she whispered.

His eyes flew open, then fluttered closed again.

"I dreamt of darkness," he murmured. "And falling...."

"Well, you're safe in bed." She traced a finger along his damp brow. "With me."

"So I am." He smiled, hands roving beneath the blankets. "And you aren't wearing any clothes. Fancy that."

Never one to neglect his duty, Culach decided to investigate further.

❧ 14 ❧
PRAETORIAN

Nicodemus raised the blade to his face and paused, studying his reflection in the murky glass. He'd never worn a beard and didn't plan to start now, though only the left half of his face showed stubble. The other.... A dark blue eye stared out from a melted ruin.

Atticus had given him a salve to put on the burns. It helped a bit. The first two days were hell, the next two barely tolerable. But his face was healing.

Not that he'd look much better once it did.

In the four days since he'd been raised to the Praetorians, King Shahak had gifted them all with shining breastplates and proper swords and shields. Nico's shadowtongue cloak, parchment-thin but tough as horsehide, had been cleaned of blood and sand. He wore soft boots laced to the knee and a fringed leather skirt beneath the cloak. Gaius said it had been the uniform of the Praetorian Guard before the war. Nico, who'd always worn trousers, was still getting used to chill drafts shriveling his bollocks.

For a fleeting moment, he wondered what Domitia would say if she saw him now. No doubt she'd laugh herself breathless. Not for the first time, he wished he'd had the courage to kill her. If Gaius loved anyone, it was his eldest daughter, and if he ever discovered her fate, his wrath would be beyond imagining.

Yet Nico hadn't been able to do it. The thought of those carcasses she'd left when he and Atticus were starving had stayed his hand. But eventually Gaius would discover that her body was not in the Umbra as Nico claimed.

Time was running out.

Nazafareen had been his greatest hope, but she was dead and the talismans lost. He considered trying to get word to the woman named Kallisto, but he had no idea where the Temple of the Moria Tree was and doubted there was anything she could do anyway.

I need to search his rooms. Nazafareen spoke of a crown....

He turned at a brisk knock on the door, by habit showing the unburned side of his face. Vanity persists, he thought with bleak humor, despite the lack of anything to admire.

The door opened before he could speak to reveal Aelia standing in the hall. She looked cleaner than when they'd first arrived, though none of the Vatras would bathe in a tub. The waste of water appalled them. Now she returned his gaze with contempt, any trace of sympathy gone. The woman who risked Gaius's ire to slip him a loaf of bread clearly didn't approve of his choice to become a Praetorian. He wished he could explain himself to her — or better still, ask if she knew the secret of Gaius's immortality — but he couldn't take the risk. It was more than possible Gaius had ordered her to pretend disloyalty to see how Nico would react.

"My husband wants you," she said, turning away. "Something's happened. I don't know what. But he's in a rage."

He noticed fresh bruises on her arms as he hurried to catch up.

"Did Gaius do that?" he asked quietly.

She gave him a level look and didn't bother replying.

I'm a son of the Kiln, he reminded himself sternly. I've seen worse. Much worse. And so has she. Pity won't do either of us any good. She doesn't want it anyway.

They found Gaius pacing up and down in his chambers. Romulus and Remus stood on either side of the door, looking impressive with their new swords.

Not that they have a bloody clue how to use them in an actual fight.

Aelia cut a quick smile at Atticus, who sat on the floor with his satchel at his side.

"Get out, woman!" Gaius growled.

Her face tightened, but she ducked out the door. Nicodemus pressed his fist to his chest.

"You called for me, my liege?"

"Something struck at me. A supernatural force."

He looked older. Haggard. And perhaps a touch frightened, as well.

Romulus and Remus looked at Nico with venom in their eyes. He knew how badly they wanted him dead, but he was a Praetorian now and there were stiff penalties for assaulting a brother. Neither understood why Gaius had spared him. Sometimes Nico didn't either. Could Gaius be his father?

He really fucking hoped not.

"I don't understand," Nico said cautiously. "Do you mean magic?"

Gaius shook his head like a bear with a toothache. "An invasive force, reaching into my very soul." He seized a ceramic figurine and hurled it at the wall, where it splintered into pieces. "I don't know! I've never felt the like." His fists clenched, eyes darting from left to right. "It's the clans. They're behind this. But I'll root them out. And when I do, they'll beg for death."

"I don't trust that alchemist bitch, nor the wind pilot," Romulus muttered. "I see how they look at us. We should get rid of them all."

"I still need Shahak," Gaius snapped. "He's crazy, but he has value. When I'm done, you can have whoever you want." He grimaced in pain. "My fucking head. Atticus, make something for me. One of your balms."

Atticus looked up. "I learned some herbcraft from the king's alchemist. She says there are healing plants that grow in the park, some with painkilling properties. Do I have your permission to search them out?"

Gaius nodded impatiently. "Go! Just make it quick." He pressed his hands to his temples. "I feel like my head's in a vise!"

Atticus grabbed his satchel and hurried out. Gaius lowered his brow like a mastiff. "None will be left alive this time. We can burn the Great Forest to ashes, that is no difficult matter. But I'll need an army to face the rest."

"The Persians—" Nico began.

"Not fucking *mortals*! I want to see terror on their faces. I want their children to piss themselves. *I want them to know what it's like.*" Gaius stopped suddenly, his chest heaving. "Yes, that's what I want." His smile sent ice down Nico's spine.

Gaius's trembling fingers touched his forehead. "But first I need something to take away this *pain*." He pointed at the twins. "Go find that fucking kid! Make sure he's doing what I told him to."

Nicodemus watched Remus and Romulus lope out the door, his thoughts churning like the great turnspits in the kitchens.

Who had attacked Gaius? Was it real, or had he simply lost his mind? And what in Nine Hells was he planning now?

"They prowl the halls like wolves," Leila muttered, skirts swishing as she strode along one of the wooded paths that wound through the parkland outside the Rock. "Shahak does nothing to rein them in. He would sell his very soul for arcane knowledge."

"The king already sold his soul long ago," Javid pointed out. "Now he sells the last shreds of his conscience." He cast her a sharp look. "Are you sure he suspects nothing?"

Leila shook her head. "All is ready. The guards at the wall know to expect the *Shenfeng* later today. I think Shahak was not displeased to have you stay here. For some strange reason, he seems to trust your advice."

They paused at the edge of the meadow where Katsu planned to land. Thick brush surrounded it, but the wind was calm and Javid thought the space should be adequate. There was a designated yard with mooring pegs adjacent to the palace, but they'd decided it was too risky. In a rare moment of clarity, Shahak agreed that it was better to make the run in secret.

"How long will it take to reach Val Moraine?" Javid asked, resting his palm on a tall oak tree.

"I will use dust to speed our progress. The Holy Father willing, no more than a day or two."

"And if Nazafareen isn't there?"

Leila turned to him. "Then we will find her trail and follow it. Katsu was a bounty hunter, yes? Surely—"

The Praetorian must have been standing behind the bole of the oak for they had no warning as he stepped forward. All Javid saw was the terrible burns, drawing his mouth down into a frown on one side, the singed, hairless flesh looping back over his left ear.

"Run!" he cried, pushing Leila so hard she stumbled. He turned to flee and a hand lashed out, grabbing the back of his coat.

"Let him go," Leila snarled, reaching for the bag of spell dust at her belt.

"Nazafareen," the Vatra grated. "How do you know that name?"

"You must have misheard," Javid gabbled. "I said Nadine...."

"Don't lie to me."

"She a friend! Just a friend."

The Vatra stared at him and his terrifying face softened. "She was a friend to me, too. But you will not find her. She's dead."

Shock made Javid stop struggling. "Dead?" he echoed.

The Vatra's head turned sharply. He pulled them off the path, deeper in the brush. Through a chink in the thick vegetation, Javid saw two Praetorians stride past, a young Vatra boy between them. He recognized them. They were the worst of the bunch.

"Move it," one snarled, giving the boy a hard shove. "Your master requires healing."

The burned face next to Javid looked murderous, but he kept quiet until their footsteps had faded into the distance.

"We must speak in private," the Vatra said, glancing around. "I have much to tell you and we cannot do it here." He saw their wary faces. "Please."

"My workshop," Leila replied. "It's near the stables."

He nodded brusquely. "I'll meet you there. Tell no one about this."

She sniffed. "Obviously."

Five minutes later, they assembled in the wooden building Leila had claimed for her experiments. Half-built mechanical devices sat on tables and wheeled platforms and the air held the acrid scent of alchemy. The Vatra eyed it all with interest, touching this and that and murmuring to himself. Javid found his patience thinning.

"What did you mean when you said Nazafareen is dead?" he demanded. He would not believe it. She was too full of vitality, her power too strong.

The Vatra turned to face him. Javid thought he looked guilty. "She tried to kill Gaius and failed."

"You mean the assassin he spoke of...."

"Was Nazafareen. I was with her." His mouth twisted. "I led her into the Kiln. I thought—"

"You bastard," Javid said in a low voice. "You *bastard*."

All the anger and frustration of the last weeks boiled over and he lunged at the Vatra, wrapping his hands around his throat. His skin seared Javid's fingers, but he dug into the windpipe with his thumbs.

"Stop!" Leila cried, leaping onto Javid's back.

They staggered around like that until the Vatra shook him off like a puppy nipping at his heels.

"I am not your enemy," he growled. "I wanted to see Gaius dead. I still do! That is why I searched you out, you fool!"

Javid's jaw set. He stood up and yanked his coat into place. "Friend indeed! You got her killed."

"She wanted to go. It was her idea." He let out a long breath. "Darius is still alive. Perhaps two of the talismans, as well. I don't know. But we might be able to help each other."

Javid's fists balled at his sides. "You're a Praetorian!"

"I swore the oaths, yes. And I plan to break them at the first opportunity." His voice took on a pleading tone. "Not all my people are like Gaius and his foot soldiers. The boy you saw in the park is my brother."

"I've spoken to him," Leila said. "He has a gentle nature." She pointed at Javid. "Sit down. He might have just saved us a wasted journey."

Javid crossed his arms. "I prefer to stand."

"Suit yourself." She eyed the Vatra. "You know who we are. What is your name?"

"Nicodemus."

"You're the one who tried to take Meb!" Javid exclaimed.

Shame flashed across his distorted features. "You know about that, eh? Well, I am not the man I used to be."

"Oh well, *that's* reassuring."

"Just listen to me.," Nicodemus growled. "Gaius had a daughter named Domitia. We came through a gate from the Kiln together." He paused. "She rose to become the Oracle of Delphi."

Javid laughed. "Come, now. If you mean to lie, at least make it credible."

"Why do you think she ranted against *witches*? It was the other clans she despised. She intended to find the three talismans and collar them to bring down the Gale. I was with her when she burned the Danai in the Umbra. It turned me against her — that and the knowledge of what really happened during the war of Sundering. I told Gaius she took an arrow through the throat, but it was a lie. I killed her." Nicodemus gave them both a level look. "There, I've just placed my life in your hands. If Gaius finds out, he'll flay me slowly with hot pincers, and that's assuming he's in a good mood."

Domitia. It seemed impossible to think of her as one of *them*. The Oracle had dark hair and looked nothing like the other Vatras. But Javid suddenly remembered the strange accent he'd been unable to place, and the pitiless blue eyes. Just like her father's.

He listened in silence as Nicodemus told them about the capture of Galen and how Domitia hoped to lure Nazafareen to the Gale and taunt her into using her power to shatter it. How he waited for Nazafareen and offered to guide her through the Kiln to Gaius's burrow. The tale struck Javid as madness, yet knowing Nazafareen, he could see her going along with it.

"I do not believe you are loyal to King Shahak," Nicodemus said at last. "But if we are sharing secrets, I would have one from you."

Leila's eyes narrowed. "Go on."

"Gaius might believe that fairytale about the source of the dust, but I don't. I watched you in the throne room when we first arrived. A look passed between you. So speak truly. Where does it come from?"

"Don't tell him a bloody thing," Javid grumbled.

Leila's brows arched. She turned to Javid. "You don't recognize him, do you?"

"What?"

"Nicodemus was the one standing in the shadows while the others ate. They wouldn't let him sit at Gaius's table. His face was whole then."

Javid vaguely remembered a Vatra leaning on a stick, but he'd been too consumed with what might spill from Shahak's mouth to pay him much attention.

"Gaius doesn't trust him, therefore I will." She turned back to Nicodemus. "Well, then. Are you certain you wish to know? The truth is ugly."

He shrugged. "It often is."

She drew a deep breath. "The dust is the bones of your people, plundered from the ruins of Pompeii. Even in death, they have power."

There was a long silence. Nicodemus paced up and down.

"Fuck me sideways," he muttered, rubbing his mouth.

Javid glared at her. "I can't believe you told him."

"Now we are both in each other's power," Leila said calmly. "What happens next?"

"I came to you because I hoped the dust could be used to discover Gaius's secret," Nicodemus said heavily. "He cannot be killed by conventional means. Could you cast a spell to find out why? We thought it must be a talisman, but I have never seen him with one."

Leila considered this, then shook her head. "That is beyond my skill. If I knew precisely what I was looking for, perhaps. But alchemy does not work for vague requests."

"What if a Vatra consumed the dust?"

She blinked. "I ... I do not know what it would do, but it's a fascinating question. Are you considering such a thing? I would not recommend it. You've seen what it's done to Shahak. For a Vatra, the effect could be a hundredfold."

Nicodemus shuddered.

"Or it could have no effect at all," Leila added. Her bright, birdlike eyes shone with curiosity. "Truly a fascinating question."

"That's all well and good, but what about Katsu?" Javid asked. "You're supposed to leave in an hour."

"I heard you speaking of a wind ship." Nicodemus's expression grew thoughtful. "You have one at your disposal?"

"We were planning to find Nazafareen," Javid replied, sudden tears stinging his eyes. "She was our last hope." He turned away before the Vatra could see his grief. "She saved my life once. The Pythia threw me inside the brazen bull and lit the pyre beneath. I knew I was going to die. And then Nazafareen opened the hatch and pulled me out."

"I heard the story," Nicodemus replied dryly. "She broke the gate behind you, to secure your escape into the shadowlands. Domitia wasn't happy about that."

"I can't believe Nazafareen is gone." Javid wiped his eyes with a sleeve. "And you say Gaius killed her? Then I will do whatever I can to see her avenged."

"There are still two talismans, one Valkirin, one Danai," Nicodemus pointed out. "They were among the party that entered the Kiln to hunt Gaius to his burrow." His face darkened. "If we had not been separated, things might have turned out differently."

"What happened?"

"The Valkirin — her name is Katrin — summoned a storm to save us from creatures called drakes. It was too powerful. The canyon flooded and swept us all in different directions. I ended up with Nazafareen and Darius. We decided to forge ahead and go to Gaius's burrow alone." He sighed heavily. "I was badly injured. When I awoke, I was Gaius's prisoner. Atticus, my brother, was sent in to examine the bodies. He lied and said Darius died with Nazafareen, but the Danai was only unconscious. I haven't seen him since."

"So he might be in the Kiln too?"

"He might." Nicodemus looked uncertain. "I didn't know either of them long, but it was clear how deeply he loved Nazafareen, and she him. I expected Darius to follow us across the Kiln, to seek revenge, though I'm glad he didn't for he would be dead now, too."

"Then it seems clear we must go to the Kiln rather than the darklands," Leila said briskly. "If we were on foot, the task would be impossible. But a wind ship can scour a large area with ease."

"I'll draw you a map," Nicodemus said. "The Red Hills are roughly parallel with Samarqand. It is not so great a distance, especially with the Gale down. Still long odds but better than none."

"The supplies for a journey into the Kiln are different than one to the frigid range of the Valkirins," Javid said. "I'd have to rethink everything."

"It's not complicated," Nico said with a touch of impatience. "Just bring as much water as you can carry."

"And what about your people? Surely there are more in the Kiln. Would they attack strangers?"

"Not if you don't provoke them. We are not all like Gaius."

The proposal made sense, but Javid had not forgotten that Nazafareen met her end following this Vatra's advice in the very same place. "Perhaps we should go to Meb," he said. "At least we know where to find her."

"You could," Nicodemus replied. "But I know the Marakai well. The Diyat will be meeting — what you mortals call The Five. They keep their own counsel and will do what is best for the Marakai. Just because they trade with the mortals doesn't mean they will rush to your rescue. The clan is cautious by nature. They will act as they see fit, whatever you tell them." He gave a brief wince and half raised a hand, then let it fall. "I'm sorry, I'm not used to speaking so much. The initiation ... I am not yet healed from it."

Javid looked away from the ruin of his face. He thought

Nicodemus must hate Gaius with every fiber of his being to undergo such a trial, and felt some of his distrust of the Vatra fade.

Nicodemus steeled himself to continue. "But I can tell you that Katrin has the heart of a warrior. If you find her, she will come."

"And the other?" Leila asked.

"Galen." Nicodemus shrugged. "I had no grievance against him, although Nazafareen did." He gave that half smile, though it made him wince again. "There was little love lost between him and Katrin, either. But the Danai built this place. If they haven't already killed each other, the two of them would tear the Rock down on Gaius's head."

Javid didn't find this particularly reassuring, but as the Vatra said, scant hope was better than none at all.

Nicodemus quickly sketched a map on a piece of parchment and gave it to Leila.

"Gaius is planning something nasty," he said. "I don't know what it is, but he will use Shahak to achieve it. Try to return before it happens."

And with those dire words, Nicodemus took his leave in a swirl of his strange sand-colored cloak.

"I'M PERFECTLY FINE WHERE I AM," MARZBAN SAID WITH A wheeze. "This is ridiculous."

"Nonsense. Javid's mother will look after you while I'm gone," Leila replied in a soothing tone, taking one bony arm as Javid took the other. "In fact, she is already preparing a nice herb tea to ease your catarrh."

"Gah! The woman made me drink that when last we visited. It's poison!" He tried unsuccessfully to shrug them off.

"You are an impossible old goat," Leila said fondly, steering her father to the door. "But I'm afraid you have no choice in the matter. I will not leave you alone, so either you come with us now, or the Vatras win and the entire city will be burned to the ground."

"At least bring my scrolls," Marzban muttered. "I can't play nursemaid to those brats all day long or I'll go mad."

Leila rolled her eyes behind his back. They both knew he doted on Javid's little sisters, Mahmonir in particular.

"I'll bring all your scrolls, father," she said brightly. "And we'll be back in a trice."

"Don't treat me like a child. I may be sick but I'm not stupid. If I was not beset with foul humors, we both know that I would be the one leading this expedition—"

"Hush, father, someone will hear you."

Marzban Khorram-Din subsided as they half-carried him down the corridor, though he continued to mutter under his breath about wayward daughters who refused to mind their elders.

It'll be just our luck to run into that pair of Praetorians now, Javid thought, sweating beneath his coat. The old man was heavier than he looked and he wasn't helping much. Thankfully, the corridor between their rooms remained empty. Javid kicked the door shut behind them and heaved a sigh as Leila eased him into the couch in the sitting room.

"I am not in need of your *cures*, woman," Marzban said imperiously, pointing a finger at Javid's ma, who stood in the doorway with a steaming cup.

"Please, call me Riza," she said with a warm smile. "Perhaps a touch more honey?"

"It is not the *honey* that I take issue with," Marzban spluttered. "It is the vile roots you steep it in. They blackened my tongue—"

"They are vile, aren't they? More honey," his ma said decisively, turning back to the small pantry, and Javid suppressed a grin.

He wished the alchemist luck in resisting her. To his knowledge, none ever had. She wouldn't argue with you outright. In fact, you'd think she was agreeing with you when all the while she was waging a quiet, relentless campaign to get her way. He shared an amused look with his father.

"We're very happy to have you here," his pa said. "Mahmonir is quite smitten with you."

"I don't know why," Marzban responded with a scowl. "Children and animals have never liked me. Nor I them."

"You must try it now," his ma said, returning with the mug. Javid could smell it from across the room. "Much better."

She sank onto the sofa and guided it to Marzban's lips, which curled back from his teeth like a snarling hound. "Just a tiny sip."

"Well then!" Leila said. "I'd best be on my way. There is much yet to do."

"I'll go with you," Javid added hastily.

"Oh my," his ma said, as Marzban bobbed and wove away from the cup. "Do take care, dear. And don't worry, I will tend to your father as if he were my own."

"Holy Father help me then," Marzban gasped. "Get that foul brew away from me, I tell you!"

Mahmohnir bounded into the room and tugged on his beard. Farima started begging for a story.

His mother was retreating as Javid eased the door shut. He heard her say, "Perhaps a soup would go down easier...."

They strode along the corridor in silence for a minute.

"I think that went well," Leila said.

"Couldn't hope for better. I'll see to it his scrolls are brought. And the worse the taste, the stronger the medicine. That's what ma says, anyway."

"It can't do him any harm. The magi would bleed him and fill his belly with emetics until he died, then say it was the will of the Holy Father." She paused. "I didn't see Bibi. Do you know where she is?"

"Sulking in her room, no doubt."

"I should have said goodbye. She deserved better." Leila hesitated. "But I don't really want to go back there."

"Nor do I. I'll tell her, don't worry."

Leila nodded. "She reminds me of myself when I was a girl. Too stubborn to heed those who tell her what she can't do. The girl has more spirit than natural aptitude, but she follows instructions and isn't shy about asking questions when she doesn't understand. To be honest, I feared she would be a burden, but she's proven surprisingly useful — though she's always *sticky*. Have you noticed that?"

"It's the candied dates." Javid frowned. "Do you really think Bibi could be an alchemist?"

The thought amused and frightened him at the same time.

Leila strode through the deserted Hall of the Scribes. "I am not teaching her alchemy. When this is over, I intend to focus my energies elsewhere. To be honest, I'm losing interest in spell dust."

"Because it's immoral?"

She laughed. "No."

"Because it's eating King Shahak alive in the most repulsive way imaginable?"

"Not that either."

"Why then?"

"Because it is a finite resource," she said in a lecturing tone. "We've already emptied many of the houses at Pompeii. I haven't told King Shahak, it would send him into a panic, but there's perhaps a year's worth left, maybe less if he continues at this rate. When it's gone, so is the magic." They neared the antechamber to the main gates and her steps slowed. "Spell dust is the past. Natural science is the future."

Leila fell silent as they approached the guards. She presented a parchment with the king's seal and they were waved through the gates.

"Do you know I've invented a wheel that turns from the force of boiling water? There could be many practical applications. I'm even working on a device to harness lightning, though I've not yet tested it."

She resumed talking as they walked through the parkland, hardly pausing for breath. Javid understood Leila needed to vent her nervous energy and listened without interruption, though she lost him when she started explaining something called *ionized currents*. At last they reached the clearing where the *Shenfeng* was to land. Javid had already arranged for new supplies to be left there and they found six barrels of freshwater, four of salted meat and crates of fruit and vegetables.

"Well," Leila said, exhaling a long breath through her nose. "I've always wanted to see the Kiln."

"I wish I was coming with you."

She took his hand. "I do, too. But you must stay and keep Shahak out of trouble."

Javid snorted. "As if he listens." He scanned the sky, nerves taut. "Where are they? I hope there wasn't trouble."

"The guards at the wall are expecting the *Shenfeng*. I made sure of it personally.... Uh oh," Leila murmured.

A shadow detached itself from a thicket of brambles and slunk towards them.

Javid sighed. "I should have known."

Bibi looked at him defiantly.

"How did you even get out of the Rock?" he demanded in exasperation.

"They all know I'm a 'prentice. I told them my mistress left her lucky satchel and she couldn't fly without it." Bibi held up a cloth bag that Javid recognized as the one Farima kept her ribbons in.

"You sneaky little—"

"Let me come," Bibi cried, addressing her appeal to Leila, who looked on with amusement. "It's no safer here than there! In fact, it's probably *safer*."

"She has a point," Leila said. "All the Vatras seem to be at the Rock now."

"Not all of them." Javid shook his head. "What would ma say?"

"Ma knows. She said that if you'd take me, at least one of her children might survive."

Whether this was true or an inspired lie, it struck its mark. Javid felt a sharp pang of guilt. Bibi saw him weaken and pressed her advantage.

"I'll be with Katsu and Leila. What could happen? We'll find the talismans and come home heroes!"

Her face shone with certainty. It was all a grand adventure to her. Suddenly, Javid found he didn't have the heart to shatter her illusions.

"It's up to Leila," he grumbled.

"Look!" Bibi pointed, bouncing on her toes.

A wind ship with an ebony air sack drifted over the trees. A giant oyster cupping a single pearl was blazoned on the side in silver thread.

"You must do as I say without question," Leila said sternly. "You may not touch the ropes or the brazier or any other part of the ship unless I tell you to."

Bibi saluted. "Yes, Leila Khorram-Din. I will be quiet as a kitchen mouse. And I'll keep my hands to myself." She made a show of wiping them on her dress. "See, they're even clean."

"Get ready to catch the mooring rope," Javid told her with a smile.

Savah Sayuzdri, their father's cousin and master of the fleet at the Merchant's Guild, tossed it over the side and Bibi scrambled to catch it. Katsu waved as the ship slowly settled to earth. The pair of them clambered down the ladder.

"Our plans have changed," Leila said. "But I'll explain in the air. I think it's best we depart as soon as possible."

Katsu looked surprised but nodded.

"I thought I'd better come along and make sure he didn't crash on his maiden run," Savah said dryly. "I've been teaching him the basics, but he's still wet behind the ears. And the conditions are tricky today."

In fact, the weather was ideal, but Savah clearly wanted an excuse to check in on them.

He lowered his voice, even though no one else was in sight.

"How are your parents and the girls?"

"Fine. They stay in their chambers. Shahak confined them to the Rock, but he's left us alone so far."

"Thank the Holy Father for that. And the *others?*"

"Their king is a brute and his guards are worse, but they've kept Shahak as their puppet. So far."

"You dance on a knife's edge," Savah remarked, shaking his large, grizzled head.

"I've done it before."

"Not like this." He clapped Javid on the shoulder with one meaty paw. "As for me, I'm too old to run away. And someone has to keep an eye on the fleet." His brow lowered. "I won't cede the Guild's property to looters. A handful have stayed with me at the Abicari, though most fled for Susa."

"So you're not going?"

Savah laughed. "Not a chance. I told you, I just wanted to make sure they got off safely. They'll drop me back at the Abicari." He cast a doubtful glance at Leila, who was helping Katsu load the supplies. "You say *she* can fly?"

"As well as I," Javid replied truthfully.

Savah watched her heft a crate of oranges to her shoulder. "Well, she has a strong back, I'll give her that. Come, let's help."

The last of the water barrels was stowed. Javid embraced Bibi and Leila, and kissed Katsu on each cheek, as was proper.

"Take good care of my little sister," he said seriously. "She's headstrong and has more courage than sense, but she means well."

"I wonder where she gets it from?" Katsu mused with a grin. Then he sobered. "Don't worry, I will return her to you, by Babana's will."

The ship's brazier was lit and the air sack filled.

Javid stood alone and watched the *Shenfeng* until she vanished beyond the trees. Four of the people he loved best in the world, and he might never see them again.

His heart ached, but it felt lighter knowing they were free.

With a last glance at the empty sky, Javid turned and trudged back to the Rock.

✷ 15 ✷

THE NAHRESI

On the day the Marakai fleet gathered, all three moons floated above the harbor on the Isle of Selk, which everyone agreed was an auspicious omen. Yellow Selene waxed gibbous to the east and Hecate's silver crescent smiled down from the west. Artemis the Travelling Moon dwarfed them both. In another week, she would reach her full splendor and the tides would lap at the feet of the Mer. Already the sea surged under her influence, driving a steady swell across the breakwater.

Meb looked out at the hundreds of square-sailed ships anchored in the harbor. Some bore the sigil of Khaf-hor the fanged eel, others the sinuous form of Sat-bu. Moonlight played over the green and blue scales of the great carp of the Jengu, whose vessels bumped shoulders with Selk cats and the galloping wave horses of the Khepresh.

Meb stared at the last in morbid fascination.

"It is time," Qenna said softly.

The rest of the Five stood at the end of the long pier on a platform wheeled out for the occasion. Meb was supposed to stand next to them while they addressed the fleet, but to say nothing.

Ahmose had been *very* clear about that.

"How are you doing, kid?" Captain Kasaika asked.

Meb met the captain's steady gaze. "Okay."

In truth, she had passed beyond fear to a strange place where nothing seemed quite real.

The night before, she'd spoken to the Drowned Lady for the first time since Tjanjin. The dream-place where they met was murky and still, the way Meb imagined the bottom of the Great Green to be. As soon as she saw that pale face, her heart lifted. The Lady hadn't abandoned her.

Am I the one? she'd asked.

I don't know, Meb. The Marakai gods keep their own counsel.

Meb's hopes faded. *Then why'd you bring me here?*

Because the world balances at the edge of a precipice. It's not my place to interfere too far, but I would tell you one thing. The clans must unite as they did before.

Three fish swam from her mouth, one blue, one silver, one green. They darted off in different directions.

Suddenly, Meb felt afraid.

Or what? she asked.

The Lady gave her a sad smile. *I must leave you now.*

Wait! Meb cried. *What am I supposed to do?*

But the Lady was gone, her white dress vanishing in the murk. Meb started to chase her. Then she saw the barracuda. Its long, narrow form hung motionless in the shadows, eyes like tarnished silver coins, mouth slightly agape. The three fish swam in circles, oblivious to the waiting teeth. Meb opened her mouth to scream and the sea poured in....

Needless to say, she hadn't gone back to sleep after that. Wide awake in the small hours of the night, Meb had gone in search of Anuketmatma, hoping the Mother of Storms would give her another sign, but the cat was nowhere to be found.

Meb took this to mean her fate would be for the Nahresi to decide.

Now she looked at Princess Pingyang and Feng Mian, who'd been given a place of honor with the viziers. Pingyang looked every inch the Jade Dragon that morning. She wore her finest silk robe and her dark hair was pinned up with ivory combs. White powder made her appear even paler than usual as she surveyed the assembled Marakai with imperious grace. Feng Mian stood at her mistress's side, head down and hands clasped. But when she glanced through her lashes at Meb, her eyes were anything but demure.

Meb the Shark gave her a fierce look in return.

The Five had been pleased that Princess Pingyang offered to help Meb get ready. All but Qenna assumed the princess to be an innocent, pampered child who would keep her charge out of trouble. Now Meb's kinky hair was washed and combed, her nails scrubbed. She wore a new leather vest and trousers without a dozen patches on the knees.

To her relief, that was all they'd done to her.

Now she walked with Qenna to the end of the pier. Together, the Five looked formidable. Tall, broad-shouldered Ramades stood with Hatshepsut, who had a beauty and grace Meb could only envy. Surely, the Blue Crown was made for that elegant head — though she'd never tried to claim it herself.

Nimlot exuded his own solid authority. The faint crease to his brow signaled that he was not entirely pleased, but Qenna said he would go along with the others. The Diyat had to speak with one voice.

Ahmose, who was neither tall nor especially striking, had been chosen to address the fleet by sheer force of personality.

The Marakai sailors clung to the rigging and hung over the rails, their faces tense with anticipation.

"Children of the Great Green!" Ahmose cried. "Two weeks ago, the Diyat convened to discuss the talisman and where the Marakai stand on the disturbing news we received from Tjanjin and more recently, from Culach Kafsnjór of Val Moraine. After giving the matter serious thought, we have decided—"

Qenna poked her hard in the ribs and Meb lurched forward.

"That I will seek the Blue Crown," she shouted.

Well, she meant to shout, but it came out more of a squeak.

Ahmose froze, then rounded on her. "Be quiet, girl," she hissed.

"It's my right," she said, her voice stronger this time. "Anyone can ask!"

The gathered Marakai looked shocked and confused.

"Speak the words," Qenna urged.

Meb took a deep breath. "I demand the test of the Nahresi. I submit body and soul to their judgment."

Ahmose looked ready to strangle someone. Her mouth opened, and then Hatshepsut swept forward.

"It's done, Ahmose," she said curtly. "There's no going back now."

Ahmose regarded Meb. "No, I suppose there isn't. Did Qenna put you up to this?"

"No one did."

Clearly, Ahmose didn't believe her, but she said nothing more, stalking away to join the others.

Hatshepsut beckoned Meb to the edge of the pier. As the representative of the Khepresh, she'd watched the last claimant meet his end, and the one before that. After Meb pestered her half to death, Qenna admitted there had only been two foolish enough to try in the last three centuries.

"You know what you just did?" she asked quietly.

Meb was surprised to see genuine concern in her brown eyes. More than that: pity.

"I know."

"And you know what you have to do next?"

Meb sighed. "Yeah."

Hatsheptsut nodded solemnly. "Good luck to you, Meb."

She hurried back to join the others at an almost-run that didn't make Meb feel any better.

It was awful with everyone watching her, so she looked down at the water below instead.

I must be mad.

Meb peeled her clothes off, dropping them in an untidy pile. Then she dove off the end of the pier, slicing cleanly into the water.

When she surfaced, she heard orders being shouted. A gentle current parted the Marakai fleet, leaving a clear path to the harbor mouth. Meb started to swim. After she'd passed the last ship, she paused to tread water and catch her breath.

The harbor was so calm she could see the three moons reflected in its surface. Meb began to shiver. She glanced back at the pier. It seemed very far away.

I could be standing there right now, safe and sound. Instead of out here, waiting for....

A cry went up from the one of the sailors. Meb's head jerked around.

She saw a line of white on the horizon.

It grew closer with shocking swiftness.

The Nahresi.

Sea foam streamed from their flanks and streaked their dark manes. Nostrils flared as they tossed their great heads, breath fogging white in the cold. Meb had seen regular horses in Susa. The Nahresi stood twice as tall at the shoulder. They galloped in perfect silence over the wave crests.

Meb counted nine.

They were beautiful and terrifying at the same time.

She watched them bear down with the helpless rapture of a small thing beneath the shadow of an eagle. The urge to call on the sea to save herself grew nearly overwhelming.

But Meb couldn't bear the shame. Better to die if the Khepresh gods willed it so.

Just before the first wave horse reached her, it reared up on its hind legs. Meb saw the powerful muscles bunch. Moonlight flashed on pointed hooves. It gave a soundless whinny that resonated in her ribcage. Then it plunged down with a mighty splash, sinking beneath the surface.

She kicked her legs frantically.

By the Mer, please don't bite me, I'd rather be trampled than have those big square teeth chomp down—

"Oh!" Meb exclaimed as she was suddenly lifted out of the water.

She wrapped her fingers in the slippery mane and dug her knees into its flanks. The wave horse tossed its head and gave a snort like a bellows. The other eight surrounded her, giving gentle nudges with their foreheads. Meb laughed, her heart filled with wonder. She ran her hands along their long, muscular necks. The Nahresi's coats were warm like real living creatures.

One held a crown in its teeth.

Meb accepted the gift, turning it over in her hands.

The crown was made of blue coral that subtly shifted from deep cobalt to a lighter turquoise. Nine flawless black pearls capped the points, just like the one she'd found inside the fish on her lucky day.

Meb put it on her head. It fit perfectly.

She almost slid off as the Nahresi beneath her leapt forward, carrying her back toward shore. She threw her arms around its neck, pressing her cheek to its weedy mane. It skidded to a halt at the end of the pier. Meb gave it a last hug and climbed off. As one, the Nehresi reared up, hooves pawing the air, then returned to the sea. She watched them gallop along the channel between the ships as if it were a road, growing ever more spectral until they dissolved into a line of white foam at the harbor mouth.

The water grew still again.

Meb put her clothes back on and turned to the Five. Hatshepsut strode forward with tears in her eyes. She pulled Meb into a tight embrace, then knelt down. Ramades and Nimlot came next, followed by Qenna. Ahmose stood alone for a long moment, her sharp face unreadable.

"And so it is," she whispered.

Ahmose came to Meb and kissed her on both cheeks. Then she sank to her knees.

A thunderous cheer went up from the fleet.

Meb looked out at their hopeful faces. She'd memorized the speech Pingyang wrote, but she knew in that moment she'd be better off speaking for herself. The folk would know it didn't sound like her, and whatever respect she'd just earned would go straight down the bilge hole.

She took a deep breath.

"Most of you know me as Meb the Mouse," she said, using a bit of air to make her voice louder.

Scattered laughter greeted this, though it was friendly.

"And you probably hoped your queen would be someone more fearsome. One of the Five, maybe." She made a face. "Or at least not a kid. But that's how it is and I guess we'd both better get used to it." Meb paused. "A friend told me the Blue Crown has another name. The War Crown. I don't s'pose any of you want war, I surely don't, but it's coming whether we want it or not."

The Marakai exchanged uneasy glances.

"I'll say it plain. The Vatras are coming back and we have to pull the clans together to face 'em. The Five agree. That's what they were going to tell you."

Ahmose and Ramades shifted, their faces grim, but they kept quiet.

"The Nahresi say I'm your queen now, but I won't make anyone go with me who doesn't want to. It'll be dangerous and we might not come back."

A murmuring rose. She heard the words *fireworkers* and *Isfet*.

"You all know of Sakhet-ra-katme and what happened to her. Well, she fought them too, a long time ago. And she beat them."

Meb only vaguely remembered the old woman she'd met once when she was little. The one who tested her. Meb thought she'd failed, but now she realized her weakness meant she'd passed the test. Sakhet knew she was the talisman, though she never said anything.

And what would I have done with the knowledge? Would I still have been Meb the Mouse? Or would it have made me angry and bitter that I couldn't touch the power?

Meb pushed the question from her mind. It was unanswerable.

"What of the other talismans?" someone shouted.

She shrugged. "We got to go find 'em."

Silence greeted this statement.

"Or you can stay landbound and hide out here while a little kid goes to war for you." Meb scowled. "But that ain't the Marakai *I* know."

For a long moment, Meb feared she'd be sailing off alone in a Stygian fishing dinghy.

Then Captain Mafuone strode to the bow of her ship.

"The *Chione* will take you," she shouted.

The other Sheut captains called out their agreement.

"And why should the Sheut have all the glory of carrying our new queen?" a Nyx captain asked good-naturedly. "There's plenty of room on the *Akela*."

"The *Akela* leaks like a sieve," a brawny Selk captain declared, to laughter from nearby boats. "Meb shall have my berth on the *Dhozer*."

"Our Nahresi gave her the crown," cried a tall Khepreshi. "We ought to get a turn!"

And one by one, the fleet came to Meb. Finally, she held up her hands until they settled down again.

"I thank you all for your generosity," she said. "And I'll pay a visit to everyone once we're underway, but my place is on the *Asperta*." She looked at Captain Kasaika, who nodded with a hint of pride. "Besides which, the cook'll have my hide if I don't gut his fish in time for supper."

The *Asperta* floated close by and everyone craned their necks to stare at the cook. He was a huge barrel-chested fellow who liked to throw things when he got mad. Meb had always been scared stiff of him. Now he grinned at her through his black beard.

"Any queen who'll gut fish is one I'm proud to follow," he declared, giving Meb a smart bow.

Meb laughed and another great cheer went up, this one even louder than the first.

"Well done," Qenna remarked, her dry tone belied by the smile on her face.

Even Ahmose gave Meb a look of grudging admiration. Then her sharp gaze fixed on the sky.

A storm petrel winged its way across the harbor, weaving with exhaustion but clearly intent on reaching the platform at the end of the pier. Meb gasped as it nearly struck one of the great masts, but it recovered at the last instant, gathering its strength for the final leg. Ahmose held out her hands, catching its tiny body as it plummeted to earth. She cradled the bird to her breast and closed her eyes.

The jesting stopped. The fleet fell silent.

When Ahmose opened her eyes and looked at Meb, her expression was bleak.

"It carries a message from the Maenads. Kallisto says.... She says the Gale is down and Gaius holds Samarqand."

THE STORM PETREL WAS TAKEN INSIDE THE MER AND REVIVED with warmth and a bit of fish. Ahmose let it rest in Pingyang's aviary until it wished to leave again.

Then the Five and Meb met with Culach and the three Danai at the top of the Mer.

"The message is difficult to interpret," Ahmose said. "Birds do not think as we do. The images Kallisto sent are fragmented." She paused. "I *think* she says Nazafareen entered the Kiln, possibly with the two other talismans, but I could be mistaken." Her face hardened. "I hope by Khaf-hor I am. For if Gaius is in Samarqand, that does not bode well for the success of their mission."

"Are you certain about Gaius?" Culach asked.

"Yes. The bird flew over the city and I saw through its eyes. A great fire destroyed one of the gates and most of the inhabitants are fled."

"The Vatras spared them?" Qenna asked in surprise.

"Save for the unlucky defenders at the gate, the city was not burned."

"Why?" Nimlot wondered.

"I don't know. But before the bird departed, it passed over the Rock of Ariamazes. It saw men in strange garb. Cloaks the color of sand with hair like beaten copper."

"Vatras?"

"One can only assume so."

"So my son might be in the Kiln?" Mina demanded.

"At least he's with Nazafareen," Culach pointed out.

Mina's dark brows drew down. "That's not reassuring."

"If the Gale is gone, we could go look for them," Meb said slowly.

"The Kiln is vast," Qenna replied. "Larger even than the darklands. And harsh. Our people would not survive long there."

"Then what should we do?" Meb bit her lip. She'd expected the Pythia and maybe Nicodemus. Not *all* the Vatras.

"Stay far from the Rock of Ariamazes," Ahmose retorted.

"No." Culach turned his face to Meb. "That's the same mistake the clans made before. Better we take them by surprise in the Rock and corner them there. If they're allowed to march on

Nocturne, it will be the War of Sundering all over again. Once the Great Forest ignites, there's no chance. But if we get to the Rock before Gaius leaves, the Danai can pull it down on his head and you can drown whoever's left."

Ahmose sniffed. "And the Valkirins? Where will they be while we're sticking our necks on the chopping block?"

"I told you what happened at Val Moraine," Culach snapped.

"The Danai took great losses, too, but they will come to our aid, will they not, Victor Dessarian?"

Everyone looked at the large man who stood apart from the others. He had a bold nose and strong jaw, though his black eyes were shadowed. Now they turned to Meb. He strode toward her and gave a respectful bow.

"My mother was Tethys Dessarian of the Danai Matrium. As her eldest son, I pledge my sword to you and all those I can gather," he said, adding under his breath, "If they don't banish me for what I've done."

"There's a fair chance of that," Mithre remarked, casting a look at Victor that was half fond, half exasperated. "Which is why Mina and I will be on hand. Don't worry, the Danai will come."

Victor rose, touched his hand to his sword hilt in a formal gesture, and stepped back.

No one spoke. Meb realized they were waiting for her.

This was swiftly followed by dread as she understood fully, for the first time, what was being asked of her.

No matter what path I take, people will die. That's what the Lady meant, though she didn't say it outright. But if we don't fight, if we try to stay out of it, we'll all be devoured.

Why did the Nahresi choose me, if not for this? To change the course of the way things might have gone?

"Thank you, all of you," she said slowly. "I think Culach is right. Samarqand is our best chance. And the clans must be united. The Drowned Lady told me so."

The Five exchanged startled looks. "You spoke to the Drowned Lady?"

"Yeah, I did. She wasn't very helpful though. And she didn't say anything about the other talismans. Just the clans."

"Samarqand lies far from the sea," Nimlot pointed out. "How can you call it against them?"

"You leave that to me," Meb said quietly. "Culach Kafsnjór. Can we talk? Alone?"

He hesitated, then nodded unhappily.

CULACH HEARD THE OTHERS LEAVE THE CHAMBER. MEB WAITED to approach until the last footsteps had faded. The girl moved like a ghost, but her scent was distinct — an odd combination of soap and saltwater.

"I know what you want," he said curtly before she could speak. "But you don't understand what you ask of me. I'm not who you think I am."

"I ain't sure *who* I think you are, Culach Kafsnjór," she replied in a slightly puzzled tone. "Besides a friend to Nazafareen and someone I trust."

Her words cut, more so because they were spoken without guile. Culach steeled himself to disappoint her. She wouldn't be the first.

"My holdfast is gone, dead, every one of them save Katrin. The others think I betrayed them to the Dessarians. They were about to lop my head off when Victor unleashed the revenants. I'm the last man you want at your side when you approach Stefán and the others."

"None of that matters now," Meb said calmly. "Once we tell them—"

"It *does* matter. You see, I knew you wouldn't understand." The raw bitterness in his voice caught Culach by surprise, but he couldn't help himself.

Meb was silent for a moment. "I did not think you a coward, Culach Kafsnjór. But I don't even know where the holdfasts are. We can sail to Nocturne, but to enter the mountains we must take your abbadax." She pronounced it awkwardly, with an emphasis on the last syllable rather than the first. "I won't let 'em imprison you again, I swear. But from what I know about your people, I doubt they'll listen to a twelve-year-old girl, talisman or not."

His fists clenched at his sides. "How can I say this plainer? I am not a Valkirin any more."

"But—"

"I cannot touch the Nexus! The power was burned out of me. I'm not even a daēva. I don't know *what* I am!"

The words spilled from him in a torrent and couldn't be unsaid. Until now, only Mina knew his secret. Culach was too ashamed to tell Victor or Mithre. Losing the power was a wound that refused to heal.

"I'm sorry," Meb said softly.

"Your pity alters matters not a whit," he snapped. "I am useless. I cannot fight. Even my sword is just for show." He turned his face away. "Leave me on the ship, I beg you. Ragnhildur will take you where you need to go."

"You promised to stand with me." Meb sounded angry now. "You promised!"

"And I meant it." Culach softened his tone. "But you cannot ask me to go back to my homeland."

Meb stepped closer. She touched his hand. "You ain't useless, don't even say that. Without your dreams, we'd be setting a course into the unknown. At least we know who we're facing. You lost your sight and I s'pose that's hard, but you can still fly."

Culach frowned. Yes, he could still fly. If not for that, he would most likely have ended things a long time ago. Mina was the other reason he lived, but even his love for her wasn't enough. He needed a purpose and he had yet to find it.

"It sounds like Victor messed up pretty bad too, but *he's* going back," Meb said shrewdly. "This is bigger than your pride, Culach Kafsnjór. It might taste shitty, but you just gotta swallow it."

Culach sighed. The girl had a knack for saying what people needed to hear. He saw her do it to the Marakai. Maybe it was no accident she'd been chosen.

"You think I don't know how it feels, but I do," Meb continued relentlessly. "Before Nazafareen broke my ward, I could barely touch water. Everyone but me could do it. How do you think I ended up gutting fish on the *Asperta*? I was an outcast my *whole life*, Culach Kafsnjór. You've only been one for a few months. And *I'm* still here. I ain't shirking my duty and neither are you."

He barked a laugh. "Maybe you're right."

"Yeah, I am. So pack your stuff. We're leaving for Val Altair first thing." She paused. "Want me to walk you back to your room?"

Culach nodded helplessly, unsure what had just happened. She tugged at his hand.

"Since you told me a story, I'll tell you one too. This one has a real grisly ending, I bet you'll like it. Once there was a sea wolf named Amen-em who fell in love with a beautiful but fickle mermaid...."

AFTER MEB SAW CULACH SAFELY TO HIS CHAMBER, SHE PAID A visit to Princess Pingyang. Feng Mian was packing their things to return to Tjanjin and trunks lay open with neatly folded silk robes and jade combs and the other accoutrements of the royal entourage.

Pingyang gave her a deep curtsy and Meb scowled. "Don't be silly," she muttered.

"You are a queen now. The proprieties must be observed." Pingyang took Meb's hands. "You were magnificent out there. And you were right to discard the speech. You must never defer to others. Listen to your own heart."

"Thanks. For everything."

"I wish we could go with you," the princess said wistfully. "But my father would be furious. And I must tell him what's happened. We will send ships to your aid, I swear it."

Meb smiled. "That's nice of you, but they'd never reach Samarqand in time anyway. This is a fight for the clans."

"I still cannot believe a Vatra was under our noses all this time." Pingyang shook her head. "He was always so civil! I used to play Senet with him. He was very good."

"I bet he was," Meb muttered darkly.

"I want you to have it," Pingyang said, handing her the ivory inlaid board. "Think of me when you play. And when you come visit Tjanjin, we can go to the aquarium together and watch the shark feeding."

"I'd like that." She gave a toothy grin.

Feng Mian laid a hand on her shoulder. "I would give you something, too." She pulled a pin from her hair. It was long and sharp. "For when your other weapons are lost." Feng Mian slipped it into Meb's dense curls.

"I have nothing to give either of you," Meb whispered, feeling guilty.

Feng Mian laughed. "The memory of you stripping off your clothes before the entire fleet and swimming out to meet the Nahresi is quite sufficient."

They embraced her, and despite everyone's efforts to keep the parting light, Meb sensed their worry. Tjanjin had a long memory. Princess Pingyang knew exactly what the clans faced and the burden that rested on Meb's shoulders.

As she walked back to the top of the Mer to finalize their preparations for departure, flanked by two Medjay, Meb gripped the board in one hand, the bag of exquisitely carved pieces in the other.

I will return to Tjanjin, she vowed. If only to beat her at Senet just *once*.

THAT NIGHT CULACH LAY IN BED, MINA WARM IN HIS ARMS. She would leave with Victor and Mithre when Hecate rose and the thought made him sick with fear that he would never see her again. But he understood. The Danai were her people and she hadn't been home since Tethys sent her as a hostage to Val Moraine.

"So Meb talked you into it?" Mina said. "I'm glad."

"More like a boulder rolling down the mountainside. It was jump the way she wanted me to or get crushed."

Mina laughed. "Well, if she can manage an obstinate creature like you, the Vatras will be damp clay in her hands."

He rolled over and cupped her face.

"Mina."

"Yes, love?"

"I've been thinking...."

"The Gods save us all."

"We might not live through this."

"No, we might not," she agreed.

"Will you...." He gathered his courage, pulse pounding. "Will you marry me? I would rather die knowing you were my wife."

"So grim! Are you thinking of Delilah?"

"A bit, yes," he admitted. "But that's not it. I love you with all my heart. I know I'm not much to look at and I have little to offer. I'll likely age like a mortal now. I haven't the least idea how I'll provide—"

She silenced him with a finger to his lips.

"First of all, we both know what an asshole you used to be. I much prefer you weak and helpless." The words were spoken lightly and Culach smiled against her hand. "And if you do age faster — which we don't know for sure yet — then we must make the most of our time, yes?"

"Yes."

"And it might help to bring our warring clans together. I don't reckon there's been a mixed wedding in a thousand years."

"Yes," he breathed.

"But those are not good enough reasons," she said sadly.

Culach's heart stopped beating. Then Mina kissed him.

"Luckily, I have my own. I will marry you because I fancy you, too. More than all the stars in the sky."

Culach smirked, folding his arms across his chest. "I don't believe you. You'll just have to prove it."

So Mina obliged.

CAPTAIN MAFUONE HELD THE CEREMONY ON THE SHORE beneath the bright light of Artemis. She performed it in the Marakai way, joining their hands and seeking Sat-bu's blessing of the union. This involved wading into very cold water, but when it was done, Culach felt like a new man. Still blind, still severed from the Nexus, but no longer adrift. For the first time since the dreams began, his heart felt peaceful.

Afterwards, Victor pulled him aside. "You're lucky," he said with feeling, though Culach was relieved to hear no bitterness in him. "I wish you both well."

"Take care of her."

Victor laughed. "I think *she* will take care of us. But I swear to die before I let harm come to Mina."

Culach found this to be a satisfying response.

"We'll get your sons back," he said.

Victor sounded weary. "I hope so. Fare well, Culach."

His parting with Mina was far more wrenching. Culach deeply regretted that they wouldn't even have a single night together as man and wife. But the fleet was eager to be gone and time was against them. Gaius might be in Samarqand, but for how much longer?

So he tasted her sweet lips one last time, embracing her until her feet left the ground and she pounded, laughing, on his shoulders.

"I will meet you at the Twelve Towers, dear husband," Mina whispered. "And we will go to war together."

He heard Meb's high voice, calling his name.

"Culach Kafnsjor! We must leave!"

Then Mina was gone and Meb was hauling him up the gangplank of the *Asperta*. Ragnhildur would fly alongside until she grew tired, then rest on the deck. He heard the smooth, liquid rush of waves splashing against the hull as the Marakai summoned a current to carry the fleet beyond the harbor. The sails snapped, filling with wind. So many new, strange sounds! Creaks and groans, the shouts of the sailors and rhythmic surge of the open sea. Culach clung to the rail, a bit overwhelmed and already missing his wife.

Sensing his melancholy, Meb took his hand again. It felt natural as his own, small but calloused and strong.

"Let's go below for a spell," she suggested. "You ain't met my cat yet. She's not mine really, she belongs to Herself, but at least I ain't afraid of her no more. Treat her nice, mind, she's got sharp teeth and we don't need more trouble than we already got on this journey."

She kept up a steady patter as she showed him how to climb down the ladder. Culach felt better in the enclosed space though his stomach remained undecided about the pitching and rolling.

"Right this way...." A hatch opened. "In here."

She must be up on her toes, for Culach felt fingertips touch his shoulder and gently press down. He sat on a narrow bunk, then jumped as something landed in his lap.

"By the Mer, don't startle her," Meb admonished.

Culach had never encountered a *cat* before. He sat stiffly as whiskers brushed his face.

"Her name's Anuketmatma. She's the Mother of Storms, mistress of smashers and conjurer of typhoons a hundred leagues wide. But she also likes a nice chin scratch. Go ahead. Don't be shy."

Culach ran his hands up the cat's lean body and she gave a low growl, back arching.

"You're petting her the wrong way," Meb laughed. "Don't you know anything about cats?"

"No."

"Here, I'll show you." She took his hand. "You got to go *with* the fur, see?"

A moment later, a strange rumble filled the cabin. It was pleasant, Culach had to admit. It reminded him of the noises Mina made sometimes when she was pleased with him.

"There, she's purring," Meb said in a satisfied tone.

Her bare feet moved toward the door.

"Where are you going?" he asked in alarm.

"Topside. I'd best talk to Captain Kasaika. Maybe clean some fish. There's always work to be done on a ship."

"But the Mother of Storms—"

"Just keep up the chin scratching, you'll do all right."

He heard Meb scamper up the ladder.

She tricked me, he thought in amusement, stroking the cat's velvety ears. Culach stretched out on the bunk, Anuketmatma curling up on his chest. She seemed to like the fur inside his coat, kneading it with her needle-tipped paws.

Well, it could be worse, he reflected. I could be at Val Altair, telling Stefán I'm *awfully* sorry my dear friend Victor Dessarian blew the horn, but won't he give me what's left of his holdfast to go fight the Vatras?

Dark thoughts crowded Culach's mind. Visions of Gerda. Of his crawl across the Great Hall of Val Moraine and the screams behind him when Ragnhildur broke free of the ledge and soared into the darkness. In truth, he had no idea what he would find at Val Altair.

I promised to stand with Meb and I will. But Nine Hells, why did Victor have to stumble over that horn?

Culach fretted, yet in the end, he proved no match for the purring cat and gentle sway of the ship, falling into a deep slumber.

🦋 16 🐍

WARRIOR WITCH

Thena extended a bare foot, studying the sketch with a critical eye.

It was the artist's sixth attempt to render an accurate portrait of Andros. The first few were hopeless and Thena had been forced to have the man flogged as a lesson. But this one.... Under her patient instructions, he'd finally gotten it right.

The unyielding mouth and icy blue eyes. The proud hawk nose.

Just looking at it made her furious.

"The water is tepid," Thena snapped. "Warm it up, you little wretch."

Domitia bowed her head, her face expressionless, and placed Thena's foot on the carpet — gently.

"Yes, Mother."

Well. The witch was finally learning to mind her manners. Thena permitted the tiniest trickle of power to flow through the bracelet and Domitia used it to heat the bowl of water. Then she dipped a cloth and lifted Thena's foot again.

"It's too hot!" Thena shrieked, kicking the bowl over. She glared at Domitia. "You did that on purpose."

The witch paled. "No, Mother. I swear it."

Fear rushed through their leash and Thena felt her own anger cool. Perhaps it had been an accident after all.

Don't forget your rules. Punishment only when necessary. She must know you are just and merciful. That is an essential part of the breaking process.

Thena sighed and leaned back in the chair. She'd taken Domitia's old chambers and arranged them to suit her own taste. Gone were the piles of dusty old scrolls and plain furnishings. Elaborately carved and gilded pieces filled the room now, as was fitting for the Oracle of Delphi. It had cost a small fortune, but Basileus controlled the treasury and he'd acceded to her demands with minimal fuss. His own tastes were even more lavish.

The sketch had crumpled in her hands. Thena smoothed it out and regarded it again.

Andros.

Darius.

He'd been her only misstep. Thena's jaw clenched. Not a misstep. A disaster.

A knock came on the door and she waved Domitia into the corner.

"Enter," she said imperiously.

The Tyrant opened the door and strode inside, shutting it behind him. He still wore the scarlet cloak, but now he carried a staff capped with a bull's head instead of the chain of the Archons. The man was even more arrogant since seizing control of the city—he'd lost no time minting coins with his own face on them—but he'd answered her summons quickly, which pleased her.

"Oracle," he said, ignoring Domitia, who knelt in the corner. "Have you had a vision?"

He never looked at the witch, Thena noticed with amusement. She scared him spitless.

"None that you need concern yourself with. But I do have a

task for you," she said, holding out the sketch so he would be forced to come to her.

Basileus's mouth tightened, but he walked over and took it.

"This is Andros. Have copies made and distributed to your network of spies. I want him found and captured."

He barely glanced at the sketch. "The witch is back in the darklands by now. It's pointless."

"Are you refusing me?"

Basileus drew a deep breath and folded the parchment. "Setting aside the fact that you permitted him to escape in the first place, I do not see why this one particular daēva matters...."

He trailed off as Thena held up a ring of iron keys. Domitia stared at it hungrily but remained on her knees. She'd learned the hard way how swift and brutal retaliation would be.

"Shall I unlock her, Basileus?"

"You'd never dare," he growled.

She gazed at him serenely. "Apollo would protect me. I am his bride. His left hand on earth. He would shield me from the flames. He told me this himself." She smiled. "But I shudder to think what the witch might do to the rest of you."

In fact, every word she'd just uttered was a lie. The god had not spoken to her since the day she was raised to the tripod, when he commanded her to get Darius back. Until the witch was properly collared, she would not be the true Oracle of Delphi.

Thena had prayed and prayed. She'd burned incense and stoked the pinewood fires. But Apollo had turned his back on her. It would be a grave offense to pretend to speak for the god, so Thena had been putting Basileus off regarding prophecies. But she couldn't keep up the pretense forever. No, she had to find Darius. Then the god would love her again and all would be well.

"You're mad," he grumbled.

"No, I have faith. You would do well to follow my example."

Basileus shook his head and turned to leave.

"I want results," she said in a flinty tone. "And I will be most displeased if you don't get them."

"Lord Nicodemus—"

"Is gone and shows no sign of returning. You will report to me in three days' time."

"Very well." Basileus stalked out of the room, the sketch clenched in his fist.

Thena turned to Domitia. "Perhaps I'll let you burn him when his usefulness wears thin. You'd enjoy that, wouldn't you?" She laughed. "Savage little beast. I know you're not tame yet, but you will be, daughter. Come, back to your cell."

A flash of impotent rage sparked through the leash and Thena laughed harder.

Six Shields of Apollo trailed them through the temple and across the plaza to the building that housed the witches. Once Domitia was safely settled into her shackles, Thena went to check on the new acolytes. They were working with the only witches who remained in her custody — both Danai, brother and sister. Rafel had gone with her to Val Moraine and tried to betray her there. His punishment was necessarily severe.

Their teenaged keepers had arrived at the temple plump and pink-cheeked and eager to serve Apollo. Now both were thin with dark hollows beneath their eyes. Thena understood. It was a burden to wear the bracelets and endure the suffering of the witches, but it was all for their own good. The girls were young and inexperienced, but soon they would learn to tolerate it. She stopped in each of the cells to give them blessings and words of encouragement.

Her steps slowed as she passed Andros's old room. Thena paused in the doorway, then slipped inside.

She drew a deep breath. She could still smell him. *Filthy witches*. Her fingers trailed across the manacles fixed to the stone wall.

It hadn't been all bad. No, not all of it.

They'd had some interesting conversations in this room. He'd seen the darkest corners of her mind, and she his. She felt sure he'd been coming to worship her until that horrible girl showed up. She'd ruined everything. Reminded Andros of who he used to be.

There would be no need to torture him for his name when he returned. She knew it now. He would be her pampered pet. Her warrior witch. Together, they would bring all the others into line.

Thena kissed the chains and returned to the temple with a lighter step.

✤ 17 ✤

REBORN

Darius rushed forward, heedless of the hissing shadows. They shrank away from his iron blade, but she sensed their hunger and fury.

"You can see me," Nazafareen whispered in wonder. "Can you?"

He nodded, his eyes never leaving her face. "I see you, my love."

Yet he looked wary. Even a little afraid.

Am I so monstrous? she thought, the anger flickering to life again. But then he gave her a tentative smile and it subsided.

"Farrumohr is gone. I banished him. The crown is broken."

Darius held out a hand. "Come to me."

Nazafareen didn't hesitate, though she was afraid he would dissolve like smoke beneath her touch. She stood and felt the seductive power of the throne slacken its grip.

"I would rather be with you in the nameless place than queen in this one," she said quietly.

He arched an eyebrow. "The nameless place?"

"Never mind. Oh, Darius, you came!"

Nazafareen reached out, her fingers trembling. Darius's closed around them, solid and real. He swept her into a fierce embrace and she staggered.

"I'll carry you," he murmured.

She gave him a stubborn look. "I walked in here. I'll walk out again."

Darius smiled. "Of course you will. I brought your sword."

He offered her *Nemesis*. Nazafareen eyed the blade askance.

Iron.

Her essence shuddered, still brittle as a husk.

"You keep it for now," she said.

The shadows trailed them to the path leading out, but they kept their distance and did not try to attack.

"I thought I'd never find you," he muttered as they hurried along. "It's a bloody wasteland."

She frowned. "You didn't see the city?"

"City? I saw nothing. Only a flat plain and a tower standing on its head."

"Oh. It's different for me."

Sorrow filled her as she understood why. To lose him again was almost more than she could bear. But he could not stay with her, nor she with him.

"The Viper said I can never return, not even to the Dominion," she said. "The Drowned Lady won't permit it. But I'll take you to the well, see you through safely—"

Darius stopped, turning to face her. "I made a bargain."

"A bargain?"

"For your life. I bought you another one. There's yet a price," he said hastily. "But whatever it is, I'll pay it gladly."

Nazafareen threw her arms around his neck. "You are not miserly with your gifts."

He held her close and the thudding of his heart echoed in the silence of the pit.

"The price. Did you say *whatever* it is?"

"She wouldn't agree to tell me ahead of time."

Nazafareen considered this. "Well then, I suppose we'll find out what it is together."

They climbed higher, the walls turning from black onyx to plain stone. At last they reached the top and clambered over the pile of rubble. Nazafareen halted.

"Do you see any Druj?" Darius asked.

Hundreds of shadows and their more substantial counterparts ringed the pit, their ranks swelling by the second. The horde stared at them both, but at Darius most of all.

Like flies to a midden.

Her heart sank. The vision Farrumohr showed her had been true.

"Many," she said. "Too many to fight. If I try, it might destroy me."

Nazafareen gazed out at the ranks of restless dead. The huo mofa flickered in her fingertips.

"You must trust me," she said quietly. "Play along and stay close to my side."

He nodded, his face pale.

She stepped up to the top of a square stone block. "Farrumohr has been cast down," she cried. "I am your queen now!"

She sensed lust and fear warring in the creatures. A few shuffled forward, greedy eyes locked on Darius. The thump of his heartbeat sounded like distant thunder.

"He's mine," she growled.

The dead stilled, though she doubted they would stay quiet for long. The lure of living flesh was too powerful.

"I will free you from this dismal place," Nazafareen shouted. They stirred in excitement at her words. "But you must obey me until we reach the portal. Any who try to take my prize will will pay a hard price. Now make way! Clear a path!"

Darius arched an eyebrow.

"Trust me," she whispered again.

Slowly, the ranks of the dead opened. She took Darius's hand

and led him into the horde. The fresher ones had pushed their way forward, leaving the shadows to drift at the outer edges. Each of their faces was distinct and she felt a stab of pity.

Not all were evil, not like the Viper. They'd stubbornly clung to something or someone in their former lives, refusing to pass on and wandering lost through the Dominion until they ended up in the Abyss. Many just seemed sad, watching them pass with empty, weary eyes.

But others were more disturbing. A naked man covered in blood, with trembling hands. A young, dark-haired girl, plump and pretty, her blue lips curling into a snarl....

She suddenly darted into their path, hands outstretched, and Nazafareen seared the girl with a bolt of blue fire. She felt another piece of her soul burn away, but it discouraged the others long enough for them to gain the other side of the plaza where the ranks were thinner.

"Hurry," she whispered to Darius, striding over a bridge and into a tangle of narrow streets, the army of dead following close behind.

"I wish I could see them," he muttered, blue eyes worried as he glanced over his shoulder. "Where are we going?"

"Back to the House Behind the Veil, or at least its mirror in the Abyss." Nazafareen searched for a landmark that might lead her to the road, but it all looked the same.

Their steps quickened as they delved deeper into the maze of streets. Some of the lanes ended in stone walls and they were forced to retrace their steps, Nazafareen walking ahead to drive back the throng. It grew steadily larger — and bolder. The worst of the pack kept trying to sneak closer when she wasn't looking.

"Where's that cursed road?" she muttered. "They're getting uppity, Darius."

He squinted into the distance. "I think I see another portal," he hissed under his breath. "Those are visible to me."

He pointed at a large building just ahead with open sides and a crumbling roof supported by pillars. A cistern sat in the center, stained and black. Nazafareen approached warily. She didn't like the looks of it.

"Are you sure? There are other places than this, Darius. Worse places."

"I think it's the same one I used. It comes out near the Lady's tower."

The dead pushed forward, shoving each other out of the way, their eyes fixed on the cistern. She opened herself to the power of the void, feeling it sizzle and spit in her veins.

Nazafareen turned to Darius with a heavy heart. She let go of his hand and took a step back. "I can't let them through. If I break the portal, you'll be stuck here too. Just remember ... remember I love you. Even if I forget."

He frowned. "What? Nazafareen, wait—"

"I promised you freedom," she shouted, as the horde ran toward them. "And you shall have it!"

A sheet of lightning erupted from her hand. It coursed outward in concentric rings, a tide of negatory magic greater than any she'd ever unleashed. She fed it with all she had left, the core of her essence.

The magic burned bright, brighter, enveloping the crush of souls surrounding the temple. When it finally faded away, Nazafareen was the last shadow standing.

And she was a shadow now, a shadow of blue flame.

She saw a dim figure, shouting, but the sounds meant nothing.

The figure reached out and seized something that was a part of her yet separate, material. It was yellow and shiny, though she had no word for it.

A darkness yawned. She did not — could not — resist as the figure dragged her inside.

NAZAFAREEN LAY ON A PATCH OF GRASS NEXT TO DARIUS. THE color was faded and it had no smell, not like real grass, but after the endless stone necropolis she found joy in it nonetheless. Above, the grey sky of the Dominion framed the branches of a fir tree.

A rock poked into her back and it *hurt*. An instant later, hunger and thirst joined the fray. Never had any of those things been sweeter. Darius laid his ear against her breast. His fist clenched her tunic, the knuckles white.

"Holy Father," he whispered. "I can hear it."

"The cuff," she cried, yanking her sleeve up.

When she saw it was still there, Nazafareen closed her eyes and waited for her racing pulse to slow again. For a terrible instant, she'd been afraid the Lady might have taken their bond away. She couldn't feel it in the Dominion, but as long as she wore the cuff, she knew it would return when they passed through a gate to the living world.

At first, her limbs felt heavy and prickled with strange sensations. Nazafareen made a wary inventory, wiggling fingers and toes. Her right hand was still gone so it was the same body she'd had before, which came as both a relief and a disappointment. She wouldn't have minded getting a new hand, though the thought of being remade from scratch was also a bit unsettling.

She touched Darius's cheek, felt the warmth of his skin.

"I saw you in the Dominion, you know," she said softly. "Sitting against a tree."

His gaze turned inward for a moment, then met hers with a flash of raw pain. "I was sharpening my sword."

She nodded. "I spoke to you, but you couldn't hear or see me. It was awful, Darius."

"I sensed something...." He barked a harsh laugh. "You've no idea the state I was in."

Darius suddenly pulled her close, his mouth covering hers, and there was nothing gentle or tentative in the kiss, just a wild possessiveness that lit her own heart afire. She tangled her fingers in his chestnut hair, surrendering to the rush of sensation. The soft scratch of his unshaven cheek against hers, strong hands cupping the small of her back. The honeyed taste of his tongue.

He finally pulled back, breathless. "Holy father, I've missed you," he said hoarsely.

"Nazafareen!"

She turned her head, her pulse still ragged. A woman barreled toward them. She knew that voice.

"Tijah!" she cried, scrambling to her feet.

They flung their arms around each other, laughing and crying.

"What are you doing here?" Nazafareen demanded, holding her friend at arm's length to get a good look at her.

"I ran into Darius. He was looking for you." She jerked a thumb at the black tower. "*She* wouldn't let us come along." Her face split into a huge grin. "But he found you and brought you back. I never doubted he would for a minute." Her gaze skimmed Nazafareen's bloody, torn tunic. "Goddess. Let's get you out of that thing. I think I have a spare..." She started rummaging through her satchel. "Here. Put this on," she said, handing Nazafareen a clean linen tunic.

Nazafareen peeled off the old one and tossed it away with a grimace. There were no scars on her chest, but she knew exactly where each one should have been. Her skin tingled as she popped her head through the collar. It smelled faintly of Tijah, like the sweet, musky oil she combed through her hair. "Thank you, sister," she said, squeezing Tijah's hand.

Darius watched them with a strange look on his face. "You remember her," he said quietly.

Nazafareen frowned. "Well, of course I do. I...." She trailed off, her face going slack with surprise. "I remember everything, Darius. *Everything*."

It was too much. Her legs gave way and she sat down hard in the grass. The memories unfurled in bright bursts, though they were all jumbled-up timewise. The most powerful came first, those that had been deeply etched into her heart because of pain or fear or joy. It wasn't like living them for the first time. They had the feel of places she'd often revisited, with some details clear and others fuzzy. But each was precious to her and Nazafareen sat for many minutes in silence, simply remembering what had been lost to her for so long.

The oil-and-iron smell of the armory at Tel Khalujah and the feel of the *qarha* as she wound it around her face. The first time she ever raised a sword in the practice yard.

She sifted through a hundred petty cruelties and small kindnesses. Her harsh but sheltered childhood, and how it all changed when the Water Dogs came. The first time she ever laid eyes on Darius. How Tijah used to fight with a scimitar. The truth about the Prophet Zarathustra. Losing her hand.

Darius knelt on one side, Tijah on the other. They didn't speak, but their presence was a comfort.

"I never expected.... I'd given up hope." She wiped her face, at a complete loss to explain how she felt at that moment.

Darius's eyes were damp, too. He took her hand, twining his fingers with hers. Tijah beamed, wrapping a strong arm around her shoulders.

"I can only imagine," she said softly. "The Lady is kinder than I thought."

"She told me the price would be paid when we came through the gate," Darius said. "But it doesn't seem like a price, does it?"

"That's because it's not," someone said.

Nazafareen looked up, still dazed. A young bearded man in purple robes approached from the tower. He held a tray in his hands, with four steaming bowls. She caught the aroma of carrots and onions.

"I thought you might be hungry," he said, placing it on the ground. "After.... Well, I imagined you might be."

"Nabu." Tijah grinned. "Always armed with stew when it's needed."

"Tijah." He winked at her. "Where's your bonded?"

"He'll be along," she said, helping herself.

Her bonded? Nazafareen wanted to ask Tijah what he meant, but the smell of the soup was making her mouth water. Darius nodded at the man, a bit warily. He seemed to know this person too.

"You must be Nazafareen," the man said, offering her a bowl.

She accepted it with a smile of thanks and dug in. It was delicious.

Darius didn't touch his own bowl. "The Lady restored her memories. I'm grateful, but I have to ask why?"

"To balance the scales," the bearded man said serenely.

"What does that mean?"

"I don't know." He looked sheepish. "It sounded good, didn't it? In truth, I think it just happened on its own." He glanced at Nazafareen. "This is, ah ... uncharted territory."

"I'm sorry," Nazafareen mumbled through a mouthful of stew. "But who are you again?"

"Nabu-bal-idinna. I've come out to speak for the Lady."

"You're that alchemist!"

He smiled. "I am. And I'm glad to see you returned from the Abyss." His voice lowered. "The odds weren't very good."

"Just tell us what it is," Darius said tightly.

He seemed anxious and Nazafareen wondered what had transpired when he went into the tower to negotiate.

The alchemist's keen brown eyes studied her. "The price is already paid. Don't you know?"

The stew soured in her stomach. Nazafareen set the bowl down. "I'm afraid I don't."

He suddenly scowled at her. "That's the ugliest pair of boots I've ever seen. And your hair! Do you never take baths?"

"I ... what?"

"Your nose is crooked."

Nazafareen touched her face defensively. "Well, it always has been."

He sighed. "Shall I insult your mother?"

She stiffened. "My mother is dead, you beastly man, and—"

Nabu-bal-idinna blanched. "Oh gods, I didn't know. I'm terribly sorry. I only wanted to make you angry."

"But why?" she demanded, thoroughly irritated now.

"So you would understand the price."

"Understand *what?*" Her gaze grew distant. "Oh. Oh!"

"Nazafareen?" Darius crouched beside her, concern in his eyes.

"My breaking magic," she muttered. "The huo mofa." She rubbed her stump. "It's gone."

Darius gave a long exhale, obviously relieved. But Nazafareen wasn't sure how she felt about that.

It was mine. She had no right to take it.

Tijah saw the turmoil on her face. "It almost killed you once," she said softly. "Maybe it's not such a bad thing."

Nazafareen nodded uncertainly. She reached for it again, that dark power that was not of the Nexus, that belonged only to her, and came up empty. She'd experienced the same thing in Nocturne but always with the promise that the hua mofa would return when she reached the sunlands.

If the Lady had asked, which would she have chosen? Her breaking magic or her memories?

The answer was not as simple as she'd once believed.

"You're right," she said firmly. "I'm better off without it." Yet the words rang false. Nazafareen resolved to set the matter aside for now. There was nothing she could do about it, and she didn't want Darius to think she was ungrateful.

"So that was the price?" Darius asked Nabu-bal-idinna.

"Part of it, yes." He held up a hand. "But we have another matter to discuss first. The Viper."

"I banished him to another plane," Nazafareen said. "Trust

me, it looked like a really nasty place. I don't think there's any way back."

She sincerely hoped there wasn't.

Nabu-bal-idinna turned to Darius, his face grave. "The bargain required him to meet my Lady's justice and cross the sea."

Nazafareen looked between them. "Don't blame *him*. He came after I'd already done it. And I didn't know about your bargain. The Viper is gone. Isn't that good enough?"

"Perhaps. It is not for me to decide," Nabu-bal-idinna replied.

"Give her a break," Tijah snapped, black eyes flashing. "She did your dirty work for you. She gave up her magic. Just let her be."

The alchemist didn't seem offended. Maybe he was used to Tijah's blunt manner.

"The Fourth Talisman did what she was meant to," he agreed. "Let us pray that Gaius meets similar justice." He turned to leave. "You must both return to the Lady in six months' time. If a balance remains in your account, she will tell you then."

"Hold up there." Nazafareen scrambled to her feet, setting the bowl aside. "What do you mean you hope Gaius meets justice? He's dead, isn't he?"

Nabu-bal-idinna looked at her in mild surprise. "Why would you think so?"

"Because I severed the thread between them," she exclaimed. "The crown tied them together somehow."

"And thanks to you, Gaius lost his immortality." Nabu-bal-idinna cleared his throat. "But I'm afraid he still has the serpent crown. The real one, that is. You broke its shadow."

"Where is he now?" Darius demanded.

"Samarqand." Another cough. "For the moment. I imagine he'll conquer the rest of the world shortly."

Nazafareen kicked the bowl of stew, sending it spinning. "Fuck," she muttered.

"Now *that's* what I was looking for," the alchemist exclaimed.

"Interesting that your temper remains despite the loss of the huo mofa. In fact, the temper might be the key factor." He stroked his beard. "Perhaps I'll write a monograph...."

Nazafareen rounded on him and he started edging toward the tower. "Yes, well, I really have to get back—"

"So you're saying Gaius *could* be killed?" she persisted.

"It's possible." His tone made this sound unlikely.

Her face darkened. "Now that I have no breaking magic to stop him?"

"Erm.... Yes."

"That's a rotten bargain," she growled.

"I don't make the rules," he replied nervously. "Look, you were dead. Now you're not. Count your blessings." He gathered the soup things and ran for the tower, spoons clattering to the ground as he went.

"What about Katrin and Galen?" she shouted after him. "Are they dead or alive?"

"Alive," he called over his shoulder, then vanished around the corner.

Nazafareen glared at the tower. "That Lady's a swindler."

"Keep your voice down," Tijah hissed, giving her a hard look. "She could still change her mind."

"I don't care," Nazafareen muttered. "It's true. She did it on purpose. But why?"

No one had an answer for that.

"What will you do now?" Tijah asked.

Nazafareen and Darius looked at each other. "I don't know," she said helplessly.

"I have to meet Achaemenes at the gates soon." Tijah sighed. "There are two, close together. You can make your decision when we get there."

Nazafareen slid her arm around Tijah's waist. "Thank you, sister."

They walked together and Tijah told her all that had

happened since she'd left. The twelve Greater Gates from the Empire to the Dominion had to be locked from both sides to prevent ghouls from slipping through. The biggest problem was that no one knew where all the gates were located in the living world. Only five had been named in Balthazar's records. The other seven still had to be found, though she believed they were all in cities. In fact, she and Achaemenes just came from Babylon, where they had many adventures before finally locating the gate and sealing it with a talisman.

Nazafareen listened to Tijah talk, the musical cadence of Al Miraj making her words leap and flow like running water. She sounded happy and purposeful. It might take a very long time to find all the gates, but the bond would extend her life to something close to a daēva's.

"Are you content with Achaemenes?" Nazafareen asked.

Tijah arched an eyebrow. "I wasn't at first. But the kid's grown on me. He's all right."

And that's all she would say about it.

"She thought I was a necromancer," Darius said with some amusement. "I was treed by the Shepherds when she rescued me."

"Did you ever find Balthazar?" Nazafareen asked.

He'd been one of the Antimagi closest to Culach's wicked sister Neblis.

"No." Tijah frowned. "He wouldn't have stayed in the Dominion. He's too smart for that." Her gaze grew distant. She had very personal reasons to despise Balthazar. "No, he's somewhere out there in the world. But I'll find him. You can count on it."

They walked in silence for a while, passing through a wood of huge old oaks with spreading boughs. Speaking of Balthazar triggered another spate of memories, a riot of images that made Nazafareen's head ache. She pushed them away; they would reach the gates soon and she needed to think.

"Do you know what happened to Nicodemus?" Nazafareen asked Darius. "I saw Gaius stab him in the leg. Then he threw him against a wall." The chain of events after that gave her a queasy sensation in the pit of her stomach.

Darius shook his head. "He wasn't in the burrow when I woke."

"So he might be alive."

Darius didn't reply.

"What happened wasn't his fault."

"I never said it was. It's just…. I wouldn't hold out much hope, my love."

Nazafareen felt a rush of pity. Nicodemus had no one to go after him beyond the veil. No one to barter for his life. All he had was his brother Atticus, and the poor boy was in Gaius's clutches, if he even still lived.

Tijah stopped. A clearing waited ahead with twin gates standing twenty paces apart. Their greenish glow burnished her dark skin.

"This is it," she said.

Nazafareen looked at the gates. One led to the world where she'd been born, the other to the one where she'd died.

"You did your duty," Tijah said, her voice pitched low and urgent. "You freed the talismans. You fucking *died* for them. You got rid of the Viper. There's nothing more you can do." Her face softened. "We're building a new world from the ashes of the Empire. A better world. Your brother Kian still lives and so do most of the Four-Legs Clan."

Tijah turned to Darius. "There are still captive daēvas out there. When Achaemenes and I finish locking the gates, we're going to help find them and free them. We could use a hand."

Nazafareen stared at the gates, first one, then the other. No one spoke for a long moment. Darius broke the silence.

"The Danai are in Nocturne," he said. "I'd be abandoning them to the Vatras."

Tijah nodded. "I understand. Really, I do. But I'd also point out that you didn't know any of them until a few months ago."

She stared ruminatively at the gates. "This world to which you fled ground you both into mincemeat. Worse than King Artaxeros ever did, and that's saying something."

"What about Gaius?" Nazafareen asked.

Tijah grunted. "What about him? The bastard killed you once. Why give him a chance to do it again?"

"She has a point," Darius said. "Even if we don't like it."

"But to run away," Nazafareen muttered. "It feels wrong."

"It's not running away—" Tijah began heatedly, but Darius raised a hand and she quieted, crossing her arms with a scowl.

"Nabu-bal-idinna said the talismans are still alive. They're the ones destined to defeat Gaius." His voice was gentle. "You're not a Breaker any more, Nazafareen."

She turned to face him. "What am I, then?"

"Yourself. The same person you've always been."

The same person. And who was *that*?

"I need to think," she said.

They left her alone.

Her heart felt torn in half. Who needed her more? Who did *she* need?

Darius, first and always. Tijah? Yes, but she had her own purpose, her own bonded. Whether or not Tijah would admit it, Achaemenes was a part of her now.

And what of the Four-Legs Clan? Could she ever return to that life?

The arduous trek across the mountains every winter. Braving blizzards and icy crevasses to reach the lower pastures, only to do it again when summer came. Death always waited around the next bend in the path.

A harsh life, but one with its own small rewards.

She thought of the spring lambs, the new animal smell of them, and the sound of ice cracking in the river when the thaw finally arrived. How pure and clean and cold that water tasted, like nowhere else on earth. She remembered curling up with the dogs for warmth, the fold of a velvety ear between her fingers. How her clan owned few material possessions, but loved fiercely and without reserve.

Yes, she thought. Yes, I could return to that.

For a long minute, Nazafareen imagined a life with Darius in the Khusk Range. He would go if she asked him to. She smiled. He'd fit in well with her people. He was not soft, and she thought he would come to appreciate the solitude and untamed beauty.

Once he'd told her that mountains dreamed, but the dreams lasted for a thousand years.

She let herself imagine it, and then, with an ache of longing, she set it aside.

She thought of Kallisto and Herodotus, of Rhea and Megaera. She thought of Javid, whom she'd left in Samarqand. Culach, who had given her his mother's sword. Galen and Katrin, who had followed her into the Kiln.

She thought about Meb.

Oh, Meb.

Nazafareen hugged herself, resting her chin on the stump of her hand.

I'm not a hero. Most likely I never was. But he's right. I am still myself.

She stood and walked over to Tijah and Darius.

"My mother used to say I had more courage than brains and I suppose she was right. I may have little to offer in this fight, but I will not turn away from it."

Darius nodded and his eyes were sad, too. She wondered what life he'd imagined for them.

"I feel the same, but I wanted the choice to be yours. It's your right. I could never ask...." He sighed. "Victor is not the easiest father to love, but oddly enough I do anyway. I would not leave him there, never knowing what happened to me."

"Damn it," Tijah said. "You're sure?"

"I'm sure," Nazafareen said.

"I have to lock this gate behind us. I *have* to. If you don't come with me now, you probably never will."

Nazafareen said nothing. Tears sprang to Tijah's eyes and she wiped them away.

"Well, shit," she said.

Nazafareen threw herself into Tijah's arms, her own tears dampening the taller woman's shoulder.

"I'll miss you, sister," she whispered, her voice cracking.

"Me, too."

Neither of them wanted to let go. In the end, Tijah was the one to step back. She kissed Darius on both cheeks.

"I don't want to see either of you here again," she said gruffly. "Not anytime soon."

"Maybe we'll meet on the other side of the sea someday," Nazafareen said with a tremulous smile.

"Yeah, maybe." She jerked her head at the gate. "So. You going?"

Nazafareen shook her head. "We have to find the one that leads to Samarqand. I passed through it once. I can find it again."

"Straight into the lion's den, huh?" Tijah drew a deep breath through her nose, the prelude to one of her tirades. Nazafareen cut her off.

"There's no time for anything else. Gaius won't stop until the world burns, but he *can* be killed now and I'll wager whatever power he has left comes from that talismanic crown. It has to be found and destroyed." She scowled. "I can't do it, but maybe the talismans can, working together. Except that they don't even know about any of this. No one does except us."

Nazafareen shared a look with Darius, who gave a brief nod of agreement.

"I promise you, we won't do anything stupid." *Like last time.* "Just find out what's going on in Samarqand. There's a slim chance Nicodemus might be there. If he's not.... Gaius's wives hate him, too. Maybe we can find a way to talk to one of them." Nazafareen remembered a young girl with a rock in her hand. Her throat tightened. "Trust me, those women would kill him in a heartbeat if they thought they stood a chance at succeeding."

Tijah let out a sigh. "If you do get close, just chop his fucking head off. That usually works."

A birdcall broke the silence, the liquid trill of a wren. But it couldn't be. Not in these woods. Tijah's head turned.

"I have to go. He's coming. I.... Ah, shit. I love you both."

And with that, Tijah strode into the trees, one hand resting on the hilt of her sword. She did not look back. But Nazafareen stared at the spot where she'd vanished for a long minute.

"I love you, too," she whispered finally, wiping away fresh tears.

❧ 18 ❧

AELIA

Nicodemus glanced up and down the empty corridor, then pushed open the door to Gaius's rooms and slipped inside.

In truth, he wasn't feeling optimistic. If Gaius had a talisman hidden away, surely he wouldn't leave the door unguarded. But Nico had to make sure. And if there *was* something, he was confident he'd find it. He had a nose for talismans.

He opened a cedar chest and quickly rifled through the contents, then ran his hands under the silk cushions on the chairs and yanked open the tiny drawers in an elegant table, which all proved to be empty. He wrinkled his nose. The place *smelled* like Gaius, cold and rancid.

He was still no closer to understanding what had happened the day before. Atticus's remedy soothed Gaius's head, though the pain returned as soon as it wore off so his brother was kept busy brewing a constant supply of the stuff. Gaius was in a foul temper and had kept to his rooms until this morning, when he'd closeted himself away with King Shahak in the royal library. Nico had hoped to eavesdrop, but Romulus slammed the door in his face when he tried to follow them inside, and left his brother Remus to watch the door.

They're plotting something, though fuck if I know what it is.

He'd passed the wind pilot in the corridor the day before, trailing behind Shahak. Their eyes met for a fraction of a second. Javid gave him the barest nod.

So the wind ship had departed.

It was the only piece of good news in a miserable week. This was the first chance he'd had to slip away unnoticed. Gaius kept him close or made sure he was on patrol with other Praetorians. Nico had to grin and nod when they talked about sacking the darklands and mortal cities, about the atrocities they would commit when Gaius finally marched. They'd been chosen for their viciousness and blind obedience, and even before he left with Domitia and learned the truth, Nicodemus had disliked them.

He moved on to the sleeping quarters, where the aroma of unwashed flesh grew stronger. He shook out Gaius's rumpled bedding, breathing through his mouth. Nothing.

Well, it stood to reason that he would carry the talisman on his person. Nico swore a soft oath.

"What are you doing?"

He gave a guilty start before he could stop himself.

Aelia stood behind him, brows drawn together, red hair falling in waves to her shoulders.

"Gaius forgot something," he said easily. "He sent me to get it."

"What is it? I can help you find it."

"Ah.... His medicine."

"I watched him drink it not an hour gone." Her eyes narrowed. "You're snooping."

"I have to go." He tried to push past her and she blocked his way. Aelia stood as tall as he did. She had broad shoulders and wasn't shy of using them.

"I know what you did in the Kiln. I watched them beat you within an inch of your life." Her intent gaze froze him in his tracks. "Why did you take the burns?"

"To save myself," he said brusquely. "Will you tell him I was here?"

"No. But only if you tell me what you were looking for."

They stared at each other.

"I owe your brother a debt," she said quietly. "When I birthed Marcus, the blood wouldn't stop. Gaius took the babe from my arms and abandoned me. Then Atticus came. He made a potion from the thorns of the catclaw and it stopped the flow. I would have died."

Nico wasn't sure what to say. "Atticus was always curious about how things worked. I'm glad he became a healer. And glad he helped you."

She tilted her head. "I remember you. When you came of age, Gaius wanted you to join the Praetorians, but you refused him. Not many had the courage to."

"He lied to us."

"I know."

Nicodemus drew a long breath. "Does he ever talk to you? About what he means to do?"

Her mouth twisted. "He treats us like breed stock. Gaius does not take *women* into his confidence."

"Then he is a fool."

"He's far worse than that," she said impatiently, glancing over her shoulder. "Tell me what you're looking for. Perhaps I can be of help."

Suddenly, Nicodemus remembered Aelia, as well. There were no villages in the Kiln. It was too dangerous to gather in numbers because the smell of so much flesh in one place would draw predators — the largest ones. When he hunted, he would sometimes see another Vatra in the distance, but they avoided each other. The single exception was when Gaius would collect them for "schooling" at his burrow.

I must have been about thirteen, Aelia nine or ten. She sat across from me, tall for her age and quiet. An orphan like me. It had just rained, the first time in months, and after Gaius let us leave she showed me a flower she'd found growing in a crevice of rock, though it was limp and crushed from her hands....

"I intend to murder your husband," he said. "Is that all right with you?"

Aelia smiled.

THEY ARRANGED TO MEET IN SECRET AFTER THAT TO SHARE ANY news. Two more days passed. Aelia watched Gaius closely when they were alone together, and recruited two more of the wives she trusted fully, though none had ever seen him with a talisman. They were forbidden to use fire around him and she said Gaius sensed it if they so much as touched the Nexus. Thankfully, his headaches left him unable to perform — and the women in peace.

"I brought him the remedy in the library today," she whispered. "He has Shahak working day and night on some conjuration, but I cannot read the scrolls. They stopped talking when I entered."

They were in one of the pantries of the enormous kitchens. Net bags of onions and garlic dangled from the ceiling and sacks of flour, salt and sugar sat piled against the wall.

"I wish I could simply poison his cup," she hissed in frustration. "Or slit his throat while he slept. But I know you're right. I've seen his fey ability to heal. Agrippa tried to leave a banded blackfang in his bed three years ago. He took four bites before killing it. One should have sufficed to finish him! His throat swelled and turned purple, yet he recovered. And Agrippa was thrown into the sea for the sharks." Her face hardened. "He made us all watch."

Nicodemus sighed. "He is not a god. His power comes from *somewhere*."

Aelia stood close enough that he noticed the light spray of

freckles across her nose.

"No, he is not a god," she agreed. "Though he fancies himself one."

By habit, Nicodemus angled his head so that the burned side was hidden in shadow. Now Aelia reached out and turned him to face her.

"Don't," he said curtly.

"You're ashamed of your scars."

"They're ... ugly."

"On another, yes," she replied honestly. "On you, they mean something else."

"I wish you could see this world before Gaius destroys it," he burst out. "The harbor of Tjanjin on a clear day, when the gulls dive for the catch of the fishing boats and the Marakai cutters fly across the waves. The forests where the pines grow so thick the sunlight hardly penetrates. There's a creature called a hummingbird that hovers in the air when it feeds. I wish I could show you all of it—"

The door to the pantry flew open, blinding them with torchlight. Nicodemus threw an arm across his face.

"I knew I'd find you here," a voice said. "I've been watching."

It was low and hoarse from lack of use.

Remus.

"You faithless bitch," he spat. "Spreading your legs for that traitor—"

Intense heat seared Nico's face, as if one of the great ovens where the cooks baked bread had been thrown wide open. When his vision cleared, he saw a greasy pile of cinders on the floor.

"I've wanted to do that for a very long time," Aelia said with satisfaction.

Nicodemus gave a ragged laugh. "His brother will come looking. They're inseparable."

She nodded briskly. "Then we'd better find a broom, don't you think?"

🪬 19 🪬

A SPRIG OF FEVERFEW

"The Rock of Ariamazes is Danai work," Nazafareen whispered. "You must have some ideas about how to get inside."

She crouched with Darius in a dense stand of trees, watching the palace-fortress. It was lucky the gate to Samarqand emerged into a shallow pond on the right side of the Rock's curtain wall. The last time she came here with Javid and the Maenads, the king's park was lightly guarded and they'd climbed over the wall using the spreading branches of a fig tree.

Things had changed.

Persian soldiers patrolled both sides. Praetorians, too, though the two groups did their best to ignore each other. Nazafareen knew they wouldn't have stood a chance of getting across without being seen.

Now they were close enough to see the towering grey walls of the Rock, but they might have been leagues away for all the good it did. Darius agreed with her that getting one of Gaius's wives alone was the most promising plan, but a contingent of soldiers guarded the entrance and the rest was seamless.

"Armies have broken against the Rock for centuries," Darius

replied. "My people made it so. I could use the power to search for a weakness, but that would bring them down on us in an instant."

Nazafareen shifted, her muscles cramping. They'd been scouting the Rock and its defenses for two full days, napping in turns and drinking from the streams that ran through the parkland. Darius found some wild berries and a few small green apples, but hunger gnawed at her belly. Nabu-bal-idinna's stew was a distant memory. She wished she'd eaten more of it before she kicked the bowl over.

"What if we knock out a couple of guards and take their uniforms?"

He glanced at her. "You're a bit short for a Persian soldier. And we'd still have to get through the front gates. They'd know."

Darius was right. Never had she felt the loss of her power so keenly. She couldn't even sense the Nexus anymore, and she hated it.

Now they were trapped, unable to find a way into the Rock nor to get past the curtain wall into the city.

They both stilled as two Praetorians in shadowtongue cloaks and shining breastplates marched along a path twenty paces away, their scarred faces watchful. Both had short red hair. The larger of the two was blue-eyed, but the other had eyes of amber.

Just like hers.

You're what happens when the bloodline of my people is polluted.

With everything else, she'd avoided thinking about what it meant. She didn't want to tell Darius, but there could be no secrets between them anymore.

"You should know something," she said softly when the Praetorians had passed and the wood grew silent again.

He turned to her, dark hair curling across his forehead.

"I have Vatra blood. That's what a Breaker is." She couldn't meet his eyes. "A mix of mortal and ... them."

"When did you learn this?"

"Farrumohr told me. He called it the law of unforeseen consequences." She sensed no surprise through the bond. "You knew!"

He shrugged. "I guessed. You have daēva blood, but so does any mortal who can wear the cuffs. There has to be something else and huo mofa translates as fire magic. You wielded all four elements. It makes sense."

"Does it?" She frowned. "It seems so ... random. If some distant ancestor of mine had never taken a fancy to a fire daēva, there would never have been a fourth talisman to break the wards." Nazafareen rubbed her forehead. "No, it's even stranger than that. My people aren't from this world. That means either a Vatra travelled through the gates to the Empire or a mortal came the other way. Did the Lady plan it or was it all just an accident? And what came first? The war or the secret love affair?"

He laughed softly. "I doubt we'll ever learn the answers to any of those questions. But you are here now."

"Yes. I'm here now." She kissed him, relieved that he'd taken the news so well. "And I wouldn't be if you hadn't—"

He put his fingers to her mouth, eyes hardening. A second later, she heard soft footsteps on the path. Only one person and the guards always travelled in pairs. Maybe it was one of Gaius's wives. Nazafareen peered through the branches. Her heart sank when she saw it was indeed a Vatra, but male and very young-looking. He had copper hair shot through with gold and walked with a limp. He didn't wear the ritual burns of the Praetorians, but the right side of his face sagged as though the muscles had atrophied.

He carried a basket and studied the ground as he walked, searching for something.

He was always frail, prone to illness. When he was ten, he caught a fever....

Recognition sparked.

Atticus, she mouthed silently to Darius.

His eyebrows quirked and he shook his head in a question.

Nicodemus. Brother.

It had to be. He fit the description perfectly. The question was whether he could be trusted.

There was no way to know for sure, but Nazafareen doubted they'd ever get another chance. The Rock was impregnable. And the longer they hung around in its shadow, the more likely they'd get caught and dragged straight to Gaius.

Darius hissed a sharp breath as she pulled free of his hand and crept from the bushes. A twig snapped beneath her boot. Atticus spun around.

He had the same eyes as his brother, a blue so dark it bordered on black.

Nazafareen stopped. He stood only a few paces away.

"Atticus?" she whispered. "Please don't call the guards. I know your brother. He was a friend. He—"

The boy's face froze in an expression of terror. His throat worked, but no sound came out.

"I won't hurt you," she said, glancing over her shoulder.

Darius stood behind her and the path remained empty, but for how long?

"Please. I came with Nicodemus to the Kiln. Looking for you."

Atticus swallowed hard. His voice was a croak. "You're dead."

"No, no." She smiled. "You're mistaken."

His eyes narrowed. "I know dead. And you were dead. Like, *hours* dead. Like *blood flies* dead."

"There's a patrol coming," Darius said curtly. "We have to get out of here."

"Listen to me." Nazafareen held Atticus's frightened gaze. "Okay, you're right. I was dead. But I'm not anymore." She held out her hand. "Touch it. It's warm. I have a pulse. I swear to you, I'm not a wight or whatever you call them here."

He stood unmoving. But he hadn't cried out an alarm, which gave her hope.

"Nazafareen," Darius said urgently, looking down the path behind them. "Four Praetorians. They're almost here."

Desperation made her reckless. She had nothing to lose now.

"I came back to kill Gaius. Please help me. For Nicodemus."

Emotions flitted across Atticus's face. Then he jerked his head. "Come on." He strode down the path in the opposite direction from the patrol, Nazafareen and Darius hurrying to catch up.

"This way."

Atticus ducked into a faint side trail intersecting the main path. They'd gone twenty paces when she heard the drumbeat of boots passing by behind them. He went a little further, to a glade of silver birch dappled with light from the low-slanting sun, then stopped and turned to face them. Wonder and fear still warred in his face.

"How did you do it, Nazafareen?" he asked. "I examined you myself."

"You know my name," she said in surprise.

"Nicodemus told me about you."

"So he's...?"

"He's alive."

The way he said it made her worried.

"What happened to him?" she asked softly.

Atticus shook his head, his mouth a thin line. "You'll see for yourself."

"Then you'll help us?" She closed her eyes. "Thank you."

He clutched the basket to his chest like a shield. "You still haven't answered my question."

"I made a bargain with the Drowned Lady," Darius replied. "She rules the Dominion. She has the power to grant second chances, if one is willing to pay her price."

Atticus rubbed the back of his neck, a slight smile on his lips. "Does she? Well, I gave *you* a second chance, Danai. I told Gaius you were dead, too."

He dropped the basket in alarm as Nazafareen threw her arms around him.

"Oh, cousin," she whispered in his ear. "You make me proud to be a Vatra."

NOW THAT THEY HAD AN ACCOMPLICE, ENTERING THE ROCK proved to be simple. Atticus explained that he'd been gathering herbs to soothe Gaius's headaches. It was a routine task he performed each day. He left them to hide in the wood while he went to fetch servants' livery. As soon as the guard changed, the three of them approached the massive gates, carrying baskets laden with feverfew, lavender and willow bark. Everyone knew of Gaius's malady and the soldiers barely gave them a second glance as they scurried inside. Apparently, escape-minded servants were their main concern — not ones trying to get *in*.

Nazafareen kept her face down as Atticus led them through the torch-lit corridors. She held tight to Darius's power to spare him the agony of passing so close to fire. The bond was another hidden advantage. The Vatras could still burn them if they were discovered, but Darius didn't need to fear close proximity to fire.

It was everywhere in the keep.

Tall braziers flared at each turning and brackets with pitch-soaked rushes lined the walls. Sweat trickled down her spine. It was nearly as hot as the bloody Kiln inside. After what seemed like five leagues of corridors, Atticus brought them to a small room and shut the door. A bed was wedged against the opposite wall, covered by a rumpled blanket. A table held a mortar and pestle and various piles of herbs. Nazafareen set the basket down.

"Wait here," Atticus said. "I'll find my brother."

"He's free to come and go?" Darius asked in surprise.

"Sort of. I'll let him explain." Atticus checked the hall to make sure it was empty, then darted off.

"He won't turn us in," she said to Darius. "He could have a hundred times already."

"I know. But he's hiding something."

They waited for several tense minutes. Nazafareen looked up anxiously as the door opened. Nicodemus stood there, a glad smile on his face.

His face.

Half was an angry red, the features melted like candle wax. Her own must have showed her shock and pity for he turned the burned side away, bitterness twisting his lips.

Nazafareen drew a breath and stepped toward him.

"I'm so glad you're alive," she said warmly.

There was no answering smile. "Aren't I the one who's supposed to say that?" he replied in a slightly mocking tone.

"Very funny," Darius muttered, watching him warily.

Nicodemus moved inside, closing the door behind him. He walked to the table and leaned on it casually, but she noticed that he stood so the burned side was averted.

Did the Vatras force that on him, or did he agree to it?

Nazafareen was afraid to ask.

"My brother says you came to kill Gaius." He shook his head angrily. "Why do I feel like we just had this conversation?"

"Are you willing to help us or not?" Darius demanded, his cool gaze sweeping over the Praetorian breastplate.

"Maybe. But I have my own plans afoot. Please don't screw them up."

"What plans?" Nazafareen asked.

"King Shahak's wind pilot sent a ship to search for Katrin and Galen in the Kiln."

"So they're still there?"

"Far as I know."

"And the king permitted it?"

"The king doesn't know." Nicodemus laughed. "His pilot

doesn't mind taking risks, I'll give him that. The kid's walking a razor's edge but he hasn't stumbled yet."

Nazafareen glanced at Darius. Wild hope stirred in her breast. "This wind pilot. His name isn't Javid, is it?"

"Yeah, that's him." Nicodemus looked startled.

Nazafareen grinned. "And he's here? In the Rock?"

"His whole family is here, the poor bastard. The king's holding them hostage, though he seems to be treating them well."

For the first time, Nazafareen knew in her bones she'd made the right decision by coming to Samarqand. Her friends were gathered here and she would help them in any way she could.

"We have a great deal to tell you, but I'd rather not do it twice," she said. "Can you bring Javid?"

Nicodemus and Atticus shared a look. "Better if you go to him," Nicodemus said. "His family's rooms are in the east wing. Gaius and his bodyguards never go there, but I can't say the same for this side."

She hesitated. "Does he know?"

Nicodemus stared at her. "That you're supposed to be dead? Of course he does. I told him everything."

She bit her lip. What if Javid reacted the way Atticus had? She couldn't bear to see him look at her with fear — or worse, loathing, like she was some unclean thing. And if she told him about the burrow, she'd have to explain all of it. Nazafareen wasn't ready to do that, not yet.

"Can you just say you made a mistake? Please?"

Nicodemus shrugged as if he didn't care either way.

"Okay," Atticus said. "I guess I can understand how you feel."

She touched his hand. "Thank you."

He flushed and nodded.

It was painful to see the two brothers side by side, their close resemblance marred by Nicodemus's terrible burns. She tore her gaze from his face as they slipped into the corridor and started for the east wing. A few frightened-looking servants crossed their path, hurrying in the opposite direction when they saw the Vatras, but the place was weirdly quiet. They passed a series of empty audience chambers decorated with faded frescoes and thick carpets, and a huge hall with two hundred tables and a great cold hearth. Gradually, the corridors narrowed and they entered a less ostentatious part of the Rock, devoted mostly to storerooms filled with clay jars.

"How much farther?" Darius muttered.

"Almost there," Nicodemus said.

They were approaching an intersection when she heard the echo of boots ahead. It was too late to turn back.

"Get behind me," Nicodemus hissed.

Nazafareen lowered her head and fell back. Darius did the same.

Just a routine patrol. They'll pass us by. We're with a Praetorian. Servants are invisible here....

"Atticus!"

The voice made her heart slam against her chest. She felt a sudden ache in her ribs. The cold icicle of a blade sliding into her body.

Nazafareen had foolishly thought she no longer feared death, knowing what lay on the other side. A tranquil voyage across the Cold Sea. She still had no idea what waited on the far shore, but she'd sensed it was a good place.

Now all the pain and terror she'd felt at the end came rushing back. Her hand clenched around the basket. She pulled her stump inside her right sleeve and hunched her shoulders, letting her hair hang across her face.

Atticus stopped. Heavy footsteps approached.

"I've been looking everywhere for you," Gaius growled. "My head is splitting. I need that remedy!"

"I'm sorry," Atticus said quickly. "I took two servants so I could make more this time—"

She heard the crack of bone on flesh, glimpsed the flash of a pale hand. Atticus stumbled back. Nicodemus took a half step forward, every muscle tense.

Don't. Please don't.

Six Praetorians strode up. She could feel the heat of them, like an open furnace.

Nicodemus knelt down next to his brother and helped him to stand.

"I'll see it's brought to you right away, my lord," he said quietly.

Gaius's cold gaze swept over them all. Nazafareen stared down at the contents of her basket, the white petals of the feverfew framing a golden eye dusty with pollen.

"You."

She girded herself to look up when Darius spoke.

"My lord?" he inquired smoothly.

"Have I seen you before?"

The tone was mild, but she detected an undercurrent of distrust.

"I've served King Shahak for twelve years, my lord. I'm his ... wine steward."

She felt the weight of Gaius's stare. "Well, now you're mine. When that concoction is done, you'll bring it to me, along with the finest cask in the king's cellars to wash the taste away."

Darius gave a low bow. "Yes, my lord."

The footsteps receded. Nazafareen trembled and hated herself for it.

They walked the rest of the way in silence, Atticus cupping a hand to his face. It wasn't far and they encountered no one else.

The door opened on a scene of domestic chaos. Two dark-haired girls came running up, yelling for ma and pa. The littlest one pulled a toy horse on a string. Chickens flapped indignantly and scattered in all directions as they crowded inside.

The chamber was large and comfortably furnished, with sofas and cushions and two gilded standing lamps. A table in the corner was piled high with scrolls. At the far end of the room, a hall led to more rooms. Nazafareen immediately felt at ease.

A slim middle-aged woman with forceful eyebrows and a blue head scarf hurried forward, wiping her hands on an apron.

"Atticus," she cried. "What did those monsters do to you now?"

"It's nothing," he muttered.

"It's not nothing. Sit down, I'll make a poultice." She smiled warmly at Nicodemus, then at Nazafareen and Darius. "Who have you brought us?"

"Is Javid here?"

"In the back with Marzban." She cast a curious look at Nazafareen. "I'll fetch him."

Nazafareen rocked on her toes, watching the doorway. A moment later, Javid emerged, looking dapper in an embroidered wool coat, if a bit careworn and thin. His eyes widened. To her relief, he didn't hesitate, but ran forward and swept her into an embrace, laughing.

"Holy Father," he said, holding her at arm's length. "I thought...."

A stern-looking man with a long beard stood behind Javid. They both regarded her uncertainly.

"I was wrong," Atticus blurted, as Javid's mother tipped his chin up to gently wipe the blood away. He gave a nervous laugh. "I mean, she *looked* dead. With the sword...." He swallowed. "Guess it missed all the important parts."

Javid studied her with a slight frown. "It must be the will of the Holy Father that you survived," he said softly.

The Persians all made the sign of the flame. Darius's hand rose to his brow out of habit, then fell to his side again. He cleared his throat, pretending to pick a piece of lint from his coat.

"This is my father," Javid said, glancing at a short man who looked to be in his early sixties, with salt-and-pepper hair and a broad, kindly face, who'd just emerged from the doorway. "You already met my ma. And my sisters. Farima and Mahmonir, this is Nazafareen and Darius."

The girls smiled shyly.

Javid gestured to the first man with the beard. "And this is Marzban Khorram-Din. A ... family friend." He lowered his voice. "We have no secrets from each other. You can trust everyone as you trust me."

She could tell he was dying to ask how they'd gotten inside the Rock and what other news they brought, but didn't want to frighten the children. Nazafareen was very glad she'd asked Atticus to lie for her. She couldn't imagine explaining the truth to a roomful of people she'd just met, even if they were Javid's family.

"Why don't you play in the back for a bit?" Javid suggested to the girls, sitting on his heels.

Farima frowned, but obediently took her little sister's hand and led her away.

"We came through the gate," Nazafareen began as they all found places to sit, though Nicodemus remained at the door, his face watchful. "There were a few soldiers, but they'd been drinking heavily. It wasn't hard to slip past them and hide in the woods."

She skirted the truth, leaving out the Abyss and the Lady entirely and making it sound as if she and Darius had gone together into the Dominion to hunt Farrumohr. She explained who he was and how she'd severed his connection to Gaius.

"The crown is the talisman that protected him. It's shaped like a serpent. We should try to find it, but I think he can be killed now either way."

Nicodemus had listened closely, though he knew better than to ask questions she wouldn't want to answer. Now he dragged a hand through his copper hair, leaving it standing on end.

"Gaius told me he was real," he muttered. "I can't believe you found him." The bitterness melted from his gaze as he regarded her. "You're certain of this? That he's no longer immortal?"

She looked at Darius and he gave a slight nod. He trusted Nabu-bal-idinna's word.

"Yes."

"I've already searched his rooms and found nothing. Who knows, maybe he hid it in the Kiln somewhere." His eyes blazed. "But it doesn't matter. Gaius never goes anywhere without a full guard of Praetorians, but you can break their fire magic—"

She shook her head. "I lost my power. It was.... It was the price to defeat Farrumohr."

"Well, fuck," Nico growled.

"That's what I said. But he'll make himself vulnerable. We just have to wait for our chance."

"It won't be easy. Gaius felt what you did. The *remedy* he hounds Atticus for is to soothe his headaches. He flew into a rage ... about four days ago, wasn't it?"

Atticus nodded.

"He blamed it on the clans. Said they were trying to kill him with magic."

"I suspect Gaius was an unwitting puppet," Nazafareen said. "He's still a monster, but he didn't *know* he was being used."

"That fits with what he told me," Nicodemus agreed. "He believed the Viper to be dead. But since you broke that shadow crown, he trusts no one except his personal guards and they're all loyal to the death. Even his wives can barely get near him."

"Maybe I can," Darius ventured. "I *am* his new steward." He turned to Atticus. "We'd better bring him what he asked for. I don't want to die my first day on the job."

"Don't even jest about it," Nazafareen said fiercely.

Darius looked chastened. "I'm sorry. I didn't mean...." He trailed off.

"You're not to leave these rooms," Nicodemus told her firmly. "I think he'll remember *your* face."

She nodded unhappily.

"Come, dear," Javid's ma said in a gentle tone. "You'll be safe with us."

I don't want to be safe, she nearly shouted. I want to help!

But Tijah was right. She'd done her part. Anything more would put them all in jeopardy.

"You'll need to stay in the servant's quarters," Javid was saying to Darius. "Don't worry, they're almost empty. I'll spread the word around that you're my third cousin. And I'll draw you a quick map of the Rock so you know where to go." They walked over to the table with the scrolls and Javid made a sketch on the back of a piece of parchment, laying out the wine cellars and kitchens, and Gaius's personal chamber. Darius memorized it at a glance.

"Be careful," she whispered, hugging him hard at the door.

"Always," he whispered back. "I'll come see you when I can."

And then they were gone, leaving her alone with Javid's parents and Marzban Khorram-Din.

"It's time for you both to take your tea," ma declared, plodding into the small kitchen she'd rigged up in an alcove and returning with two steaming cups.

Both Javid's da and the alchemist groaned softly, but she cajoled them into drinking most of it. Javid's father suffered from swelling in the joints of his hands and she had to help him hold the cup, though he was nicer about it than the alchemist, who spluttered and cursed.

That task accomplished, ma eyed Nazafareen critically. "You look healthy enough, if a bit thin. Can I fix you something to eat?"

Her stomach growled and ma smiled. "I have some leftover rice. I'll just warm it up for you."

The rice had saffron and raisins. She ate every last grain, washing it down with watered wine. Nazafareen carried the bowl to the little kitchen. Her eyelids were suddenly so heavy she could barely keep them open.

"Why don't you curl up on that cushion, dear? I'll get a bed ready in the back. You can sleep with the girls."

"Thank you," Nazafareen said gratefully, stifling a yawn.

She sank down on the cushion, listening with half an ear as Mahmonir and Farima sat at Marzban's feet and he began to teach them their letters. Perhaps after she took a quick nap, she'd pay attention and learn something. Might as well use her time wisely.

Her thoughts drifted to Katrin and Galen. She imagined them marching for Samarqand, an army at their backs and Katsu flying above in his wind ship.

I misread them both, she thought ruefully, just before sleep dragged her under. They're the heroes the world has waited so long for.

❧ 20 ❧

WHAT A WONDERFUL WORLD

"Go fuck yourself," Katrin muttered through cracked lips.

Galen stopped walking. The hood of his cloak was raised against the brutal sun and sweat gushed from every pore. It made the half-healed burns he'd taken from the drake sting like a bastard.

"I only asked if you could make it rain again. Is that so unreasonable?"

Green eyes flayed him. "And what about *your* power? Oh, I forgot. It's fucking useless."

"I should have left you wandering in circles," he muttered. "But I was nice enough to stop and see if you needed help."

Katrin snorted. "Sure you were."

"What's that supposed to mean?"

"It means you wouldn't have made it this far without me, Dessarian."

They'd been staggering through the Kiln for days, keeping the sun to their backs. Three times, Katrin summoned drenching storms, but only Rhea had managed to keep her water skin in the flood and a single skin didn't stretch far among three people. Now

Katrin said the weather was screwed up and she couldn't call more rain. Somehow, she made it sound like his fault.

"It's complicated," she snapped. "The nearest clouds with any moisture are all the way out by Val Altair and the White Sea, that's almost a thousand leagues away."

Rhea laid a hand on her arm and Katrin quieted. What the Maenad saw in her, Galen would never know, but she was the only one who could make Katrin listen to reason. When he found them in the Red Hills, Katrin had wanted to continue hunting Gaius even though their guide was gone. Galen didn't want to abandon Nazafareen and Darius so he'd agreed to mount a search. But they found no sign of their companions, nor of any Vatra settlements. And without supplies, even Katrin had conceded they had no choice but to hike out.

It had been a profoundly miserable experience so far.

"We must be near the edge of the Kiln," Rhea said, leaning on her staff. Unlike Katrin, who was red and blistered, her fair skin was untouched by the sun — one of the advantages of being a child of Dionysius. "It can't be many more leagues to the border, though we'll likely come out farther south than we went in. Midway between Samarqand and Delphi, I'd guess."

Galen still found it hard to believe the Gale had fallen, but it seemed the only explanation. When they'd first entered the Kiln, the wards had dampened elemental power. But shortly after they'd lost their companions, that stricture had vanished. How or why, none of them knew. Galen just hoped it meant Nazafareen succeeded.

"Once we reach Solis, I have to find my father," he said without thinking — and instantly regretted it.

Katrin's expression hardened. He knew part of her relentless hostility stemmed from the fact that he was the spitting image of Victor, with the same raven hair and black eyes, the same bullish build. He could see it in her face every time she looked at him, mingled fury and shame that her holdfast had fallen to the Danai.

Galen understood. If the tables were turned, he'd probably feel the same way. But he was hot and starving and at his limit.

"Don't," he said warningly. "Eirik was far worse, we both know it. What's done is done. Get over it."

Katrin smirked. "I hope Runar strung him up by the—"

Galen flew at her and they rolled around in the sand, grunting and punching. Gods, she was strong. He seized a fistful of hair just as she kneed him in the balls. He sucked in a ragged breath and caught her jaw with an elbow. If he wanted to, he could have used earth to crack every bone in her body. He supposed she could use air to choke him, but by unspoken agreement, they just beat the hell out of each other the traditional way.

"Stop it!" Rhea yelled, whacking them with her staff until they broke apart, panting and covered in sand. "I'm sick of your constant bickering. The Vatra was right. You're fucking children!"

Galen spit bloody sand and wiped his mouth. His tongue found a loose tooth.

Katrin stared at the ground, not even bothering to stanch her own nosebleed.

"You should be ashamed of yourselves," Rhea said more quietly. "Is this why the Lady gave you the power? So you could continue the mindless feuding that destroyed your clans in the first place?" She poked Galen in the chest with her staff. "Tell her you're sorry."

He scowled but muttered an apology. He respected Rhea, and even if he hadn't, she was right.

"Now you," she said to Katrin.

Katrin raised her chin. Her eyes flashed defiantly.

"Do it, or I swear I'll never speak to you again," Rhea growled.

"I'm sorry," Katrin whispered, not looking at Galen.

Rhea nodded in satisfaction. "Now there has to be water around here somewhere. The Vatras survived with nothing but their wits."

"We need a Marakai."

Rhea looked down at Katrin. "Well, we don't have one, do we?" She turned to Galen. "Can you bore a hole into the earth? There might be water down there."

He rose to his feet with a wince. His groin felt like it had been trampled by a warhorse.

"I'll try." Galen slid into the Nexus, sending his awareness through the strata beneath their feet. First sand, then shale and bedrock, and then.... Yes, he sensed the resonance of liquid water. Very, very deep down.

In truth, he'd been afraid to test himself. Part of him still expected to hit his old block, but a torrent of power infused muscle and flesh, more than he'd ever dared to imagine. I could build a mountain, he thought with wonder, or tear one down. I could flatten a city. I could shake the very bones of the earth....

He chose a point some distance away and released a fraction of what he held, focusing it in a narrow line. A geyser of sand fountained into the air, followed by chunks of rock. Katrin swore under her breath and backed away. When he judged the hole to be deep enough, Galen released the Nexus. It was a heady feeling to wield so much earth. His body ached like it did after he'd been running for leagues with Ellard through the forest, but nothing was broken from the strain. Any other daēva would have died attempting what he'd just done with ease. It should have been a moment of triumph, yet Galen felt empty.

He still thought often of Ellard, though his ghost no longer lingered. Galen worried more about Rafel, who languished at the temple of Apollo, and his father, Victor. If they did manage to get out of the Kiln, he would free Rafel and Ysabel first, then decide what to do. The Danai needed him, but how could he return to the forest after what he'd done?

"I hear running water!" Rhea shouted. She stood next to the jagged rent in the ground, peering into its depths.

Katrin gave him a measured look, then joined her. "Give me the water skin," she said.

She used air to lower the skin into the crack and submerge it in the underground river. A minute later, the full skin flew back up and slapped into her palm. She eyed it longingly, then turned to Galen.

"Here," she said, handing it to him. "You earned the first drink."

He accepted it and gulped down a mouthful. It was one of the sweetest things he'd ever tasted, slightly metallic but colder than the rainwater they'd gathered. He handed the skin back and she tipped it over her mouth, then passed it to Rhea. They refilled it until they couldn't swallow another drop, and used a few more skinfuls to soak their salt-stiffened clothes.

The momentary relief from thirst and heat put everyone in a better mood. Katrin actually clapped him on the shoulder.

"It's a strange world, Dessarian," she said with a laugh. "I honestly don't know why either of us was chosen. Maybe the Marakai girl has a steadier temperament."

"Gods, I hope so," Galen replied with a wry smile.

"Megaera told me she seemed like a sensible child," Rhea remarked. "She's in the Isles. Kallisto will help us find her."

Katrin stared back in the direction they'd come from. "Do you think Nazafareen and Darius found the burrow?"

"My brother's a good tracker. I expect they did."

"Hope she killed that fucker."

"Same here," Galen agreed.

Without looking at him, she said in a low voice, "You met the Lady, right?"

"Yeah."

"What did she tell you?"

"Nothing. She kissed me and pushed me back through the gate." Even standing in the furnace of the Kiln with the sun blazing overhead, Galen shivered as he remembered those cold lips on his.

"Me, too. She said whatever I did was my decision. That was it. Not much help, was she?"

"Maybe she figured she'd already done her part and the rest is up to us."

Katrin just shook her head. They turned east to start walking again and froze.

In the wavering heat above the next dune, at least seventy Vatras stood in a ragged line. Their shadowtongue cloaks made them almost invisible. Who knew how long they'd been watching? Now the hoods were thrown back. Intent, feral eyes stared at them in hostile silence.

"Ah, shit," Katrin said.

✣ 21 ✣

THE TYRANT'S REVENGE

Basileus gazed at the scorch marks on the opposite wall. Servants had scrubbed them with lye, but traces remained. He hadn't bothered to replace the bed Domitia had reduced to ashes. He'd never sleep peacefully in this chamber again. But he still liked the view of the Acropolis from his favorite writing desk. And his palace afforded utter privacy.

Basileus dragged his eyes back to the man who stood on the other side of the desk.

"And you heard this from whom, exactly?"

"Two dozen different people, my lord."

Basileus nodded calmly, though inside he was close to panic.

The informant was a merchant trader who had run a barge along the Zaravshan River between Samarqand and Delphi before the Pythia's embargo. For more than twenty years, Basileus had paid him to relay news and gossip. His information had generally proven accurate and he knew better than to exaggerate.

Now he claimed a band of Vatras had taken the Rock with King's Shahak's blessing.

"But you didn't enter the city itself?"

"Gods, no. I spoke to those who'd fled. They told me the

Carnelian Gate burned and I could see it if I wanted to, but...."
He shrugged. "I'm sorry, my lord, but I have a family to think of."

At first, Basileus had chalked the story up to wild imagination.
He'd seen the Gale with his own eyes only a short time ago. And
Nicodemus claimed to hate the Vatra king. Surely he wouldn't
have enabled his escape.

But the merchant's report was the fifth he'd received saying
the same thing. One came from servant inside the Rock itself
who'd managed to flee. He said Shahak surrendered without a
fight.

"I came straight to you," the merchant said, his hands twisting
together. He looked like he hadn't slept since he heard the news.
"Can it be true, Tyrant?"

Basileus gave a thin smile. "I have little doubt King Shahak
planted these rumors to strike fear into our hearts." He took his
time pouring a cup of wine, keeping his hand perfectly steady. "He
is reputed to be an alchemist and skilled at illusion. Never fear,
the Vatras are safe in the Kiln. If it were true, our venerable
Oracle would have foreseen it."

"Of course," the man said uncertainly.

"The Gale has protected us for a thousand years, and I'm sure
it will stand for a thousand more. But tell no one of this. I pay you
for discretion as well as information."

He handed his informant a heavy bag of silver. The man
bowed.

"As you say, my lord. I will carry it to my grave."

Basileus watched him leave, knowing he'd be spending the
money in a tavern within hours and telling anyone in earshot that
the Vatras had returned to exact their revenge. Word would
spread like wildfire.

He had very little time left to make a decision.

Basileus drained the cup and poured another, but set it
untouched on the desk. As much as he wanted to gulp down the
whole decanter, he needed to keep his wits.

The obvious choice would be to flee. At least he'd get out ahead of the stampeding herd. But where would he go? After the comforts of his position, he didn't relish life as an exile in the Isles of the Marakai. All the gold in the world couldn't buy more than a dark, cold hovel there, not to mention the company of unwashed simpletons.

I've navigated treacherous currents before and stayed afloat. There must be a way to salvage this.

Basileus tapped his fingers on the desk, staring out at the Acropolis. If King Shahak cut a deal with the Vatras, perhaps he could too. Clearly, the Persians were trying to outmaneuver him. But Basileus knew the rules of the game better than some upstart young king.

The main obstacle to any alliance was the Oracle. She was unhinged and obsessed with punishing the "witches." Personally, he held no particular grudge against the daēvas. He'd only gone along with it all because the last Oracle insisted. And she'd turned out to be one of them!

Basileus hated the fact that Thena used the bracelets to control him as surely as she did her unlucky charges. He'd wanted to dispose of her for a long time now, but the Shields remained loyal to the Oracle and Domitia would incinerate him in an instant if Thena gave the order.

He picked up the cup, intending to drown his sorrows, when his eye caught on the edge of a parchment. It sat at the bottom of a stack he'd been going through when the merchant arrived.

Basileus set the wine aside and smoothed the crumpled sketch Thena had given him. A slow smile spread across his face. He'd never bothered to have copies made. The daēva was gone whether she accepted it or not, and he'd had other business to attend to.

Now the last piece of the puzzle snapped into place.

In his mind, Basileus began composing the message he would send to the Vatras. He'd pledge to open the gates and welcome them with laurel wreaths and trumpets. Once the dust settled, he'd find a way to propose himself as regent. Conquerors rarely wanted to shoulder all the mundane tasks of running an empire. And the title didn't matter to him, only the authority. He'd tell them how he cooperated with Lord Nicodemus. Perhaps Nicodemus was even with them. Feeling pleased, Basileus drank the second cup of wine to steady his nerves. Then he summoned his litter bearers and ordered them to carry him to the Temple of Apollo.

The streets were crowded and he saw no signs of mass panic — yet. But surely it wouldn't be long. Even if the merchant kept his mouth shut, the news would trickle in. Basileus urged the muscular bearers to hurry, gritting his teeth as the litter jounced up the temple stairs.

He found Thena in the adyton, slumped on the tripod. Her dark eyes seemed to stare straight through him. She did not look well.

"Your report is overdue, Basileus," she muttered.

Once he would have bridled at her failure to use his proper title. But nothing could dispel his good mood. He bared his teeth in a smile.

"I have tidings, Oracle. After an intensive search, I finally located the witch you asked about."

She leaned forward, her gaze intent. "Where?"

"At the Rock of Ariamazes with King Shahak. It is certain. He matches the description in every respect. And my source says he moves with an otherworldly grace." This was a last-minute addition, but Basileus thought it a nice touch.

Thena frowned. "He's with the Persians?"

"They must be plotting against us," Basileus replied smoothly. "I'm not surprised he went straight to our greatest enemy. No doubt he is sharing all your secrets right now." Basileus paused. He'd thought long and hard on the way over. If he pushed her, she might suspect something. "But I beg you, Oracle. Don't do anything rash. We cannot risk your safety."

Thena's eyes narrowed. "The god watches over me, Basileus. I am the Pythia. Even the heathens will tremble before me."

"Of course, of course, I meant no disrespect."

She stood and strode toward him. Basileus flinched as she reached out, but it was only to take his hands in hers. The dead-eyed creature had transformed and her face shone with confidence.

"I will demand an audience with King Shahak and tell him to hand Andros over."

"And if he refuses?" Basileus asked, wishing she'd let go.

"Domitia will teach him a lesson. It would be no great loss. He's a heretic who condones the use of spell dust. It is Apollo's will that the Persians be brought to the light, but I will deal with that in due time." She gave his hands a last affectionate squeeze and stepped back. "You've done well, Tyrant."

He gave a heavy sigh. "As you say, it is the god's will. From what I heard, news of his presence has already spread. Honest folk who know the witches as evil are abandoning the city in droves, fearing his influence on their king. You may wish to make haste."

Thena inhaled sharply. "Yes, I must leave for Samarqand immediately. Will you see me off?"

Basileus bowed. "Nothing would please me more, Oracle."

He followed her out, nodding his head as she rambled on and trying hard not to laugh.

Let her go to Samarqand. She'd find an interesting reception for her fanaticism there. Once she was dead, he'd make it clear that he renounced her completely and that she'd acted of her own accord.

And so it came to pass that Basileus waved goodbye from the temple steps as Thena and Domitia trundled off in a wagon with four Shields of Apollo as their escort. She'd wanted to take more, but he convinced her that a larger force might be viewed with suspicion and she'd be unlikely to get an audience with the king.

As the wagon vanished down the ring road, Basileus felt a happy peacefulness settle over his heart. He might go to a tavern himself, one of the more upscale ones, and have a celebratory drink or two. The future was still uncertain, but by all the blessed gods of the pantheon, at least he didn't have Thena to contend with anymore.

22

HOUSE BARADEL

"I no longer care for honor," Victor said, his voice breaking. "My sons have vanished. My wife and mother are both dead. I should have died with them, but my own arrogance and madness saved my miserable hide. Yet I will not roll over and bare my throat to the Vatras. I wish to fight. To stand with the clans as they go to war together." He spread his hands on the oak table. "Culach Kafsnjór, once my greatest enemy, has gone to rouse the holdfasts. They will join with the Marakai and sail for Samarqand, where Gaius waits."

The seven young women across the table regarded him impassively. He'd found the new Matrium at House Baradel on the shore of the White Sea. They greeted Mina warmly, he and Mithre a tad less so. During the sea journey, Victor had prepared a speech that he thought deftly combined humility and contrition with a rousing call to arms. He *had* to convince them to see past their dislike of the messenger and grasp the urgency of the situation. The old Matrium would have deliberated for days, and they didn't have the time for that.

"I know you have already sacrificed too much," he said. "Hundreds of lives were thrown away on the plain and it is partially my fault. But if we do not act now, that catastrophe is only the beginning. The Umbra separates us from Gaius's wrath for the moment, but he will cross it, and when he does, the forest will burn." He paused to let that sink in. Now for the clincher. "The clans set their differences aside and fought together once before. We must do it again, not for glory but for—"

"Peace, Victor Dessarian," Analee Suchy said briskly. "We already know all that. Do you think we've been sitting around doing nothing in your absence?"

He opened his mouth, then closed it again.

"The houses are already gathering. We sent runners out as soon as we saw the Marakai masts on the horizon. This development is not unexpected." Victor saw mingled pity and irritation in her brown eyes. "Daníel of Val Tourmaline came here weeks ago and told us your sons went into the Kiln to hunt Gaius."

Victor paled. "A bird came to the Mer carrying a garbled message that said as much, but I'd hoped it wasn't true."

Analee glanced at the other women. "And the Valkirin talisman, too. Daníel thought it a fool's errand and I heartily agree."

"What about the mortal woman, Nazafareen?" Mithre asked.

"It was her idea." Analee shook her head. "As they have not returned, the Matrium agree we must face this threat ourselves."

"But you will not lead our house," Gavriella Dessarian said firmly. She was a distant cousin of Victor's, olive-skinned and black-eyed with a fiery temper.

"You will do as Gavriella tells you," Lin Baradel added with a scowl.

Nika Martinec patted his hand. "Don't fuss about it, Victor, or we'll have to leave you behind."

Victor heard a snorting sound as Mina stifled a laugh.

Seven sets of eyes watched him warily. He stiffened. The women were holding earth in case he threw some kind of temper tantrum!

"Fine," Victor muttered. "I expected no less."

This was not entirely true. In fact, Victor had imagined himself leading the charge. But the Matrium clearly had other ideas.

"You can wait down at the ships," Nika said with a smile. "Tell the Marakai we should be ready to board in a few hours."

Mithre leaned over. "I think we've been dismissed," he whispered.

Victor stood and gave them a bow. "Matrium," he said curtly.

They nodded, already turning away to hammer out the details.

"I thought that went well," Mithre said as they walked down to the shore. "They didn't send you packing."

Victor barked a laugh. He'd thought to find the Danai in disarray, but these women seemed to have things well in hand. Then he sobered, recalling what Analee said about the Kiln.

"What the bloody hell were they thinking?" he said softly. "How did they even pass through the Gale?"

"They must have had a good reason," Mina replied, though her face was tight. "You may despise our son, but he was obviously trying to redeem himself."

"I don't despise him," Victor muttered, and it was true. He wanted both his sons back in one piece so he could try to make up for his own loutish behavior.

"I've been an awful father, haven't I?"

Mina said nothing.

"Well, I won't believe they're dead." Victor cleared his throat and looked away. The loss of Delilah was a heavy stone in his chest. Their child was his last link to her and he wasn't sure he could survive it if he lost Darius, too. "If I must go into the Kiln to search for them when this is done, I will."

"I'll join you," Mina said.

"And I," Mithre sighed.

Mina drew a deep breath of fir-scented air. "It's good to be home. I wish I could stay longer."

Lumen crystals shone in a few windows of the tree-homes of

House Baradel as they walked through the compound, but many were dark and empty. The lights had been dimmed in the dwellings of those who died on the Umbra, leaving black gaps in the forest like missing teeth.

Victor thought of Val Moraine and what he'd unchained there. It hadn't been purposeful — even he wouldn't wittingly have summoned revenants — but he'd known in his heart that the horn would do something terrible and he hadn't cared. Perhaps the Matrium was right to keep him on a short leash.

His mouth curved in a sardonic smile. He and Culach made a fitting pair. They both were an object lesson in the penalties of hubris.

"I wonder if your husband is finding a warmer reception at Val Altair?" Victor murmured.

Mina snorted. "If Meb weren't with him for protection, I never would have let him go." A flicker of worry crossed her face. "But he'll be fine. Even those bloody-minded Valkirins have to come around."

A boat waited to take them out to the fleet. Victor watched the shore as a current swept them straight out from the pebbled beach. Shadows moved in the forest. The houses were gathering. He only prayed it wouldn't be for the last time.

23

THE HOLDFASTS

"I never imagined you'd have the nerve to turn up here."

The master of Val Altair was smaller than the Valkirin guards who had escorted Meb and Culach into the darkened chamber. He had a clean-shaven, foxlike face and shrewd grey eyes.

"I'm not thrilled about it myself," Culach replied. "But you must hear what I came to say."

Meb was accustomed to bitter cold, but the air inside the keep had a dank, close quality that made her shiver. Stefán sat in a high-backed chair with fur blankets on his knees. Val Altair perched at the northern tip of Nocturne, where the winds from the White Sea howled like a banshee. The wall behind him was a transparent shield of air and Meb could see a field of stars twinkling in the night.

"Who's the girl?" Stefán squinted. "Is she Marakai?"

"Mebetimmunedjem is the chosen talisman and heir to the Blue Crown. She commands the fleet now."

Stefán grunted. "Do you know where Katrin is?" he asked Meb, a plaintive edge to his voice.

She shook her head. "I wish I did."

"She never returned," Stefán muttered. His gaze fell on Culach. "Speak," he said harshly. "You have two minutes."

"First, how many escaped Val Moraine?" Culach asked.

The hollows beneath Stefán's eyes seemed to deepen. "Perhaps a tenth of those who entered."

Meb felt sick. Culach had told her about the revenants as they flew over the mountains with Ragnhildur. She'd never suspected such things could exist.

"And Runar?" Culach asked.

Stefán stared at them, his face unreadable. "Runar used the diamond to seal Val Moraine again so the risen couldn't get out and attack the other holdfasts."

"Did he return to Val Petros afterwards?"

"You misunderstand. He was *inside* the keep at the time."

"Bloody hell," Culach muttered. "And his riders?"

Stefán shrugged. "Who knows? Those of us who managed to escape did not look back."

"How many fighters are left here?"

"Enough questions, Kafnsjor," Stefán snarled. "You will tell me why you've darkened my doorstep with this child."

"King Gaius of the Vatras broke out of the Kiln," Meb said quickly. "He's in Samarqand. The Marakai are willing to fight, but we need help."

Stefán absorbed this news without any visible reaction.

"I can call the sea," Meb said. "Flood the Rock of Ariamazes before they know what hit 'em."

Stefán's thin lips pressed together in what passed for a smile. "Then you don't need Val Altair."

Meb realized she was slouching and stood up straighter, meeting his wintry gaze. "The Drowned Lady said you had to go." She thought of the three fishes. "Or it won't work."

He laughed. "The *Drowned Lady*? You are a fanciful child."

"She's real," Meb growled. "I met her twice."

"I have never heard of such a person. No, my holdfast has seen enough of death. I won't lead them into another disaster based on the imaginings of a little girl."

"She's not imagining it," Culach growled.

"It makes no difference. This is not our fight."

"But we may never get another chance!" Meb said. "What happens when the Vatras come to your mountains?"

"We build with stone. Val Altair can withstand an assault."

"You haven't seen what they can do," Culach said urgently, "but I have. The fire they summon is beyond your understanding. They'll crack the very walls—"

"Get out of my keep."

"Please, just listen," Meb began desperately.

"Get out!" Stefán shouted, his composure crumbling. "Or I'll have you thrown into the cells. Out!"

Culach's face set into a mask. "Let's go," he said to Meb. "We'll try Val Tourmaline."

They turned to leave when a younger Valkirin strode through the door. He wore his hair in three long plaits adorned with jeweled pins. He gave Culach a wary nod of greeting.

"They're right, father," he said. "We must fight."

"Eavesdropping, were you?" Stefán spat.

"I wouldn't have to if you invited me to your counsels."

"This is no *counsel*. The last of the Kafsnjórs came to beg for a bone and I'm sending him on his way."

"That's not what I just heard. The scouts say half the Marakai fleet is anchored off the coast. Let me take a force and join them."

"No."

Father and son stared at each other.

"I must follow my conscience," the latter said at last.

"You would defy my wishes, Den?" Stefán said softly.

"In this, yes." Den glanced at the Valkirins at the door. Both nodded. "Mebetimmunedjem is the Marakai talisman. We must heed her. And whatever grudge you hold against Culach, I've known him a long time and still count him a friend."

"You do not command this keep!" Stefán railed, half rising.

Den just shook his head and signaled at Meb and Culach to follow him out. Stefán's curses chased them into the corridor, but he remained in his chair.

"I fear my father was broken by what happened at Val Moraine," Den said, his face pained. "I cannot say I blame him. As the heir I remained behind, but I heard the story from those who got out. Is it true Victor Dessarian blew the Horn of Hellheim?"

"It's true," Culach conceded. "But he had no idea what the horn did. He regrets it."

"He's gone to rally the Danai," Meb said, walking fast to keep up with her companions' long strides. Culach seemed to know the route back to the stables for he didn't need her assistance. "They'll meet us."

Den drew a deep breath. "I can't say I relish being Victor's ally in all this, but the alternative seems worse. If *you* can forgive his sins, I can, too. He killed your father, yes?"

"It's the one thing I have to thank him for," Culach replied grimly.

Den looked shocked, then laughed. "Yes, Eirik was…. Never mind. I will take all who are willing and help you gather the others."

"That would speed things along," Culach said. "If you go to Val Petros, we will seek out Daníel at Val Tourmaline. Have you had any word from him?"

Den shook his head. "Not since the disaster at Val Moraine. Katrin left, as well. My father said something about a ward on her power could only be broken in Solis." His face grew hopeful. "If she's back, we will have our talisman. Katrin would rain death on the Vatras."

Meb and Culach exchanged a grim look. "A message came just before we left the Isles," Meb said. "A party went into the Kiln to hunt Gaius and Katrin may be among them."

"Into the Kiln?" Den exclaimed. "How is that possible?"

"We don't know," Culach said, stopping at the heavy door to the stables. "But I will learn more at Val Tourmaline."

Den seemed shaken. "They went to the Kiln, yet you say Gaius is in the mortal cities. This is ill news, Culach."

"I know. But we must fight regardless. If we delay, the war will come to us, and I fear the outcome would be a lost cause."

Den nodded slowly, though his face was grave.

"Meet us at the Twelve Towers and make haste." Culach opened the door to the stables and an icy wind blew into the corridor, carrying skirls of fresh snow. "How many riders can you bring?"

"We have a hundred or so here. I imagine the same at Val Petros."

"So few," Culach muttered.

"Most would shudder at the thought of two hundred Lords of Air flying to make war," Den said, a trifle haughtily.

"Yes, well, perhaps not Gaius. But it will have to be enough."

They clasped elbows and Den strode away, bellowing orders to the Valkirins who were gathering to hear his news.

"Poor Stefán," Meb murmured as the door closed behind them, leaving only the starry darkness of the ledge. "He must have seen some awful things. But I'm glad his son saw sense." She smiled. "And he pronounced my name right on the first try."

"Den is a good man." Culach whistled for Ragnhildur. "I'm not sure what we'll find at Val Tourmaline. Halldóra used to be in charge, but she was killed by Gerda Kafsnjór. The keep descended to Halldóra's grandson, Daníel. I saw him at Val Moraine not long ago, fresh from a year of captivity in Delphi. He was still recovering from brutal treatment, but he had the courage to go with Nazafareen and Darius to hunt the Pythia."

They mounted Ragnhildur, Meb in front. Culach raised his hood against the foul weather, pulling on thick gloves, and Meb did the same. The abbadax of Val Altair watched from their nests with slitted eyes.

"I hope Nazafareen is well," Meb said. "If not for her, I'd be in Delphi wearing one of those collars."

"Don't even think about that," Culach admonished her quietly.

But Meb couldn't help it. She remembered what Nicodemus said when she asked him to tell her where they were going, and he'd replied that knowing would be worse.

He'd probably killed her parents, along with Sakhet-ra-katme. How could she ever have fallen for his lies?

"Why do they hate us so much?" she asked Culach as Ragnhildur scrabbled her way across the ice to the edge of the stables. Hecate drifted in and out of the clouds above the White Sea.

Culach's breath smoked in the chill air. "I will tell you the whole story if you wish to hear it, Meb."

"You know?" she said in surprise. "I thought it was all so long ago. No one ever told me about the Vatras before." She frowned. "If they had, I might have been more careful."

"I didn't know about them either. Until I lost my sight and was plagued by strange dreams. It all began with an odd boy named Farrumohr. A Vatra gifted at forging talismans but with a deep bitterness inside him...."

The white glaciers rushed by as Culach told her the story of the Viper and Julia, of their father's feud with the other clans over a single well, and how they lost their homestead and were taken in by Gaius's family. How Farrumohr orchestrated Gaius's rise to power and controlled him with a talismanic crown, all the while plotting his revenge. How it ended in the war, the Sundering, and the Viper's slow death in the desert outside Pompeii.

By the time he'd finished the long tale, she could see the holdfast of Val Tourmaline, perched on a peak deep inside the Valkirin range.

"So Gaius has been waiting in there all this time," Meb said with a shiver. "Do you think he still wears the crown?"

"Whether he does or not, he is poisoned by hatred that has seeped into the other Vatras, as well."

"We're here, Culach Kafsnjór," she said, twisting in the saddle. "I see Valkirins in the stables!"

When Daníel came out himself to greet them, Meb's spirits lifted. But once they were settled in one of the inner chambers, warming their feet on the summerstone floor, he confirmed what Kallisto had said in her message.

"I told them it was madness," Daníel muttered. "But Nazafareen was bent on punishing the Vatras for what happened in the Umbra. And you know Katrin, she couldn't resist going along. The Danai talisman, too."

"But how could they even find Gaius?" Culach demanded. "The Kiln is enormous."

"A Vatra led them. A man named Nicodemus."

Meb stiffened. "Nicodemus? He's the one who tried to kidnap me!"

"He claimed to regret that. He said he'd killed the Oracle and wanted Gaius dead, too. Something about his brother being in the Kiln, and Nicodemus wanted to rescue him." Daníel sighed. "They shouldn't have trusted him."

"No, they shouldn't have," Meb agreed. "Will you help us?"

"You are the Marakai talisman, eh?" Daníel asked, a note of skepticism in his voice.

"She had the courage to summon the Marakai wave horses and face their judgment," Culach snapped. "Meb might be young, but I am proud to follow her, and so is Val Altair."

"Easy," Daníel laughed. "I meant no offense. We were both young when we first flew to battle, yes?"

Culch's lips curled. "It was more of a skirmish, as I recall. Over some old iron mines on Grímsvötn glacier, wasn't it? Your sword was bigger than you were, but you managed to get in a few jabs."

"A few? I nearly cut your harness away. But Ranghildur was too fierce. I think I still wear the scar from her beak." Daníel's smile died. "Yes, we will come. Halldóra would have done the same. She never shied from a fight, even if the odds were poor."

"I'm so sorry about what happened—" Culach began.

"It was not your doing." A strange expression crossed his face. "I spent some time with Gerda, before her madness overtook her. She helped me see the truth. So it is not for me to hold a grudge against the Kafsnjórs." Daníel stood. He was as tall as Culach but wore his silver hair long and unbound. Faint marks still ringed his neck. "Yet I do hold one against the Vatras. The Pythia said she was Gaius's daughter and that his hand directed all she did. Val Tourmaline will ride with you."

They went to the armory, a vast chamber with all manner of vicious-looking weapons fixed to the walls with invisible bonds of air. Meb hadn't seen many Valkirins before Culach and she'd expected they all wore swords like he did. But there were also spiked maces, iron-tipped lances, blades shaped like a scythe and others.

"I'll muster all who are able to fly," Daníel said.

"Did Frida make it out?" Culach asked.

"Barely," a woman's voice said curtly from the dooway.

Daníel gave her a steady look. "Frida, this is Meb, the Marakai talisman. Meb, this is my second-in-command."

Meb nodded a greeting. The woman eyed Culach with an unreadable expression. She had short silver hair and bright green eyes, though they held a shadow.

"I heard you came back," she said, addressing Culach.

He stiffened. "You threw my wife in the cold cells. You tried to make her watch my execution. I'd say we're even, Frida."

"I don't hate you, Kafsnjór," she replied with a brittle laugh. "You aren't the one who called the dead against us." She walked forward. "I know what you think of Runar, but he sacrificed himself so the rest of us could cut our way out. He led the revenants away from the stables, deeper into the keep. Gave us a five-minute head start and then sealed it with the diamond." Angry tears shone in her eyes. "I lost at least fifty good soldiers in there. Kin and friends."

Culach was silent. He looked sad.

"I do not hold the Danai responsible for what Victor did. He acted alone." Her lips thinned. "But I will never forgive him for it."

"I don't ask you to," Culach said quietly. "Only that you set aside your feelings until we've dealt with the threat of the Vatras. Victor will be with the Danai when we join them." He paused. "Assuming they haven't exacted their own retribution. I understand the Matrium was not well pleased with him."

Frida nodded, then turned to Meb, her face solemn and respectful. "I'm sorry, talisman. I'm glad you've come." She seemed about to say something more, then turned away and strode out the door.

"Frida was one of the few to return from Val Moraine," Daniel muttered. "She has not been the same since."

Culach sighed. "None of us have."

Daniel left them in a chamber with some food and drink while he mustered the holdfast. Two hours later, they were back at the stables with Ragnhildur. She greeted Culach with a happy burble. The snow fell thick and fast as riders took off from the ledge in pairs, hovering above the windswept valley. Valkirins disdained armor as a mortal fetish, wearing only their white fur-lined leathers, but each bristled with weapons.

Their numbers were far fewer than Meb had hoped for.

Daniel was the last to leave. His mount was called Wind from the North. She was a magnificent creature, larger than the other abbadax and with iridescent green feathers on her breast. He buckled into his harness and soared over the chasm, his hood thrown back, fierce joy on his face.

Meb thought about the marks on his neck. What he must have endured in Delphi.

What almost happened to her.

She smiled, her throat tight. It didn't matter now.

Daníel was finally free.

"WHY ARE THEY CALLED THE TWELVE TOWERS?"

Meb stood with Culach and Mina atop the rugged series of cliffs that marked the far southeastern edge of the Umbra. The Gulf of Azmir stretched out below, offering a sheltered harbor for the fleet to anchor. A steep switchback trail led down to the shore where longboats were ferrying the Danai out to the ships. Above, formations of abbadax wheeled across the twilit sky.

"My mother told me the Umbra used to be an inland sea," Mina replied, "before the Sundering caused a great drought and remade it into a barren plain. The tops of these cliffs were islands in an archipelago."

Meb had never thought much about the Sundering. It was hard to picture the sun moving across the sky. How different the world must have been! She tried to imagine it now, but the thought of bright light in the Isles for half the day was too bizarre to contemplate.

"Where's Den?" Culach muttered. "He should have been here already. We can't wait much longer."

"I think I see them!" Meb bounced on her toes.

The riders from Val Tourmaline raced to meet their cousins with shouts of greeting. As promised, Den had mustered both Val Altair and Val Petros. The few dozen abbadax swelled to several hundred.

"I'm going down," Meb declared, running pell-mell along the rocky path to the water.

At the bottom, she stopped to catch her breath. The last of

the longboats reached the ships and unloaded its passengers, clad in the brown and green of the forest dwellers. Selene began to rise over the Twelve Towers. The hubbub aboard the ships died down as the Danai joined the Marakai sailors at the rail. Even the abbadax quieted, hovering on updrafts above the fleet. More than a thousand sets of eyes fixed on the skinny, wild-haired figure who stood alone on the shore.

The Mouse in her — who wasn't gone, not entirely — twitched its whiskers unhappily. But Meb didn't pay it any mind.

"Lords of Earth!" she cried.

The Danai held up their bows.

"Lords of Air!"

The mounts screeched and their Valkirin riders dropped the reins to raise gloved fists.

"Lords of Water!"

Prayers were shouted to the eel, the cat, the carp, She of Many Arms and No Face, and the wave horses.

"You're what's left of us," Meb called. "So I'll ask only one thing. Forget your clans. We're all the same today. We are the people of the darklands!"

The host roared back at her.

"And I've been thinking," she added with a sly grin. "Maybe we don't have to take the long way 'round after all."

Meb raised her arms and turned her face to the sky.

The sea began to rise. It crept up the shore, surging into the honeycomb gaps in the cliff walls.

Gentle now, she thought, her veins singing with power. Or you'll dash 'em to bits.

She spoke to the Austral Ocean and it obeyed her will, pouring into the Gulf of Azmir in a steady torrent. Meb let the tide carry her until it crept over the top of the cliff. Then she summoned a current to sweep her back toward the ships. Waiting hands grabbed her vest as she floated past a ladder, hauling her aboard the *Akela*.

"Hold on to something!" Meb yelled.

Shouts of alarm erupted as hulls scraped along the bottom. A moment later, the fleet lifted free. The newborn sea surged eastward across the Umbra, carrying them at great speed toward Samarqand.

Daniel of Val Tourmaline banked sharply and flew down next to the *Akela*. Half his riders were already winging away to the north.

"I've a quick stop to make," he called. "But we'll catch up!"

Meb nodded and scrambled to the bow, watching in delight as the wave devoured the land ahead, dashing itself against all obstacles and quickly submerging them.

The captain of the *Akela* joined her. He looked at her askance.

"I did say I'd be honored to have the talisman," he remarked. "But I didn't expect *that*."

Meb grinned. "You ain't seen nothin' yet," she said.

KALLISTO STOOD ON THE WIDE STONE STEPS OF THE TEMPLE OF the Moria Tree, watching the water rise. The twilit shore of the Cimmerian Sea was a barren place, but Dionysus had blessed this small piece of earth with rich soil and a variety of grape that needed no sunlight to flourish. For centuries, the temple's vineyards had provided a lush, green oasis where the Maenads drank and danced and lured mortal men for their lovers.

If Dionysus approved of the union, the man's seed would quicken and he would be sent back to wherever he had come from, his time here fading like a sweet, half-remembered dream. And when the girl child was born — for it was always a girl — Kallisto would guide her in the mysteries of the cult until she came of age.

Their numbers had dwindled over the years, but she still counted a dozen Maenads. Three were deep in mourning for their lost daughters. The twins Alcippe and Adeia, slain by the Pythia's Shields at the tender age of sixteen. Charis and Cyrene, killed on the Umbra in a desperate bid to free Galen from his chains. Megaera was last of the parthenoi — the virgin warrior-girls — save for Rhea, who had not returned from the Kiln.

"We cannot stay much longer, my dear," Herodotus said quietly, laying a hand on her shoulder.

Kallisto nodded, clasping it in her own with a heavy heart. "All the worst I foresaw came to pass," she said. "The end approaches, husband, yet even I cannot read it clearly."

"You sent a message to the Marakai. Surely this flood means they heeded it."

The tide lapped at the upper steps now. She watched as the vineyards drowned in black saltwater. They could be sown again, but not if Gaius triumphed.

All my plans are dust in the wind.

Kallisto had always known the Vatras would return someday, but she expected it to be like last time. The talismans would be gathered and they would face the threat together.

Nazafareen had been the maggot in the good dog's eye.

No, that wasn't fair. The girl's intentions were good. And they'd needed her power.

But as soon as Kallisto learned there were not three but *four* talismans to contend with, and one of them a Breaker with a Breaker's wild, dark heart, she'd known that it would *not* be like last time.

She'd hoped Nazafareen would rise to the occasion, but the girl had chosen wrong. And she had died for it.

Kallisto still felt sick with guilt and regret.

Should I have told her more? Did she ever stand a chance? And if not, why was she sent to suffer a terrible end?

The Drowned Lady had come to her in a vision and commanded her not to reveal anything of importance before Nazafareen departed, and Kallisto had obeyed. Only a fool crossed the Lady. But now she wondered what secret game the keeper of the Dominion played at — and worse, whose side she was truly on.

"I fear the time for escape has passed," Herodotus observed, stroking his beard as he did when he sat at his desk, scribbling away with a stylus. "We appear to be trapped."

She turned to him. How she loved this brilliant, gentle man. Others mistook him as a scholarly innocent who buried himself in scrolls and histories to avoid living in the present. But he had courage and loyalty of the quiet sort that was easily overlooked.

Kallisto sighed. "I've mucked everything up, haven't I?"

"You've done nothing of the sort." Herodotus lifted the hem of his robes as a wave washed over his sandals. "But I suggest we climb to the roof, my dear. Your daughters are already there."

Kallisto followed him to the rickety ladder fixed to the trunk of the Moria, passing him her staff as she clambered up the final rungs. From her vantage atop the temple, she could see the full extent of the deluge. It poured in relentlessly, churning in whirlpools around the columns and climbing higher with each minute.

The roof had a large opening so the crown of the Moria could pass through. It was an olive tree, but the seedling had been planted by Athena's own hands, so it towered as high as an oak. The Maenads gathered beneath its spreading boughs were a fierce sight, clad in thigh-length fawn dresses, staffs at the ready.

Unfortunately, their foe was a hundred and fifty leagues away in Samarqand, all of it now underwater.

The wind whipped Kallisto's hair as she surveyed the Umbra. Armies gathered, dark power swirled, forces converged for a final reckoning. And she had delayed too long, hoping one of her birds would return with a message. She'd sent ten into the Kiln to search for Rhea, three more to the Valkirin holdfasts, and seven to the Danai houses.

"We should have gone to Samarqand earlier," she muttered. "Now it's too late...."

"Mother!" Megaera cried.

Kallisto followed her pointing finger.

Dark shapes descended from the clouds. Her eyes widened as she recognized Halldóra's grandson at the tip of the phalanx. After they'd left Nazafareen and the others at the Gale, Daníel had escorted her, Herodotus and Megaera to the Temple of the Moria Tree. He had an inquisitive mind and asked many questions during the journey about the Maenads and the task they'd been set by their god to watch over the talismans should the Vatras ever return. She knew of his ordeal as a prisoner in Delphi, but he'd seemed to be recovering well.

Now Kallisto felt gratified that not *everyone* had forgotten about her.

The riders alit on the roof and Daníel strode over, his white leathers bright in the gloaming.

"Kallisto," he murmured, inclining his head politely, as if the sea were not rising all around them.

"My Lord of Val Tourmaline," she replied dryly. "You're a welcome sight."

When Daníel left them two weeks before, he hadn't tarried. He still had an injured Danai to see home, so he had bid them goodbye on the roof and flown off without even pausing for food or drink. Now she sensed her daughters studying him with interest. He was an uncommonly handsome man, and many of them had always hoped for a Valkirin lover, though none had ever turned up on the doorstep until now.

"The clans are sailing for the Rock of Ariamazes," he said. "I thought you might wish to join us."

Kallisto arched an eyebrow. "And here I was starting to worry we'd miss the whole thing. But you'll find it worth the delay."

She gestured to the Maenads, who removed the pine cones

from the tips of their staffs to reveal gleaming spear points. Strong and fit, they had been born for war and looked it.

"Gaius will find us no easy meat," Kallisto said with a sly smile. "In fact, I think his Praetorians will be in for quite a surprise when they discover their fire magic cannot touch us."

"I look forward to it." Daníel's answering smile warmed as he met the gaze of Rhea's mother, a striking woman with her daughter's long elegant neck and grey eyes.

This one will be trouble, Kallisto thought with amusement. Though for him or her, I cannot say.

"I'm afraid I am no warrior," Herodotus remarked. "But I would still like to come along. Someone must record this epic battle for posterity."

"You shall ride with me, scholar," Daníel said immediately. "Come, there is little time. We must catch up to the fleet."

"Meb is with them?" Kallisto asked.

He laughed. "She wears the Blue Crown. I never thought to follow a child into battle, but this one is ... special."

The riders beckoned and the Maenads vaulted onto the abbadax behind them, securing their staffs and exchanging quick greetings. Kallisto saw her husband settled with Daníel, then joined a Valkirin woman named Frida who was his second-in-command.

And so begins the end, she thought, sending a silent prayer to Dionysus. At least we have fulfilled our duty.

With anxious screeches, the mounts rose into the air just as the sea gathered the Temple of the Moria Tree into its cold embrace.

24

SKY GARDEN

Nazafareen watched the chickens peck at a bowl of grain with glassy eyes. A heatwave had descended on Samarqand, penetrating even to the inner recesses of the Rock. She blotted sweat from her brow, hoping for even the faintest breeze, though it was wishful thinking in the windowless chamber.

Javid's parents were kind, his sisters adorable, but she was starting to go a little mad. Three days could be an eternity when you had to sit around while everyone else took all the risks.

At first she'd been glad for the respite. So much had happened and she needed time alone to think on it. She'd slept in one of the back rooms for an entire day. When she awoke, she'd lain there for a long time, sifting through her memories again, trying to weave them together into a whole that made sense. It felt like returning to a childhood home full of cobwebs, each object precious and meaningful but badly in need of dusting. She was still getting used to the new — old — Nazafareen, yet she no longer chafed so much at losing the huo mofa. On balance, she would rather be herself than the woman who had tortured Nicodemus.

Or the one who died in the Kiln.

But now she was growing antsy. Nazafareen was not accustomed to doing nothing. And she missed Darius terribly. He hadn't been back to see her and she understood why, it was too dangerous if someone saw, but she worried about him all the time. She held his power tight through the bond, careful not to let it slip for an instant. The Rock was full of fire and the Vatras were prone to use it unexpectedly. The situation had her on edge — a state that was not improved by the other unwilling resident there.

Marzban Khorram-Din pored over scrolls at a table in the corner. The old alchemist snored like a wood saw and talked to himself just loud enough to be annoying. He complained about the food, the quality of his bed, the foul taste of the tea Javid's mother poured into him twice a day. Nazafareen was starting to dislike him very much, though he was decent to the children.

She'd tried to engage him in conversation several times with no luck. But she thought she ought to practice being the new Nazafareen. The one who was kind and patient and gentle.

The poor man is probably as worried about Leila as I am about Darius, she thought. *They've been gone for more than a week now.*

"I'm sure your daughter will return soon," Nazafareen said.

Marzban grunted. He didn't look up.

"Were you very close? I imagine you must be, if you were training her to be an alchemist."

"She's the least stupid of my children," he muttered. "Though unfortunately, also the most froward."

Froward? "What does that mean?"

"Ask somebody else."

They were the only ones in the sitting chamber. The girls napped with their father in a back bedroom and Javid's mother had gone down to the kitchens to scavenge what she could for supper.

A muscle in her jaw tightened. "I'm asking you."

Beady, malicious eyes flicked her way. "Headstrong. Disobedient. Willful. Unruly. Recalcitrant. Do you understand any of those words?"

"Yes." Nazafareen smiled. "I wonder where she gets it from?"

He turned back to the scrolls. "I haven't the slightest idea. Now I would ask you to cease your incessant chattering and permit me to work."

She took in his long beard and ink-stained fingertips. He looked a little bit like Herodotus, but any resemblance ended there. The Greek scholar was a nice person. He would have been asking her all sorts of questions about the shadowlands and the Empire. But Marzban Khorram-Din seemed to have no interest in anything except spell dust and the squiggly lines covering his scrolls.

She leapt to her feet at a knock on the door, two short raps followed by a third.

Darius slipped inside, dressed in the garb of a steward, his red-and-white tunic bearing the roaring griffin of King Shahak. She threw her arms around him and kissed him, to the evident disgust of Marzban Khorram-Din.

"Any news of the wind ship?" Marzban demanded when Nazafareen stepped back.

Darius shook his head and the alchemist's shoulders slumped. He *was* worried about Leila, even if he wouldn't admit it.

Marzban Khorram-Din turned his back to them and Nazafareen drew Darius to the far corner of the room, where they sat down on a couch.

"What's been happening?" she asked. "Javid is hardly ever here. The king calls for him at all hours of the day and night."

His gaze drank her in. "First, how are you?" he asked softly.

"Bored and anxious, but very glad to be wholly myself again," she replied after a moment. "I wish I could help you search for the crown. I don't suppose there's been any progress?"

"Gaius is always surrounded by a full complement of guards.

He has a child taste all his food and drink now, even Atticus's concoctions." He gave a hollow laugh. "I managed to meet with Nicodemus a few times. We've thought of a hundred ways to kill him, but apparently, Gaius has, too. And if we make an attempt on him and fail...."

"What are his plans? He won't stay here forever."

"He keeps them close. But I fear he will act soon, one way or another." Darius's lips thinned. "His Praetorians have already killed half the nobles and most of the servants, always on the pretext of some petty offense. I'm pretending to be simple lest they wonder why I don't try to run away."

Her gut clenched. "Are you serving Gaius personally?"

"Sometimes." She sensed his unadulterated rage, though his voice remained even. "You cannot imagine what it's like being so close to the man who hurt you and being unable to do anything."

"You can't take a chance, Darius," she said hoarsely. "Don't you dare."

Her gave her a sudden smile. "I'm only pretending to be simple, my love. That doesn't mean I am."

"I thought it would be easier," she growled. "The bastard can die. We know what the crown looks like."

"His wife Aelia turned his rooms upside-down again looking for it. It's not there."

"So we wait for our chance and hope it comes before Gaius marches." Nazafareen lifted the sweaty hair from the back of her neck and fanned it with her stump, which didn't work very well. "Gah! What about Meb? The other clans?"

"On that score, I know no more than you do. But I'm not sure a single talisman would be enough anyway. The Vatras are too dangerous. We need the three of them together."

"So our hopes are pinned on Katsu and Leila."

"Or Gaius making a mistake." Darius's face grew grim. "If he lets his guard down for an instant, we'll kill him. Though we'll still have the rest of them to deal with." He took her hand and gave her a tender kiss. "I must get back. There's only a handful of servants left, my absence will be noticed. But I had to see you."

"Thank you, my love. You've made that nasty old man's company bearable," she said lightly, though her heart was heavy with all he'd told her.

She followed Darius to the door. The moment he opened it, the golden-feathered chicken shot between his legs and ran squawking into the corridor. Nazafareen swore an oath as Darius took off after it. Marzban glanced over from his scrolls, looking annoyed at the interruption. He really was the most unpleasant creature.

"Hold her with the wings folded down or she'll struggle like ... like a froward toddler!" Nazafareen called after him.

Unlike her more docile sisters, the golden hen made an art of escaping at any opportunity. She was fast, but not faster than a daēva at full sprint. Darius retrieved her at the end of the corridor and delivered her into Nazafareen's arms, a low grumble of discontent in the bird's throat.

"I love you," he said with a grin.

"Be careful," she whispered, watching until he vanished around the corner.

Nazafareen shut the door and glanced at Marzban Khorram-Din, who'd gone back to pretending she didn't exist. She sat down on the couch, one foot tapping the carpet as the walls closed in again.

JAVID SCANNED THE EMPTY SKIES TO THE WEST, A WARM BREEZE ruffling his hair. Nothing stirred in the streets beyond the curtain wall. Samarqand had the feel of a tomb — or a plague city. Even the legions of stray cats and dogs had vanished, sensing the wrongness that emanated from the stone fortress on the hill.

For the first time in memory, no smoke rose from the blacksmith's quarter. No horses thundered around the racing oval. Canopies fluttered listlessly over empty stalls in the market. Abandoned carts clogged the larger avenues, some tipped onto their sides with the contents strewn across the ground like the detritus of some great flood.

Shahak no longer bothered to fill the garrisons at the outer walls. If there was a looter with the balls to enter Samarqand, Javid had yet to spot him.

We'll run out of food soon, he thought. If most of the nobles and servants and all the rest of them hadn't fled, we would have done already.

Of course, starvation was the least of his problems.

Each morning, he came to the rooftop gardens, searching for any sign of the *Shenfeng*. Shahak, who thought Leila had gone to collect spell dust, was also impatient, though for different reasons. The king had managed to put Gaius off for days, but now the Vatra would wait no longer.

"You said it yourself," Gaius growled. "The supplies you have are adequate to the task."

He stood with the king on the lawn where the royal brood used to play chaugan with stick-horses and tiny gold-handled mallets. The grass had gone brown without the attention of the gardeners, dying in large patches. Four of Gaius's Praetorians flanked them on either side.

"Yes, but my stores are dwindling," Shahak replied, a plaintive edge to his voice. "I *need* it."

"And they will be replenished when your alchemist returns! Do you not wish to learn the making of talismans?"

"Yes, yes—"

"Then do this thing I ask of you and we will begin your training immediately."

Shahak drew a sharp breath, a greedy light in his eyes.

"Well, then, I think all is ready. We shall begin. Do you have the items I requested?"

Javid watched as Gaius handed him a parcel wrapped in cloth. The king unrolled it on a stone bench. A twist of hair and a vial of dark red liquid lay inside.

"This will bind them to your will," Shahak said.

Them? Javid felt a stab of fear. He had been barred from their councils at Gaius's insistence, until an hour ago when King Shahak demanded his presence in the gardens. Who did he plan to summon? Javid suddenly remembered the chimera, needle teeth the clear color of water, and suppressed a shiver.

The king opened his lacquered box with a shaking hand and spooned out some dust. He turned his back and Javid heard a sharp inhalation, followed by a sigh of bliss. He set the box aside, spots of rose blooming in his sunken cheeks.

"This is the most complex and difficult conjuring I have ever attempted by far," he said gravely. "There must be no disturbances. The consequences would be dire."

Gaius inclined his head and took a step back. A strange excitement lit his face.

"Proceed," he said.

Shahak forked his fingers at the hair and it burst into flame. He muttered words to himself as he opened the vial and shook a few drops of blood into the fire, making it hiss and sputter. Tendrils of smoke curled upward. Shahak coaxed them to rise higher, his hands fluttering like bats.

"Anzillu la minam. Tamabukku la minam."

The smoke writhed like a serpent.

"Qitrubu anzillu. Qitrubu tamabukku."

Energy crackled in the air like invisible lightning, lifting the fine hairs on Javid's neck.

"Anzillu tamu. Tamabukku tamu."

A single bloody tear traced a path down Shahak's face. He continued to chant, his eyes glowing with an unholy power.

Qitrubu. To draw near.

Tamu. To make swear.

La minam. Without number.

Javid did not know the meaning of *tamabukku*, but he had heard the word *anzillu* once before, the day Shahak seized the crown.

Abomination.

"Anzillu la minam. Tamabukku la minam...."

The smoke boiled and thickened. A wind rose, tearing the tender petals from the rosebushes and screaming across the exposed battlements of the Rock. It did not touch the smoke. Javid sank down against the stone wall, drawing his knees to his chest. Shahak's terrible voice seemed to come from inside his own head. He clamped his hands over his ears.

"Anzillu tamu. Tamabukku tamu."

On and on it went, the king's voice ringing above the tumult of the wind. Javid peeked through his fingers and saw Shahak, arms outstretched like a supplicant, darkness pouring from his mouth and joining with the smoke. *Feeding it.*

"Arhis, wardum. Arhis!"

Quickly, slaves. Quickly!

And as suddenly as it came, the wind died. The pall of smoke hanging over the Rock raced away to the west, spreading to a thin line as it went. Shahak sank down onto the stone bench.

"It is done," he whispered.

The flush in his cheeks faded to an ashen grey. A thin, watery substance trickled from his eyes, his nose, his ears. Javid had never seen him so ghoulish.

"How long will it take?" Gaius demanded.

"Soon, soon," the king whispered. He gritted his teeth and pressed a hand to his belly. Black blood seeped from beneath the nailbeds. "Now will you teach me the secrets of the ancient adepts?"

Gaius gave him a look of utter contempt. "Only those of pure Vatra blood can make talismans." He nudged Shahak with a toe. Just that slight pressure toppled the king. He slipped from the bench and lay on his side in the parched grass, his breath coming in harsh rattles.

"But you... you promised...."

"You're dying, you mortal fool," Gaius spat, turning away. "Give it up."

Shahak grasped at his foot. "But we are ... brothers," he wheezed.

Gaius spun back, rage on his face. "How dare you—"

"The dust, it...."

Javid's heart took off at a gallop. The linen bindings flattening his chest suddenly felt far too tight.

Holy Father, don't tell him the truth.

"It *what?*"

"My liege!" Two Praetorians walked toward them across the lawn. "A mortal woman has arrived seeking an audience with King Shahak."

"Kill her," Gaius replied, scowling in irritation. "Or have your sport with her, I don't care."

"She claims to be the Oracle of Delphi."

Gaius's eyes narrowed. "The bitch who outlawed magic?" He pulled his foot from Shahak's grasp and kicked his hand away. "This idiot spoke of her." Sadistic glee curled his lips. "I could do with some amusement. Tell her the King of Samarqand will see her in the throne room."

The Praetorians pressed fists to hearts and strode off. Javid hoped he'd been forgotten, but now Gaius's pale eyes turned to him. His skin prickled with fear.

"My lord," he said quickly, rising on watery legs.

"Inform me immediately when the shipment of spell dust arrives."

Javid bowed, not rising until the party of Vatras had departed. He thought Shahak was dead, but then he heard the king whisper his name.

Shit.

"Majesty?" he said, kneeling down.

"Help me...." His fingers scrabbled for the lacquered box, which lay just out of reach.

Javid looked at the king, then at the box. He raised the lid. It was half full of sparkling dust. He still feared Shahak — who knew what magic might linger in his corrupted body — but he'd finally had enough.

I am not your servant anymore.

"Hurry," Shahak gasped, his red eyes dimming. "It's not ... too late...."

Javid sat back on his heels. "You have done an evil thing, Majesty," he said softly. "May the Holy Father grant you mercy."

"Give me the box!" the king grated, but his voice was weak and frightened.

Javid closed the lid. Shahak gnashed what was left of his teeth. He tried to form the words of a spell, but his tongue shriveled before Javid's eyes like a scrap of cured meat. The frantic look in his eyes almost made Javid pity him.

Almost.

He watched with mingled horror and relief as the king's body slowly shrank within the heavy purple robe, settling in upon itself until all that remained was skin and bones. The eyes were the last to go, hardening to small, opaque marbles in the sockets. When it was over, Javid made the sign of the flame.

His feet led him back down into the Rock, though without any destination. He walked the corridors in a daze, the echoes of Shahak's sorcery still ringing in his mind.

Anzillu.

Arhis, wardum.

Arhis.

The hustler in him didn't want to face the truth. There had to be an angle. Some crack he could get his fingernails into. Some way to reverse whatever Shahak had begun.

But if there was, he couldn't see it.

If I hadn't been such a coward, I would have stopped him long before. Now it's too late....

A soft voice from the shadows jolted him out of his dark reverie.

"Javid."

Nazafareen approached, silent as a wraith in her soft boots.

"Are you mad?" he exclaimed. "What are you doing here? Someone might see you!"

She gave him a stubborn look that reminded him of Bibi. "I just had a row with Marzban Khorram-Din. He yelled at me for *fidgeting*. He's an awful old thing. I will go mad if I stay there any longer." She paused. "Nicodemus told me the Vatras never come to this side of the Rock. The gardens you spoke of.... I thought I'd go up and look for Katsu. Get a breath of fresh air."

"I just came from the gardens." He shook his head, glancing down the corridor. "We can't talk here. The new Oracle of Delphi has arrived. Gaius is meeting with her."

Nazafareen frowned. "Do you know who she is?"

"Not a clue."

"Then no one's up there. *Please*. Just for a few minutes."

Javid hesitated. He certainly didn't want to go anywhere near the throne room. What could it hurt? At least he knew Gaius and his Praetorians were occupied elsewhere. In truth, he was glad for Nazafareen's company. And she needed to know what he'd witnessed.

"All right. The stairs aren't too far."

They hurried along the corridors, passing near the inner court and Shahak's personal chambers. Javid heard a plaintive *carrr* through the half-open door. Pity filled his heart.

"Wait a moment," he said to Nazafareen.

Javid ducked inside. The crow sat in its cage, eyes bright. When it saw him, it began to hop up and down, pecking at the bars.

"You must be very quiet," he told his former master.

The crow cocked its head. Javid unhooked the cage and slipped back out.

"I'll explain later," he whispered to Nazafareen, who lifted her eyebrows. "Let's go."

25

FECKLESS DAUGHTER

Darius stood in the shadows with a pitcher of wine, his face arranged in a semblance of meek obedience. Inside, he boiled with frustration. It ran against every part of him to do nothing as the Vatras terrorized the keep, but he had no choice. Now a Praetorian flicked a finger and he hurried forward to refill the man's cup.

Twelve of them sprawled at four tables, drinking and dicing. The mingled aromas of rancid fat and stale wine wafted from the filthy floor. Bones from old repasts had been tossed aside, to be fought over by a trio of bizarre creatures the Praetorians treated as pets. Javid said they'd been Shahak's mother and brothers who'd defied the prince when he sought his father's crown. As punishment, he transformed them into beasts resembling badgers — if a badger had a beak and scales. They scurried under the tables, gulping down scraps and nimbly dodging the occasional kick.

Nicodemus sat at the farthest table, his boots propped on the back of a chair, eyes hooded. He'd taught the others the art of gambling to keep them occupied and it was working, up to a point. Before he'd produced a pair of dice, the Praetorians found their sport with Shahak's courtiers. Charred heaps of ash showed how *that* game had ended.

Looted jewelry changed hands as they argued over whether the little beasts could be taught tricks. Darius made the rounds, filling cups and ignoring jests about his withered arm.

"How long do you think the gimp would last in the Kiln?" one asked, drinking deeply.

"Depends. His legs work. I'd say a day or so."

"Not if he ran into a wyvern." Laughter. "Or anything else."

"I'd like to see that. Give him a spear and let him loose. If he even knew which end to poke them with."

Darius fixed a mild, incurious smile to his lips as he refilled their cups. If they didn't wield fire, he'd be happy to show them what he could do with a spear. It wasn't his preferred weapon, but he'd trained with one for years. Given the choice, he might have preferred the Kiln to his own childhood.

Chairs scraped back and the Praetorians rose to their feet, pressing fists to breastplates as Gaius entered with his bodyguard. Darius melted back into the shadows.

"We have a guest," Gaius declared in a jovial tone. "The Oracle of Delphi has come to our fair city."

Nicodemus choked on his wine. Darius shot him a sharp look, but he seemed oblivious. The unburned side of his face was white as parchment.

"Pardon, my lord," Nicodemus muttered, setting his cup aside.

So they appointed a new one, Darius thought. She must be insane to come here. Maybe *all* the Oracles are insane. He braced himself for bloodshed, knowing this audience wouldn't end well. The poor woman.

"Show our visitor some decorum, you dogs," Gaius snapped, though he seemed amused.

The Praetorians formed up into two facing ranks, most of them reasonably steady on their feet. Gaius walked between them and climbed the dais leading to the throne. He sat down and crossed his ankles.

The patter of bare feet signaled the arrival of the Hazara-patis. The man was no longer Master of a Thousand. He wasn't even master of his own clothes. Gaius had ordered him stripped naked except for his chain of office, and his bony, wrinkled form looked pathetically small next to the burly Praetorians flanking the doors.

"I present to His Royal Highness the Oracle of Delphi, Keeper of the Divine Mysteries and Voice of the Sun God Apollo," he cried in a thin voice.

A woman strode confidently into the throne room. She wore a white dress and her dark hair fell in a long, loose braid down her back. The torchlight caught her face. Darius's hand clenched around the jug. His thoughts raced, tumbling like pebbles in a landslide.

A sister, it must be....

"King Shahak," she said, gracefully inclining her head, and the voice was unmistakable.

Darius had heard it a thousand times.

What is your name?

I want you to remember this is your doing, Andros.

Someday we'll be very good friends.

I don't wish to be cruel....

"King Shahak is indisposed," Gaius said, hauling Darius up from the well of unpleasant memories. "I am his regent."

She raised her chin. "He has a witch in his custody. I demand that you hand him over at once. This witch is the property of the Temple of Apollo. He escaped not long ago and I have reason to believe he came here."

Escaped. The lie spilled smoothly from her lips, but Darius knew better. Black mirth bubbled up and he bit his lip to keep from laughing aloud.

"A witch?" Gaius frowned. "What sort of witch?"

"A daēva witch," Thena snarled, her composure slipping. "One of those foul creatures from the darklands."

"Oh, my." Gaius looked around in mock terror. "Do you think he could be hiding in this very room?"

The Praetorians snickered. Thena bristled.

"You mock, regent, but I am entirely serious. You are in greater danger than you imagine."

Gaius's smile died. "How fortunate you came to warn us then. I will confess, there are rumors that such a monster might be lurking about. You might have noticed how empty the city is."

Thena nodded, a trifle uncertainly. "I'd heard the good citizens of Samarqand fled his evil shadow, but it did seem—"

"You are the Oracle who outlawed magic, yes?"

"It is heretical," she replied sternly. "All power must come through the god."

"Of course." He paused. "And where is your retinue? Surely you didn't travel unattended."

"Outside in the hall. The guards said I had to come in alone."

Gaius gestured and the Praetorians at the door stepped aside.

"Let's have you all together," he said with an agreeable smile. "Then we can search the Rock for this witch."

Thena nodded, pleased. She still hadn't turned in Darius's direction, though he could see the scene clearly from his vantage against the wall. Four Shields of Apollo entered the throne room, a hooded and cloaked figure between them. The lines of the body suggested a woman. Nicodemus stood with his back turned in the closer line of Praetorians, but his shoulders stiffened as they passed.

Thena unrolled a piece of parchment. "I have a sketch of the witch, regent. I suggest we make copies and distribute them to the servants."

"An excellent idea," Gaius replied, leaning back in the throne. "I have only the greatest respect for your sun god. Fire is without a doubt the purest element. I understand you burn unbelievers?" He glanced at the withered skins tacked to the wall.

"Only when the god wills it so," she said primly.

"Now *that* is a fitting punishment. It has a certain nobility, to die scoured in flame." He rose and stood at the edge of the dais, his pale eyes gleaming. Gaius cupped a hand to his ear. "In fact, I think I hear the god whispering to me right now." More laughter from the Praetorians. "What is it he says? Ah, yes."

Gaius pointed, a lazy, contemptuous gesture, and the Shields of Apollo burned.

They burned with a heat so fierce it reduced them to blackened shards of bone in the space of four heartbeats. Swords and helmets clattered to the ground, along with an iron collar. Darius's skin crawled, though he had no love for the temple soldiers. It must be the collar she'd brought for *him*.

Thena's face froze, the wheels in her brain spinning but failing to gain traction.

Gaius laughed. He stepped down from the dais. "I'm sorry," he said. "It gets away from me sometimes."

Thena spun to the hooded woman and hissed something. The woman hunched into herself, refusing to look up. Thena slapped her and Darius saw gold glinting at her wrist.

"Burn him," she snapped with an edge of hysteria. "I command you!"

The woman screamed, a full-throated shriek. Sharp talons raked Darius's heart. He took half a step forward. Someone had to stop it, they *had* to....

Gaius strode forward and Thena stood her ground, rage and fear mingling on her face. But he went straight past and approached the cloaked figure kneeling on the ground. With a flick of one finger, he pushed the hood back. His eyes widened slightly.

Darius knew her, too. She'd murdered his mother and grandmother, and hundreds more Danai. His pity evaporated.

"Father," she whispered, raising a trembling hand. "Please. Help me."

Gaius stared down at her, his mouth a slash. There was genuine emotion on his face for the first time since this bizarre audience began, though Darius couldn't make out what it was. Pity? Anger? Regret?

"How did you fall into the hands of the mortals?" he asked softly.

Thena had wisely given up trying to coerce her slave and there was perfect silence in the throne room. The Praetorians all stared at Domitia, too. They knew her well, Darius realized.

She looked around in a daze. Her gaze slid past Nicodemus, then flicked back.

If Darius had any doubts, the look in her eyes banished them. He didn't know how the Vatra had managed it, but he'd tricked them all. And if he hadn't, they never would have gone into the Kiln. They would have gone after Domitia. And none of it, fucking *none* of it, would have happened.

Say it, he thought savagely. Say his name.

Domitia turned back to Gaius. "That bitch poisoned me," she said hoarsely, casting a hateful glance at Thena, who quaked some distance away. Domitia's fingers fluttered against the collar. "Get this off me and let me have her. There's a key, she keeps it in her pocket." She searched Gaius's eyes, trying on a smile. "I got you out of the Kiln, father. We did it."

He didn't smile back. "Nicodemus said you were dead."

"He must have thought so." She yanked at the collar, a note of desperation in her voice. "The key. *Please.* But don't kill her. I've earned the right. I want her alive."

"My poor daughter," Gaius murmured. He bent down as if to smooth the hair from her forehead. Darius saw the flash of a blade. Red bloomed on her chest, a deadly rose spreading its petals. Domitia's mouth widened slightly but she made no sound.

"That's for being weak." Gaius stabbed her again. "And

stupid." He gave the dagger a twist. She fell to one side, her limbs drawing up. Crimson pooled around her.

In the hush that followed, Gaius's heavy breath was like a bellows. Even his own Praetorians looked a bit amazed at the depths of his savagery.

"My feckless daughter has brought shame on all of us," he roared, a dark flush creeping up his cheeks. He flung the dagger away and pointed a finger at the Hazara-patis, who waited wearily to fulfill whatever order came next. The old chamberlain seemed to have reached a place beyond fear where anything could be endured if it bought him another hour of life.

"Tell my wives to ready my armor and bring the mounts from the stables," Gaius rasped. "Come, dogs."

He turned his back on his daughter and stormed off. The Praetorians trotted in two lines after him — all except Nicodemus, who stood rooted in place, staring at Domitia.

Darius pushed off the wall, intending to shake the Vatra until his teeth rattled, but then he saw a flash of white. Thena was at a small servants' door on the other side of the huge chamber, skirts hiked up and running for her life. Gaius had either forgotten about her or he didn't care — most likely the second.

Darius no longer feared her. Since his encounter with the Drowned Lady, the old demons Thena had woken inside him were gone. He didn't even hate her anymore — that would require giving a damn. But the woman was insane and dangerous and she had the spark, enough to collar another daēva if she ever got the chance.

But you won't get the chance. I'll make certain of that.

Darius dropped the wine jug and ran after her.

❧ 26 ❧

DOMITIA'S EPITAPH

Blood slicked the floor of the throne room. Nicodemus stepped around what remained of the Shields of Apollo and made his way to Domitia. He shrugged off the shadowtongue cloak and laid it over her, pulling it up to cover the iron collar around her throat. He thought she was dead, but then her eyes opened and a sound that might have been laughter escaped her.

"That's mine," she managed. "Bastard."

Torchlight flickered on the lines of her face, making her look very young one instant and impossibly old the next.

"You didn't tell him," Nico said. "Why not?"

She didn't answer. Her eyes fixed on something distant.

"Why not, Domitia?"

He needed to know. It mattered.

"I should never have left the Kiln." The words were a hoarse croak. Sweat slicked her pale forehead. "I belonged there."

Nicodemus took her hand, not for the woman she became but for the girl he once knew, the one who told him he had eyes like the summer sea on a moonlit night. For the one who'd saved him from the crab.

For the one who'd just saved him from Gaius and been punished in his stead.

"I wish...." he began.

What did he wish?

Nicodemus wasn't sure, but he understood. He carried the Kiln inside him, too. It had shaped him in its image, tempered him with pain and want and envy. But his love for Atticus had altered the casting.

All she'd had was her monstrous father.

Their eyes met. He saw her spirit was fading, but also that she wanted to tell him something. Her lips moved, the words too faint to make out. Nicodemus leaned down, straining to hear as her breath tickled his cheek.

"Let go of my fucking hand," Domitia whispered, and died.

❦ 27 ❦

THE SUN GOD SPEAKS

When Darius reached the servant's door, the corridor was empty in both directions. He swore under his breath and chose the right-hand turning, sprinting to the next junction. His daēva ears heard faint footsteps and there she was, vanishing up a staircase that led toward the east wing of the keep.

He was forced to slow and press against the wall in deference when a contingent of Praetorians came from the opposite direction. They didn't give him a second glance. Darius ran flat out again as soon as they had passed, taking the stairs three at a time.

Part of him wondered where Gaius was riding to. Things were coming to a head. He needed to find Nazafareen and tell her what had happened. A disquieting feeling of failure made his stomach roil. They were no closer to finding the crown, if it even still existed. And Gaius himself was as invulnerable as the Rock.

Thena, on the other hand, could meet the fate she so richly deserved. Killing her might not alter the larger course of events, but it would certainly cheer him up.

She was faster than he expected and he nearly lost her in another large hall with many doors leading out. But then he heard her panting breath and caught up with her again in a long hall. She'd slowed, looking around fearfully. She was lost.

"Thena," he called.

She turned and saw him. A beatific smile lit her face. She appeared perfectly composed, but he'd seen that expression before. It was a thin veneer over a simmering cauldron of madness.

"Andros," she said, nodding to herself. "The god has brought you to me. I knew he would."

Darius made a show of looking around. He scratched his head. "I don't see your Shields, Thena. Where are they?"

"They were not part of his plan," she replied serenely. "So the Archon spoke true. I wondered if perhaps...." She shook her head. "Never mind. You have come to me. That's all that matters now."

He began walking toward her, wary in case she had a hidden cache of spell dust. "You collared the Pythia. I assume Nicodemus helped you?"

"Apollo helped me. The others were merely his pawns." Her eyes shone with unshed tears. "He is still angry with me for losing you. He will not speak to me, Andros." She stood up straighter. "But all that will change once we return to the Temple. I have atoned for my sin. That's what he's telling me by bringing you here, don't you see?"

Darius stopped. Could he really kill such a mad creature in cold blood? She was unarmed. His power was blocked by the bond, but she possessed only a tenth of his strength....

"I'm glad to see you rid yourself of that one-handed bitch," Thena added. "You never belonged to her anyway."

One quick twist of the neck, Darius decided. Quiet and reasonably painless. If she did suffer — well, he'd find a way to live with himself.

"I don't have a collar with me, but we'll find you one, don't worry," she said warmly. "And if you're very good, I'll let you use your old name. I know it now. Your father told me." She paused, savoring the moment. "*Darius*."

He'd underestimated his own feelings, because hearing his name on her lips made Darius go cold with loathing. Thena saw it. Her mouth trembled. The tears spilled down her cheeks. Perhaps part of her was still sane enough to have suspected the truth all along.

Darius would never know, for at that instant a chicken raced down the corridor, half flying, half running. It got tangled up in Thena's gown, squawking, then broke free. A small child followed, pelting heedlessly after her pet. Before Darius could move, Thena's hand shot out and grabbed her by the braid. Mahmonir's head yanked back. A bloody blade appeared in Thena's fist, pressed to the child's throat.

It was the same one Gaius had used on Domitia. She must have picked it up and hidden it in her sleeve.

"Not a single step closer," Thena snarled.

Mahmonir writhed in her grip and she gave the girl a hard shake. The child began to cry.

Ten paces separated them. Darius could never reach her before she slit Mahmonir's throat. And he knew she would, without hesitation.

"On your knees, Andros." Her voice was devoid of emotion now, her eyes blank holes.

Darius complied, cursing himself for not just killing her when he had the chance.

"Treacherous witch," she muttered. "You thought to trick me twice. But Apollo has intervened." She threw her own head back and howled, a sound of tortured agony. "Why does he toy with me this way? What does he want? I did all he asked of me!"

Darius inched forward and Thena's attention snapped back. She pressed the point of the blade to Mahmonir's eye.

"If you test me," she said quietly, "I will start with the left one. Then the right."

He held his hand up, searching for some sign of humanity in that empty face. "Let her go. Please, Thena. She's only four."

"You abandoned me. Lied to me. Beg my forgiveness, witch."

"I'm sorry. But I spared your life. Does that count for nothing?"

Thena's pupils dilated. Her gaze lit on the torch fixed to the wall. She gave a soft exhale.

"Yes," she whispered. "I see now. Our destinies are entwined."

Ice trickled down his spine.

"I'll do whatever you ask," he said. "Just let her go."

Dead eyes stared at him. "We must die together, purged in flame." She jerked her chin toward one of the iron brackets on the wall. "Take the torch," she ordered. "Bring it to me."

He glanced at the flames. The bond kept him from reaching for them, but he felt the wild power like an ache in his bones. "Let her go first."

Laughter rasped from her throat. "Do you take me for a fool? I will release the child once you're alight. You must have *faith*, Andros." The knife moved a hair closer to Mahmonir's eye. "She's a pretty girl, but she won't be for long."

He took a step toward the torch, sick with regret, his hand moving for it —

A molten glow filled the corridor, as though a piece of the sun had fallen to earth. Darius threw an arm over his eyes, dazzled. The light blazed even brighter for an instant, then faded. Thena drew a sharp breath.

A golden-haired youth stood before her. A quiver of arrows hung across his broad back and he wore a crown of laurel leaves. Softer ripples of light still clung to his form, gilding his bare torso and sensuous face.

"Oracle of Delphi," the god intoned in a voice deep and terrible.

Thena's face shone with ecstasy. "Apollo," she cried. "Have you come to carry me to Mount Olympus?"

His brows drew together in displeasure. "What transpires here?"

Thena's face went slack. She glanced down at Mahmonir. Her mouth worked soundlessly.

"I placed my trust in you. Raised you above all others. Yet you abused your authority."

"I followed your commands," she said quickly. "Led the witches from darkness, showed them the true path—"

"All the creatures of this land are my children," the god thundered. "It is your own madness and ambition that led you to this end." Shafts of blinding light shot from his eyes. "You were to be my bride. But you have failed me utterly."

Thena shook her head in denial. "No, no, please—"

"I cast you down."

His voice seemed to shake the stones of the Rock. Horror contorted Thena's face. Inarticulate noises bubbled from her throat.

"I strip you of all authority and blessings. I banish you from my temples—"

With an anguished cry, Thena shoved Mahmonir away and seized the torch.

"I condemn you to Tartarus, to languish in chains among the adamantine columns and suffer the lash of Tisiphone for all eternity." The god's handsome aspect twisted in fury. "I renounce you, Oracle!"

Thena's hair caught first, then her white gown. She stumbled down the corridor, blazing in counterpoint to Apollo's fierce glow. Darius stood frozen in shock, watching as she finally collapsed and lay unmoving.

The golden light around the god faded. His form shimmered, though not before Darius saw a faint smile on his lips. In the next instant, Apollo vanished, leaving an old man in a tatty robe.

Marzban Khorram-Din reattached the bag of spell dust to his belt and brushed his hands together with an air of satisfaction.

Mahmonir ran to him, pressing her cheek against his side. He patted her head.

"Don't look, child," he said in a stern tone that carried a hint of Apollo's authority. "She can't hurt you now."

Darius gave a shaky laugh. The illusion had been perfect. Even *he* had believed it. For Thena.... Well, it was her worst nightmare come to pass.

"How did you know her heart so well?" he asked, still amazed.

Marzban Khorram-Din scowled at Thena's lifeless form.

"Fanatics," he muttered. "They're all the same."

———

WHITE CLOUDS DRIFTED THROUGH THE SKIES ABOVE THE ROCK. From her vantage point at the western edge of the gardens, Nazafareen could see the spiraling streets of Samarqand, the patchwork of fields and farms beyond its walls, and finally the drylands where the civilized world started bleeding into the waste of the Kiln.

Nothing else stirred in the sky.

Javid told her what he'd witnessed. What had King Shahak done?

And where was Katsu?

"He'll come," Javid said quietly at her side, and she realized she'd spoken the last aloud.

Nazafareen glanced at him. "I know he will. And you still haven't thanked me for getting you thrown into the dungeons. You wouldn't have met him otherwise."

Javid laughed. "It's true. I take back all the awful things I said about you." He raised a brow. "*Ashraf.*"

She made a face. "Look, I could have killed you and thrown you out of your own wind ship, but I decided to be nice and ask for passage. We'll call it even."

"Fair enough. But tell me one thing."

"What?"

He studied her with a disquieting intensity. "How did you come back from the dead?"

Nazafareen stilled. "What kind of question is that?" she blustered.

"Because your story makes no sense. It's only been a few days and you have no wounds. Not a scratch. Yet you were supposedly left for dead. I've been around Atticus long enough to doubt he'd ever make such a mistake."

She stared out at the deserted city. "Darius brought me back," she said at last. "He followed me behind the veil and he brought me back."

Javid nodded. She suspected he'd press for details later but, for now, he seemed content to hear the truth.

"Now that's true love," he observed wistfully.

"Damn right it is."

He glanced at the crow, hunched in its cage at his feet. "I used to wish I was Izad Asabana. I wanted to be rich and powerful. To own a huge estate and have a fleet of wind ships."

"But you don't anymore?"

"No, I still do."

Nazafareen laughed. "That's a relief."

"But I want Katsu more. I should never have let him go."

"You had to."

"I could have gone myself."

She laid a hand on his arm. "Don't. He'll return."

"And if he doesn't?"

"I'll help you find him."

"Thanks, Nazafareen." He hefted the cage. Asabana's beady eyes watched him intently. The crow pecked at the bars.

"Perhaps you'll forget you were ever a man," Javid murmured, unlatching the door. "I can't change you back. But at least I can grant you freedom."

The crow hopped to the edge of the balustrade. It perched there for a moment, then spread its wings and flapped away.

"I suppose he brought it on himself," Javid said heavily. "But I still feel sorry for him. He did help me when—"

"Javid?"

She could still see the crow, a black dot against the blue sky. But something was descending from the clouds, a great shadow arrowing down, scales glinting in the sunlight.... Massive jaws gaped, then snapped shut. The crow vanished in a puff of feathers. A screech of triumph echoed through the silent buildings below.

Nazafareen and Javid looked at each other.

"Holy Father," he said, making the sign of the flame. "What the hell was that?"

Nazafareen's fingers went white on the balustrade as she scanned the sky. "A drake," she whispered. "It's something called a drake."

❧ 28 ❧

ANZILLU

Meb watched the horizon brighten. The Valkirin scouts said the fleet was less than twenty leagues from Samarqand. She'd never been north of Susa before, but she'd heard about the Rock of Ariamazes. A fortress like no other, built to outlast the ages.

She turned as Ragnhildur skidded to a landing on the deck of the *Akela*. Culach slid easily from the saddle but kept hold of the harness. The abbadax settled down on the deck, folding her wings.

"Meb?" he called.

She took his enormous hand and led him to the bow, guiding him to the rail. His cheeks were flushed from the wind and his silver hair stuck up in all directions like an unruly boy. But when he spoke, his voice was serious.

"I've been thinking," he said. "My inability to touch the Nexus could be an asset. I won't be drawn to reach for fire." He paused. "I'd like to be your bodyguard when we get there. Ragnhildur can serve as my eyes. She's a clever girl and she'll kill anything that comes close."

"That suits me," she said, touching his fingers to her face so he could feel her smile.

Culach seemed to find this new habit amusing, for his own lips quirked in response.

"Is everyone ready?"

He knew a great deal about waging war — Valkirins did little else — and he'd given sound advice to the hastily assembled council of clan leaders that met on the *Akela* during the journey. A woman named Astrid commanded Val Petros now. She, Den of Val Altair and Daníel of Val Tourmaline had gathered with the new Matrium and the Five, of course. Meb had mostly listened. She wielded raw power, but martial strategy was new to her.

"As we'll ever be."

"Tell me the plan again," he said. "Eirik used to drill me over and over. It's the best way to find holes."

Meb ticked the points off on her fingers. "The Five will command their own fleets. Your Valkirins can fly between the ships and pass on orders and information. Once we're close enough, the Danai will join together and attack the Rock. The Valkirins can protect the Danai by battering the fortress with winds strong enough to suffocate any flames the Vatras summon. The Marakai — me, mostly — will submerge the rubble, drowning whoever's left inside."

Some of the words were new to her. *Submerge* and *suffocate*. But she'd listened closely at the council and understood what they meant.

He rubbed his jaw. "It's a good plan. The main thing I'm worried about is the Danai. Working earth breaks bones. That fortress is huge and the walls are thick. It won't be a simple matter to destroy it."

"But they just have to crack it enough that the sea pours in. I think it's the best we can do." She glanced over at the *Chione*, which now carried a contingent of mortal women called Maenads whom Daníel claimed were impervious to fire.

Culach sighed. "If the Vatras weren't holding the Rock, I wouldn't attempt it. Meeting them out in the open would be suicidal. But if they're trapped inside.... Ah, well. At least the mortals already fled. Susa must be bursting at the seams with refugees."

It sunk in for Meb that they were talking about the likely destruction of an entire city — the oldest one in Solis. They were both quiet for a minute.

"Would you like to hear about Katrin, the Valkirin talisman?" Culach asked. "I know her well."

"Yes," Meb replied eagerly. "Was she weak in air?"

"Apparently so, though she hid it well. She was Val Moraine's most fearsome fighter. I suppose she wanted to make up for her weakness." He tilted his head. "Galen, the Danai, betrayed his clan to my father. At the time I thought he was just mercenary. Now I wonder if he was driven by his own demons."

"I didn't know that about Galen," Meb said, disturbed by this revelation.

"Don't mention it to Mina," Culach added hastily.

Meb frowned. "I never would."

"Honestly, you're the only normal one of the bunch," Culach said with a smile. "Were you really an outcast?"

"I felt like one. Captain Kasaika treated me decent, but it was hard being so different."

"What about your family? Did they know?"

"If they did, they never told me. I don't know what happened to them. My parents disappeared when I was little and I got sent to Captain Kasaika." She didn't want to talk about Nicodemus and how he tricked her. It still hurt.

"I'm sorry, Meb."

"It's okay. I'll be thirteen soon." She looked at the sky. "Artemis is almost full. She helped me raise the tides. I used to worry about what would happen when I came of age, but I guess I don't have to anymore. If we live through this."

"You'll be a good queen," Culach said. "Better than if you'd never known hardship. My father led Val Moraine for more than three hundred years and no one mourned his passing."

"He was that bad?"

"Worse."

"How come you're not like him?"

"I used to be," Culach admitted. "Mina changed me."

She glanced at him. "That sounds backwards. She wouldn't love you if you hadn't changed *first*."

Culach laughed. "Maybe you're right. She says I used to be an asshole."

Meb grinned and took his hand again. "Well, I'm glad you're not one anymore." She hesitated, feeling suddenly shy. The Princess and Feng Mian had been kind, but she'd never felt totally at ease with them. Not like she did now. "I think you're my first real friend, Culach Kafsnjór."

He looked startled, then dewy-eyed. "Oh, Meb." Culach cleared his throat. "I...." He squeezed her hand. "Thank you. I'll do my best to live up to it."

Anuketmatma twined between his legs and leapt to the rail. She stared toward Samarqand, green eyes intent.

The features of the Umbra grew clearer with each passing minute. Wind-carved escarpments flashed past, and gullies that spewed jets of foam as the sea poured in. Meb felt tired and jittery at the same time. She hadn't slept since they left the Twelve Towers. Her power was the only thing carrying the fleet forward and if she let her link to the Nexus slip, the wave would disperse. At first it had been almost effortless, but now she was starting to feel the strain. The song of the Great Green wound through her blood, but it had a will of its own — and it didn't much like what she was making it do. The Umbra was a plateau between the Cimmerian Sea and the Austral Ocean. In forcing the water to rise, she'd broken fundamental natural laws. They exerted their own force and Meb knew that eventually, they would win.

I only have to hold on for a little bit longer, she thought.

Up ahead, a Valkirin scout sped toward the fleet. Culach heard the wingbeats, tipping his face to the sky. Meb recognized Stefán's son, Den. He wore jeweled pins in his braids, emeralds and rubies that she secretly admired. She still missed her old knife. It had been the only thing she owned of any value.

Maybe the Valkirins will trade me for a new one, she thought. I bet they have a fancy dagger or two lying around.

As Den neared, Anuketmatma hissed, arching her back. Meb frowned.

"What is it, Mother of Storms?"

She thought it prudent to address the cat in a respectful tone, rather than her usual "cat." It might have been tolerated on the Isle of Selk, but Meb wouldn't test the storm deity's patience on open water.

Anuketmatma's fur bristled and she laid her ears back. At that instant, the sun broke above the western horizon. Meb cupped a hand over her eyes and squinted, letting them adjust to the dazzling brightness. She hadn't seen the sun since Tjanjin nearly three weeks before. Shouts erupted from the nearby ships and she glimpsed other daēvas shielding their faces, some with both arms.

At least I'm Marakai and used to traveling between the light and dark sides, she thought. I bet a lot of Danai and Valkirins ain't never seen the sun at all.

When Meb's vision cleared, the grey walls of Samarqand loomed ahead, its palace-fortress rearing above the city like a small mountain.

"Culach Kafsnjór," she began excitedly, breaking off as Den landed on the deck next to Ragnhildur. The two mounts eyed each warily, neck feathers flaring. Culach — who had an uncanny ability to sense Ragnhildur's mood — gently chastised her and she let out a mournful puff of air before settling her feathers again and ostentatiously looking away.

Den slid from the saddle, peeling his gloves off and tucking them into his coat. Meb knew right away that something was wrong. He was easygoing for a Valkirin and always had a smile for her, but his face was grim.

"There's an army ahead," he said without preamble. "A large one. I couldn't risk getting too close. Some of the creatures have wings."

"Creatures?" Culach demanded, his white brows drawing together. "What the bloody hell is up there?"

"Looks like they came from the Kiln," Den said flatly. "I only saw them from afar, but there's thousands of the things."

"We have to turn back," Meb said, fear fluttering in her chest.

"She's right," Culach agreed in a decisive tone. "We're not prepared for this." He swore. "How did they appear so quickly? The last scouts saw nothing."

"I don't know," Den replied. "They must move fast." He paused. "It was hard to tell for sure, but I think I saw spiders. Huge ones. There's dark magic at work here, talisman."

Meb drew a breath. "I'll inform the Five and the heads of holdfasts and houses that we're returning to the Twelve Towers."

With each passing moment, the city grew larger. Meb could see dots in the sky now, wheeling over the Rock. The walls blocked her view of whatever waited on the ground. If the Valkirin scouts hadn't given advance warning....

She pushed all that from her mind and tuned her senses to the body of water surging around her. It was at least ten fathoms deep and a league or more wide. Meb tried to reverse its flow, but her energy was flagging and she found it difficult to control. The massive moon Artemis wasn't helping any. It hung low in the west, visible even in the sunlight. Doubts crowded her mind. The Nexus wavered.

No!

She stilled her thoughts and the link strengthened, but the current swept the fleet forward. Meb groaned. Samarqand sat on lower ground. The water was naturally flowing down a gradual incline and would continue to do so even if she released the power. She realized with something close to panic that making it climb again was beyond her abilities.

Maybe if I'd had more time to practice, she thought angrily. *But the Five forbade me from trying.*

"What's wrong, Meb?" Culach asked quietly.

"I can't," she said, tears stinging her eyes. "It's too late."

"Then we will fight," he replied calmly. "Plans rarely turn out the way you expect. But we still need you to be strong."

She nodded, wiping her face. Den waited, his gaze steady. She was grateful he didn't seem angry or disappointed.

"Shall I relay new orders, talisman?"

"Yes." Meb's expression hardened. "I'll drown as many of 'em as I can. I think the clans know what to do with the rest."

He grinned and it wasn't the amiable smile Meb had grown used to. This one had a brutal edge.

"That we do, talisman."

Den leapt into the saddle and flew to the next ship, hovering to relay the news, and then moved on to the next. In twos and threes, abbadax took off from the decks of the Marakai fleet until all the Valkirins were airborne. Danai crowded the rails, bows at the ready. Meb sensed deep, heavy currents of earth swirling around them.

Samarqand sped closer.

Meb turned to Anuketmatma. The cat gazed back, green eyes aglow, and Meb could have sworn she saw a smile.

✤ 29 ✤

WATER DOGS

The horizon stirred. An army massed there, thousands upon thousands in an endless sea. White wyrms with segmented bodies. Lizards and scorpions the size of horses. Doglike beasts with mirrored scales. Other things Nazafareen had no name for. They crawled, flew, loped and scuttled on jointed legs.

"Shahak did this," Javid whispered. "He summoned them. *Anzillu*. Abominations."

She heard distant shouts as the skeleton guard of soldiers standing watch on the walls deserted their posts, fleeing back toward the Rock.

The Kiln had disgorged its children, but magic made them even deadlier. Larger, faster, and unified behind a single purpose. But what was it? The Vatras had been their prey for a thousand years. Surely such an army would savage anything in its path. Nazafareen watched in numb shock as it approached the outer wall. She doubted even the Rock would hold against so many.

But Shahak had been mad. And now he was dead. There was no way to turn them back....

A white charger rode out from the stables below, flanked by a guard of Praetorians. Gaius galloped through the gate in the inner curtain wall, his shadowtongue cloak streaming behind. The Vatras raced straight for the horde and Nazafareen smiled grimly at his arrogance.

Then the first ones reached him, creeping low, heads bowed in submission, and she understood.

They were his to command.

She sensed Darius behind her and turned. His face paled as he surveyed the scene at the walls. Then he gripped her arm and pointed.

Coming from the opposite direction, she saw what looked like masts in the distance. It was such a strange vision she could scarcely believe her eyes. Storm clouds moved in from the Umbra, lightning flickering in their depths. The heat that had gripped the city for days was whisked away on a fresh, cool breeze. A few droplets of rain spattered the stone balustrade.

The ships drew closer and she realized they were carried on a huge, curling wave that devoured the land before it. Hundreds of abbadax flew ahead of the fleet, swooping down to do battle with the drakes. Gaius and his Praetorians wheeled around and galloped back through the gates, heading for higher ground.

"It's Meb," Nazafareen said, tears stinging her eyes. "She came with the clans."

Darius swore. "They're outnumbered a hundred to one. A thousand to one. Not counting the Vatras."

So the final reckoning had come. The darklands against the Kiln. It might be a lost cause, but the die was cast.

"We have to get out there, do what we can to help," she said urgently. "Maybe if Gaius is killed, whatever power he wields over them will disperse."

And what will the monsters do then? she wondered, though she didn't say it aloud. Go meekly back to the Kiln? Well, it was a slender hope, but better than none.

"I'll come with you," Javid said tightly.

"You'll die in a second out there and we both know it," Nazafareen said firmly. "But your family needs you. Go to them and barricade the doors."

Javid nodded, his face anguished. He ran for the passage down into the Rock.

"Thena is dead by her own hand," Darius said quietly. "I just saw it happen."

Nazafareen thought nothing could surprise her after seeing a drake eat Izad Asabana. She was wrong. "Thena came to the *Rock*? I thought she was bloody dead!"

"Nicodemus lied. I'm still not sure how, but he set us up. Domitia was here, too. Thena got herself appointed the new Oracle of Delphi and she had Domitia with her, collared. So it's not like the Vatra didn't suffer." His jaw set. "But I still plan to have a nice, intimate chat with him about it."

"And Domitia?"

"Her father killed her. Said she'd brought shame on him by getting herself captured."

Her eyebrows lifted. "That's harsh. Well, they deserved each other, didn't they?"

The ships were nearly at the wall. It began to rain harder.

"I'll tell you all about it later," Darius said. "I came straight here — after a quick stop in your rooms."

He handed her *Nemesis*. She slid the baldric over her shoulder, feeling the cold fury that always settled over her just before a fight with the Druj. She might not be a Breaker anymore, but she could still draw blood.

Every sense sharpened. She smelled the sharp tang of ozone, heard the distant thunder of water.

"Release me," he said. "I'll need the power for this."

She glanced at the battle now raging below. Gouts of flame shot from the knots of Praetorians. Some of the Marakai ships were already alight.

"But—"

"Nazafareen." His voice held a note of warning.

She sighed. "Of course."

She opened her fist on the bond and felt power flow between them, drawn from the deep well of the Nexus. It was like standing on the banks of a raging river. She couldn't touch it herself, but the raw force of it still shook her to her core.

Darius exhaled and closed his eyes. When he opened them, she saw death lurking in those blue irises.

"Let's show them how Water Dogs fight," he said with a crooked grin.

BLACK CLOUDS RACED IN FROM THE NORTH AS THE CURRENT swept the Marakai fleet toward the walls of the city. Anuketmatma's tail lashed in fury. The Mother of Storms perched on the rail at Meb's elbow. Jagged bolts of lightning shot down, stabbing the roiling mass of creatures that encircled Samarqand.

"What do you see?" Culach asked in a low voice.

Meb peered into the gloom. "Monsters, Culach Kafsnjór. Some of 'em have spiky skin and lots of legs. Others look like giant crabs. The flying ones are the worst."

He frowned in worry. "Are they abbadax?"

"No, I don't think so. They look more like … dragons. But I thought those were made up."

He was quiet for a minute. "We don't know what lives on the other side of the Gale. If that's where they came from." He gave a subdued laugh. "I suppose we'll find out shortly."

With Anuketmatma's help, she gave the wave a final burst of power. It broke over the first ranks, sweeping them under. Then the walls loomed ahead, tall grey stone five paces thick. Samarqand had nine gates, but all save one were closed. Meb sucked in a breath. They'd agreed it would be up to the captains to navigate the currents and the Danai to clear the way. Everyone knew their part, but it was still a close thing.

The *Akela* was seconds from smashing to bits when the gate wrenched from its hinges and hurtled high into the air. It landed on a cluster of spiders, driving them beneath the waves. And then they were through, the sailors steering for the Rock. There was no direct approach. The streets circled around the Rock in a spiral and it sat on an elevation above the city. Meb had to make the water climb.

She fought back exhaustion as she coaxed the sea to obey her. Saltwater flooded Samarqand, devouring the lowest ring of streets. It was a poorer district of cheap inns and markets, all shuttered tight. Meb glanced back. The other Marakai ships made it through the gates and followed in her wake — but so did Gaius's ghastly foot soldiers. They poured inside, skittering and leaping across rooftops. Shiny carapaces gleamed. Multi-jointed legs moved with nimble speed. Claws and teeth snapped. She felt a thousand hostile eyes fixed on the ships.

And the flood was starting to slow.

Meb tried to draw more water, but the Austral Ocean lay fifty leagues away. In her weakened, terrified state, gravity could no longer be denied. The *Akela* finally came to rest in a vast oval several tiers down from the Rock itself. She'd seen a similar place in Tjanjin. The emperor would stage horse races there on sunny afternoons, watching from a raised pavilion with his wife as they sipped rice wine.

The instant the ship's keel ground into the dirt, a huge spider with dripping fangs vaulted onto the deck. Three Danai rushed up to slash at it with their swords. Above, a squadron of Valkirins engaged the flying creatures. The Marakai sailors scrambled to surround her. She heard cries of "Protect the talisman!"

"Meb," Culach said urgently. "To Ragnhildur."

Anuketmatma leapt into Meb's arms. She tucked the cat into her leather vest and let him drag her to the saddle. Culach settled her in front of him and whispered to his mount. She spread her wings, leaping over the rail. Moments after they were airborne, a gout of white flame hit the *Akela* and the sails caught. Meb's gut tightened as she heard brief, agonized screams, followed by a terrible silence.

"Don't look at the flames," Culach hissed. "Push them away. Think of anything else."

Meb squeezed her eyes shut, but unfamiliar heat singed her skin. A wild, flickering energy tried to lure her, daring her to touch it. If she did, Meb knew she would die.

Higher and higher Ragnhildur climbed, until Meb sensed the danger had passed. She opened her eyes just as the sky broke open. At least a dozen ships burned. The rain dampened the blazes but didn't put them out. The fire was too hot.

From above, she could see the full extent of what they faced. The monsters flooding through the shattered gates were only a tiny fraction of the army pressing against the walls. It looked endless, stretching back toward the Kiln for leagues.

Culach swept them around in a wide circle, the reins loose in his hands. Wherever she could, Meb summoned water to douse the fires breaking out everywhere. She saw the Maenads rush forward to engage a group of Vatras in long cloaks, their staffs whirling, unhindered by the balls of fire the Vatras threw at them. As she passed overhead, Meb caught a glimpse of a man on a white charger, shouting orders. The monsters cringed before him. She knew it must be Gaius.

One of the winged creatures arrowed toward them and Ragnhildur slashed with claws and beak, her serpentine neck dodging as it spit venom at her face. As it passed, she clipped it with the razored tip of a wing, slicing its throat. The creature dropped like a stone. Ragnhildur screamed in triumph.

"Ah, my darling," Culach cooed. "The stupid things think you're built like them. You'll have to disabuse them."

The Danai sent missiles of broken stone at their enemies. The Valkirins used air to send the flying things tumbling. The Marakai conjured walls of water to drive them back. But Meb could see they'd be overwhelmed in minutes. And they weren't even near the Rock. It stood untouched on higher ground. The Danai couldn't attack the fortress when they were fighting for their lives.

"It's bad, Culach Kafsnjór," she shouted, a painful lump in her throat. "Real bad."

The tide was already receding. Only a few inches of water remained in the racing oval, though the streets below were still flooded.

The cat nipped her ear and Meb frowned. Then her spirits lifted.

A dozen Danai were about to be swamped by a pack of enormous lizards when tentacles rose from the shallows, each one clutching a limp monster. Sat-bu gave the beasts a savage shake and flung them away, reaching for more and dragging them under.

The Nahresi galloped out of a side street, black manes flying, hooves trampling the monsters in their path. A huge mouth opened in the center of a whirlpool and the giant carp of the Jengu swallowed fifty spiders in a single gulp. Anuketmatma purred against Meb's chest. Lightning streaked down again, lancing through a Praetorian with his hand raised and fire dripping down his arm. His blackened body fell. The sailors he'd been about to burn gave a ragged cheer.

The aid gave the daēvas hope and they regrouped, Danai and Marakai fighting together, Valkirins swooping low to protect them from the peril in the skies. But still, she saw Praetorians striding among the monsters, their cloaks billowing, sending streams of fire at the clans. She saw men and women burning. She saw the last of their ships fall to ash. And for every monster that died, ten more took its place.

It was supposed to be three of us, she thought, fighting back tears. The clans together aren't enough. *I'm* not enough.

She turned her cheek to Culach, a warm, solid presence at her back. "The sea gods came to help us," she said softly as they swooped around the Rock. "We kept the faith and they didn't abandon us."

He smiled. "With the blessing of the gods, we cannot fail."

Meb felt like she'd aged ten years in the last ten minutes. She knew the truth, even if those below couldn't see it.

"It'll buy us some time," she said. "But the water's going down. I can't stop it. And when it's gone, the sea gods will be gone too."

DOMITIA'S SKIN COOLED, THE POOL OF BLOOD AROUND HER thickened, and still Nicodemus crouched beside her, feeling strangely bereft.

Perhaps it was her final act of vengeance. To leave him full of guilt and regret and questions that would never be answered. That would be exactly like Domitia.

Footsteps made him turn. Aelia stood behind him, staring with empty eyes. Ash streaked her gown.

He stood and gently turned her to face him. "What happened?"

"He killed them all," she whispered.

"Who?"

"The women. He ordered us to assemble as he donned his armor. He was ranting, nearly incoherent." A single tear ran down her cheek. "He turned his back and Livia pulled out a blade. She was always the bravest of us. Romulus walked in at that very moment. He burned her. Gaius came undone. He slaughtered the rest in an eyeblink." She put her hands to her face, her voice breaking. "I ran, Nico. I left them."

He took her in his arms. "We'll kill him, Aelia." He paused, sudden dread filling his heart. "And the children?"

"I locked them inside one of the storerooms with Atticus."

"Good."

She pushed away. "The other clans have come to take back the city. But that's not all. I heard him talking, before." She swallowed. "He used magic to call the Kiln against them. Wyrms, drakes. Every one of the creatures that persecuted us."

Nico drew a sharp breath. So that was why Gaius had shuttered himself away with the alchemist king. Rage set his veins on fire. Yet he could see exactly why Gaius had done it. He'd as much as said it plainly that day, if Nico had only listened.

I want to see terror on their faces.

I want them to know what it's like.

"Run," Nico said, taking her hands. "I'll find you."

Aelia shook her head. "No. If you mean to fight, I'll go with you."

He pressed his forehead to hers, copper hair spilling through his fingers.

"I'm sorry," he said softly. "Sorry I didn't come back sooner."

Her hand cupped the scars along his jaw. "Don't be," she said with a sad smile. "You didn't have to come back at all."

ANOTHER BONE-RATTLING BLOW STRUCK THE DOOR.

Javid eyed the teetering pile of furniture they'd pushed in front of it. Three beds. Both sofas. Ma's pots and pans and every knickknack they could lay hands on. It wasn't enough. Whatever the hell was out there seemed determined to get in.

"I'm almost out of spell dust," Marzban Khorram-Din said in a funereal tone.

His words were punctuated by another blow. The stout oaken door shuddered in its frame.

"Son?" his da called from one of the back rooms.

Javid raised a trembling hand to his forehead, trying to keep voice even. "Yes, da?"

"Can you come back here for a second?"

"Go," Marzban Khorram-Din told him, pulling his robes

tighter around his frail body. "I'll hold it off." He peered into the dwindling bag of spell dust. "For a few minutes, at least."

Javid heard the alchemist intoning words to fortify the door as he entered the stripped-down chamber where his parents huddled on the floor with Farima and Mahmonir. The chickens were running around in a frenzy. Whenever they passed too close to his ma and da, the creatures on their laps snapped hungrily.

"Are you sure they won't bite?" his ma asked. She was holding up well, all things considered.

"No one's saying you didn't do the right thing, son. It's just that...." His da winced. "They're a little feisty."

On his way down from the gardens, Javid had heard the scrape of claws in the shadowy corridor. He'd looked back, heart pounding. But it wasn't the monsters King Shahak had summoned.

It was Shahak's brothers.

Dadash, the littlest one, had tufted ears like a fox kit and the scales of an armadillo. The older one was even stranger, with grey hide and snaggly yellow teeth set into a short beak. Javid didn't know where the Queen Mother was, but he didn't think she would abandon her children unless something terrible had happened to her.

They'd trailed him to his family's rooms, slinking ten paces behind. He had no intention of letting them in, but when a roar echoed through a nearby corridor and the little one squeaked in fear, his heart softened. He beckoned and they scooted forward with pathetic eagerness, making it through the door just as he glimpsed something huge and white slither around the corner.

He assumed that was the same *something* now doing its best to break the door down.

Javid crouched before Dadash and patted its misshapen head. He couldn't tell if they still understood words, or if they were truly animals. He wasn't sure which would be worse.

"Just keep the chickens out of reach," he said.

Mahmonir, who'd already suffered a traumatic experience just an hour gone, sucked her thumb and stared into space. Farima stroked her back mechanically. Caring for her little sister seemed to be the only thing keeping her from dissolving into hysterics.

"What's happening out there?" his da asked in a level voice.

"Don't worry," Javid said with false confidence. "Nothing will get in, I promise."

Another tremendous crash resounded from the sitting room.

Farima looked at him with wide eyes. Mahmonir crawled over to pet Dadash, who rubbed his beak against her chubby hand.

"You'd better go help Marzban," his ma said quietly. She forced a smile. "I love you, my son."

He smiled back, his heart aching. "I love you too, ma."

Javid hurried back to the sitting room. Marzban caught his eye. His thick grey brows were drawn down. The relentless thudding ceased, but now he heard a wet, squelching sound coming from the corridor outside. A long minute passed in silence. Then a worm wriggled under the door. It had a tiny pink mouth that opened and closed, blindly seeking flesh to attach itself to. Javid's mouth twisted in revulsion and he stomped on it. Four more oozed through the crack, then six, a dozen, each the length of his palm. The alchemist grabbed a small figurine and they threw themselves into destroying the tide of pale worms.

"Holy Father, what are they?" Javid panted, his boots slippery with the foul things.

Marzban sighed. "I think the big one just gave birth," he said.

✿ 30 ✿

TO THE ROCK

Six bodies sprawled at the entrance of the Rock, so savaged only the scarlet tabards identified them as Persian soldiers. Nazafareen and Darius exchanged a wordless look. The men had not died by fire or blade. Something from the Kiln had done this, though it seemed to have moved on.

Darius picked up one of their swords, testing its weight in his hand. They stepped from the fortress into heavy rain. Storm clouds pressed down on Samarqand, the underbellies lit with an orange glow. She smelled smoke and wet leaves. The sounds of fighting were distant, somewhere beyond the curtain wall.

They ran through the wooded park, alert for any signs of movement. Water dripped from the branches in a steady patter. Every few seconds, a fireball traced across the sky like a shooting star, raining death on the city below. In those brief flashes, she saw dark shapes flying through the columns of smoke. Flights of arrows hissed in dense volleys from the rooftops. The earth groaned and trembled. Voices shouted in defiance. And above it all, Nazafareen heard the dull roar of ten thousand chitinous legs jostling together as Gaius's army tightened its grip.

They neared the final stand of trees before the wall when a

huge crab scuttled sideways from the undergrowth. Nazafareen hacked off the snapping foreclaw as Darius drove his blade down into the soft juncture where the carapace met the head.

The crab died. More came. Nazafareen let her breath and heartbeat fall into rhythm with her bonded, losing herself in the whirl of blades. They fought as one, anticipating each other's movements, and the *anzillu* fell before them until the space around the curtain wall was quiet again.

Darius flicked greenish blood from his sword. She remembered him doing the same after beheading a revenant and for an instant the world lurched, two places superimposed over each other — one here and now, the other a killing ground on the Great Salt Plain of the Empire.

Darius touched her arm. "Are you all right?"

The vision faded. There had been men, too, in leathers of human skin. Necromancers....

Nazafareen nodded. "It's just the memories still take over sometimes." She bent to wipe her blade on the grass. "Come, we'd better find out what's going on."

They climbed to the top of the gatehouse, taking the stairs two at a time. The scene beyond nearly made her lose hope. daēvas fought in small, isolated pockets spread through the four tiers of streets winding down from the wall. Whatever strategy they'd planned, it had fallen apart.

She turned to Darius. Courage flowed into her through the bond.

"To the Rock!" Darius bellowed, his voice slicing through the chaos.

The nearest daēvas heard him and began to rally. She saw Mithre, bleeding from a dozen wounds, lay waste to a spider with his sword. Two Maenads ran at a Praetorian, unhorsing him with their staffs. Fire engulfed them, but when it faded, the Maenads still stood and the Vatra lay unmoving on the ground. More voices shouted "To the Rock!" The cry spread from group to group as a new purpose took hold.

"We just have to hold the gates while they fight their way clear," Darius said, eyes blazing. "Gaius abandoned the fortress. It's ours now."

She nodded and they ran back down, standing shoulder to shoulder before the gates.

The daēvas weren't the only ones to heed his call. A tide of monsters skittered forward.

Nazafareen and Darius raised their blades to meet them.

SMOKE BURNED MEB'S EYES AS RAGNHILDUR CIRCLED AROUND the battle raging below. Despite her best efforts to hold it, the water had slowly ebbed away and she hadn't seen any of the sea gods for at least an hour. Even the cat was gone. Meb had felt her dissipate like mist in the sun, leaving a cold, empty place inside her vest where warm fur had been.

She was so tired, she could hardly sit up straight, but Culach held her tight against his chest.

They passed over the Rock and skimmed the trees inside the curtain wall. Sooty tears ran down her face and she wiped them away with the back of her hand. Without any water, there was nothing she could do. As they cleared the wall, she saw daēvas fighting at the gates. And the flash of a young woman's face, her blade singing as she cut down one of the wolflike creatures....

"Nazafareen," Meb exclaimed. "I think I saw her down there."

"Where?"

"Go back around," she said in excitement. "She's behind us now."

His communication with the abbadax was too subtle for Meb to decipher, but Ragnhildur wheeled over the racing oval and sped back toward the Rock. Meb leaned forward in the saddle, intent on the gates of the inner wall to the Rock. Her heart lifted as she saw Darius fighting at Nazafareen's side.

"She's come! She's—"

Meb screamed as the abbadax rolled upside-down. A jet of smoking venom shot past inches from Meb's face. Culach let go of the reins to steady her, but some of it must have hit the harness because she could hear leather straps snapping, one by one.

Another jolting impact knocked her clean out of the saddle. Culach felt her go. His hand closed around hers as she dangled above the seething mass below.

"I've got you," he shouted.

Her heart hammered in her throat. Another strap broke away. The last ones groaned under his weight as Ragnhildur struggled to right herself. But the mount was overbalanced and weary from hours of flying. Meb knew that if she held on much longer, she'd drag them both down. And Culach was blind. If he was unseated, the monsters would kill him in an instant.

She tried to pry her fingers free, but his grip was like iron.

For when your other weapons are lost.

Meb fumbled for the pin Feng Mian had given her. It was stuck in a tangled knot. She yanked hard, her eyes watering as it pulled loose, along with several strands of curly hair.

"What are you doing?" he growled. "Meb, no, stop—"

She jabbed the pin into the back of Culach's hand. His fingers spasmed open.

Meb fell.

She missed the curtain wall by two paces. A mound of bodies, monsters and daēvas, lay piled against it, and that's what she landed on. Her breath rasped as she clawed her way free. She looked up and saw the drake that had attacked them fighting with Ragnhildur. Culach was screaming her name, but his voice receded as the battling pair soared higher into the smoky gloom.

Nothing stirred in her immediate vicinity, but Meb's skin crawled to be on the ground, alone. She looked up at the wall, thinking she could scale it like the Mer. It was sheer and high, without a single toehold. Meb hugged her arms around herself.

I just have to make it to the gatehouse. I *did* see Nazafareen. And it's not so far.

She shrank into the shadows, making herself small and inconspicuous.

And just like that, she was Meb the Mouse again. Meb the Skulker and Meb the Sneak.

Mud coated her feet as she slipped like a specter along the wall. By unspoken agreement, the two sides seemed to have taken a pause to regroup. She saw *things* scuttling around through the rain, heard the distant drumroll of hooves, but there was a lull in the unending ferocity of the last few hours.

She estimated that she was about halfway to the gatehouse. The charred husks of what looked like spiders were scattered in her path, their long, spindly legs black and twisted. A Praetorian lay on his back in their midst. He was all bloody and she thought he was dead, but when she was a few paces away his eyes opened, fixing on her.

"Meb," he croaked.

She couldn't breathe.

Nicodemus.

She hadn't recognized him because of the cloak and the burns on his face. But it was him, all right.

Run! Her mind shrieked even as her feet failed to move.

Run!

Run....

"Run, Meb," he growled, his gaze moving behind her. "For fuck's sake, run!"

She spun and came face to face with another Praetorian, this one very much uninjured. He was hulking and reeked of death.

"Marakai girl." Flames licked at his open palm. He smiled, the scars twisting his lips. "Taste it," he said, thrusting his hand toward her.

She turned away, fighting the suicidal urge to accept his offer, when she felt the flames vanish. Meb looked back in time to see a blade erupt from the center of his chest and twist viciously. He toppled to the ground. A tall Vatra woman with a sword stood over him.

"I killed your brother, too," she spat as his eyes dimmed. Then she saw Nicodemus. She fell to her knees beside him, her face tight with grief.

But his eyes never left Meb's face.

"I'm so sorry," he whispered hoarsely.

Her thoughts raced too fast to make sense of them. The spiders were charred. Nicodemus must have burned them. But he was dressed as a Praetorian, and he'd tricked her once before. Meb looked from one to the other, wary and confused. This woman saved her life. A Vatra saved her life.

"I have something for you," he whispered.

His fingers fell open, revealing her best knife. The one she'd bought with the black pearl.

"Take it," he said, his head falling back into the mud. "It's yours."

She hesitated, then darted forward and snatched it away.

"Please, forgive me, Meb." Blood bubbled from his lips. "I never meant...."

Meb looked up. Two drakes soared overhead, screaming their unearthly cries. A wind rose. The earth trembled.

The battle was starting again.

❧ 31 ❧

CALIGULA

Nazafareen staggered back, barely getting her sword up as a lizard darted forward. The blade glanced harmlessly off the creature's armored hide and she cursed herself. She knew better. She'd already killed two dozen of them. The eye was the only vulnerable place. But she was so tired, she could hardly think straight. It lunged for her again and Darius materialized out of nowhere, dispatching it with a clean thrust.

"You need a rest," he said — as if he weren't exhausted himself.

She shook her head and tried to lift *Nemesis*, her arm trembling. Darius gave her a flat look.

"You're no use like this," he said bluntly. "You'll just get killed. Go up to the gatehouse and sit down for five bloody minutes. Drink some water."

The fighting had raged for hours. If the first group of daēvas hadn't reached them quickly, they would have been overwhelmed within minutes. But now they had reinforcements — Danai, Valkirins, a few Maenads, though none she knew. Once she'd caught a glimpse of Victor, dealing death to anything that crossed his path. She shouted his name and he'd turned, an improbable smile flickering over his lips. She beckoned, but instead of joining her at the relative safety of the curtain wall, he strode away towards a bunch of Danai trapped on a rooftop. She hadn't seen him since.

The battle ebbed and flowed, drawing friends near and then dragging them away again. Kallisto, lightning shooting from her staff. Captain Mafuone, a broken mast in her hands, holding back a pulsating wyrm. Daníel on an abbadax with Herodotus, the scholar's beard whipping in the wind as they pursued a drake.

She'd seen Gaius, too, astride his white charger, but always in the distance, surrounded by his Praetorian Guard.

"Come." Darius pried the sword from her numb fingers and led her to the gatehouse. A lull had fallen over the muddy oval but she knew it was the false calm, before the storm broke in earnest. They made their way up the narrow, winding stairs to the top of the wall.

The rain still fell, though softly. Everywhere, fires burned, giving the city a hellish red glow. Their plan to gather the daëvas and retreat to the Rock had stalled. Twenty had made it. The rest were too far away. An ocean of death lay between them.

This is what the world will look like when the last of us fall, she thought numbly. Nothing but char and *anzillu*.

The knife in her heart twisted as she saw a full legion of Vatras, sixty or seventy, loping up one of the broad avenues. The rest of the Kiln had arrived.

Darius saw them at the same time. He twined bloody fingers with hers. Love bloomed in the bond, sweet and achingly sharp, with the knowledge that at least they would die together this time.

She turned to kiss him one last time when his grip tightened painfully around her hand. A dark silhouette dropped out of the western sky, just clearing the outer wall. Two drakes flew to intercept it and Valkirin riders swooped down in pursuit, buffeting the creatures with wind. They screamed in fury, rolling away.

A ship emerged from a thick column of smoke. Nazafareen's breath caught as it landed hard in the muddy racing oval, the air sack deflating. From every direction, the spawn of the Kiln closed in. A child's terrified face peered over the edge. Nazafareen caught a glimpse of Katsu as he snatched her back and lifted her into his arms.

"Javid's sister," she whispered, pressing her hand to her mouth. "No...."

And just like that, Darius was gone, leaping from the top of the wall. He landed in a crouch and raced for the ship, his blade gleaming red in the firelight. The Vatras had nearly reached it too, short spears clutched in their hands. Their faces were hard, though she didn't see the ritual burns of Gaius's personal guard.

Nazafareen had resigned herself to death hours ago. What terrified her was that Darius might leave her behind. That she would come to the shore of the Cold Sea too late. Even minutes could make a difference; who knew how it worked?

She couldn't drop down from the wall as he did, it was much too far. Nazafareen was about to turn for the stairs, to join him in his final sacrifice, when she saw two tall figures vault over the ship's rail.

Raven hair and silver.

They stood together like avenging angels and wherever their gaze fell, monsters died. Galen tore them limb from limb, Katrin tossed them high into the air and back over the walls. They wielded the power with brute force but not indiscriminately, and she understood that they could have obliterated everything within the city, but there were still pockets of resistance and the talismans were shielding them. Rhea was with them, tall and regal, her staff spinning as she leapt into the fray.

None saw the four Praetorians charge from the shadow of the curtain wall. They rode wyverns, the powerful haunches bunching and lengthening as they devoured the distance. Nazafareen screamed a warning, knowing it was too late. Lines of flame raced across the ground — and the four Praetorians burned, cloaks streaming out like fiery banners.

It's the Vatras from the Kiln, she realized in perfect astonishment, tracking the fire to its source. They're fighting on *our* side.

And in that moment, the tide of the battle irrevocably turned.

The Vatras spread out to hunt any surviving Praetorians. She saw Darius reach the wind ship and embrace Katsu, then turn to a small woman in a green dress who must be Leila Khorram-Din. Nazafareen remembered saying goodbye to the Stygian in Tjanjin, never really expecting their paths to cross again. Yet he had come to their aid. And he'd brought the talismans.

Nazafareen scrubbed a sooty hand through her hair, brushing away tears.

It was a bitter victory, every inch of ground paid for in blood. But a remnant of the clans endured and that was better than none.

Then she noticed a lone figure stumbling along the road to the Rock.

Gaius.

He'd lost his horse and must have climbed the wall, though she could tell from his stiff gait that he was injured. The four Praetorians he'd sent after the talismans must have been the last of his personal guard. His back was turned, but she recognized the ridges of scar tissue on the side of his head, pale against the bright red of his hair.

On the other side of the wall, Katrin and Galen strode deeper into the city, pursuing the retreating army. Small battles still raged through the lower streets and their Vatra allies followed the talismans at a safe distance, sending streams of flame against the drakes. The defenders who'd helped hold the gate now surrounded the wind ship, finishing off anything that moved.

Nothing stirred within the curtain wall. The monsters were dead.

All except one.

Nazafareen's hand crept to her ribs. She could still feel the blade sliding in.

You shouldn't have come here, Breaker.

It's a bad place to die.

She might be part Vatra, but the magic in her blood was gone. She couldn't even sense the Nexus. Darius's power shimmered in the corner of her eye, but it didn't belong to her.

I am a mortal, nothing more, she thought firmly. Gaius will tear me to shreds — if I'm lucky enough to get that close before he burns me. I must wait for the talismans. Let them finish him.

Gaius was nearly at the Rock now, heading straight for the open gates. Nazafareen frowned. The fortress would be a trap. He had to know that.

Why isn't he fleeing?

There could only be one reason.

Because he has some evil purpose. And by the time you get help, it will be too late.

Nazafareen tried to swallow, but fear dried her tongue.

If she hadn't glanced toward the Rock on her way down, she would never have seen him. Yet she stood at the perfect vantage point — the *only* vantage point — he'd be visible from.

It felt like fate and she didn't like it.

She wished she'd jumped from the wall with Darius. Then she'd be lying at the bottom with two broken legs and a legitimate excuse to stay there.

But she hadn't.

Destiny?

Or just shitty luck?

Nazafareen walled off her emotions lest Darius sense her turmoil and come to investigate. It was one thing to die together on the field of battle, another to drag him along with her own stupidity.

And part of her knew this was meant for her, and her alone.

"Okay, then," she muttered wearily, knowing that if she failed this time, there would be no coming back.

A TRAIL OF FRESH RED DROPLETS LED THROUGH THE UNGUARDED gates of the Rock. They were spaced several paces apart, which meant Gaius was still running. Nazafareen followed them, silent as a cat. The trail led deep into the fortress and then toward the upper levels. Some of the *anzillu* had gotten inside for she saw bodies sprawled in the intervening corridors. On the third tier, a lizard exploded from the shadows of an empty room. She drove her blade into its eye and through the brain. It died instantly.

She stalked down a long corridor and up a flight of stairs to the very top of the Rock. Nazafareen smelled roses and jasmine as she slipped through the half-open door to the Sky Garden. She crept along the path, following the crimson droplets. They were closer together now. Gaius had slowed to a walk.

Then she saw a cloaked figure. He stood at the balustrade, watching the final defeat of his army. In the skies beyond, a pair of drakes spiraled toward the ground in flames. The horns of the Danai blared a brazen victory cry. Abbadax and their Valkirin riders soared over the rooftops, hunting stray *anzillu*. The only gouts of fire she saw now were directed at the drakes.

Nazafareen took another cautious step forward, *Nemesis* gripped firmly in her left hand. Twenty paces separated her from Gaius. He was muttering to himself, though she couldn't make out the words.

Some instinct made her drop into a crouch behind a rosebush as he suddenly turned. She followed his gaze to the body of King Shahak. It was a husk, dessicated and fleshless as though it had lain in the desert sun for a month. A lacquered box sat on the ground next to his corpse. Gaius picked it up. He opened the box and stared at its contents for a long moment.

Rage and bitterness marked his face, but that's not what made her blood go cold. His eyes glinted with a kind of desperate cunning as he thrust a hand into the box and shoveled the contents into his mouth. At the first taste, Gaius made a wet choking sound. His eyes bulged and his throat worked as he forced it down. He swallowed another handful, and another, all the while emitting those repulsive gasps.

Nazafareen studied him from her hiding place. Gaius hunched over, the box falling from his hands. His shoulders heaved and he looked like he was struggling not to vomit.

She hoped there'd been poison in that box.

Really fucking nasty poison.

A sudden cramp in her calf forced her to shift slightly. Gaius's head snapped around. Glittering ash coated his lips. She turned to run but he was on her in a heartbeat, wrenching the sword away and putting the tip to her throat. He stared at her, blood oozing from the corners of his eyes like tears.

"You," he whispered.

His breath steamed. Blisters rose on her arms where his fingers gripped her. Nazafareen struggled wildly and Gaius threw her to the ground. She smelled smoke and realized the grass was smoldering around them. His foot lashed forward, cracking ribs. Nazafareen rolled away and pushed up to hands and knees, pain biting into her side with each breath. His eyes glowed like live coals.

"Little Breaker." He raised his hands to the heavens. "It's a miracle! You came back to play with me." Gaius chuckled. His tongue was black. "Would you like your sword? Go ahead. Take it."

He watched in amusement as she crawled over and curled her fingers around the hilt.

"Get up," he said.

She pushed to her feet, using the sword for leverage. Before she could lift the blade, his open palm slammed across her cheek, driving her down. A sonorous buzz filled her head. Nazafareen ignored it and found her feet again. The gesture was futile, but she refused to grovel.

My mother used to say I'd argue with a goat.

The memory came from nowhere, as they often did. She saw her mother's face, exasperated at whatever stupid thing she'd just done, but with a hint of pride. And at that moment, Nazafareen knew she'd rather die as herself than live as a stranger — even one with dreadful power.

She swayed, pretending a bout of dizziness, then lunged and managed a shallow slice across his forearm before another tremendous blow knocked her sideways. She lay on the ground, stunned. One eye wouldn't open, but the other saw boots approach. Flames licked at the grass around them. They wound up his legs like snakes. His foot drew back and she saw what was coming but couldn't stop it, or even roll out of the way. A half second later, the blow connected. Her face exploded in a white burst of agony. Nazafareen spit blood and tried to breathe through her mouth. Her nose wasn't working right. Nothing was working right.

"You're a tedious opponent," Gaius rasped, and his voice sounded different. Thicker. "I'm not even using magic. You're just too fucking slow."

He gave her another desultory kick. Her cracked ribs screamed. The boots strode a few paces away. He bent to pick up the sword. She thought he'd use it on her but he walked to the edge of the roof.

"Shahak was a fool," Gaius muttered. "The dust was never meant for mortals. It was meant for us. The power.... It's like nothing you can imagine, little Breaker. It sings in my blood."

Spell dust. So Gaius had added cannibalism to his litany of sins.

Did he even know what it was? Javid had told her the truth after supper one night when they were alone. He'd seemed ashamed.

Nazafareen lifted her head, her vision doubling. Gaius surveyed the city, hands propped on the balustrade. She could feel it now. Unseen lightning crackled around him as some unimaginable force gathered.

"I could lay waste to all I see," he said quietly. "Every last league from the Kiln to the darklands and beyond. Burn it all to ash." He laughed. "And here they are, gathered together celebrating their great victory. The talismans returned, but it will do them no good this time."

His body jerked in a sudden spasm. Nazafareen dug her toes into the earth and dragged herself forward, broken in a hundred places but still arguing with that goat.

Inch by inch, she drew closer to Gaius. Waves of darkness threatened to drag her under. She fought them with all she had.

You just have to tell 'em that you're more stubborn than they are, she'd explained to her bemused mother, young enough to take the words literally. When her brother Kian had found out, he'd teased her about it for weeks.

Nazafareen was two paces away when Gaius's tremors stopped as abruptly as they'd begun. He straightened. Through a hazy tunnel, Nazafareen glimpsed his face. Fire burned in his eyes, in the cavern of his mouth. He was something else now. Not a single Vatra. A thousand of them in one body.

Gaius raised a hand wreathed in dazzling white flame. It flowed down his arm, hot as the sun, bright as an exploding star.

Nazafareen knew he was about to unleash it. So she did the only thing that came to mind, grabbing his leg and sinking her teeth into it until she hit bone. The taste of his sour flesh made her gag, but she tore a chunk free and spit it out with the doomed ferocity of a rat nipping at a pack of terriers.

Gaius shrieked and seized her by the throat. Nazafareen scrabbled for a rock, a stick, anything at all, but all she felt was dry grass. Then her fingers brushed a smooth surface. The lacquered box. She smashed it down on his head, battering him until the wood splintered and the ridged burn scar on his brow split open.

Gaius roared with rage, throttling her harder. Darkness rushed in, devouring everything but his face, twisted into a grimace of hatred. She was about to close her eyes, unwilling to let Gaius be the last thing she saw on this earth — yet again — when Nazafareen caught a glint of gold, like the last sliver of sun before it sunk below the horizon. It winked at her through the gash in his head.

The serpent crown.

It had melted to his skull when he fled the fires of Pompeii. His leash to Farrumohr saved him from dying and eventually scar tissue covered it, but it had been there all along, welded to his head like a second skin.

Boiling blood dripped from the wound, spattering her face. Gaius's viselike grip trapped the scream in her throat.

"I am fire and scourge," he hissed. "I am the whirlwind. Do you see?"

Her stump caught him across the cheek and he winced, though the blow was glancing. In the depths of his burning gaze, she thought she saw a flicker of pain.

I hurt him.

The thought came sluggishly through her own agony.

How?

The crown was a talisman of pure malice. It couldn't be broken even if she had the power, Nazafareen sensed this truth in her bones. Just as with Farrumohr, her hatred would only make it stronger.

And Gaius was so much more now....

Kallisto's parting words suddenly rang in her mind, clear and strong.

You must be more than the huo mofa, or it will not serve you at the end.

As her vision failed and her body grew cold with shock, Nazafareen thought she understood.

I am a reflection of this world. *That* is the true nature of a Breaker. I am the light and the dark both. But I can choose.

I can choose.

And she knew why Gaius had flinched.

She still had her own talisman left — one forged in envy and fear but turned to a different purpose.

The antithesis of the foul thing the Viper had wrought.

Gaius loomed above, a blazing god. With her last ounce of strength, Nazafareen reached up and pressed the cuff to the crown, letting all that was pure and good in her flow through it. Her bond with Darius flared bright.

To fight as one. To live as one.

She'd spoken the oath all those years ago without an inkling of what the words truly meant. But she did now.

Gold met gold in a shower of sparks.

Gaius's eyes flew wide.

The puckered skin covering the crown cracked all the way open, revealing the scaled coils of the serpent. He let go of her and clutched his head. A keening sound tore from his mouth, high-pitched and sharp as a blade.

Nazafareen sucked air through her parched throat. She coughed and tasted blood, though the pain felt distant.

She watched as the metal softened, running down his face in a molten waterfall. It quivered with power, buzzing like a thousand maddened flies. There was a sudden crack, like a whip striking flesh, and a woman's scream, clear as a bell. Gaius howled, falling back against the wall. He looked down at the rivulets of gold with a strange expression, a mixture of astonishment and rage.

His gaze lifted and met hers. His eyes were a pale blue again. She saw his terrible realization.

"All this time," he whispered. "I never...."

Nazafareen's own eyes slid shut, then flickered open at a

hoarse cry. The magic that had sustained Gaius for a thousand years was fading. Bit by bit, his body fell away to ash, borne on the wind, until all that remained was a misshapen lump of gold.

She rolled to her side on the blackened grass. Her eyes closed again.

And that is how Darius found her minutes later, with a serene smile on her face.

32

REUNIONS

J avid surveyed the sitting room, trying not to retch.

Slime covered the floor. His calf burned where some of the worms had managed to crawl up into his boot and suction to his leg. They'd almost been overwhelmed when the tide suddenly ceased. Now silence reigned in the corridor outside.

"What's next?" he muttered to Marzban Khorram-Din, who slumped against the barricade. "Your guess is as good as mine."

"The Kiln must be an unpleasant place," the alchemist said thoughtfully. "It's rather amazing the Vatras managed to survive all this time. I wonder if these monsters were created during the Sundering, or evolved independently?"

"Does it matter?" Javid grunted.

"Well, certainly it does. If the former, the Vatras' grudge is easier to comprehend. It does seem a bit excessive to not only wall them off in a hellish desert but to unleash hordes of monstrous carnivores on them. If the latter, we must consider that the magic itself had unforeseen consequences which rippled outward through the centuries, though that might not be as far-fetched as it..."

Javid stopped listening. It was maddening not to know what

transpired outside. If the *anzillu* were inside the Rock, it didn't bode well for the daēva army. He had to face the truth. There might be no getting out.

Will we have the strength when the time comes? he wondered. To die together, a quick cut of the knife....

He flinched as a blow hit the door. But it was followed by a human voice.

"Javid?"

He wrenched the door open, his pulse hammering, to find Katsu, Leila and Bibi standing behind him. Katsu's fist was raised to pound on the door again and he nearly stumbled inside.

"Thank Babana," the Stygian exclaimed in a low voice.

And then they were all tangled up, laughing and crying in relief that they'd all found each other again. Even old Marzban wiped back a tear as Leila clasped his hands.

The commotion drew Javid's parents and sisters to peer tentatively from the back room. Bibi ran towards them and his da swept her into a fierce hug, twirling her around. His mother beamed and the girls chased the royal brothers back down the hall before they could eat the chickens.

"What happened out here?" Katsu asked, eyeing the remnants of worms on the floor.

Javid shook his head. It was a story for later. First, he needed to find out what had happened.

"We saw those horrors passing beneath the wind ship," Leila said as they all retreated to the bedroom.

"And we almost turned back to bring a warning," Bibi chimed in excitedly.

"But then we saw something strange in the distance, sand spewing high into the air, so we decided to investigate," Katsu finished. "We found the talismans and the Maenad with a large group of Vatras. The two sides looked like they were about to attack each other." He rubbed his beard stubble with a wry grin. "Personally, I would have headed the other way as fast as possible.

But Leila landed the ship right in their midst and calmly explained that Gaius was in Samarqand and anyone who didn't like him should come fight."

"I decided to trust what Nicodemus claimed," Leila said. "That they were not all like their mad king. It seems the Vatras had already realized they'd been abandoned and weren't very happy about it. Once they learned where Gaius had gone, they sprinted off ahead. The rest of us followed in the wind ship. I made as much haste as I could, though the Vatras were still faster." She paused. "Why did the beasts of the Kiln come to Saramqand?"

"Shahak summoned them," Javid said. "It was his final act of magic. The shock of it killed him, but not before he completed the spell."

He glanced at the royal brothers. Mahmonir had found some dried scraps of meat and they were wolfing them down. Javid's parents made the sign of the flame.

"So the battle is won?" his ma asked hopefully.

"The monsters have been driven back," Katsu agreed. "I fear the daēvas suffered heavy losses, but we saw survivors. All the Praetorians are dead."

"There was something just outside the door," Farima whispered, still fearful. "It was trying to get in to eat us."

Katsu met her gaze with steady reassurance. "I promise you, we saw nothing on the way in. If Gaius is dead, whatever sway he held must be gone as well. Those that were not destroyed have returned to the Kiln."

Javid stood. He suddenly couldn't bear to remain within these thick, sunless walls for another moment. "What do you say we leave this place and never return?"

No one argued. Farima and Bibi each grabbed a flapping chicken, thrusting the third at Marzban Khorram-Din, who accepted it with a grunt of ill humor. His ma glanced at the royal children, who snuffled at her feet.

"We can't leave them," she sighed. "The poor dears."

"I'll take care of them," Leila said quickly — a bit too quickly. Javid gave her a sharp look as she scooped up the beasts, wedging one under each arm. Motherly kindness was not Leila's strong suit. But he was too tired to bother challenging her intentions, and in all honesty, he was grateful to cede the responsibility to somebody else.

As they reached the door, Katsu took his hand, drawing him to a halt. "When I saw that army encircling the Rock, I thought...." He trailed off, his grey eyes searching Javid's. "I thought my heart would tear from my chest—"

Javid quieted him with his lips. He'd intended it to be a discreet but passionate "I love you too" kiss, but once they started, it was hard to stop. He could hear Bibi and Farima giggling like maniacs and his ma's sharp reprimand.

"Leave your brother alone," she snapped. "Javid deserves a little peace."

🐝 33 🐝

POMPEII

Artemis shone over the desert, so bright in her fullness even the sun couldn't steal her glory. The Traveling Moon would soon begin her year-long journey into the heavens, dwindling with each passing day until she was just a dot in the sky, but she was here now to bless the multitude below and herald the start of a new era.

A small, skinny figure walked to the center of the plaza and raised her brown arms. Water shot from a hundred fountains, washing away the dust of centuries. A cheer went up. Beneath the sightless marble gazes of the clans' ancestors, the feast began.

Danai, Valkirins, Marakai and Vatras sat together in the shade of two dozen pavilions for the first time in a thousand years, eating and drinking and celebrating the restoration of the Vatras' capital, Pompeii. The lords of air had swept the encroaching sands away. The lords of earth completed work on the half-finished towers. And now the masters of the sea had raised water from the depths of the desert so the glass city would live and breathe again.

"Happy birthday," Culach said, as Meb rejoined them at the table.

She smiled. "I get my first tattoo today," she said proudly. "From Captain Kasaika."

"And what will it be?" he asked.

"The Mother of Storms, of course." She took his hand and touched his fingers to her cheek. "Right here."

"You're brave." He chewed thoughtfully on a piece of bread. "I don't think I'd like a needle being jabbed into my face."

"No?" Mina asked. "I thought you might get my portrait inked on your chest. Then I can look at myself while I scold you."

He grinned. "Only if you get my...." He seemed to remember Meb was sitting there and groped for his cup of wine. "... sword on *your* chest."

"If you do, I'll disown you both," Galen said with a laugh. He turned to his father. "Quit hogging the fruit salad."

Victor plucked out an apricot and pushed the bowl toward him. "Here, O Mighty One. I saved you some canteloupe."

Galen scratched his head, suppressing a smile. "How long do you to plan to call me that?"

"I don't know." Victor frowned, but his eyes danced with amusement. "Katrin seems to like it."

"That doesn't surprise me."

They glanced over to the next table, where the Valkirin woman sat with Rhea and a few other Maenads. She said something and Daníel of Val Tourmaline laughed, gesturing with his knife.

Galen smiled as Rafel's hand landed on his thigh under the table.

"I think it suits you well," Rafel said, his face innocent.

Rafel's sister Ysabel sat to his left. Galen had found them both in the Pythia's cells with two trembling teenaged girls who'd wept with gratitude when he took the bracelets away and unlocked the collars. Ysabel hadn't spoken a word since her rescue, but her face was slowly coming to life again. Now she watched the daēva children race each other around the plaza with a wistful smile.

Kallisto and Herodotus sat with a group of Vatras, the scholar ignoring his plate as he leaned in to ask questions about the new city and the talismanic workshops planned for the eastern quarter. Megaera crouched on the flagstones, playing some sort of game involving daggers with Mithre and Keyln. The Maenads were the first mortals ever to attend the Feast of Artemis, but they'd earned a place. Half the Praetorians had fallen to their staffs and they'd kept the others from incinerating the last pockets of resistance. Without them, the talismans might have arrived to find no one left alive.

Yet there were missing faces. Analee Suchy, who had died drawing too much earth when she pulled a building down on the *anzillu*. Frida of Val Tourmaline. Ramades and Ahmose of the Five. Many others.

The wine flowed and soon the singing began, first among the Valkirins and then the Danai.

"That pickled eel isn't sitting right," Nazafareen muttered. "I knew I shouldn't have eaten it."

Darius winced. "I warned you. Now we *both* get to suffer."

"Maybe Meb will heal me."

He laughed. "They're leaving soon, my love. If you plan to beg for mercy, best do it now."

She walked over to their table and slid into a chair. In truth, she felt distinctly odd.

"Culach Kafsnjór," she said in a husky voice. "We meet again."

His head turned toward her. "Nazafareen! Where have you been hiding?"

"Beneath a platter of pickled eels."

"Ouch."

"I thought they'd be disgusting, but then I couldn't stop eating them." She cast a hopeful glance at Meb, but the girl was talking animatedly with Stefán of Val Altair — of all people. He had some nerve to show up, she thought, acting as if nothing had happened.

Then again, if he'd stayed away, it might imply he held a grudge.

Nazafareen sighed. She was weary of daēva politics.

"I thought you might want the sword back," she said to Culach. "It did belong to your mother."

He shook his head. "It's yours now. My only wish is that you never have to use it again."

"Me, too." She paused. "Where will you go, now that Val Moraine....?"

Mina rested her head on his shoulder. "We leave with the Marakai," she said.

Nazafareen raised her eyebrows. "Truly? I will miss you."

She looked at the Vatras. They were no longer so thin and ragged, but not all wished to stay in Pompeii. The desert wasn't exactly the Kiln anymore, but it had been their prison and some wished to find a new homeland, so Meb had offered to send some of the Marakai ships across the White Sea to discover what lay on the other side.

There had been some discussion of whether the talismans should try to reverse the Sundering and free the sun to move across the sky again, but in the end, everyone agreed it was too risky and could result in a cataclysm — besides which, they were accustomed to the current arrangement and didn't particularly want to change it.

"And Katrin?"

"She will remain at Val Tourmaline. She's pledged to Daníel now." Culach frowned. "I am glad she chose his holdfast. He won't try to abuse her power."

"Would Stefán?"

Culach raised his cup in a toast. "Happily, we'll never know. To old friends and new beginnings!"

They all rose to their feet. Nazafareen lifted the cup to her lips, but the smell of the wine made her stomach roil. "Excuse me," she muttered, setting the cup down and pushing away from the table.

Darius looked concerned and she gave him a sickly smile.

"I just need a little air."

"I'll come with you —"

"Not for this," she replied grimly, marching over to some newly planted bushes ringing the plaza and emptying her stomach.

"Gah," she whispered, wiping her mouth with a sleeve. "They should call that dish Khaf-Hor's Revenge."

She stood up and saw a figure standing alone by a fountain, his back to the festivities as he gazed out at the western desert. Naza-fareen looked over at Darius, who watched her with a worried frown, and waved reassuringly. Victor, bless him, laid a hand on his son's arm and drew him into conversation. She straightened her tunic and walked to the fountain.

"Nicodemus."

He turned. When Meb had saved his life, she'd also healed the worst of the burns on his face, though the right side still looked stiff.

"You should join us," she said.

It was the first time she'd seen him since she learned what he had done. At first, she'd been furious. But since that day on the roof with Gaius, she'd resolved to be a better person. Which meant forgiving him for denying her the satisfaction of dancing naked with the Pythia's head on a pike.

"I thought you'd hate me," he said quietly.

The shadowtongue cloak was gone. He wore a simple white shirt with the sleeves rolled up and blue breeches tucked into low boots. The sun gilded his copper hair, though his eyes were dark as rainclouds.

"I did," she admitted. "For a while. But I think everything happened the way it did for a reason. Don't you?"

"Yes." He paused. "But mine is selfish. If I hadn't gone back to the Kiln, Aelia and Atticus would still be there. With *him*." Nicodemus sighed. "Yet if we'd left the wards alone, Gaius might never have escaped. A lot of people died because of it."

"No, I think he would have eventually. Just as you said."

She remembered the army of restless dead Farrumohr was building. His plans to seize the Lady's tower and gain control of the Nexus.

"It doesn't matter now," Nazafareen said. "We're still here and Gaius isn't."

Nicodemus broke into a sudden smile. "I have a gift for you." His tanned skin flushed. "It was meant to be a peace offering. Atticus and I made it together. We're learning the art of the ancient adepts." He fished into his pocket and drew out a silver chain with a disc the size of a coin.

Nazafareen examined it, surprised and touched. One side bore an image of the moon, the other of the sun.

"It's a talisman. As long as you wear it, you'll never fall ill."

She laughed. "I wish I'd run into you ten minutes ago. But thank you, Nicodemus. It's a precious gift." Nazafareen grinned at him. "I'm part Vatra, you know. Your people gave me the Breaker's blood."

His brows lifted. "I never imagined.... Well, then you could stay here if you like. Aelia and I took one of the empty houses. There are plenty to choose from. The Valkirins swept them clean of the poor souls who dwelled here before." His face darkened. "There will be no more looting of the dead. Their remains have rejoined the desert sands."

Nazafareen studied the forest of sparkling glass towers. It was beautiful, but not to her taste.

"That is a kind offer," she said. "I will think on it. But I'm glad *you're* staying."

"I wish more of us were." Nicodemus smiled, his gaze straying to the pavilions. "Come, I'll walk you back before Darius gets jealous."

Nazafareen laughed. "He's not the type." She noticed a tall, red-haired woman staring at them intently. "Aelia, on the other hand...."

Artemis beamed down on them as they ambled across the plaza, mutual loathing having produced the happy result of a true friendship.

A STIFF BREEZE FROM THE WHITE SEA RUFFLED CULACH'S HAIR as he dismounted from Ragnhildur. It blew the last remnants of wine from his head. He'd already said goodbye to Daníel and Den, Katrin and Victor and Nazafareen. Pompeii lay twenty leagues from the sea and the Vatras who were leaving waited aboard six Marakai ships anchored at a safe distance off the coast. The cliffs were high here and jagged reefs lurked beneath the waves.

"Culach Kafsnjór." Fingers tugged at his coat. "I came to see you off."

"Meb." He bent down and laid a hand on her shoulder. "Thank you."

"For what?" she sounded baffled.

"Making me brave again."

"You always were." She kissed his beard-roughened cheek. "Come back and visit sometime, okay?" Her voice sounded small and sad.

Culach's throat tightened. "I will. Be a good ruler."

She laughed. "If I'm not, I don't 'spose I'll last long." He heard her step back. "Fare well, Culach Kafsnjór."

He felt the warmth of the sun on his face as he climbed back into the saddle. "Fare well, Queen Mebetimmunedjem."

Mina waited on Ragnhildur. She slid her arms around his waist, careful not to jostle the three eggs tucked into his coat. Like a few of the daēvas, Ragnhildur had found a mate at the Feast of Artemis and laid a clutch of eggs. She'd hissed when

Mina pointed them out, but finally allowed Culach to take them and keep them warm against his body

Abbadax gestated in the shell for forty-one days. By that time, he hoped they'd be on the other side of the White Sea. If not ... well, the ships would just have to deal with the hatchlings until they could fly on their own.

Culach picked up the reins. In his mind's eye, he saw the sea as it was that night long ago when he and Ragnhildur flew north as far as she could go. The waves far below, tipped with spindrift and moonlight. A million stars strewn across the sky. The sense of a world wide open and bursting with possibility.

"This time, we won't turn back, my darling," he whispered in her ear. "This time, we'll find out what lies on the other side."

Ragnhildur dove from the cliff, the air catching her wings, and then they were gone.

🝳 34 🝳

MERCHANT PRINCE

Sunlight poured through six enormous windows, casting yellow rectangles across a long table piled with tools and various bits of machinery whose purpose Javid could only guess at. Marzban Khorram-Din sat ensconced in a comfortable chair with Bibi perched on a low stool at his elbow. They were going over a parchment covered with complex mathematical symbols. Bibi turned out to have a good head for such things, and she followed his murmured explanation with bright, curious eyes.

It was the first free time Javid had found to visit their workspace in a new building near the Rock. The days had been a flurry of activity as Samarqand's populace slowly trickled back into the city. The dead *anzillu* had been carted away and burned. A new monument rose in the racing oval, dedicated to the daēvas who had turned them back. It was a simple iron spire visible from all directions to travelers approaching the gates, forged from the swords and arrows of the fallen. People left offerings there, or simply stopped to touch it and whisper a quiet prayer.

Javid made sure the Guild knew what Shahak had done — and that Katsu was the one who'd brought the talismans back to save the city. They granted the Stygian a full license to conduct trade throughout Solis, a privilege that usually took a decade or more, and much greasing of palms.

The hull of the *Shenfeng* had been damaged beyond repair, but once the Abicari was up and running again, Katsu had commissioned another ship, one even larger and grander. They'd both been delighted to find Savah Sayuzdri still holding court in the main hangar, bellowing orders at his carpenters and limping through the yard like a grizzled old lion defending his pride. He'd been one of the only mortals to hold out during the battle, wielding a heavy mallet against any *anzillu* that came near his wind ships.

Javid's parents were back in their old house near the Abicari. The sodden carpets had to be replaced, and all the furniture on the first floor, but his ma was already planting tomatoes in the garden.

In the markets and inns and shops and brothels, people were picking up the pieces. Hammers rang through the city and the forges of the blacksmiths' quarter belched smoke at all hours of the day.

With all the rebuilding and trade flowing with Delphi again, they had more contracts than they knew what to do with. Katsu had already commissioned two more ships. But as much as he liked nice clothes and fine food, Javid would have been happy sleeping in the streets as long as the handsome Stygian was there to make him laugh.

He'd always believed living as a man would require giving up any hopes of intimacy. His birth identity was a secret to be protected at all costs. But Katsu had opened doors he thought forever closed.

Javid quietly used some of his new wealth to help the poorest families resettle in Bildaar, that infamous slum where his old boss got a start running gangs of slag-pickers. In some strange way, he still felt he owed Izad Asabana a debt.

After the new king was crowned, he'd offered Asabana's

estates on the Zaravshan River to Javid. They were a prime piece of land and worth a fortune, but Javid politely declined. If he'd learned one lesson, it was that the higher you climbed, the harder you fell. He wanted nothing to do with royalty. No, he was quite content to share a snug cabin on the *Shenfeng II* with Katsu.

Some of the nobles had grumbled when the young king gave him an official pardon for helping Shahak gain the throne — but after all, Javid had saved the boy's life at the end.

"You never told me how you managed it," he said to Leila, who fixed a sphere to a metal axis and gave it an experimental spin. "I thought the transformative powers of spell dust could only be achieved if you ingested it directly."

She gave him a small smile.

Javid closed his eyes, flashes of Shahak's final days playing like a nightmare in his head.

"Please tell me you didn't."

She tested one of the nozzles projecting from the sphere and made a small adjustment, blowing away tendrils of hair escaping from her braid. "There was no other way. If the line of Cambyses ended, the surviving nobles would have fallen on the throne like a pack of wolves and like as not, we'd have a civil war on our hands. It had to be done."

"You truly are insane," he said flatly.

She tried on a sympathetic tone. "Come, Javid. Those poor children. How could I leave them like that?"

Javid remembered the older boy — now king — when he'd first seen him in the throne room. He'd shown courage in the face of his elder's brother's madness and Javid had privately regretted supporting Shahak.

He crossed his arms with a sigh. "I know you. You just wanted to see what it was like."

Leila laughed. "Shahak had a weak will. Inhaling the dust was an interesting experience, I'll grant, but not one I'd care to repeat.

Besides which, it's banned now. I couldn't get any even if I wanted to."

"Thank the Holy Father for that."

She glanced at him and stood, pressing her palms to the small of her back.

"What will it do?" he asked, nodding at the contraption she'd been assembling.

"Boiling water will shoot steam from the nozzles and make the sphere spin."

"And?"

"That's it."

He raised his eyebrows. "And the king is paying for this?"

"Unlike you, flyboy, he has vision. Someday, you will pilot a ship powered by steam. But I must start small."

"So you are no longer an alchemist," he said teasingly. "What do I call you then?"

"I am ... a natural philosopher," she murmured, stooping back to her sphere. "And how are Nazafareen and Darius? Is she quite recovered?"

The extent of her injuries had been devastating. Shattered bones, massive blood loss. If not for the quick intervention of the Marakai healers....

"She's well. Katsu and I plan to visit them soon." Javid smiled. "She says they're having a baby."

🔆 35 🔆

THE COMPACT

Nazafareen kicked her feet up and gazed through the window at the harbor of Susa. The town hugged the cliffs overlooking the cobalt waters of the Austral Ocean and the smell of the sea filled all the rooms of the narrow three-story house. Upstairs, she heard the rasp of a saw. Gulls wheeled and squabbled along the Corniche, white wings flashing in the sun.

They'd chosen to live in Solis for the bond, but she was glad for the light and warmth, too.

The house they bought was whitewashed with bright blue shutters and a red tile roof. Darius used the top floor for his workshop. The living quarters occupied the second, and the first was given over to their business, which was selling wooden figurines of the Prophet Zarathustra. Nazafareen came up with the idea and when Darius finished laughing, he'd gone out to the market and returned with a cartload of new tools and some fine boles of ash and chestnut. She sensed fine trickles of earth power flowing through the bond. An hour later, he'd produced his first faravahar, which he presented to her with a flourish.

Even with the infirmity that withered his left arm, Darius's work was so fine that soon he had more orders than he could fill and took on one of Javid's nephews as his apprentice, a gentle boy named Parizad. Nazafareen enjoyed chatting with the customers and arranging his carvings to their best advantage. In quiet moments, she practiced her letters, with the goal of someday reading Herodotus's multi-volume history of the world.

Sometimes, as she sat and watched the sea, she thought wistfully about Culach and Mina and wondered what sort of adventures they were having. When this restlessness came, she'd remind herself that she'd had enough of that sort of thing. She loved Darius, she loved Susa and their sun-filled house, and she had her hands full getting ready for the baby.

Javid and Katsu visited often, as they were frequently in town for business. They knew all the juicy gossip and reported that Delphi's Ecclesia had been restored after a mob stormed the Tyrant Basileus's palace and threw him in the dungeons. The Maenads rebuilt their temple — and were delighted when their pet snake returned to nest in the bull's head altar. A new Oracle had been chosen by the assembly, but this one was a nice middle-aged lady who stuck with giving people advice.

And so the days passed in peaceful harmony, neither of them mentioning Darius's promise to the Drowned Lady that he would return. Nazafareen hoped she might forget. Farrumohr was banished and Gaius dead. The clans hadn't started any new wars with each other yet. Surely their debt was paid.

Then they started getting visitors.

Galen came first, bearing a beautiful cradle made from silver birch. He chatted for a while about the goings-on at House Dessarian and then his face grew solemn.

"She wants to see you," he said.

Darius blinked. "Does she?" he said faintly, not needing to ask *who*.

"'Fraid so. Just passing it on."

Galen stayed the night and they spoke of it no more,

promising to come visit the forest after his niece or nephew was born.

A week later, Katrin arrived. She brought a tiny ruby bracelet and the same message.

"Good luck," she whispered in Nazafareen's ear when she departed, giving them both a warm hug.

When Meb showed up two days after that, Nazafareen nearly slammed the door in her face, queen of the Marakai or not. But Meb held out a striped grey kitten and she softened.

"Come on in," she said with a sigh. "Let me guess. The Lady sent you."

Meb gazed back with her usual deadpan expression. "I really think you'd better go see her, Nazafareen. But I didn't come just for that. The Mother of Storms birthed a litter a few weeks ago and I thought the baby might want to have one."

Nazafareen regarded the kitten warily. "Is it safe?"

Meb shrugged. "You know cats. They're unpredictable."

The kitten yawned. Nazafareen fetched a saucer of milk. The kitten dipped a paw into it, growling, then scampered away to do battle with an imaginary foe.

"I can't stay long," Meb said regretfully. "Ship's waiting. Oh, but I also have this for you." She gave Nazafareen a pink spiral shell. "It's a Talisman of Travelling that will bring you straight to the tower. Now you don't even have to find a gate."

So much for the Lady forgetting about them, Nazafareen thought.

"What if it does something weird to the baby to take it behind the veil?" she asked anxiously.

"It won't," Meb said. "I already asked her that."

She sat down for a cup of chai and showed off her new tattoos. Anuketmatma graced one high cheekbone, the eel coiled around her wrist, a Nahresi reared up on one shoulder, faceless Sat-bu waved her tentacles from the other, and Hammu the carp flicked

its tail across her slender back. The artist had used special iridescent ink to make the blue-green scales glitter.

"One for each clan," she said.

Meb had grown since they last saw each other. She would be a
beautiful woman someday, like Tijah — who, Nazafareen realized,
probably had Marakai blood.

"They suit you," she said with a smile.

She laid a hand on her belly as she watched Meb slink back
down to the harbor.

When Darius returned from the market laden with baskets of
her favorite foods, he saw her face and stopped in the doorway.

"Let's just get it over with," she said.

He laid the baskets down and wrapped his good arm around
her, resting his chin on the top of her head.

"Tomorrow," he said.

They were together that night for the first time since her belly
had swollen, and she fell asleep to the sound of his heart beating
against her ear.

THE TALISMAN REQUIRED ONLY A POOL OF LIQUID TO CREATE A
passage to the Dominion — water, wine, blood, any of these
things would do. So the next day, they waded into the goldfish
pond in the back garden. Normally, it was only a pace deep, but
with the shell in her fist, the pond became a temporary gate much
like the fountain outside Apollo's temple at Delphi.

"Don't worry, we'll be able to breathe," Darius said as the
tepid water reached their chests.

"I know."

Nazafareen took a final look at the house. The kitten watched
them in fascination from the windowsill. Then she slipped
beneath the surface.

She remembered the sensation of featureless gloom, like walking along the bottom of the sea. A forest of tall grey weeds swayed in an invisible current. They followed an upward slope and emerged from another quiet pond in the woods of the Dominion. A short distance away, the Lady's octagonal tower soared above the trees.

"Ready?" he asked.

"No."

"Me neither."

Nazafareen waddled toward the tower. They found the archway on the back side and Darius led her down a long corridor with many closed doors. He counted them as they walked and stopped at the one hundred and sixth door.

"I think this is the one," he said. "The Chamber of Souls."

"Whether it is or not, I need to sit down," she replied. "My feet are bloody killing me."

He rubbed her back with a sympathetic look. Of course, he already knew that.

She pushed open the door.

A cavernous chamber filled with flickering lights waited on the other side. A woman strode among them, stooping here and there to more closely examine one of the sparks. Water trickled from her thin slash of a mouth. Her hair slithered down her back like strands of seaweed.

"You're late," she said, turning to regard them.

Nazafareen gripped Darius's hand tighter when she saw that bone-white face.

"Well, we're here now," she said. "As you commanded, Lady."

The Lady beckoned and they followed her through the chamber, ghostly rivers and lakes and mountains shimmering at their feet, to another door and another chamber, this one smaller and lit by warm yellow crystals.

Nazafareen sat on a couch, sighing as the weight eased. The child inside her kicked as if sensing her disquiet. Darius sat rigidly, his eyes fixed on the mistress of the Dominion.

"I like you two," the Lady said, reclining on another long couch and helping herself to a bowl of grapes. "You did well."

They waited in silence.

"I've decided that when the talismans die, the power will die with them," she confided. "It's too much for any one person to handle. Frankly, it was a close thing with Katrin and Galen, although Meb had more sense." The Lady smiled. "She's a scrappy little kid, isn't she?"

"What do you want?" Darius asked bluntly.

"Oh my, yes," the Lady mused. "What do I want?"

Nazafareen laid a protective hand over her belly. "You can't have my baby."

The Lady stared at her for a long moment. "Please. I have absolutely no interest in your baby, or any other." She ate a grape. "It's something else."

"I already paid your price."

"No, you broke even," the Lady said patiently. "You got something and you lost something. But you still owe me. You didn't bring Farrumohr back like you promised."

"You tricked us," Darius growled. "You knew all along who Nazafareen was. You knew she had to die to defeat Farrumohr, and then come back to defeat Gaius. There was no other way."

The Lady made a face. "Don't be melodramatic. I didn't trick you."

"You knew she'd have to use her breaking power in the Abyss and that it might destroy her utterly. Isn't that enough?"

"I'm afraid it's not. There's a compact. I won't go into the details, they don't concern you, but the bottom line is that the dead don't come back. Not ever. For any reason. Obviously, I broke it." She smiled. "But I found a little wiggle room."

"Here it comes," Nazafareen muttered.

"You spend half the year with me. I need a couple of swords around here." She waved a hand. "Part-time mercenary work. Right up your alley."

"You already have the Shepherds," Darius said flatly.

"And they're quite dedicated. But not the brightest, if you get my drift. I need someone to round up the souls who try to linger. Most of them get caught, but a few are clever enough to elude my hounds." She shot a look at Nazafareen. "You know a little something about that, don't you?"

Nazafareen scowled.

"Half the year?" Darius demanded incredulously.

"You can live here. I have plenty of room. Nabu makes a very nice lamb rutibaya." She arched an eyebrow enticingly. "It has pistachios."

Nazafareen and Darius looked at each other. "But I'm having a baby," she said faintly.

The Lady gave her a warm smile. "Congratulations." The smile faded. "Or you can break your promise and go back to being dead. Take your pick."

"Wait!" Darius pleaded. "We have to think about it."

The Lady stood and took Nazafareen's hand, soaking the end of her sleeve. "You can have your six months in the world first. Come back to me after the child is born."

Darius opened his mouth to argue, but Nazafareen touched his knee.

"We'll talk about it later," she said softly.

The Lady rose. "Well, thanks for stopping by. Good luck with...." Her long fingers fluttered at Nazafareen's enormous belly. "However that works."

They left.

"She's insane," Darius stormed as they strode through the corridors. "How can we leave our child for half the year? What if we don't come back?"

Nazafareen had already considered this. "The Maenads will take her."

He stopped, his eyes suddenly soft. "You know it's a *she*?"

"No, but I'll confess, I'd like a daughter." She paused. "Did you hope for a son?"

He smiled, though she knew he was still furious. "A daughter, actually. But I'll be happy with either one."

Nazafareen thought of *Nemesis*. She kept the sword clean and sharp, but only when Darius wasn't around. She thought of her own restlessness, and the submerged fear that it would grow when she had nothing to do but dust figurines and change diapers.

"Well, I do like a nice lamb rutibaya," she murmured as they waded into the pond.

SHE HAD THE BABY A MONTH LATER, A HEALTHY, RED-FACED creature. They named the child Delilah. She'd inherited her grandmother's black hair, her father's blue eyes, and Nazafareen's mulishness. In short, she was perfect.

When she was five months old, they dutifully brought Delilah and her cat to the Temple of the Moria Tree and entered the Lady's service. They never encountered Farrumohr again, but there were plenty of restless dead creeping about and they managed to drag a fair number of them to the Shepherds waiting at the boats. Once they ran into Tijah and Achaemenes and made camp together, sharing stories and laughter as the Shepherds lolled on the ground. Nazafareen liked him very much. She thought Tijah did too, though they couldn't be more different, Achaemenes quiet and reserved, and Tijah, well ... *Tijah*.

When the six months expired, they returned to the temple, picked up the baby and the cat and went home to Susa. Parizad had kept the business running in their absence, and all things considered, it went fairly well, though Nazafareen cried a bit when Delilah failed to recognize either of them. That was the hardest year.

Time passed and Delilah grew older. Thanks to the gift from Nicodemus, she never knew a day of sickness. The routine became well-established and Delilah looked forward to her season with the staff-wielding aunties because they all spoiled her horribly. When she turned six, the pain of parting became too great and Nazafareen decided enough was enough, bringing her along to the Lady's Tower. Delilah was perfectly safe there, though at first the Lady herself was less than enthusiastic about having a headstrong young person running wild through the halls. But Delilah charmed the Lady into telling her stories, and Nabu-bal-idinna into teaching her the art of cartography and baking her favorite cookies.

To Nazafareen's great relief, the child showed no sign of having special powers, although the devil only knew what might happen when she was a teenager.

❧ 36 ❧

THE BEGINNING

Rain pattered against the windows, the third day of it in a row. Business at the shop was so slow, Papa had decided to close early. They'd played endless games of Senet and hide-and-seek while Mama sharpened her sword. Delilah wanted to go down to the harbor and watch for Marakai ships, but Papa said it was too wet out.

Now she rolled to her back on the carpet, dark hair spreading out like a fan.

"I'm bored," she declared.

"Then go clean your room," Mama said. "It looks like a goat pen."

"Goats are neater," Papa remarked, his blue eyes twinkling.

Delilah scowled. Mama had a way of turning everything around so you did what she wanted.

"I'll do it later. I want to hear how you met Papa."

Her parents glanced at each other in that secret way they had.

"I already told you, mouseling," Mama said with a slight frown, as she wiped an oiled cloth down the blade. "A hundred times."

Mama loved her fiercely, although she wasn't always patient.

Papa was the patient one. He drew Delilah into his lap and tickled her ribs. But she wouldn't be deflected this time. It was just the right sort of afternoon for one of Mama's tales, the sky grey and heavy, the house snug and warm.

"I want the whole story this time," Delilah said. "I want the parts you leave out!"

Mama's eyes narrowed. "How do you know I leave anything out?"

"Because you rub the place your hand used to be and get all dreamy-looking."

Papa smiled. "You're too clever for your own good." He leaned over and kissed Mama on the forehead. "I think she's old enough, don't you?"

Mama set the sword aside. Her gaze softened and Delilah could see she was gathering the threads of memory. "Perhaps." She studied her daughter with a grave expression. "It has scary parts. In fact, I think I'd better skip ahead—"

"No! Start at the beginning," Delilah insisted.

Mama reached over and joined Papa in tickling her ribs, her toes, under her chin. Delilah squirmed and snorted. "The very beginning, eh?" She poked a finger behind her knee and wiggled it. "The very, very beginning?"

"Yes," she said, breathless.

Mama thought for a moment. "Very well, mouseling. Our story starts in the Khusk Range, the mountains of my childhood. We were nomads and had to move from place to place, following the changing seasons, or our animals would starve and the people with them. It was a hard winter that year. The snows came early. I wasn't much older than you are now."

Delilah settled back against Papa's chest, her imagination conjuring the ice-clad peaks, as Mama began to speak in her special story-telling voice, low and dramatic.

"The wind whistled through the high passes as we picked our way up the trail...."

CHARACTERS IN THE SERIES

Mortals

ARCHON BASILEUS. The head of civic religious arrangements in Delphi.

ARCHON EPONYMOS. The chief magistrate of Delphi.

HERODOTUS. A Greek scholar and former curator of the Great Library of Delphi.

IZAD ASABANA. A wealthy merchant and dealer in spell dust.

JAVID. A wind ship pilot from the Persian city of Samarqand.

KATSU. A Stygian thief-catcher.

KORINNA. An acolyte at the Temple of Delphi.

LEILA KHORRAM-DIN. Marzban's daughter.

MARZBAN KHORRAM-DIN. Asabana's alchemist.

NABU-BAL-IDINNA. An eccentric alchemist of the golden age of Samarqand who claimed to have traveled in the Dominion and met the Drowned Lady.

NAZAFAREEN. A wielder of negatory magic.

PRINCESS PINGYANG. Daughter of the emperor of Tjanjin. Her maidservant is FENG MIAN.

THE POLEMARCH. The commander of Delphi's armed forces.

PRINCE SHAHAK. Heir to the crown of Samarqand.

SAVAH SAYUZHDRI. Javid's old boss at the Merchants' Guild.

THENA. An acolyte at the Temple of Delphi.

Daēvas

Avas Danai (Children of Earth)

DARIUS. A daēva of House Dessarian who was born in the Empire on the other side of the gates.

DELILAH. Victor's wife and Darius's mother.

GALEN. Victor's son with Mina. Half-brother to Darius.

MITHRE. Victor's second in command.

MINA. A Danai hostage at Val Moraine.

RAFEL/NIKIAS. A daēva who was kidnapped by the Pythia.

TETHYS. Victor's mother, head of House Dessarian and one of the Matrium.

VICTOR. Darius's father.

Avas Valkirins (Children of Air)

CULACH. Once the heir to Val Moraine, he was blinded and lost his power.

DANÍEL/DEMETRIOS. Halldóra's grandson and heir, he was abducted and brainwashed by the Pythia.

EIRIK. Culach's father and the former lord of Val Moraine.

ELLARD. Galen's friend. Raised as a hostage at House Dessarian in exchange for Mina.

FRIDA: Halldóra's second in command.

GERDA. Culach's great-great-grandmother.

HALLDÓRA. Mistress of Val Tourmaline.

KATRIN. Culach's former lover.

PETUR. Culach's best friend. He tried to kill Nazafareen and was killed by Galen.

RUNAR. Lord of Val Petros.

STEFÁN. Lord of Val Altair.

SOFIA: One of Halldóra's riders.

Avas Marakai (Children of Water)

AHMOSE. Leader of the Nyx fleet.

HATSHEPSUT. Leader of the Khepresh fleet.

KASAIKA. Captain of the *Asperta*. Selk Marakai.

MAFUONE. Captain of the *Chione*. Sheut Marakai.

MEBETIMMUNEDJEM, a.k.a. Meb the Mouse. A 12-year-old orphan of the Selk who does grunt work on the *Asperta*.

NIMLOT. Leader of the Jengu fleet.

QENNA. Leader of the Sheut fleet.

RADAMES. Leader of the Selk fleet.

SAKHET-RA-KATME. The oldest Marakai and one of the original talismans. A distant ancestor of Meb.

Avas Vatras (Children of Fire)

AELIA. One of Gaius's wives.

ATTICUS. Nicodemus's younger brother.

DOMITIA, a.k.a. The Pythia, a.k.a. the Oracle of Delphi. Gaius's daughter.

FARRUMOHR, a.k.a. the Viper. Gaius's advisor. Haunts Culach's dreams.

GAIUS JULIUS CAESAR AUGUSTUS, a.k.a CALIGULA. Former king of the Vatras.

ROMULUS AND REMUS. Two of Gaius's Praetorians.

NICODEMUS. A survivor of the Kiln.

Maenads

KALLISTO. Head of the Cult of Dionysus, she seeks to protect the talismans from harm. Her followers are RHEA, CHARIS, CYRENE and MEGAERA. Two others, twins named ALCIPPE and ADEIA, were killed by the Pythia's soldiers.

GLOSSARY

Abbadax. Winged creatures used as mounts by the Valkirins. Intelligent and vicious, they have scaled bodies and razor-sharp feathers to slash opponents during aerial combat.

Adyton. Innermost chamber of the Temple of Apollo, where the Pythia issues prophecies and receives supplicants.

Anuketmatma. Worshipped by the Selk Marakai as the spirit of storms, she takes the form of a small grey cat with dark stripes. The Selk carry her on their ships and lull her with milk and honey.

Avas Danai. Children of Earth, known for their dark hair and eyes and strength in earth power. The Avas Danai are divided into seven Houses located in the Great Forest of Nocturne. Their primary trade commodity is wood. Qualities of earth: Grounded, solid, practical, stubborn, literal, loyal.

Avas Marakai. Children of Water. Dark-skinned and curly-haired, they are the seafaring daēvas. They make their home in the Isles of the Marakai and act as middlemen between the mortals and other daēva clans. Their wealth derives from the Hin, equal to one-tenth of the goods they transport. No one else has the skill to navigate the Austral Ocean or the White Sea, so they enjoy a monopoly on sea trade and travel. Qualities of water: Easygoing, free, adventurous, cheerful, cunning, industrious.

Avas Valkirins. Children of Air. Pale-skinned and silver-haired, they live in stone holdfasts in the mountains of Nocturne. The Valkirin Range is the source of all metal and gemstones in the world. Qualities of air: Quick to anger, proud, changeable, passionate, ruthless, rowdy, restless.

Avas Vatras. Children of Fire. Red-haired and light-eyed. No one has seen the Avas Vatras for a thousand years, since they tried to burn the world and were imprisoned in the Kiln. The only clan with the ability to forge talismans. Qualities of fire: Creative, ambitious, generous, destructive, curious, risk-taking.

Bond. The connection between a linked pair of talismans that allows a human to control the power of a daēva. Can take the form of two matching cuffs, or a bracelet and collar. A side effect of the bond is that emotions and sensations are shared between human and daēva. A bond draws on fire and will only work in Solis, not in Nocturne.

Breaker. See *negatory magic*.

Chimera. Elemental hunting packs, they're made from water, earth and air, seasoned with malice, greed, sorrow and fear. Chimera cannot be killed by any traditional means and will track their quarry to the ends of the earth.

Daēva. Similar in appearance to humans with some magical abilities. Most daēvas have a particular affinity for earth, air or water and are strongest in one element. However, they cannot work fire, and will die merely from coming into close proximity with an open flame. Daēvas can live for thousands of years and heal from wounds that would kill or cripple a human. Regarding clan names, *val* means mountain, *dan* means forest, *mar* means sea, *vat* means fire. *Avas* means children of.

Darklands. The slang term for Nocturne.

Diyat. "The Five." The governing body of the five Marakai fleets.

Dominion, also called the gloaming or shadowlands. The land of the dead. Can be traversed using a talisman or via gates, but is a dangerous place for the living.

Druj. Literally translates as *impure souls*. Includes Revenants, wights, liches and other Undead. In the Empire, daēvas were considered Druj by the magi.

Ecclesia. The popular assembly of Delphi. Open to all male citizens over the age of twenty. Elects the Archons and votes on matters of law and justice.

Elemental magic. The direct manipulation of earth, air or water. Fire is the fourth element, but has unstable properties that cannot be worked by most daēvas.

Empire. A land reached through gates in the Dominion, it is a mirror world of Solis and Nocturne in many ways. Nazafareen and Darius come from the Empire. It is the setting of the Fourth Element Trilogy.

Faravahar. The symbol of the Prophet, revered by the Persians. Its form is an eagle with outstretched wings.

Gale. The impassable line of storms created to imprison the Avas Vatras in the Kiln.

Gate. A permanent passage into the Dominion. Temporary gates can also be opened with a talisman.

Gorgon-e Gaz. The prison on the shore of the Salenian Sea where the oldest daēvas were held by the Empire. Victor Dessarian spent two centuries within its walls before escaping.

Great Green. What the Marakai call the collective oceans.

Hammu. A giant carp that causes undersea earthquakes and tsunamis. Worshipped by the Jengu Marakai.

Hin. The tenth of all goods shipped by the Marakai, taken as payment. Most is thrown into the sea for their deities, but the remainder is closely guarded within the treasure chambers of the Mers.

Infirmity. Called the *Druj Curse* in the Empire, it is the physical disability caused to daēvas by the bonding process.

Isfet. The time of chaos. According to Sheut Marakai prophecy, it heralds the return of the Avas Vatras.

Khaf-hor. Giant fanged eel with slimy, viscous skin. Worshipped by the Nyx Marakai.

Kiln. The vast, trackless desert beyond the Gale where the sun sits at high noon. The prison of the Avas Vatras.

Lacuna. The period of true night that descends when all three of Nocturne's moons are hidden. The timing of the lacuna varies from seconds to an hour or more depending on the lunar cycle.

Magi. Persian priests who follow the Way of the Flame.

Medjay. The half-human, half-daēva mercenaries employed by the Marakai to guard their treasure chambers. They wear shark-skin coats and carry short spears.

Moons. Selene, Hecate and Artemis. Selene is the brightest, Hecate the smallest, and Artemis has the longest orbit, taking a full year to complete. The passage of time in both Solis and Nocturne is judged by the moons since they're the only large celestial bodies that move through the sky.

Matrium. The seven female heads of the Avas Danai houses.

Nahresi. Skeletal horses that gallop across the waves. Worshipped by the Khepresh Marakai.

Negatory magic. A rare talent that involves the working of all four elements. Those who can wield it are known as Breakers. Negatory magic can obliterate both elemental and talismanic magic. The price of negatory magic is rage and emotional turmoil. It derives from the Breaker's own temperament and is separate from the Nexus, which is the source of all elemental magic.

Nocturne. The dark side of the world.

Parthenoi. Virgin warriors. See *Maenads*.

Rock of Ariamazes. The fortress-palace of the Kings of Samarqand. It was scorched in the Vatra Wars but never destroyed.

Sat-bu. Like the mythological monster Charybdis, she makes a whirlpool in the deep ocean that sucks ships down. Tentacled and faceless, she is worshipped by the Sheut Marakai.

Shadowlands. See *Dominion*.

Shepherds. Hounds of the Dominion, they herd the dead to their final destination at the Cold Sea. Extremely hostile to anything living, and to necromancers in particular.

Shields of Apollo. The elite unit of Greek soldiers that hunts and captures daēvas.

Solis. The sunlit side of the world.

Spell Dust. A sparkling powder; when combined with spoken words, it works like a talisman to accomplish any number of things. Only trained alchemists are fluent in the language of spell dust. Extremely addictive when consumed directly. Source unknown (except to the Persian merchant and dust dealer Izad Asabana).

Stygians. Mortals who dwell in the Isles of the Marakai. They're the only humans to live in the darklands, surviving by fishing and diving for pearls. The Stygians worship a giant oyster named Babana.

Talismanic magic. The use of elemental magic to imbue power in a material object, word or phrase. Generally, the object will perform a single function, i.e. lumen crystals, daēva cuffs or Talismans of Folding.

Talismans (*three daēvas*). They ended the war with the Vatras by creating the Gale and sundering Nocturne into light and dark. Their power passed on through the generations.

Umbra. The twilight realm between Solis and Nocturne.

Viziers. The Marakai administrators respon.

Water Dogs. Paramilitary force of bonded pairs (human and daēva) that kept order in the distant satrapies of the Empire and hunted Undead Druj along the borders.

Way of the Flame. The official religion of the Empire, and also of Samarqand and Susa. Preaches *good thoughts, good words and good deeds*. Embodied by the magi, who view the world as locked in an eternal struggle between good and evil. Fire is considered the holiest element, followed by water.

Wight. A Druj Undead with the ability to take over a human body and mimic the host to a certain degree. Must be beheaded.

Wind Ship. A conveyance similar to a hot air balloon, but with a wooden ship rather than a basket. Powered either by burners or spell magic.

AFTERWORD

Dearest Reader,

It feels bittersweet to be at the end of this long storyline (two linked series, eight books!), but I'm excited to return to my gaslamp fantasies, which blend the worlds of the Fourth Element/Fourth Talisman with Victorian paranormal mysteries. Yes, there are daevas and some characters you'll already know from the earlier series, plus all manner of nasty ghouls and undead things. I'm thinking of the stories as Sherlock Holmes meets The X-Files...with magic, of course.

The next book, *A Bad Breed*, is due in early summer 2019. Without giving away too much, I can tell you it begins in the Carpathian mountains of Transylvania with a series of vicious attacks on a remote village that bear all the hallmarks of a *pricolici* (that's what werewolves are called in Romanian folklore). Of course, you already know there will be plenty of twists in store for our fearless investigators from the London-based Society for Psychical Research....

In the meantime, if you're curious about how Vivienne Cumberland met Alec Lawrence, the history of the daëvas, and

Balthazar's checkered past, you can take a journey back to ancient Persia in the Fourth Element Trilogy where these characters first appear. Book #1 is *The Midnight Sea,* I hope you'll check it out.

Join my mailing list at www.katrossbooks.com and I'll send you a FREE copy of *The Thirteenth Gate*, a fantasy romp through Gilded Age London and New York with daevas, cane-swords and the quest for a dangerous Egyptian amulet.

Cheers, Kat

ACKNOWLEDGMENTS

My eternal thanks to Laura Pili, who understood the Viper better than I did, and who read and re-read key scenes until I finally got them right. Cara, you are the best.

To Sara Fonaas, my very first reader, who caught mistakes and gave me a boost when I desperately needed it.

To Christa Yelich-Koth, whose advice has guided every single one of these books.

To mom, my sharp-eyed proofreader.

To the lovely team at Acorn, for cover advice, moral support and all-around amazingness.

And to all my readers, thank you, thank you for letting me do what I love the most.

ABOUT THE AUTHOR

Kat Ross worked as a journalist at the United Nations for ten years before happily falling back into what she likes best: making stuff up. Join her mailing list at www.katrossbooks.com to claim your free book and so you never miss a new release!

ALSO BY KAT ROSS

The Fourth Element Trilogy

The Midnight Sea

Blood of the Prophet

Queen of Chaos

Gaslamp Gothic Series

The Daemoniac

The Thirteenth Gate

The Fourth Talisman Series

Nocturne

Solis

Monstrum

Nemesis

Inferno

Some Fine Day

Printed in Great Britain
by Amazon